Prologue:

The First Incident

National Petroleum Reserve, AK
In the near future

W hat exactly is this?" the co-pilot asked. He held the mouth-piece tight in hand to get above the roar of the plane's engine. "Nothing natural can register these readings. Have you ever seen this before?"

He turned to the pilot, who was still dumbfounded, gazing at the arctic skyline in front of them. Whatever it was, they were close to it, and it seemed to come out of nowhere. The Aurora appeared to be on fire, ignited by something. The usual slow, silent watercolor appearance had lightning overlays with bursts of new color. The pilot instinctively pulled down and away from the atmospheric disturbance. The lights reached downward, fingerlike, toward the ground with crackling light rippling along their lengths.

They were only a mile or two from the strange phenomenon when the pilot brought the plane into a circular pattern around the cyclone shape forming before them.

"I can honestly say," the pilot said, "I've never seen anything like this before. Here, use my phone to take video."

Then, as quickly as it came, the phenomenon disappeared. Without a sound, without a flash, as if a light switch turned off. The Aurora was back to normal, as were the readings on the compass and magnetometer, but a significant, circular impression remained on the ground with dis-colored vegetation.

"There's a good spot." He pointed. "That small lake over there."

"We're landing?" the co-pilot asked, afraid, still shaking from what he had just seen.

"Don't worry," Ethan grinned. "I do this all the time."

The plane glided in and slowly dropped onto the calm arctic lake. As the plane's pontoons splashed through the water, Ethan reversed engines and coasted the aircraft to the shoreline. The two men popped off their headsets, unbuckled, and stepped out on the pontoons.

Jumping onto a muddy bank, they hiked a short way through the grassy tundra. When they reached the trampled grass line, Ethan bent over and rubbed the grass between his fingers.

"Looks wilted, like old lettuce," he said.

Then the co-pilot bent down and pulled some grass. "Hmm, it's dead," John said. "All of it."

They looked in all directions. Nothing bright green; all vegetation was the pale-green color of seaweed.

"John, look here," Ethan said, pointing at water puddles left by their footprints. "The water is bubbling."

Ethan pulled off his glove and touched the water.

"No heat," he marveled. "But it appears to be boiling. It must be gas, a natural gas emission."

"Do you think that killed the grasses?" John asked.

Ethan did not respond, taking in the dead zone's size.

"I don't think we should stay here any longer," he warned.

The two quickly made for the plane. At the water's edge they noticed the same condition, water bubbling all along the bank. They studied it momentarily, then hopped into the plane. Ethan fired up the engine and taxied out across the water.

"The whole lake is bubbling," John exclaimed. The plane accelerated, skipped across the water, and lifted to the sky.

"Did you get those coordinates?" Ethan asked. "That has to be investigated further."

***

Ethan Sites was a recent college graduate, skinny, dark-haired with glasses, and an ever-changing expression on his face. Still growing out of teenage insecurities, he often found himself with a lowered head in social situations. But on technical topics, he was outgoing and talkative. He grew up in Boulder, Colorado, home of the National Oceanic and Atmospheric Administration (NOAA). He interned as an undergraduate and was now on permanent assignment in Alaska, studying polar anomalies.

The Magnetic Poles have always moved, like the axis of a gyroscope. But now it was moving faster than ever, so the Administration decided to put a surveillance crew in the air to check for anything unusual. Ethan had the equipment to track magnetic field changes, barometric pressure, temperature, Aurora patterns, and electrical disturbances.

Working the tundra was a challenging, sometimes monotonous effort. Nine months out of the year, it was dark and frozen; the other three were daylight 24/7.

Native Americans had fished the waters of this delicate ecosystem for 10,000 years, but in the twentieth century, the U.S. Government set the region aside as the National Petroleum Reserve.

***

"I've never seen anything like that before," Ethan explained. "Can't be natural. It has to be a side effect from drilling or blasting."

"But that's not allowed in the refuge," John said.

"Wouldn't be the first time somebody broke the rules." Ethan grimaced.

They flew east toward their base in Perishton, more than three hundred miles away. They had put in a long day of surveillance, the sun was low on the horizon, and the Auroras were dancing overhead.

"This damn compass is still messed up," John said. He smacked it on the side a couple of times, but it did not reset.

"Maybe it's because you hit it all the time," Ethan joked.

"It doesn't matter anyway; I'm using GPS," John said, miffed by Ethan's comment. "Maybe it's because we're right on top of it."

"We've been right on top of it a few times this spring," Ethan said. "And the compass spins. That's what it's supposed to do at the Pole. And now we're close to the Pole again, so …"

"Yeah, I get it." John smirked.

Then it happened again. The compass started spinning.

"Something is happening," Ethan said. "Look at the magnetometer. It is spiking, like a giant heartbeat… There it is again."

The magnetic bursts were so high they did not register, disappearing up, then down off the viewscreen.

John held out the phone and moved it from side to side as they flew. The plane kept its distance as the light grew more intense.

"This has to be what killed the grasses," Ethan told. "Look at the vertical striations, like lines painted on a tower, but unchanging laterally. They're not generated by wind. Hurricanes and tornados swirl sideways, but these lines are vertical. They have to be magnetic, like field lines from a magnet."

"No pressure changes," John said, checking the primary flight gauges. "No change in wind speed or shear."

"It's all energy, magnetism, or both," Ethan said. He made for a landing in a small pond near the dead area.

"Grab the magnetometer," Ethan directed. "Look, more bubbles."

"It will be pretty sloppy out there," John said.

"We won't be long," Ethan said.

They hurried toward the one-mile-diameter dead area in the marshy, spring tundra. Vegetation lay wilted and spoiled, worse than in the last location. The damage had no pattern; nothing laid down, just an even field of dead, partially burnt vegetation. Small patches of exposed surface water had the signature bubbles from the last site.

"What's the magnetometer read?" Ethan asked.

"Spiked," John answered. "Completely spiked."

"So, this is the North Pole," Ethan said.

"Or a crop circle." John smirked.

"Yeah, right," Ethan returned. "Do you hear that? Sounds like seabirds."

Flocks of seabirds chirped and cried as they approached by the thousands. As they drew nearer, they turned counterclockwise, circling the dead area. After a few minutes, they settled down and landed on the perimeter of the dead zone. Ethan took video with his cell phone.

"Let's get back to the plane," he said.

John did not argue.

"Why are seabirds out here?" Ethan asked. "Could the magnetic displacement have that much effect on them?"

They noticed something peculiar about the birds; some were sitting, others wandering.

"Look, we step right through them," John said. "They don't even acknowledge us."

A new scent filled the air while their feet made cautious steps.

"Do you smell that?" Ethan mumbled. "Is something burning?"

They turned to see small fires flashing up throughout the dead zone and spreading. Their eyes met in disbelief as they raced for the float-plane and lifted off. The seabirds took to the air as flames engulfed the entire area and spread out beyond the dead zone. Ethan circled the plane, going upwind of the smoke towering above the tundra.

"Can you believe this?" Ethan asked.

John just tightened his seat belt.

"Take video while I circle," Ethan said. "Then we need to start tracking again. Where is it going? Why did it stop here and do this?"

"How did that fire start?" John asked, still breathing heavily. "How is that possible?"

"Fire needs an ignition source and something that burns," Ethan explained. "That's it. The scorched grass was still hot, and those bubbles are probably an accelerant."

"The bubbles?"

"Yes, probably methane gas from melting permafrost," Ethan said.

After a few more minutes of observation, the small plane headed back on its southeast trajectory, following the strange magnetic readings. Before long, they came upon a large herd of caribou stampeding across the tundra in the same direction.

"A couple more hours to Perishton if we turn now," Ethan said. "But I want to go southeast and follow its current path. I can't believe the Pole is moving this fast."

WESTERN LIGHTS

C. P. SCHAEFER

WESTERN
LIGHTS

C.P. SCHAEFER

Library of Congress Catalog number: TXu002399305

ISBN 979-8-9890608-4-9
eBook ISBN 979-8-9890608-3-2

Printed in the United States of America

Edited by Claire Ashgrove
Cover Design by Jeff Brown
Interior design by Sabrina Milazzo, www.sabrinamilazzo.net

First Paperback Edition

For mom

For more information and to stay up-to-date with
tour dates, new releases, and book signings, please visit
www.cpschaefer.com and sign up for the mailing list.

"Wait," John blurted. "We lost signal. We went from spiked to flat, instantly."

"Keep your eyes open," Ethan said. "It's starting to flicker up there."

"I don't see anything," John said.

Ethan looked over his shoulder and saw it again. "Why is it getting so bright?"

The Aurora exploded with bright vertical fingers reaching to the ground. This time, it had even more striations, and the sheer light curtain changed color around its perimeter. He pulled back on the stick and flew around toward the silent tempest only a few miles out in front of them. The vertical bands reached up through the atmosphere, cutting the Aurora as it passed up out of sight.

The plane's instruments flashed and spiked, as did the compass and magnetometer. Digital readouts on the plane's console froze with non-descript reverse-image lettering.

"I'm having trouble with the handling," Ethan grunted. "It's locking up."

"What!"

"I'm going for that pond up ahead," Ethan grunted again, red-faced, pulling hard on the stick.

"We're coming in too fast!" John shouted, clinging to the overhead strap.

The small Cessna made for an emergency splash landing with no down flaps or reverse engine thrust, hoping the pontoons could handle the impact. The plane limped along with the grace of an old man falling down a staircase. The initial impact shocked the plane as it bounced off the water and made a jet-tail splash. The right pontoon broke away on the second impact, causing the plane to roll and tumble over the water. When it finally stopped, only the fuselage remained intact. Pontoons, wings, and the tailfin all floated behind or ended up in the grassy tundra. The fuselage floated on its side near the shoreline.

John lay unconscious and bleeding; Ethan felt dizzy and had pain in his back. He could smell smoke and quickly unstrapped.

"John, wake up," Ethan shouted, shaking him.

Ethan reached behind the seats and pulled out his computer bag and a survival kit. He pushed open the door above and tossed them up on the side of the fuselage.

"Wake up, John!" he shouted, but no response. "We've got to get out of here!"

Water poured into the lower parts of the cabin as it creaked and whined. John would drown in minutes if Ethan could not unlatch him and pull him free. The severity of the situation hadn't sunk in yet, however. Ethan was young, and this was just another adventure, another game to win before going home to supper.

Ethan reached down and unbuckled the seat harness to pull John up. The smell hit him again; brush fires marched away from the tower of light to the pond's edge. Ethan frantically pulled at John's arms and coat to get him up, but the boy was limp and unresponsive. Then the fire hit the water's edge.

"Come on! Wake up! This can't be happening," Ethan shouted. "Can't be happening!" Ethan turned to see fire racing across the methane-rich water.

Ethan pulled John through the door and laid him on the fuselage with one last tug. His unconscious body lay face down, his limp legs dangled in the cockpit.

"Wake up!" Ethan shouted again, slapping him on the face. Ethan grabbed his gear and continued shaking John.

"Wake up!" Ethan shouted. "We have to go now!" Ethan noticed a subtle reaction; at least he was alive.

Reality set in as the fire reached the plane. The intense heat was too much to take, so Ethan instinctively jumped out into the fiery water.

A few feet through surface flames, he reached the grassy bank, threw off his coat, and rolled on the ground. The fire came toward him; he ran a few yards to keep his distance, then heard a terrible scream. Through the smoke, he saw John's body lurch and roll.

Then it blew. The plane's fuselage exploded into a fireball. Ethan felt the intense heat and ran back.

"John!" Ethan shouted, then fell to his knees sobbing.

Young men never consider their mortality until it becomes reality. He had no idea what to do next, but he had to keep moving away from the spreading fire.

The giant tempest in the distance continued to change color, flashing and flickering as the fire spread. The great caribou herd stood on a distant ridge, watching. Seabirds circled the peculiar wall of bright light as if drawn to its power.

Ethan looked in all directions for options, but Alaska's tundra was the most remote and desolate place in North America; roads did not go there, he had no choice.

Ethan Sites picked up his computer bag and hurried off through the marshy tundra.

PART 1

Core rotation — Due North

Earth's magnetic field protects us from damaging cosmic rays. Invisible field lines are pushed from their natural hourglass shape by solar wind and stream away from the Earth in a comet-shaped tail.

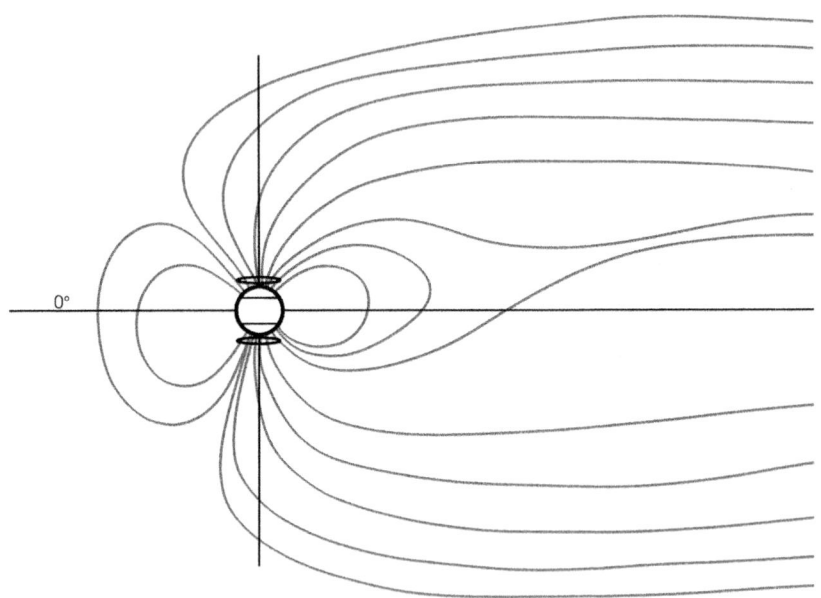

Chapter 1
The First Conference

Washington, D.C.

A black limousine made its way up Pennsylvania Avenue toward Capitol Hill, inching through stop-and-go traffic for a Congressional hearing on climate change. A single passenger sat in the backseat, staring out the side window. Julia Gathers was a refined woman in her late sixties, highly respected by her scientific peers, but her name brought mixed reviews in political circles. This hearing would undoubtedly focus on breaking news stories about strange atmospheric phenomena and flash fires in Alaska.

Julia was the Director of NOAA, a high-pressure position in the late 2020s as environmental crises became monthly issues. Once only a scientific government organization, NOAA quickly stepped into the political spotlight. And fortunately, Julia Gathers was the right person at the right time in history to be leading the Administration. Not your typical government appointee; she had been at the helm for decades. Julia spent most of her life protecting the environment; it was her driving force, and she had the pedigree to back it up. Julia was well educated and attractive, short on words but always got her point across, never wavered on any decision, and did not take crap from anyone. She held sway over her Administration and even at Congressional hearings when requested to offer opinions.

Her cell phone rang, and she sifted through her purse. There was poor reception, but she could still make out the name that appeared.

"Hello, sweetheart," she said. "Thanks for calling back. How are you?"

A scratchy voice cut through the static.

"Hello, Mother," a voice replied. "I'm fine. I wanted to let you know that I'm packing for an excursion. There's a pod of stranded whales a couple hours' drive from here, so I could be out of pocket for a few days. It's always poor reception out here, but lately, even worse; it might be a while before I check in with you."

"Sara, darling," Julia said. "I can hardly hear you. But I had to get in touch. Have you heard anything about the flash fires up in Perishton? I know you are hundreds of miles south, but—"

Communication cut in and out.

"Flash fires," Sara responded. "Do you mean forest fires? Happens all the time in the forests north of Denali."

"No, sweetheart," Julia followed. "In the northern tundra, no trees. I need to get feet on the ground and might send you that way."

Communication broke. Frustrated, Julia stuffed the phone back into her purse.

The limousine pulled up to a curb where a large crowd of protesters jammed up near the vehicle. They lined the streets and scores of steps leading up to the Capitol Building. Riot security held them back as a guard opened the side door for Julia.

In years past, a climate change hearing went almost unnoticed, but a recent report by the Army Corps of Engineers had been leaked on the Internet, most likely by hackers, and it could not have been worse timing. Calls came down from the highest authority to diffuse the ticking time bomb. The 'Overland Project' included detailed construction plans, schedules, and budgets for the multi-trillion-dollar construction of "Super-Levies," elevated-overland highways, and locks for boat transport in and out of major cities in Florida and the Florida Keys. The project was on a fifty-year timetable to protect major coastal cities from imminent sea-level rise.

Six of the Florida Keys from Largo to Key West would have thirty-foot-high concrete fortresses built around them, all inter-connected with elevated highways that ran directly over other keys, considered non-essential or non-strategic. The future submerged Keys would become fish sanctuaries in newly created 'cold water' reefs.

A similar fate awaited mainland Florida that lay less than fifty feet above sea level, and the Everglades would simply disappear. The Miami dikes were the most complicated piece; 300 miles of earthen and concrete barricades would encase the southern Florida supercity from Coral Gables up to Palm beach. The levies would be mainland only, leaving the Barrier Islands to nature.

Elevated highways would connect all major cities with no account for smaller towns, Rural Florida would disappear. A cold vision of future coastal conditions with small cities and coastlines blanketed under the pale blue ocean.

Even though the Florida Project leaked, the public assumed similar plans for all coastal regions were in place. Protests and news media broadcasts turned the hearing into a spectacle. Panicked public officials looked for answers as Julia Gathers scaled the steps of the Capitol Building.

Two hundred or more people inside the hearing room, mostly news media, political activists, and security, jammed in tightly. Protesters who managed to push their way into the back of the room were holding anti-Overland Project posters. Public presence was meant to be a show of transparency.

At the head of the room, a panel of faces sat behind an ornate wooden bench, looking out over the audience. An old wooden balustrade separated the crowd from the hearing area. Two small utility tables positioned in front of the balustrade had seats facing the panel. Seated at one table were military officials, at the other table representatives from big oil, all in a discussion on the Alaskan wildfires.

"We're not going off-topic," Senator O'Connell said, rapping a gavel in response to shouts about the Overland Project. "Let's stick with the agenda. And let me remind all of you that I will have this room cleared if there are any further outbursts."

"Colonel Jackson," Senator O'Connell continued. "I know it sounds like I'm beating a dead horse, but could these ever-expanding fires in northern Alaska have anything to do with the reported atmospheric phenomenon?"

"We have nothing to confirm that, Sir," Colonel Jackson said. "Most of the reports are civilian. Our station commander in Barrow has confirmed that the Auroras are brighter than normal, but that's it. There have been no thunderstorms or lightning strikes reported."

"What about a meteor impact?" O'Connell asked.

"We would have tracked that, Sir," Colonel Jackson responded.

O'Connell paused and flipped through papers.

"So, Mr. Duncan," Senator O'Connell redirected to the next table. "You're telling the panel that the oil industry has no explanation for these fires."

"That's correct," Duncan said. "There are no drilling operations in that area. Never have been, by any oil company."

"Yet these fires are all in the Northern Alaska Oil Preserve," Senator O'Connell said. "Seems coincidental. An area devoid of trees, and this time of year, nothing but cold, damp grasses. There are reports that these fires are expanding as if fueled by an accelerant."

Duncan shook his head.

"It was permafrost long before the Government declared it an Oil Preserve," a voice arose from the crowd.

O'Connell peered over his reading glasses.

"Ah, Director Gathers," he critiqued. "So nice of you to join us this morning."

The panel, military men, and oil men all politely stood as Julia Gathers made her way through the crowd. Confused onlookers dropped their pitchforks momentarily to take in this unusual show of respect for a person they did not recognize, but who clearly had the undivided attention of the powers-that-be. She wore a loose-fitting dress with a drawstring at the waist to fit her skinny frame. A long, black sweater draped to her ankles, and her hair was shoulder length and mostly gray. She wore a dark beret, multiple bracelets, and reading glasses that hung from her neck. Not exactly elegant, but true to her 1970's roots.

Mr. Duncan stepped over to open a swinging access gate. Colonel Jackson extended his hand as she passed through, then gestured for her to take his seat. He pulled out his chair, and she accepted. Colonel Jackson stood behind her, facing the panel.

O'Connell dropped his glasses to the desktop.

"Do you get this kind of treatment everywhere?" he sarcastically remarked. "I mean restaurants, hotels, everywhere?"

Julia broke a smile.

"As I mentioned, Senator O'Connell," she said. "Permafrost has been there for millennia. It's on the surface, but your oil fields are far below."

"Your point being?" O'Connell asked.

"As Mr. Duncan pointed out, there are no oil operations in the region," she continued. "Not now or ever. So, we rule out that piece of the puzzle. However, the permafrost is on the surface, and now it's changing."

"In what way?" he asked.

"As higher CO2 levels continue to raise atmospheric temperatures," she said. "Climate changing side effects begin to unfold. The most noticeable up to this point has been extreme weather conditions around the globe. But other, more subtle changes are starting to reveal themselves."

She paused.

"This state of climate emergency has gone unchecked. Climate change has reached a tipping point because human activity lacks balance with the ecosystem. And now the permafrost is melting," Julia pointed out. "We've been monitoring it for years, and it's starting to reach a critical point. Melting permafrost releases methane gas into the atmosphere, a much more lethal greenhouse gas than CO2, so the atmosphere warms even more quickly. As a result, we now have methane bubbling out of arctic lakes, rivers, and streams, like soda fizz." She pointed to a bottle of Perrier water on the table.

"That's certainly a grim environmental picture," O'Connell said. "But what's that got to do with—"

"Methane is a highly flammable gas," she cut him off. "I'm in the process of getting feet on the ground to investigate, but I suspect methane gas is causing these fires to spread."

Curious silence filled the room.

"OK, so if it is methane gas," O'Connell said, "then what's the ignition source?"

"That," Julia conceded, "I'm not sure."

"OK, how long do you think these fires will go on?" he asked.

"At this point, there are too many variables to decide," Julia said. "The ignition source, for one. But it's been drought level in that region for two years now, so the permafrost grasses are comparatively dry, and the soil is leaching methane. Bubbling methane could allow the fire to spread across open water, lake to lake, through rivers or streams. There is no proof of that, but it is a possibility. Either way, I suspect the fires should burn out in days; if not, we need to act."

"With all due respect, Director, I find this hard to believe," Senator O'Connell said, then redirected. "However, you're the last person I'm going to question on a technical topic."

He shuffled through papers.

"There are two major fires currently fanning out," he continued. "Both in circular patterns and approximately one hundred miles apart. Is it possible this is arson?"

Eyes turned to the military and the oil executives. All were shaking their heads.

"Senator O'Connell," Julia said. "I will have feet on the ground in hours. We will know the answers to some of these questions at that time. I suggest we reconvene after that, so we can provide you with substantiated answers."

Chapter 2

Bristol Bay

Southwest Alaska

The line's tangled!" the old captain barked. "Pay attention!"

Two deckhands bragging about last night's exploits jumped to work.

"What am I paying ya for? Here they come now, here they come!"

Fishing nets rolled over the stern rail, filled with squirming salmon. The captain was relieved when they finally hit.

"Can't get good help anymore," he grumbled.

The longline reel of the Gillnetter boat coiled up as its hydraulic reel whined louder and louder. *The Nordic Warrior* was an old model Gillnet boat, thirty-two-feet long, and tugboat-shaped, its longline spindle reel held hundreds of feet of net.

"Hahn," the captain shouted. "Where the hell are ya?"

A tall man in his early thirties stepped out from the lower deck and handed a thermos of coffee up to the captain.

"I'll take this side now," Hahn told the deckhands. "You've got a dozen on the floor already. Get 'em up in the pan."

Captain Ray Barron was a thin man in his sixties with a chiseled, weather-beaten face and a wispy beard. A cigarette hung from one side of his mouth and rattled as he spoke.

"That's it for now, boys," Ray said. "We'll be drafting too deep if we take on anymore. Good job!"

"We keep this up, boy," Ray shouted. "And it'll be a record year!"

"I thought they were all record years," Mason smirked.

They pulled into port at Pelham, where fishing boats waited to unload their haul. The *Nordic* had some twelve tons of salmon bagged in its hatches. The *Nordic* finally got through, unloaded, and pulled in to dock. Mason tied the last anchor rope to a heavy steel cleat and headed down the long, wooden dock. A loud horn blasted with the sound of a freight train. Mason instinctively bent over, clutching his ears.

"Really, Cap?" Mason shouted.

"Where's ya going?" Ray followed.

"You know, when you're in front of that damn thing," Mason shouted. "It blows your ears out."

"That's why I'm back here," Ray said. "Where's ya going?"

"The usual." He pointed. "I'll hold you a seat."

"What about clean-up?" Ray asked.

Mason kept walking.

The King Crab was a decades-old restaurant that served up everything from smoked salmon to king crab. Old wooden floors, walls, tables, and ceilings gave it an Alaskan back-country look.

Mason grabbed a seat at the bar; the server came up quickly.

"Hi, sweetie, today's special is salmon cakes and bisque," she said with a pointed smile. A large woman in her late fifties, Rita had graying hair that she pulled back during work hours.

"With a beer," Mason replied. "Oh, and the usual for Cap, thanks."

"Where is the old grump?" Rita asked. "I heard that damn horn."

"He'll be along shortly." Mason chuckled.

A newscast showed angry protesters throwing plastic bottles filled with oil at a line of armed police.

"What's this all about?" Mason asked.

"Over in Valdez," Rita replied, handing him a beer. "Been on all morning. They arrested a bunch of protesters and hauled them off."

"Thanks." Mason lifted the beer. "So, this mess is up here now. You'd think it was another Exxon oil spill."

Climate change rallies rose to epidemic levels in the late 2020's. Not since the war and race riots of the 1960s have people so organized for a common cause. Last month, a group staged two major rallies, one on the Brooklyn Bridge and another on the Golden Gate. At peak rush hour, fifty cars on each bridge stopped and threw their keys over the side.

"So, a whiskey for Ray?" Mason nodded.

Mason kept to himself and had a serious nature. He felt like he needed a life change after fourteen summers of fishing and fourteen winters of mudlogging. He worked in Perishton during the winter months as a mud-logger, checking sediment samples from drill rigs. It was great money—two weeks on the rig and two weeks off but paid 24/7 while on.

He sipped on a cold beer and stared at the mirror over the bar; something did not look right. It might have been the unshaven face, the routine, or the beer in his hand. But Mason Hahn needed a change.

"Hey, young man." Ray slapped his back. "Daydreaming again?"

Mason snapped out of it. Rita walked by as if on cue and pushed a shot of whiskey in front of Ray. He threw it back in stride.

"They're all cleaned up out there," Ray continued as Rita dropped off a new shot. "Weighed in at nearly twelve tons." Ray lifted the new shot in the air.

Mason raised his glass with a broken smile.

"What's troubling you, boy?" Mason shook his head.

"Ya ain't worried about money," Ray said. "And I know you ain't worried about some woman. Doesn't fit ya."

"I'll be fine, Cap," Mason said. "Tired, I guess." They both knew it went deeper than that but let it lie.

Rita laid plates in front of them and another shot for Ray.

"By the way, take a look at that top deck compass," Ray added. "Not workin' and GPS is all I have left, except this." He pointed to his head.

"Wouldn't trust that last option," Mason replied. "Is it foggy, might be condensation?"

Ray shrugged. "Then it probably needs replacing."

A crowd of tourists entered the restaurant, chattering away.

"So, what's your plans?" Ray continued, ignoring the newcomers. "Going up to the Yukon this winter?" An odd question from Ray, who never pried into Mason's private life.

"Not sure yet," Mason answered. "Why?"

"Just asking," Ray said.

Rita laid down another shot. "You hear what they're talking about?" she asked.

Mason looked across the room at the tourists, all focused on their smartphones.

"Something about beached whales up near Clovis," she said.

Mason walked over. "Excuse me, is there a problem?" he asked.

"Yeah, beached whales," a man said.

"May I take a look?" Mason asked.

A boy held out his phone. There was an entire pod of whales laid up on the beach with people nearby.

"What in the world?" Mason mumbled and gave the phone back.

"What is it?" Ray asked. "Really got some big beasties washed up?"

"Yep," Mason said. "And probably not enough rescuers."

"Well, good luck to 'em," Ray said. "Probly be Coast Guard or Conservation folks out there soon."

"Maybe," Mason questioned. "But Clovis is pretty remote."

"Ah, only a bunch of big fish anyway," Ray said. "And all they do is eat my fish. Let 'em be. Who really cares anyway?"

"Who cares?" Mason shouted and shoved his plate aside. "They're beached whales. No different than a herd of cattle running off a cliff!"

"Hey, I was only saying—"

Mason walked over to talk to the boy again. "Hey, kid," he said. "Do you know the people sending that footage?"

"Yes, sir."

"Can you get their GPS location?" Mason asked, holding out his cell phone. "And send it to this number?"

"Yes, sir," the boy answered. "I'll send them in a few minutes."

"Thanks," Mason said, he left Rita a ten and made for the door.

"Where the hell are you going?" Ray shouted.

"I'm going out to rescue some *big fish*," Mason shouted sarcastically, pushed open the door, and trotted up the road.

Mason called ahead to the Pelham Airport to have his floatplane prepped and ready. It was a small, private airport with more tour plane personnel than staff members. He briskly walked to the gate.

"Afternoon, Mason," the gate man said.

"Afternoon." Mason passed with a salute. "Plane ready?"

"Yes, sir," the man responded. "Where you off to?"

"Clovis," Mason replied. He crossed the airfield, checking his cell phone. A text popped up with GPS coordinates.

"Good boy," Mason mumbled, checking the data as he walked.

Momentarily, he was dockside with the Cessna 185 Floatplane, dropped the tie ropes, and fired up the engines. The Cessna lifted off, dropping a long trail of water as it rose. Mason mounted his cell phone on the dash and typed in the directions. It read back—Destination: 32 minutes.

Perfect, he thought.

Mason did not know what he was getting himself into; the idea of saving whales was exciting, but how do you do it? His mind wandered. Then something caught his eye. The compass pointed southwest, but the GPS read northwest. He tapped it on the side, nothing adjusted. He pushed reset on the GPS; it confirmed northwest— Destination: 8 minutes.

No whales in sight, but a rocky point blocked the view. He pulled farther out and turned back toward the coast. Then he saw them—whales!

An old Jeep was parked near the beachhead and a flatbed trailer sat halfway between it and the whale pod. The Cessna pulled in low and away, skipped a couple times, then throttled down and banked into the sand. Vultures circled in the sky, so he grabbed a pistol from under the seat and stuffed it in his coat pocket. Mason jumped out with heavy rope over each shoulder, tied off to nearby trees, and started away.

When he reached the whale pod, he could not believe their size. Even Mason, at six feet four inches, could not see over the large one. A woman in her early thirties stepped out from the crowd.

"Who are you?" she asked sharply, wiping her hands.

Taken by her striking appearance, he was momentarily speechless. "I'm Mason Hahn," he managed to stumble out. "I heard about the beaching and flew right out."

"I'm Sara Gathers," she said. "Any useful supplies on that plane?"

"Odds and ends, really, but I have this," Mason answered, pointing to the gun in his jacket. "Might come in handy with the vultures."

"Probably scare whales more," she scoffed. "Look, we're working against the clock here. We have to get the whales covered, so they don't sunburn and dehydrate. Go get the rest of the burlap on that flatbed and help us cover them."

She turned and walked back toward the whale pod while Mason watched her walk. Star-struck, love at first sight, whatever you call it, Mason had a momentary lapse of thought. So, with mouth hung open, he re-grouped and marched over to the flatbed.

Chapter 3

Sara Gathers

Clovis, AK

Mason unloaded dozens of burlap rolls. Some rescuers worked the burlap, some dug trenches, while others poured water over the gigantic cetaceans. The rescue effort had structure and all volunteers looked to Sara for guidance.

When she cut through heavy brush to the beachhead, Sara brought a Native Alaskan who knew the area. She made it clear that she needed help, but she was the only one authorized to direct a rescue effort.

"Hey, can I get your attention?" Sara shouted. "Let's stop digging for a while and focus on keeping the whales hydrated."

"Stack shovels on the flatbed, anything sharp near them can get caught up under their bellies. We don't want to add to the problem. And no water near the blowholes, you'll drown them."

***

Sara Gathers was thirty-one years old, slim built with straight, dark hair pulled back in a ponytail, diamond-blue eyes, and a no-nonsense demeanor. She graduated college with honors then completed her post-graduate work in Cetacean Biology. Sara's mother hired her to work for NOAA (drafted as her ex would say). But Julia had worked there most of Sara's life and knew it would be a perfect fit for her daughter.

Five years ago, her college love left her. She was heartbroken. He held back on most of the details but said their long-distance relationship simply did not work. He was an accountant with a stable position, and she traveled wherever the job took her.

***

Mason unrolled his first bale of burlap over the dorsal hump of the largest whale. He worked quickly, overlapping each piece as he went along. He stopped momentarily near the eye, deciding what to do.

"Don't get too close to his eye," a voice came up from behind. Sara reached over, petted him near the eye, and poured water over it.

"You think this bull is the leader?" Mason asked.

"No doubt," Sara said. "But it's kind of a curiosity. Males don't usually travel with the pod, must be mating season."

"Are they humpbacks," Mason asked. "Is that right?"

"No, sperm whales," Sara said. "You can tell by their gigantic foreheads; full of oil."

"Oil?"

"In the nineteenth century," Sara explained, "they were almost hunted to extinction because of it. The oil was used for lamps."

Mason nodded, then redirected. "Why bottled water?"

"Seawater dries out quickly," she said. "The salt crusts up and damages their eyes. We have no choice but to use seawater everywhere else because of their enormous size."

"So, you keep a shed full of burlap and bottled water around for a rainy day?" Mason asked.

"Sort of," Sara responded. "You'd be surprised how often this happens. Burlap, water, buckets, and shovels are the bare essentials."

Mason cut another piece of burlap and tossed it over the mammoth whale's snout. Sara helped pull and straighten it out.

"I'm surprised how relaxed they are," Mason commented. "I expected them to be jerking and thrashing with people around."

"Right now, they're exhausted," Sara said. "If we were harming them, even one of them, trust me, they would all be fighting for their lives."

Sara walked off to survey the rescue progress. The whales were all covered by late afternoon, so Mason picked up a shovel to help with trenching. Seemed to be a clever idea: make trenches that would fill with seawater. But the trenches were between the whales, not behind them. Something did not add up.

Mason noticed it was quiet, no people-sounds for the first time since he got there, only calm, monotonous work. He looked for Sara; she was down the beach with a book, staring out across the water. Then farther down the beach he saw his plane floating out in the surf. He trotted toward the plane, right past Sara, thinking he went unnoticed.

But she did notice, craning her neck as he passed. He was a resourceful guy, she thought, and could make a difference. Another thing crossed her mind, too—he looked at her in a way no man had in a long time.

The plane's ropes were slacking, so Mason pulled the plane back to the water's edge. He heard rustling in the brush that stopped each time he turned. He felt for his gun, re-secured the ropes, and headed back down the beach toward Sara.

"So, now what?" Mason asked.

"We wait for high tide," she responded, absorbed in thought and scribbling notes.

"I'm sure they got here at high tide," Mason said. "So maybe …"

"The tides will take them back out," Sara followed, still looking seaward. "Up here, we get the highest tides in the world, and yesterday was a full moon with unusually high tides, but tonight might not be so."

"So, these trenches," he said. "Will they channel them back out to sea?"

"Ha, no," she chuckled, but realized that was a bit condescending. "I'm sorry. Trenches help buoy them, so when the tide comes in, we push them into the trenches."

Mason pointed over his shoulder. "Even the big ones?"

"That concerns me," Sara owned. "Never pushed one that big. Not even half that size." She looked away, noticeably upset.

"What about the Coast Guard?"

"Not for strandings," she said. "Only in the water, distressed, or tangled in fishing nets. But once they hit land, Coast Guard is off-limits."

"Why do you think they're beached here?" He changed the subject.

"Stranded," she pointed out. "And it's because they're lost."

Mason studied her body language as she walked and talked about the problem in a self-analysis mindset.

"It doesn't make any sense," Sara continued. "I can't figure out why they're here. A male with the pod is highly unusual, but sperm whales on a beach in Alaska? This has never happened in the historical record. Not once in five hundred years has there ever been a sperm whale stranded in these waters. Why now? What's different?

"Sometimes they get confused by synthetic sounds. I've been checking, and there are no drill rigs nearby, no military operations, and no recent seismic activity. These are relatively untouched waters.

"It could have something to do with the warming ocean. The temperatures are up two degrees in the last ten years. They could have been looking for cooler Arctic waters. I don't know."

Mason digested her explanation. "Do you record all this in your journal?" he asked.

She thought about it for a minute.

"I used to keep a diary when I was younger," she said. "I found it easier to handwrite than to type into a computer. In the same way, I can quickly track facts in a journal. It's a better 'scope of work' tool that way."

"So, you have a lot of mysteries to solve here," Mason said. "I get it. But the first order of business is getting these whales back out to sea."

Sara looked back toward the whale pod, then to the tree line.

"The first order of business," she clarified. "Is protecting these whales from predators until the tide comes in."

Chapter 4

NOAA

Magnetic Field Tracking Facility
Perishton, AK

Perishton, Alaska, was a staging town for oil operations near Prudhoe Bay on the Arctic Ocean. It's where the Alaska pipeline begins the long run south through permafrost, forests, and mountains to Valdez on the southern coast. Oil riggers, mud loggers, engineers, technicians, and maintenance people are all housed there. Pipes, fittings, steel framing, food, and water are all stocked there. There is also an airport and paved roads, used by snowmobiles and half-tracks most of the year. A town prepared to hunker down through the harshest winters and keep the oil moving.

Nestled at the south end of town is a small, utilitarian structure that seems out of place, with no windows and one metal entry door. The masonry block building is tiny compared to the radio tower standing next to it and the array of satellite dishes stacked on its concrete roof.

Two men inside work frantically in a room with multiple computers and wall-mounted view screens. They roll from station to station on their wheeled office chairs. Both men are middle-aged, one balding, the other prematurely gray, both wear reading glasses from years of squinting at computer screens. The room has a glass separation wall that isolates a large Cray Exascale-Class, AI Supercomputer. They have as much computing power as NASA, but the space is disorganized and cluttered, hardly Mission Control-esque.

"Did you see that?" Paul Moore asked. "There it is again."

"Where is that kid?" David Thomas asked.

"Haven't heard from him all day. Ethan was supposed to report in every four hours."

"Look at this," Paul continued. "Have you ever seen anything like it before? These readings are off the charts. Normally 60,000 nanoteslas at this latitude, but it's spiking well above 1,000,000 nT. The magnetic field is all over the place. These ejections of magnetic power create spikes that resemble tectonic plate shifts."

"These readings can't be right. The Earth's core doesn't generate that kind of magnetism. It's got to be something else."

"What can it be then?" David asked.

Paul sighed, still focused on the viewscreen.

"Anything yet from the Solar people?" he redirected.

"No, lines appear to be out."

"Maybe a solar flare hitting the upper atmosphere," Paul wondered. "We've got satellite disruption, and cell phones are spotty."

"Could explain a lot," David said.

Then, a pounding at the front door. Paul walked that way.

"That kid is going to give me a heart attack one of these days," he barked. "OK, where the hell have you been?"

But it was not Ethan Sites at the door.

"Ben," a shocked Paul said. "What are you doing here?"

Ben Hadley, a chemical engineer from a lab down the street, was out of breath.

"Have you seen this," he pointed.

Paul stepped out and looked up. "What the hell is going on," he asked.

"At least that explains why everything is going haywire," David said, stepping across the threshold to view the crackling Auroras.

"What's happening?" Ben asked.

"We're not sure." Paul shrugged.

Two military jets roared past in the distance. Seconds later, they heard a sonic boom as they raced westward.

"OK, that seals it," David said. "Martians are attacking. See, we can all rest easy now."

Paul was not amused. "We need to get back in there," he said. "And get a hold of the outside world. I don't care how you do it, but we need communication."

"Nobody has it," Ben pointed out. "I've been trying all afternoon. Everything is dead. Satellites must have been knocked out."

***

In time, cell phone disruption minimized. There was still no contact with Ethan Sites, but they contacted Colorado's Space Weather Prediction Center. The Solar Group confirmed that radiation from two massive coronal mass ejections slammed into the Van Allen, matching the times of the spikes that registered on magnetometers.

Another knock at the door. Paul popped up and crossed the room.

"Ben, what's up now?" Paul asked.

"There's talk around the camp," Ben said. "Those fighter jets found two enormous wildfires out in the National Oil Preserve.

They don't know what started them, but they are circular-shaped and about 100 miles apart."

"See," David said. "Martians. Told ya."

"There's nothing out there but tundra." Paul frowned.

"Oil fire?" David asked.

"No, they don't drill out there," Paul argued.

Paul stared at a tracking monitor.

"We've been caught up with these strange magnetic readings," he said. "But when was the last time we checked Pole movement?"

"It's been a few days," David said. He took a seat at a different station across the room.

"Is this right?" he asked.

Paul and Ben walked over to take a look.

"It's moving again." David pointed to the monitor. "At better than 100 miles per day and accelerating. Something extraordinary is going on here. It made landfall and traveled almost 400 miles in two days."

"What does that mean?" Ben asked.

There was utter silence as they all considered the implications.

"David, can you overlay the magnetic readings onto this path?" Paul asked.

"Give me a minute." David typed away.

When the two images appeared, the spiked magnetic values were quite far apart.

"Scale that," Paul said.

"It's about ninety miles," David responded.

"I have a creepy feeling that's where we'll find those two fires," Paul said.

"Oh my god," Ben panicked pushing his hands through his hair. "Oh my god."

"What?"

"One of the guys heard that fighter pilots reported small plane wreckage near one of the fires," Ben said.

"David," Paul directed. "Call Ethan and keep calling him until you get through."

***

A few more hours passed but still no contact with Ethan. The unusual magnetic readings tapered off to normal and the Northern Lights faded away. The Magnetic North Pole stabilized less than 100 miles southwest of Perishton.

They welcomed a temporary relief from the bizarre events of the past few days. The men inside the tiny NOAA facility were the only people on Earth who had managed to put the puzzle pieces together, but they were still studying data to confirm their findings. Clicking keyboards, rolling chairs, occasional coughing, and the background hum of the Cray computer filled the air.

A new sound interrupted the background noise. Both men turned their attention to a ringing they had not heard in a long time, the landline. Paul and David exchanged confused expressions.

David picked up the phone. "NOAA, Perishton."

"Julia Gathers here, calling for Paul Moore," the voice said.

"Paul, it's for you." David nervously held one hand over the mouthpiece. "The Director."

"Julia?"

"Yes."

Paul rolled across the room and reached for the phone.

"Director Gathers," he said. "Nice to hear from you. I thought you might be calling soon."

"Paul, so you know why I'm calling," Julia said. "What can you tell me about the fires up there?"

"We're still piecing things together," he explained. "But here's what we know so far. The Magnetic North Pole has jumped out of the Arctic Ocean and is racing across northern Alaska at over 100 miles per day. Nothing like this has ever happened, not even close, and then it suddenly stops. But during shifts, we believe there was an atmospheric interaction with the solar wind.

"Each time the core jumps and moves, there is an enormous release of magnetism. The coronal mass ejection that caused satellite disruption also coincided with these jumps. The energy and magnetic interaction created the most brilliant Auroras we've ever seen. This may have caused the fires because the spikes in magnetism plot out at the same locations as the fires."

A brief silence.

"That's extraordinary," Julia said. "Have you sent anyone out to investigate these sites?"

"Yes, Ma'am," Paul said. "We've had a survey crew in a small plane, studying magnetic Pole movement for a few months now, but we lost contact with them yesterday. And, uh ...we are afraid their plane might have crashed. There are rumors that fighter jets spotted plane wreckage near the second fire."

"I need more definitive proof of what's going on," Julia said. "Get someone out there in the next few hours. I believe methane emissions from melting permafrost are causing the fires to spread, but we need feet on the ground to prove it.

"There is another climate change hearing in Washington tomorrow afternoon, so I need a detailed report of your findings by noon."

"Julia," Paul clarified. "There are no roads in that area, and our plane is apparently down. All I can do from here is continue our efforts to contact the survey team. In the meantime, we'll assemble a detailed report of our findings."

"I need on-site knowledge of those fires," Julia demanded. "No excuses."

Paul thought about it for a moment. He understood where she was coming from, but he also knew she asked for the impossible.

"I'll do what I can, Julia," Paul replied.

Chapter 5

Twilight

Clovis, AK

Alaskan summers never get dark, and predators stalk their prey in daylight or twilight hours. Wolf packs, bears, coyotes, raptors—they all must eat and can pick up the scent of a stranded whale for miles.

The tide slowly rolled in, and by midnight, the breakwater was only a few feet from the tailfins. Sara paced nervously; would it rise enough?

"The sun is low now," Sara said, "and things change at twilight."

"Predators?" Mason asked.

"Right," Sara responded. "By moon-up, they'll be coming."

"Maybe I should round up firewood," Mason offered. "Make campfires, form a perimeter."

"I have five gallons of kerosene in the Jeep," Sara followed.

"Why am I not surprised," Mason joked.

He approached the others to collect recruits. "We need help collecting wood," he stated.

"I'm Rick Morris," one man said, extending his hand.

"I saw you in the video," Mason said. "Thanks for staying."

"No problem," Rick said. "These are my boys, Marc and Rick Jr. We camp up here every summer. We usually have phone service, but Auroras are making it worse."

"No reception on mine either," Mason grimaced.

"I'm Tulok." Another man stepped up. "I help Miss Gathers with chores, supplies, and wildlife problems in general."

Collecting enough wood took time. They picked up every piece of wood in sight, and the campfires were soon crackling.

"You've done this before?" Sara complimented.

"Oh yeah," Mason responded, and finished a burlap torch.

"You seem to have a lot of common sense," Sara replied. She had rescued whales before but defending them was something new.

"Shouldn't it be high tide now?" Mason pointed down the beach.

"Should be," she said. "But you never know with these waters."

"You must live around here," Mason inquired. "Otherwise, how did you get here so quickly? I mean, it's a half hour flight from Pelham."

"And a two-hour drive," she answered. "I just knew sooner."

Good to know, Mason thought.

"Let's try this," he said. "Stand back." He poked the torch into the fire, and it lit up big and bright."

Sara patted his back.

"For what it's worth," Mason added.

"So, you're a bush pilot?" Sara asked.

"Not really," Mason replied. "I'm a fisherman in the summer, work on a rig Perishton in the winter, and I fly back to the valley."

"The valley?" she asked. "California?"

"That's right," he said. "My folks have property in Cibolo with a grass runway for Dad's aircraft, so I learned to fly when I was young."

"I know the area," she said and reached for Mason's torch. "So, how did you hear about the stranding?"

"Those guys." He pointed to the hikers. "I heard their friends talking about whales at a restaurant, and they gave me the location."

"So, you sit around waiting for animals to rescue?" Sara asked, swirling the torch around.

"No." He chuckled. "I have an appreciation for whales. Sometimes, people get in their way, and it's not the whale's fault."

"People get in their way," she followed. "Like, fisherman?"

Mason nodded, in thought.

"Have *you* gotten in their way?"

"It happens," he replied. "You just have to keep your distance. It's their ocean, not ours, but some people don't see it that way."

"I take it you know some of these people," Sara said, handing him back the torch.

"Hmm, yeah." Mason nodded. "The older generation."

Sara studied his face. "Good torch."

By two a.m., an eastern moonrise brightened the sky while the sun hovered in the west. The quasi-fortress was ready. The defenders easily ran off the wolves with torches when the first attack came.

"Any ideas, Tulok?" Sara asked.

Tulok watched the retreating wolf pack make for the cover of brush. "They were scared off," he said. "But they'll be back."

"How long do you think we have?"

"Not sure," Tulok answered, and started away. "I need to see if that was the whole pack or only scouts." He disappeared into the trees.

"What do you think, Mason?" Sara asked.

"Let's form a line behind the campfires," Mason said. "Everyone grab a torch. You boys stay behind us and look out for a side attack."

Their father nodded, and they stepped back.

"They're afraid of fire," he said. "So, it will keep them at bay."

"And if that doesn't work?" a male voice asked.

"They're also afraid of loud noises," Mason said and pulled his pistol.

Minutes seemed like hours as the group silently waited at post.

"I bet you boys never thought hiking could be so boring," Mason joked, breaking the silence. Smiles filled all faces, even Sara's.

Silence again, more time passed, torches re-fueled. Then, up the beach from the encampment, the entire wolf pack charged out in force.

"Twenty or more!" Tulok shouted, bursting from the brush.

Mason charged toward the rushing pack. Yelling and swinging his torch. Tulok grabbed a torch and followed.

"The rest of you stay back," Mason shouted, as they ran.

In seconds, they clashed. They took Tulok down quickly and jumped on Mason's back as he threw his torch into the pack. Mason reached for his pistol, shot it in the air, and the pack ran off into the brush.

"You all right?" Mason asked, pulling Tulok to his feet.

"Yeah," Tulok said. "They got my arm. Not too bad."

"Are you crazy?" Sara shouted. "That could have killed you both!"

"Would you rather fight them back here?" Mason gasped for breath. "They were charging. We had to charge back, force on force."

"I agree," Tulok said. "We have to keep them away from the pod."

"Hey, guys." Mason pointed. "We need more wood on these fires."

"Got it," Rick followed. "Come on, boys."

Minutes later, they charged again, straight on. The boys were still toting wood. Mason quickly fired shots in the air, they ran again, but stopped short of the beachhead.

"How many bullets are left?" Sara asked. "Don't be a cowboy."

"I think I may be out," Mason said, checking his pistol.

The wolf pack started a slow approach on the flanks where the smaller calves lay. Mason jumped out in front of the campfires to head them off, and the others followed, side by side.

"You boys stay back now," Mason shouted. "Stay with the calves."

They attacked all at once. The outnumbered defenders yelled and swung torches wildly. Sara's went out as two wolves darted from the line toward her. She beat them back with a bare stick.

"Come on!" she shouted.

Yelping in pain, one wolf ran off, and the others followed.

"I can't believe you just did that!" Mason shouted.

The wolf pack stopped at the beachhead; their fear of the defenders gone. Mason searched for options, then took a long stare down the beach.

"I'm going for it!" he shouted.

"Going for what?"

Mason ran for the floatplane; the watchful pack made chase. He ran full stride through breaking water and stumbled in the surf. The pack darted for him but was slowed by the water. They dove for him as he reached the pontoons. He kicked away at them, opened the door, and pulled himself inside. He sifted furiously through the rear of the fuselage until he found it. Then splashed back into the water, aimed a flare gun at the center of the pack, and pulled the trigger.

An enormous fireball blew up, dead center of the pack. The wolves ran full speed off the beach, whining and yelping. Mason made his way back to the campsite and dropped a bag of flares.

"This should buy us time," he said.

Tulok patted his shoulder.

More time passed, no howling, no nothing. Sara studied the eye of the bull whale. Her fixed gaze, flickering in the campfire glow, was no longer hopeful. One day left.

"These creatures are in pain," Sara sighed, noticing Mason's shadow. "I don't want to watch them die in pain or be eaten by wolves."

"What do you mean?" Mason asked. "We're winning here, right?"

"We're only keeping nature at bay," she scoffed. "But other forces are at work. If we don't get them out to sea soon, they will die. Did you notice the tide? It's going back out. I lost track in all the chaos."

Mason walked over to the bull and reached out to pet its enormous snout. Sara followed. The whale lay motionless, eyes hardly open, unmoving. The flickering Aurora made a strobe-light effect, casting long shadows across the beach, giving the whale an animated appearance.

"Beautiful creatures," he offered. Sara nodded. "I was wondering, how did you ever find this place?"

"Tulok," Sara said. "He fishes these waters and radioed yesterday."

"Radioed?"

"Short wave," she said. "Still the best way to communicate. So, I informed NOAA about the situation, packed supplies, and here we are."

"Yeah, here we are," Mason replied. He really liked her—a short-wave radio *and* an old Jeep.

"You know. I've never seen Auroras this bright in June," he redirected. "And they're out of the east, not the north, strange."

"I hadn't noticed," she said.

"Over there, due east," he pointed. "The arc in the sky should originate from the north."

"Mason, I'm not out here to study the heavens," she said.

"Just look."

"All right." She tilted her head. "They are bright. But I don't have a good sense of direction."

She needed a break, and Mason knew it, but they did not have the luxury of time, so he switched the subject.

"Ray told me a story once," he remembered, petting the whale's snout. "He came across an injured whale, a calf. It was drifting, so he decided to end its suffering. He roped it and drove a harpoon into its heart. He thought that would kill it instantly, but it rolled so fast it pulled the harpoon out of his hands. Its mouth opened as if it were screaming in pain. It thrashed for a few seconds, then stopped."

Sara looked away. "Why are you telling me this?"

"I've known Ray for fourteen years," he replied. "And never once heard him tell a heartfelt story. Always a big fish story or a girl he met at a bar.

"But he only told this story once. I think it haunts him, the way that calf died. He'd never admit it, but at that moment, he realized that he'd killed one of God's creatures, not just a fish. And it changed him."

He looked in Sara's eyes. "We'll find a way to save these whales," he said. "I won't end up like Ray."

Tulok stepped out from the line of campfires, flare gun in hand, silently watching the beachhead.

"They're back," he said. Glassy, yellow eyes reflected by the firelight stood ready to pounce.

Mason stepped up beside Tulok. "What now?" he asked. "There's only a couple flares left."

"When they attack," Tulok said. "You fire at the center of the pack. I'll chase them and take the last shot. Maybe that will do it."

Mason picked up a dead torch and handed another to Tulok.

"And I'm coming with you," Mason told, Tulok smiled.

Then the wolves charged. Mason fired straight into the pack; they scattered, whining and yelping. Tulok and Mason ran after them. Soon, the pack stopped and turned. Mason and Tulok yelled and waved their dead torches. But the pack leader growled and slowly moved toward them. Mason's heart raced as the pack started to circle.

Tulok fired directly at the pack leader. The explosion reflected off nearby trees and ignited grasses. The pack leader was down and injured, but slowly limped away. The rest of the pack ran off, yelping. Relieved, Tulok and Mason stepped out the flames and made their way back to camp.

Chapter 6
The Second Conference

Washington, D.C.

I n 1859, a strange cosmic phenomenon caused telegraph lines in New York City to crackle and burn. The Northern Lights were visible in the Caribbean, and the Auroras were brighter than ever at both Poles. But the strange lights in the night sky disappeared quickly and did not return, so life went on, and the event soon passed from public memory.

Back then, we were still in the Pre-Industrial Age. The only dangerous forces of nature were hurricanes, volcanoes, and earthquakes. In a world of horse-drawn carriages and oil lamps, there were no secondary effects from the solar energy blast that lit the Auroras. But today, that same event would take out most of our communication satellites and shut down substantial portions of our power grid for years.

Imagine waking up in a world with no access to cell phones or the Internet. It could happen tomorrow, with little warning, and there is nothing we can do about it.

"Julia," Paul said through phone line static. "We still haven't heard from our survey crew, and it's more and more likely we lost them in the second fire. The e-mail I sent summarizes everything we know about the phenomenon, except for visual confirmation."

"And there is no way to get out there?" Julia asked.

"Flights are grounded up here until things get sorted out," he said.

"Senator O'Connell has called an emergency session to discuss our findings," she stated. "He will demand answers."

"Then tell him the truth," Paul said. "You lost your recon team in the second fire, along with all their data. Good drama. They'll love that."

"I'm not one for showboating," she said.

"Politics is all about showboating, Julia," Paul returned.

✳✳✳

It was a charged atmosphere, crowds wrapped the Capitol Building, covering the West Front Lawn, extending out to the Reflecting Pool. Senator O'Connell called for a closed session due to the sensitivity of the material, but more people than ever filled the hallways outside the hearing room. All eyes were on Senator O'Connell and Julia Gathers as they entered the room. O'Connell called the session to order, and the crowd went silent. The well-respected lady at center stage had risen from relative obscurity to a household name since the first hearing.

The group of panelists busily read the report submitted by NOAA. They exchanged concerned glances, murmured a few words, and pointed to specific underlined paragraphs through their reading glasses. Julia patiently waited for the group to summarily reach a closure point. The military staff and oil executives flanking her simply sat, motionless. About thirty minutes had passed when Senator O'Connell finally broke the silence.

"I have to admit, Director Gathers," Senator O'Connell said. "The content of this report is not what I expected. If anything, it adds even more mystery to the problem.

"The summary says that the North Pole is moving, amazingly fast, in a start-stop motion. And there are, in your words, 'magnetic interactions with coronal mass ejections in the upper atmosphere,'" O'Connell continued. "Coronal mass ejections from the sun?"

"That's correct, Senator," Julia said. "The two solar events that caused power outages and communication disruption around the world also occurred at exactly the same time as the magnetic surges and the fires.

"The Magnetic Poles are moving at rates never seen before, and while moving, the magnetic field strength is so high that it can't be measured."

"Excuse me," another Senator interrupted. "The North Pole is the North Pole, right? How can it move?"

"Senator, you are partially correct," Julia said. "There are two kinds of North Poles, well three if you believe in Santa Claus.

The group chuckled. O'Connell did not.

"There is the geographic North Pole, the one you see on globes, a manufactured reference point that never moves. But the *Magnetic* North Pole is generated by the Earth's molten core. Its location always changes—having done so since the times of Magellan.

"But its movement was always subtle, maybe a few miles per decade. In the past decade, its movement accelerated, sending it into Siberia. But now it's reversed course, back across the Arctic Ocean into Alaska, and moving more than one hundred miles per day."

"OK, so what does that mean?" O'Connell asked.

"Well, this electromagnetic interaction certainly caused the two fires," Julia said. "But why there is so much rapid movement of the core is not understood."

"Speculate, please," O'Connell asked.

"It may only be a hiccup," she said. "A small adjustment or correction back to its normal location."

"Ha!" One Senator smirked. "It prefers U.S. soil over Russian."

O'Connell sighed, not happy with the remark but more concerned with the tone of Julia's last comment. She seemed uncharacteristically unsure of herself.

"What else?" he asked.

She turned away, then looked back.

"It could be something entirely different," she admitted.

O'Connell leaned forward, peering over his glasses.

"Go on."

"The start of a core shift," she said.

There was a murmur from the panelists.

"A core shift?"

"Yes, where the Poles flip," she said. "North goes south, and south goes north."

Silent stares from the panel.

"Say again?" O'Connell asked.

"Throughout Earth's history," Julia continued. "The molten core has flipped about once every 780,000 years. There are no serious effects on the environment that we know of. And there is no evidence of the timing of how long it takes to flip. It could take 1,000 years or only a few decades. We simply don't know."

"Director Gathers," O'Connell said. "If this happens regularly every 780,000 years, then why do you speculate this could be happening now?"

"Because, Senator O'Connell," she replied. "The last *major* core shift was about 780,000 years ago. So, we're due, and the Magnetic Poles have never traveled this fast before."

You could hear a pin drop. O'Connell's blank stare summarized the look on all faces in the room.

"Let's take a ten-minute break," O'Connell said.

***

An occasional cough and the smell of coffee filled the air. The panel shuffled papers and whispered comments to each other. Julia exchanged words with the colonel, who handed her a small, bound document. O'Connell rapped his gavel to restart the session.

"Let's move on to another topic," he said. "Director Gathers, per minutes from the last meeting, you stated that you would have feet on the ground to investigate 'possible methane emissions,' but I don't see that discussion in this document."

"As it turns out, we did have feet on the ground," she said. "And actually, before the last meeting. Our survey team was following the Pole movement. They were, no doubt, eyewitnesses to the phenomenon. However, we lost them in the second fire, along with their findings."

"Lost?"

"Yes, we believe both were killed in a plane crash," Julia said. "Not far from the second fire as reported by military reconnaissance aircraft."

"So, you had men out there," O'Connell questioned. "But they didn't bother to radio in what they saw?"

"With all due respect, Senator," Julia said. "That would have been impossible with the electromagnetic interference."

"I see," he said.

Julia flipped through the report from Colonel Jackson. This caught Senator O'Connell's attention.

"Excuse me, Director," he said. "Is that the document Colonel Jackson handed you during the break?"

"Yes, it is."

"I noticed," O'Connell critiqued. "You know, it can be handed to me as well."

Colonel Jackson walked a copy up to O'Connell.

"Thank you, Colonel," he said. "Can you please brief us on this, Sir?"

"Yes, Sir," Colonel Jackson said. "On 06/16 at 1856 hours, we scrambled two F-16s from Patterson. They made visual contact with the smoke plumes at 1920 hours and did a flyby on the eastern plume at 1929 hours. They first commented that it was a forest fire, about two miles in diameter at the base and spreading on its perimeter. An enormous cloud up to 5,000 feet drifting eastward. They reached the western plume at 1954 hours. The base was more prominent there, but the plume appeared to be diminishing. Then they headed east in search of more potential fires. Everything clear to the Canadian border.

"We followed that up at 2050 hours by dispatching a Chinook transport helicopter. It arrived at the eastern plume at 2185 hours. Landed one mile upwind at 2212 hours, with feet on the ground at 2216 hours. They did confirm the bubbling water that Director Gathers spoke of but could not prove it as an accelerant.

"With permission from the panel, we intend to initiate water airdrops with DC-10 tankers to contain and extinguish the fires."

"Permission granted," O'Connell said. "These efforts should be coordinated with Alaskan Fire/Conservation Officials."

"Yes, Sir."

***

Another brief break while O'Connell conversed with the other panelists.

"So, we have two large fires," Senator O'Connell said. "And now we know the cause of these mysterious fires and the communication satellite disruption. But we are still unsure of how they are spreading so quickly."

"As we all heard from Colonel Jackson," Julia said. "The methane emissions are confirmed. We will send another team to figure out if it is the ignition source. But I think it highly likely."

"What are the chances of more of these fires starting?" O'Connell asked.

All eyes turned to Julia Gathers.

"Senator, this is completely unprecedented," she said. "It's difficult to say whether it will happen again. But if the core continues to move, then it's possible."

"Are you tracking its movement?"

"Yes, we are," she answered. "But currently, it's stationary. And remember, it took interaction with the energy released from a large solar flare to cause these 'Super Auroras,' so the two things have to coincide."

"And what are the odds of that?"

"Normally, I'd say very low," Julia said. "But we are currently in an era of a Solar Maximum, an eleven-year run of higher solar temperatures and activity, so anything is possible."

Chapter 7
Last Stand

Clovis, AK

Sara went over all workable options. She had a kit to euthanize, complete with syringes and gallons of chemicals. Should she leave these poor creatures to the wolves? These options were too unbearable to consider.

She sat between the bull and the mother, within eyeshot of each, their large eyes curiously moving again. The dry trench below Sara's feet and the receding tide beyond symbolized her growing hopelessness.

Mason and Tulok sat by the bonfire, eating jerky and passing a fresh pot of coffee. Rick Jr. walked up to them with a bucket in hand.

"Mason," he said. "I got us some rocks."

"Rocks," Mason replied. "For what?"

"For throwing at the wolves," the boy said. "If they come back."

Mason stared at the boy. "Is that our kerosene container?"

"Miss Gathers said I could cut the top off," the boy replied.

"Good thinking, kid," Mason grinned. "Better than nothing."

Sara sat quietly. Mason sensed her anxiety and was giving her space, but decided it was time to break the ice.

"Hey, would you like some coffee?" Mason asked. "It's fresh."

"Sure," she sighed, he poured a cup. "Thanks."

"You know," he continued, relieved that she accepted. "The next time you try to fill that kerosene can, it'll probably leak."

She grinned. "It was a sweet gesture," she said. "He thought that up, to help protect these creatures. You don't see that very often in young boys."

"Those two have hung in there," Mason said. "Real troopers."

"Yes, they have," she replied. "I'm hoping this has a happy ending, so their effort is worthwhile."

"Hey, that Jeep over there." Mason pointed. "Keys in it?"

"Yes, they are," she answered. "Why?"

"Not sure," he said. "Might be of some use if they come at us again."

She turned. "The Jeep?"

"Better than throwing rocks," Mason followed. "I mean, if I roll the Jeep chasing them, you'll forget all about that can of kerosene."

She lost it at that point, really laughing.

"But seriously," he asked. "What is our next move?"

Reality returned, along with Sara's long face. "Euthanize," she said.

"What?"

"You heard me," she replied. "Look out there. That water is where they live, and we can't get them there. And now we're endangering human lives. I can't have that on my conscience, too."

"No!"

"No, what?" Sara shouted. "Heroics are played out, and the tide is gone. These creatures will die a painful death in the heat today.

Meanwhile, their enormous body weight is crushing and suffocating them since they're not floating in water."

Sara headed across the beach toward the Jeep. Once there, she found the bag on the floorboard. The one thing she never believed she would use.

Then she heard something and looked up to see everyone motionless, staring in the other direction. Coyotes.

They lined the underbrush at the top of the beach; their growling signaled an attack. The defenders launched a volley of rocks into the bush.

Sara felt a rage well up inside her that she had never experienced before. She tossed the bag in the passenger seat and fired up the Jeep. The coyotes made their charge. But with the whip of a high-speed boat, all four wheels spraying sand behind, Sara darted through and cut them off. She hit two coyotes on the first pass, and with an impressive 360-degree turn, came around again, sand flying in all directions. The pack made for the bush as she grazed past their feet. She turned for one last pass, but they were nowhere in sight.

Wow, Mason thought. *She can really drive, too.* He really liked her.

Sara stopped and reached for the duffle bag, but it was gone. It had rolled out on the big turn. She jumped out and marched toward it.

"Sara!" Mason shouted. "Sara!"

"This has to be done," Sara agonized, bag in hand. "Maybe you should all leave now. Mason, can you take them back in your plane?"

She knelt next to the bull whale and opened the duffle bag. Multiple syringes lay in factory-packed plastic cartons, along with two-liter containers of liquid. She gasped as tears welled up in her eyes. Mason approached but stopped short.

Sara reminded herself it was for the best as a thousand ideas raced through her mind. In a few minutes, it would all be over, but was it really for the best? Then a very loud noise snapped her out of deep thought.

"WOO-WOOO!"

"Hey there, boy! Could ya use some help!" Ray Barron shouted.

"Who the hell is that?" Sara asked.

Chapter 8
The Marines

Clovis, AK

"Hey-hey!" Mason shouted, splashing out into the surf. A fleet of Gillnetters cruised close to shore. Men from each boat jumped in the water, striding for the beach. Mason was reborn with energy.

"You came all this way?" Mason shouted. "For some big fish?"

"Big fish still on the beach, I see!" Ray shouted.

"Still on the beach," Mason chuckled.

Sara stepped up through a crowd of gawking sailors.

"I'm not sure what you think you can do here," she said.

"Whatever it is you need," Ray offered, removing his hat. "Miss?"

"Gathers," she said. "Sara Gathers." She felt intimidated by the old pirate, but he did respect a lady.

"These whales have to get to water today," she stated. "Or that's it."

"I have an idea." Mason beamed. "We'll use the reels to pull them out."

"Excuse me," Sara interjected. "How would that work?"

"Those big spindles on the boats," Mason said, "have a lot of pulling power. If we can get the net around their bodies, we can pull them out."

"Thrust from the motors will help, too." Ray sported a proud grin.

The wheels were turning now in Sara's mind. "You can't grab their tails," she said. "Wrap them up past the dorsal to evenly distribute their weight."

"Then, we'll dig trenches under them," Mason said, "and thread the line and net around them in a spiral."

"OK, Sara contemplated. "This might work."

"You heard the man," Ray shouted. "Let's get to work."

"We want to get the bull out first," Sara directed. "He's the leader and will start thrashing if we pull on one of the others."

They gently pulled the netting around the large whale, clasping it off tight. Mason checked the work, pulled lines, and snapped them back.

"I'm concerned about the beach," Sara said. "A whale's underside is soft and cuts easily. Lets' roll out burlap along the whole pathway."

The sailors jumped to it and were ready for the first pull. Ray engaged the hydraulic controls that creaked and whined as they brought tension into the lines. The large bull thrashed, and the lines started to slip.

"Hold it! Hold it!" Mason shouted. "It's slipping too much."

"It's not strong enough," Sara said. *Maybe the Marines landed too late*, she thought.

"How many ratchet straps do you have?" Mason shouted to Ray.

"Plenty," Ray replied.

"OK, back it off!" Mason shouted. "We'll fish the straps around him through the dig-outs and ratchet them tight; this will do it."

"Too tight, and you could hurt them," she said. "If this works, I want to tag him with a radio transmitter. I have one in the Jeep."

With ratchet straps in place, Ray engaged the longline reels, and the net lines started stretching. The boat pulled astern, but Ray throttled up to compensate, and the giant whale started to move. Metal creaked, engines whined, and the whale slowly inched backward, sliding over the burlap.

"Some of you guys go up front," Sara said. "And push on his snout."

The farther he slid, the easier the pull. At the breakwater, he really started moving out in the surf.

"OK, let's stop the boat for a minute," Sara said. "We need to get these straps off him before he gets buoyant and tries to swim off."

All men jumped into knee-deep water and unlatched the straps that rolled off quickly. The fishing net around him was the only restraint left.

"Ray!" Mason shouted. "We'll bring a boat around and follow you out. When he gets deep enough, I'll snap the clasp loose."

Mason turned to Sara. "Want to go for a ride?"

"I'm not missing this," she said.

Ray put the *Nordic* in gear and motored out. Mason motioned to have the second boat pull alongside the whale. The water deepened, and soon the big bull was floating, his eyes below water.

Sara's heart was happy for the first time since she set foot on this beach. She could not believe what she was seeing.

"Get me closer!" Mason shouted. "I have to lean way over to grab it, so you'll have to hold me from falling out."

Two men grabbed his ankles, and one man held his belt as Mason stretched out. Seawater splashed in his face as they pulled alongside the giant whale, and reaching for the clasp, he snapped it open.

"Pull me back!" Mason shouted.

The net line uncoiled, and it was free! The whale swam away with no signs of fatigue. It swam in large circles, diving in and out of the water.

"We did it!" Sara shouted. "It worked! It really worked!"

Exhausted, Mason sat down and took a breather.

"What are ya sittin' around for, boy!" Ray shouted. "We got more whales to save!"

With a proven system and three boats to work with, they quickly pulled the rest of the pod out to sea. They were out in the bay by late afternoon. Crews readied the boats, and all said their farewells. Mason and Tulok loaded burlap on the flatbed and re-attached it to the jeep.

"You know, if you hadn't flown in here," Sara said. "I probably would have used this stuff."

Mason saw the red duffle bag sitting on the floorboard. "I've learned that the longer you keep things in play, the more chances you get. It doesn't always work out, but this time it did."

"Yes, it did. Thank you." Their eyes met briefly.

"WOO-WOOO!" Ray's horn interrupted the moment. "Ya need anything else from me?"

"Excuse me," Mason said. "I'll be right back."

Mason waded through the surf and pulled himself up on deck where Ray was leaning on the longline reel.

"I hate to admit it, boy," Ray confessed. "But I guess ya do learn somethin' new every day. Ya come up with something new for Little Missy over there to write about."

"Hmm, maybe," Mason said. "I'm just glad it all worked out."

Splashing nearby caught their attention. Out in the bay, spouts and tails elevated against the horizon.

"We've really done something good here today, Cap," Mason said.

"Well, kid, ya got me thinkin'," Ray said. "Whales do have a place in the sea, and it's different from the fish. Thought I owed 'em one."

Ray smiled and patted Mason on the shoulder. The two men embraced. Then, Mason hopped overboard into the surf.

Back at the Jeep, Sara had the engine running with Tulok riding shotgun and the back seat jammed with gear. Mason's heart sank as he approached, thinking he might never see her again.

"Hey, they're all out there swimming around," he said. "We can still see them from the boat. They look happy."

He tried to make eye contact with her but knew Tulok was looking.

"Yep, it's truly a wonderful day," Sara had one hand on the gear-shift. "One I need to catalog as soon as possible."

"Hey, would you like to see them from a plane?" Mason pointed to the floatplane. They made eye contact.

"I wouldn't miss it for the world," she said with a beaming smile.

"I'll take the Jeep back and unload," Tulok added.

Chapter 9

Take a Chance

Clovis, AK

Minutes later, the floatplane throttled up and moved out across the bay.

"Put this headset on," Mason said. "And plug it into the console."

Sara quickly got it adjusted and motioned thumbs up. Mason noticed she seemed nervous when she grabbed the overhead safety strap.

"It's a little bouncy till you're in the air," he said.

"Just a little," she reluctantly agreed.

The plane popped out of the water and throttled up over treetops, then headed out across the bay. Seconds later, they saw spouts and the whales popping in and out of the water.

"There they are!" Sara shouted. "They're beautiful!"

"I think that's all of them," Mason said. "Let's take another pass."

They turned in a circular pattern while Sara busily took video.

"Looks like they're moving out to sea," Sara said.

"Well, I certainly hope so," he said. "At least until I rest up."

"You're a hero, you know," Sara offered, with a grin. "Like someone in a movie that came out of nowhere, and so is the captain."

"I'm no hero," Mason replied.

They made eye contact as Sara squeezed his arm. Mason felt a rush come over him.

"We did good today, didn't we," he said.

Sara reached for his hand. "I think you're a special person," she said.

They followed the pod out to open water. A fitting end to a miraculous day that Sara had feared would end in disaster. And in all the excitement, she forgot about the tracking monitor.

"Do you have a USB port in here?" she asked.

"This plane is thirty years old," Mason answered.

"Got it," she said, and stowed it behind the seat.

"You ever fly over the mountains?" Mason asked.

He pulled the plane toward the coastline, lifted to 3,000 feet, and headed inland. Mason held her hand tightly as they cruised in among the peaks where the mountains reached 4,000 feet.

"When you're right on top of 'em," Mason said. "They're unreal."

Sara could see a relaxed, confident look in his eyes, a man that seemed content with everything about him.

"So, you've been flying all your life?" Sara asked.

"Pretty much," Mason answered. "My dad's a pilot, so he took me up a lot. Anyway, it makes the commute to Cali a lot easier."

Mason noticed the compass spin back and forth. His concerned gaze caught Sara's attention, but she did not say anything.

"So, how long have you been saving whales?" he asked.

"Most of my life," Sara said. "When I was thirteen, my mother and I were walking a beach and found a dead gray whale. I could just tell it was so out of place, lost and scared before it died."

"So, it traumatized you," he said. "Set you on a course."

"You could say that," she replied. "I don't like to see innocent creatures put in harm's way."

Mason turned back toward the sea, the compass still spinning.

"And how do you know the captain?" she asked, starting to get concerned about the compass.

"I came up here looking for work after high school," he said. "Ray was the first guy I asked for a job."

Mason flicked the compass with his finger, but no change.

"What does that mean?" Sara finally asked.

"Not sure," he replied. "Compasses have been acting funny all week."

They cruised for a while and dropped in for a landing back at the beach where Tulok waited by the Jeep.

"Toss me the ropes!" Tulok exclaimed. "I'll get it tied off for you."

Sara and Mason walked toward the Jeep. There was an awkward silence as Mason looked for words.

"I suppose you need time to re-group after this," he said.

"Oh yeah," she said.

"We could exchange numbers," Mason offered. "If our cell phones had power."

Sara jumped in the Jeep and fumbled through the glove box. "Not a pen to write with," she said.

Mason thought about the plane but knew it would be easier to find a needle in a haystack than to find a pen in that plane. "Well, you can always find me in Pelham at the King Crab," he said.

"I like that idea." She smiled.

"I'll keep an eye out for you," Mason said. He felt a rush as they made eye contact and embraced. He wanted so much more but was still a little intimidated by Sara and couldn't figure out why. He didn't want to overstep his boundaries so early in a relationship, so he pulled away, grinned the best smile he could, and let fate take a hand.

Tulok tied off the plane for a second time.

PART 2

Core rotation – Southern Alaska near the 60th parallel

As the axis of the core rotates, subtle environmental changes occur. A thinning ozone layer follows the rotation as do the Auroras and higher radiation levels.

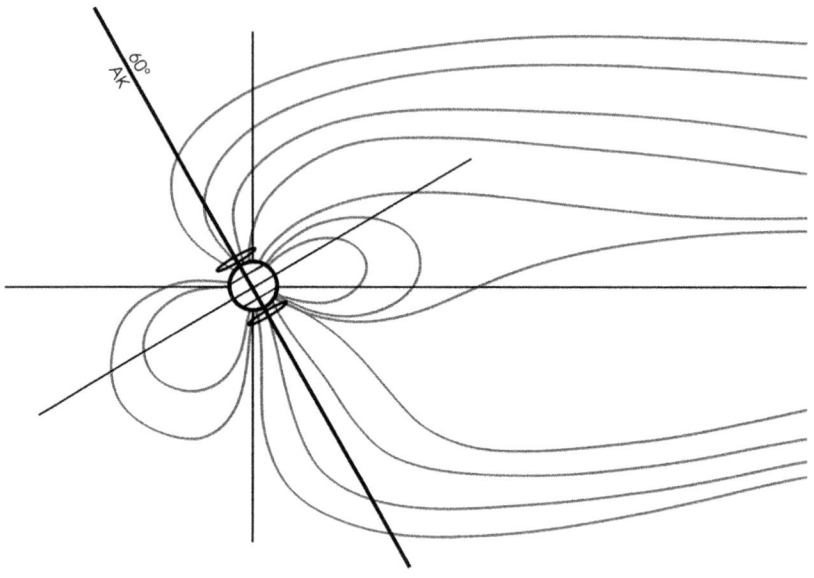

Chapter 10
The King Crab

Bristol Bay, AK

M ason made his way back to Pelham Airport and walked
back to his apartment. The twenty-minute walk seemed
like an eternity. Had he let something go? Should he have said
something different to her? Suddenly, the guy who had no cares
in the world found an unfamiliar knot in his stomach. An uneasy
confusion rushed through him. Had he lost her? Why did that
even matter? It kept circling through his mind.

Mason stood in his apartment, beer in hand, staring out across
Pelham Bay, watching fishing boats motor in and out. He was exhausted but could not sleep. Finally, he pulled the curtains to dark-
en the room, plugged in his dead cell phone, flopped on the bed,
and drifted off to sleep.

A few hours had passed when Mason awoke to Ray's loud
passing by. Ray knew his apartment and knew that Mason would
be sound asleep after his long adventure. Mason checked his cell
phone for the time; he had slept through to the next morning.
He stumbled out of bed, put on a pot of coffee, and took a quick

shower. Three cups of coffee later, he headed out to the King Crab.

***

The Crab was its usual self as the lunch crowd filed out. Mason smiled and nodded to people as he walked up to his regular seat at the bar. The excited server hurried over.

"Well, you're the talk of the town," Rita said. "Everyone's going on and on about rescuing those whales."

"I guess news travels fast," Mason groaned. "But it wasn't only me. Ray and a lot of other people showed up to help."

"True," she said. "But you stayed out there for twenty-four hours, fighting off wolves and coyotes before they ever showed up."

"You heard about that?" he asked.

"Yep, so did everyone else," Rita replied. "I think Ray is spreading the good word."

Mason smirked and motioned for a beer.

"Hey, you clean up nicely," she continued, noticing his new shirt and shaven face.

A tall beer in a handled mug landed on the old wooden bar in front of him.

"I get tired of smelling like fish," Mason replied. "Can I get the special?"

"Sure can."

Mason sat at the end of the bar with his familiar reflection looking back at him. He turned away. The room was empty.

"So, tell me all about it," Rita asked. "There's nobody here now. What else do you want to talk about?"

Mason sighed and rolled his eyes.

"Come on," she queried. "I heard you were fighting wolves bare-handed, riding whales like a cowboy, and you met a girl."

Mason wondered how she knew all that and gave a wry smile.

"And I leap tall buildings in a single bound, too," he said.

Rita chuckled. Mason took a big slug of beer and wiped his mouth.

"OK, it was pretty intense," he offered. "Hungry wolves are hard to fight off without guns. But we managed to fight them off for hours. If Ray hadn't shown up when he did, we'd have had to leave the whales to the wolves."

"I heard your girlfriend was going to put them to sleep so they wouldn't feel anything," she said. "The way they do at the dog pound."

Confused and dumbfounded again. "Where do you hear this stuff?" Mason asked.

"One of the Boy Scouts told me that," she said. "And Ray's all over that one."

Mason sighed.

"Did you really ride on a whale?" she asked.

"Noooo!" Mason blurted. "I think these stories you've heard are a bit exaggerated."

"You're being too modest," Rita said, walking back to the kitchen.

Mason slugged down his beer, then stood and walked around the room. He was still thinking about Sara but felt better about the whole situation now that he had a chance to sleep on it. He looked out over the bay, no activity. All the boats were still out, but the mid-day runs would soon be over, and the sounds of fishermen would fill the air.

"Here you go, sweetie," Rita said, placing a plate of food on the bar.

"Thanks," he said. "I'm starving."

"So, are you going to tell me about this mystery girl?" she asked.

Mason caved to the inevitable and decided that actual facts would help dispel crazy rumors.

"Not a whole lot to tell," Mason said. "She's basically a marine biologist. I liked her the first time I saw her, but we were in the middle of this rescue effort. There were a few times we talked when things calmed down, and I thought we had a connection.

"Then I took her for a plane ride to watch the whale pod make their way out to sea. It was a great ride. She really enjoyed it; she took video of the whales. Then we flew inland around the mountains. She'd never done that before."

"Did you get her number?" Rita asked.

"No," Mason said. "Neither cell phone had power, and we couldn't find a pen."

"What?"

"But I think it might work out," he admitted.

The sound of boat motors and horns filled the air. Mason turned to see the fleets making port with the day's catch.

"Ray will be here soon," Rita said, patting Mason on the shoulder.

***

Mason had finished the daily special and a second beer when fishermen started filing in. This crowd had, in recent months, become background noise, just cars going by on a freeway. But now, it was a refreshing sound to his ears. Everyone was full of life and happy to be there. Gloating about the day's catch, who pulled in the most fish, who had mechanical trouble, who caught something they were not supposed to, and the usual bellyaching about the Alaska Department of Fish and Game. Mason took it all in with a grin on his face and another beer in his hand.

A few minutes later, Ray slapped him on the back. "Where's my whiskey, boy?" he asked. "Don't ya think I deserve one?"

Mason made a swirling motion with his finger. Rita laid down two shots and left the bottle. The two men threw backs the shots; Mason poured another round.

"Ray, I owe you an apology for the way I acted in here the other day," Mason said. "And a thank you for helping us out there."

Ray grinned. "Don't worry about it, boy," he said. "I could tell ya have too many things on yer mind these days. Besides, it felt good to save those beasties."

He threw back another shot.

"Ya knows," he continued. "Even old men learn new lessons.

Right some wrongs."

Mason smiled as Rita busily wiped down the counter, eavesdropping on the conversation. She broke a smile, too.

"So, what's next for ya?" Ray asked.

"Not really sure," Mason replied.

"I'm talkin' 'bout the lady," Ray said, leaning in Mason's face.

Rita's ears perked.

"I'm not sure where we stand." Mason shook his head. "But there was chemistry."

"So, ya like her?" Ray asked, with a quick glance at the 'fly on the wall' washing glasses.

"What's not to like," Mason said. "She's beautiful, she's smart, and she drives an old Jeep."

They took another shot.

"She cares about the world, the environment, and animals," he continued. "She doesn't care about material things. Do you know any people who are that way? I don't know any, except her."

"So, am I losing a good first mate?" Ray asked.

"You're not losing anything," Mason said.

"It's all right, boy," Ray conceded. "Not all men fall in love with the sea. Most men fall in love with a woman."

"Who said anything about—"

"I can see it in your eyes," Ray stopped him mid-sentence. "And in everything about ya."

Rita popped up from behind the counter.

"I see it, too," she said. "And it's about time. Hearts will be breaking all over town."

Mason had that dumbfounded expression again. Ray placed a hand on Mason's shoulder.

"I'm happy for ya, boy," he said. "See ya tomorrow on the boat?"

"Sure, I'll be there."

***

Mason left the restaurant for the airport to check on his plane since he had dropped it off in a hurry the day before.

It was a mess inside, but nothing needed immediate attention. The dried mud on the pilot seat surprised him at first, then he remembered the wolves and the struggle to get the flares. He looked behind the front seat for a rag or an old shirt to wipe it down, but his hand hit something else. It was the radio tracking device that Sara stuffed back there and something that would need to be returned.

***

When he got back to the King Crab, the dinner crowd had started to roll in. He made his way toward the bar and noticed his usual seat occupied. Rita stood nearby, taking a table order, grinning at

Mason as he walked past. When he reached the bar, he had to look twice. There she sat, Sara!

He could not believe how attractive she was. He had only seen her covered in mud. But she had let her hair down and wore a nice leather jacket over a white cotton top, and she smelled heavenly.

"I wasn't sure you would show up," Mason said. "You look beautiful."

"You clean up nicely, too," she said. "And you shaved."

He fumbled for words, then held out the tracking device.

"I found this in the Cessna," he said. "Thought you might want it."

She took it from him and placed it on the bar. "Did you find anything else?" she asked, standing from her stool.

She reached both arms around his neck and pulled him close. They kissed, and Mason tried to keep himself as his heart pounded. He fumbled for words as he pulled out a bar stool for her.

Rita made her way over and sat a beer in front of Mason. "What will you have, honey?" she asked Sara. "I know you've been sipping on water, but this occasion calls for something with a kick."

"Bourbon and Coke?" Sara asked.

"Coming right up!"

Mason was awestruck by her: she is beautiful, brilliant, drives a Jeep, has a short-wave radio, saves stranded animals, *and* drinks Bourbon. Sara caught the expression on his face.

"Everything OK?" she asked.

"Fine," he answered. "Why do you ask?"

"Nothing," she said. "It appeared you wanted to say something."

When he didn't respond, she changed the subject.

"You know, I've been thinking about that whole experience at Clovis. What you guys did with those pulleys is a new technique, and it worked perfectly. That procedure must be published. It could save whales all over the world."

"I've never felt better about anything in my life," Mason said. "I couldn't believe we pulled that big bull out into the water."

"I know; we were all exhausted and surrendered to their fate," Sara responded. "I had nothing left."

"It really was a miracle," Mason said. "Wasn't it?"

"Yes, it was," she replied. "It started the second you landed on that beach."

They made eye contact as their hands clasped. Rita placed a tall bourbon and Coke in front of Sara.

"On the house."

"Thank you," Sara politely replied.

Mason's eyebrows were raised in surprise.

"Don't give me that look," Rita said. "I comp your beer all the time."

Rita walked on to check tables.

"So, where's the captain this evening?" Sara asked.

"Ray only comes in for lunch," Mason said. "He spends half his time working on the boat and the rest sipping whiskey."

"He seems to be quite a character," she said.

"He certainly is," Mason responded. "So, did you drive out here in the Jeep?"

"Sure did."

"Two-hour drive, right?" he asked.

"That's right."

"You know, there's a way to cut that return trip this evening down to almost nothing," Mason said.

"Down to almost nothing?" she asked. "Are you going to perform another miracle?"

"No."

"Are we flying again?"

"No."

"Does it involve reeling me in with one of those spool boats?" she asked.

"No spools," he returned. "But I am trying to reel you in."

"Reel me in?"

"Sure," he said. "You stay here tonight and drive back tomorrow."

Sara took a sip of Bourbon.

"Hmm, does that mean I can start writing that procedure?" she asked. "With all this extra time?"

"Depends."

"On what?"

"You'll need something to write with," he said. "Do you have a pen in the Jeep?"

Sara burst out laughing.

***

The next morning at Mason's one-room flat, they lay in his bed warm and spooned under blankets. A cool breeze blew in from the bay through a partially open window. Seabirds cackled and flew circles as Gillnetters made their way out of the harbor. Mason and Sara awoke to the sound of Ray's deafening horn.

"Does he do that on purpose?" Sara asked.

"Only when I'm not on the boat," Mason said. "Not sure if he's mad at me or playing around, even on days off."

The rumble of boat motors filled the cool morning air. It was a new day for both Sara and Mason.

"How did you sleep?" he asked.

"Slept great," she replied. "I haven't slept in someone's arms in years. Thank you."

"My pleasure," Mason said. "Would you like some coffee?"

"That sounds wonderful," she said.

Mason pulled on his pants and walked over to the kitchenette. He set up the coffee machine and pulled cups from the cabinet. Both cell phones lay charging on the countertop.

"How about some eggs?" he asked.

"Love some." Sara sat up in bed.

"Coming right up," he said. "Do you want to check your phone?"

"Not really," she said. "But I probably should."

Mason pulled out the USB line, and her screen lit up with several unanswered text messages.

"Somebody's looking for you," he said, handing her the cell phone.

"Probably my mother," she said. "Oh yes, my goodness, twelve texts."

Mason went back to the coffee and eggs.

"How about some toast?" he asked.

"Oh my God, something's happening up north in the National Oil Preserve," Sara said. "She wants me to fly up there to investigate fires spreading in the tundra. This must be what she called about before I left for Clovis."

"What do you mean?" Mason asked. "Fires on the North Slope? That's impossible."

"Evidently not," she said. "I need to call her."

She hit the speed dial.

"By the way," she continued. "Can we take your plane up there if she needs me to go—Hello, Mother?" Sara said.

Mason gave thumbs up.

"Hello, sweetheart," Julia Gathers replied. "And I can finally hear you, clearly."

"So, what's going on up there," Sara asked. "With these wildfires."

"It's a bit complicated, dear," Julia said. "There are two large fires, started by an unusual atmospheric phenomenon and, I think, spreading by methane gas releasing from melting permafrost.

"I've been in front of a Congressional committee twice now, and they are demanding answers. Our survey crew was investigating, but we lost them in one of the fires. It's a dangerous situation.

"Our Atmospheric Sciences team has determined the cause of the fire, but I need proof of the methane emissions.

"Can you fly up there to look into this for me? I don't want you near the fires, but from a few miles away, you should be able to get soil samples."

Julia Gathers was Mother, Matriarch, and head of a national organization. When she asked for something, you simply did it. She never raised her voice or stomped her feet. No one crossed her in personal or professional life, and Sara was part of both.

"I have access to a floatplane," Sara said. "I should be able to get up there in …"

Mason scribbled on a piece of paper 'normally twelve hours with fueling, but there's a flight restriction notification on my cell phone—No-Fly Zone.'

"Is that normal?" Sara asked.

"Sorry, dear?" Julia said.

"Sorry, Mother. I wasn't talking to you," Sara said. "About twelve hours flight time, but there are flight restrictions in the area. It's a no-fly zone."

"I can get you flight clearance," Julia told. "But you might have to go through Fort Patterson. I'll text you the instructions later. Thank you, sweetheart. Take care."

Sara hung up and turned to Mason.

"Is this OK?" she asked. "I mean, I feel like I'm seriously imposing here."

"One thing I learned at Clovis," he said. "I don't want to get on your bad side. You're as strong-willed as they come, and I'm sure the nut doesn't fall far from the tree, so I'm not going to irritate your mother either."

Sara smiled.

"I had the plane checked out and fueled," Mason said. "So, it's ready to go. We can stop by your place to load up your gear."

"We shouldn't need much," she said. "Can I leave the Jeep here? That will save a couple of hours drive time."

"Sure, it will be fine here," he said. "This is turning out to be one hell of a week."

Chapter 11

Fort Patterson

Crossing the Alaskan Range

W e'll follow the coastline north for a few hours," Mason said over the headset. "Then stop for fuel in Isolene. But we'll need that flight plan to Ft. Patterson before we leave Isolene."

"Understood," Sara said. "I should have that text anytime."

"Are you sure we have everything you need for this expedition?" Mason asked. "I mean, a few buckets, a shovel, and some matches?"

"That's right," she replied. "I assume you have a knife, right?"

"Always."

They continued up the western Alaskan coast for two hours and finally had the town in sight.

"I'm glad this compass quit acting up," Mason said. "Made the trip a lot easier."

"Mother said there were atmospheric disturbances," Sara said. "Maybe that explains the compass problem and why we lost communication in Clovis."

"So, if it acts up again," Mason asked. "Could be more trouble?"

He pulled the plane around toward the docks at the end of town near the airport. It was a smooth approach in a cloudless sky.

"By the way. Who *is* your mother?" he asked. "Not just anyone can get military clearance to enter a No-Fly Zone."

"She's the Director of NOAA," Sara said. "A highly important position in this day and age."

"I guess so," Mason acknowledged, making a tight turn. "Hang on."

The floatplane made a gentle splash in the bay, slowed to a stop, and idled to the docks. Two men waited to tie it off as Mason and Sara hopped out.

"They'll fuel it up," he said. "We can catch a ride to town and grab something to eat."

They made it to a local burger joint and placed an order. Sara rechecked her cell phone, no text.

"I'm calling her," she said. "We need that information before we fly out of here, right?"

"That would be nice," Mason said. "But Patterson is in Fairbanks, so if we're heading that way, there are non-military airports where we could land temporarily."

Sara sighed. "I'm still calling her."

She hit the 'mom' button again, and momentarily she got an answer.

"Sara, sweetheart, is that you?" Julia Gathers asked.

"Yes, Mother, we're enroute and need that security clearance," she said. "Have you had any luck with that?"

"I've just spoken with Colonel Jackson at Ft. Patterson," she said. "You need to check-in at the base first, then you can fly north. He's expecting your call. I'll text his number."

"We're in a floatplane," Sara said. "It lands on water. I don't know if it can land on a military runway."

"It has wheels, too," Mason interrupted.

"Really?"

"Excuse me?" Julia asked.

"Sorry, Mother," Sara said. "I guess it can land on runways."

"Perfect," Julia said. "Will you send me a report? There is a NOAA base in Perishton. They are expecting you. You can send the report from there."

"OK, Mother," Sara said. "We should be leaving for Ft. Patterson soon."

"Thank you, sweetheart," Julia said. "I love you."

"OK," Sara explained to Mason "A Colonel Jackson is expecting my call. We will land at Ft. Patterson, they will re-fuel us, and we'll be on our way."

"You're not kidding," Mason said. "She really does have connections. I wonder what the tower at Patterson will think when they see a floatplane coming into land?"

"So, does this plane really have wheels?" Sara asked.

"Sure does," Mason said. "Most floatplanes are for water only, but the Cessna has wheels that lower down for ground landings. I even have on-board ski attachments for snow landings."

Sara nodded. She liked versatile equipment.

"OK, I'm calling that Colonel before we take off," Sara said. "We have a good signal here."

A server brought out their orders. Mason started in without saying a word. Sara excused herself to make the call.

"This is Sara Gathers calling for Colonel Jackson," Sara said.

"Yes, ma'am," a voice responded. "He is expecting your call. Please hold."

"Jackson here," the colonel answered.

"Colonel Jackson," Sara said. "Sara Gathers here. My mother mentioned you could get me flight clearance to investigate wild-fires on the North Slope."

"Yes, ma'am," he said. "Have you contacted the tower here on ETA and plane registration?"

"No, we haven't yet," she said. "But I know we will be leaving Isolene within the hour."

"That's good enough," he stated. "We'll be expecting you."

"Thank you, Colonel," she responded.

"You sound just like your mother," the colonel said. "I've known her since before you were born. I have a lot of respect for that lady. It will be a pleasure meeting you this afternoon."

"I look forward to meeting you, too, sir," Sara said.

Sara walked back inside to a waiting burger and fries.

"Are we squared away?" Mason asked.

Sara reached for the hamburger and motioned a thumbs up.

"Good burger isn't it?" he asked.

Thumbs up again, with a mouth full.

"OK, then," he said. "We should be fueled up anytime."

The four-hour flight across the Alaskan interior was uneventful. No issues with the compass or any other instruments. Sara did not appreciate the bumpy ride and started to feel nauseous. Mason told her downdrafts and up currents from the nearby mountains caused the turbulence. But soon enough, they could see Mt. Denali in the distance, and Ft. Patterson was not far away.

Mason radioed the control tower and received clearance for landing. He pulled the plane into position two miles out from the runway but could not shake the feeling that something was wrong.

Civilian aircraft do not land at military installations, there were no fighter jet fly-bys or escorts, and the runway looked empty. So, he dropped the plane in and made a gentle landing.

Two men with red flags directed them toward the main hanger, where they came to a stop outside the hanger door. Mason and Sara stepped down onto the tarmac. An official vehicle pulled up at once. Four officers filed out and approached. The older officer walked over to Sara.

"Miss Gathers," he said, extending his hand. "Colonel Matthew Jackson. It's a pleasure to make your acquaintance."

Colonel Jackson was a tall, broad-shouldered man with the thickness of age in face and waist, but he still displayed a healthy military presence. His crew cut had, no doubt, not changed since his enlistment decades ago. He was formal, respectful, and to the point.

"The pleasure is mine," Sara replied. "We can't thank you enough for allowing us access to the North Slope air space.

"This is Mason Hahn," she continued. "He will be flying me up there."

"Colonel," Mason said, extending his hand.

"We'll get you on your way shortly," Colonel Jackson said. "I assume you need fuel. Any other supplies?"

"No other supplies, thank you," Sara said. "But maybe something to eat before we leave."

Jackson turned to the other officers.

"Captain, bring up another car," he ordered.

"Miss Gathers," he continued. "You get to try the Officer's Mess Hall. It's not bad food, but it's the best we got."

"That would be wonderful, thank you," she returned. "I'm not used to flying in small planes and turbulence near the mountains."

"Sounds like you could also use a bicarbonate," the colonel stated. "Dramamine, or even a good stiff drink."

That brought a smile to Sara's face.

***

Colonel Jackson and many of his staff accompanied Sara and Mason to dinner. The colonel discussed how water airdrops with DC-10 tankers successfully extinguished the wildfires. He also recommended an aerial escort to the North Slope.

"That's a generous offer, Colonel," Sara said. "But our work up there is pretty straightforward, so I don't think we need assistance on the ground."

She looked over to Mason.

"I've flown from Fairbanks to Perishton dozens of times, Colonel," he related. "So, unless another magnetic storm hits, we should be OK."

"A Chinook will get you there a lot faster," the colonel said. "And a lot smoother ride. No offense, Mr. Hahn, the Cessna is a fine plane."

"None taken," Mason said.

"Besides, your mother would never forgive me if didn't make the offer," the colonel followed.

"We also need to meet with the NOAA group in Perishton," Sara said. "And that could take time, maybe a day or two."

"As you please," Jackson said. "So, how is the salmon?"

"Excellent," Sara said. "Five-star restaurant quality."

"I have some connections." He smiled. "We get it flown in daily."

"Speaking of connections," Sara said. "How do you know my mother?"

The colonel paused and smiled.

"Many years back," he started. "Before you were born, I was in the Corps of Engineers—Military Haz-Mat section. In the late 1980s, the United States and the Soviet Union agreed to destroy many weapons of mass destruction: nukes and chemical weapons mostly. VX nerve agent was stored at bases all around the country. It's a highly toxic nerve gas developed during the Vietnam War.

"Anyway, lots of public outcry about it. How to safely dispose of something so lethal when a single grain can kill a person in three seconds? And the plan was to burn it, so where do the ashes and smoke go?

"Long story short, the whole thing went to court. Big media hoopla. We tried to convince people that our plan was safe, but then your mother stepped in on behalf of the EPA, and she cleaned our collective clocks. In the end, a new facility had to be built, and all VX from around the country shipped to one location for proper disposal.

"She represented herself, the EPA, and the public so well and carried herself so eloquently that, in the end, I even rooted for her. The cost was high, and I took a bit of a career beating, but it was the best solution for the country."

"You seem taken by her," Sara teased.

"Who wouldn't be?" he reflected. "And from all appearances, Julia groomed you in her image."

"I can vouch for that," Mason said.

That brought out a chuckle from the table.

"What is she sending you up there to do, if I may ask," Colonel Jackson said. "The methane?"

Sara's eyes perked up. "How do you know about that?" she asked.

"Your mother discussed it at the hearing," he said. "Then some of my team saw it first-hand the next day."

Jackson motioned across the table.

"Captain," he said. "Please describe your findings to Miss Gathers."

"Yes, Sir," he said. "We landed about one mile upwind of the eastern fire. The ground was swampy, lakes and streams everywhere. Water was bubbling but mostly from the lakes. As we walked along, we heard occasional splashing sounds. We thought it was a fish jumping from the water. But when we got up close, it was giant bubbles popping out of the water, released from gas pockets below."

"And the water was bubbling everywhere?" Sara asked.

"Yes, ma'am," he replied. "Even in our muddy boot prints."

Sara looked concerned, contemplating. "Did the fire appear to be expanding?" she asked. "Maybe jumping across the water?"

"We couldn't get close enough to tell," he said. "The flames were too intense. I've seen grassfires before, but not like this. Something else had to be feeding it."

Sara could realistically land anywhere for soil sampling. But now, she was intrigued by the wildfires. At first, she did not fully understand Julia's request, but now it had taken on a whole new light. And since the fires were out, she could get a first-hand look.

"Colonel," Sara redirected. "Thank you for dinner and the briefing. But I think it's time we gather our things and head north."

They all exchanged goodbyes and good luck. Minutes later, the Cessna made a rolling lift-off and headed north.

Chapter 12

St. Elmo's Fire

Heading North

Seafarers in wooden ships centuries ago charted waters with handheld sextants and compasses. Navigating long voyages was impossible without these two essential devices and two natural constants, the North Star and the Magnetic Pole.

Occasionally, sailors faced strange atmospheric disturbances on the open sea, exotic light displays caused by thunderstorms, volcanoes, and Auroras. These were bad omens in an age devoid of scientific knowledge. Survivors of these encounters paid tribute to St. Erasmus, the patron saint of sailors. They called these phenomena St. Elmo's Fire.

***

"Did you believe that story about the bubbles in the water?" Mason asked.

"We'll find out soon enough," Sara said. "I had no idea this could happen. Mother has mentioned a few times that melting permafrost would lead to methane release. But she didn't say it was this advanced."

"We should reach the North Slope in three and a half hours," Mason said. "And the compass is holding steady. If you start feeling bad, let me know, and I'll find a place to land."

"I'm fine for now, thanks," she said. "By the way, I had a great time last night."

Their eyes met.

"Me too." He smiled.

* * *

Eventually, they reached the Brooks Range, the northern Alaskan Mountains that extend to the vast tundra plain. The sun sat low on the horizon, and hues of the blue sky darkened to a twilight color. The unusual June Auroras started to flicker into sight and increased with every passing minute.

"There it goes again," Mason said.

"Yes." Sara gawked. "They're beautiful."

"Yes, they are," he said. "But look at the compass. It's spinning again."

"Can you still find your way?" she asked.

"GPS is still good," he said.

When they finally passed, the Brooks Range trees disappeared, and slopes flattened out to grassy tundra that stretched to the horizon. Sara started to feel nauseous again. Mason searched for a lake to land on for a break. Sara decided that landing would be worse than flying, so they continued.

In time they were on it. "I can see it," Mason said. "There, straight ahead, that flat red patch."

The tell-tale sign of water drops on wildfires is a red chemical retardant. The red patch seemed to grow as they approached. It was a three-square-mile patchwork of red stripes, overlaid on a pitch-black canvas of burnt-out vegetation. The red lines criss-crossed at angles like brush strokes on canvas. Obviously, Colonel Jackson's effort was thorough.

"We'll try that small lake to the west," Mason said. "How does that look to you?"

"That should do," Sara returned.

Mason pulled the plane around and dropped down to the water surface. He taxied up to the water's edge and throttled the plane up to the grassy bank. The marshy soil made for tricky footing, but soon enough, the obvious was in front of them. Sara bent over for a closer look at the bubbling water. Mason approached with shovel and buckets in hand.

"This is incredible," Sara worried. "If not frightening."

Mason had been flying up here for years and never seen it, but the lakes were frozen during his winter stints in Perishton. Even so, there were never discussions or even rumors about this phenomenon.

"OK, how are we doing this?" Mason asked.

"Fill three buckets with soil," she said. "One sample from the bank, one with undisturbed tundra soil, and the third from the charred area. I need the fourth bucket and your knife."

Mason tossed her the knife and was impressed with how well she handled it.

Mason started digging at the shoreline while Sara carved a tiny hole in the bottom of the bucket, then plugged it with an old gum wrapper. Mason looked on while she carefully placed the bucket on the water, open-end down, and held the bucket in place for a few minutes. Then she pulled a matchbox from her coat pocket, removed the gum wrapper from the hole, struck a match, and held it over the hole. It lit into a blow torch, burned for a few seconds, and died out.

"That's a nice trick," Mason noticed.

"This is what my mother was afraid of," she said. "There's a lot of methane release up here. Certainly, enough to fuel fires. And at this rate, cause many other problems. Let's gather these samples and head to Perishton for testing."

"OK," Mason said. "One down."

They walked toward the charred spot but stopped halfway for the tundra soil sample. Mason dug it out, vegetation and all. The roots were still tough to cut through, but they eventually pulled away from the marshy soil.

They got this creepy crop-circle feeling when they reached the charred spot. They were standing in something unnatural, otherworldly. The charred soil was a wet, crunchy chemical mess. The intensity of the fire damaged the root system and left the ground abnormally soft and fluid. They did not move far into it, fearing a quicksand effect. Meanwhile, the Aurora was getting brighter and starting to crackle.

"Let's wrap this up and get out of here," Sara said.

They found a small black area with almost no red chemical stain to pull the last sample, nothing but mud and black char. They walked quickly back to the plane, loaded up, and taxied out for take-off. Sara popped tops on the buckets and labeled them. The plane headed east toward Perishton, compass spinning and Auroras crackling across the sky.

"What is this?" Sara asked.

"I don't know," Mason replied. "Never seen anything like it before. No wonder it's a no-fly zone."

"This went from breath-taking, to frightening," she said.

"You ever hear of St. Elmo's Fire?" Mason asked.

"No, what is it?" she asked.

The Auroras suddenly illuminated with sparkling bursts of light. Sara reached for Mason's hand.

"Sailors in the old days," he explained. "Back when they first started exploring the oceans, came across all kinds of unexplainable things; northern lights, thunderstorms, meteor showers, you name it. It was all a mystery to them, especially on small wooden ships at sea with nowhere to hide. Heck, they called the tip of South America the land of fire, but it was only the southern lights.

"Anyway, they prayed for St. Elmo to see them through."

More crackling and flashing off in the distance.

"And they called the lights," Mason squinted, "St. Elmo's Fire."

Sara lifted a hand to shade her eyes.

"So, I should start praying to St. Elmo, right?" she asked.

Chapter 13

Rescue

National Petroleum Reserve, AK

Imagine a world where Corporations have carbon-neutral footprints. They balance CO_2 output with CO_2 absorption by acquiring forests and farmland. Western Europe and Japan have used this system since the 1990s, but the superpowers will not agree to such legislation.

***

Suddenly another bright flash. There was an explosion in the sky, down in front of them at low altitude. Then another bright flash.

"Those are flares," Mason realized. "Somebody's in trouble."

He flew in low and circled. He saw a man crossing the tundra on foot, waving his arms to signal them. Mason circled in low a few times, signaling thumbs up, then made for a landing in a pond not far away. By the time the plane came to a stop, the man was close by, sloshing through the tundra.

Mason quickly jumped out of the plane and ran toward him. The man was young and on the edge of collapse, his clothes ragged and filthy.

"Are you all right?" Mason asked.

The young man collapsed. Mason picked him up and carried him to the plane.

"He's just a kid," Mason said. "Help me get him in here."

Sara pushed things around to make room in the back of the plane. She managed to clear out one side enough for him to lie down.

"My bag." The boy sighed softly. "Do you have my bag?"

"This one?" Mason asked lifting the bag.

"That's it," the boy whispered.

They carried him into the back seat.

"What in the hell are you doing out here?" Mason asked.

"Perishton, take me to Perishton," he whispered and passed out from exhaustion.

"I'll get us back in the air," Mason said. "And radio ahead that we rescued a man who needs medical attention. Check him for identification. Maybe there's something in that bag."

"Got it," Sara replied. "He's probably dehydrated. Do you have anything for him to drink?"

"There should be power drinks or water in the cooler," Mason said. "Back there somewhere."

Once in the air, Mason tried the staticky radio but had no luck. Sara jumped in the back and searched his pants and coat pockets. She found a saturated cell phone in his front pocket that did not work. There was nothing else on him, no watches or jewelry, so she opened his satchel bag.

She pulled out a laptop computer that looked surprisingly dry and a notebook. Then she noticed something around his neck. It was tucked inside his shirt. A lanyard, the kind for access to official buildings or events. She pulled it out from his shirt collar.

Ethan Sites
Asst. Mgr. – Operations
NOAA – (NCEI) Magnetic Field Tracking Facility
Perishton, AK

"Oh, my God," she blurted.

"What?" Mason asked. "What did you find?"

"I don't believe it," she said.

"What is it?" Mason asked.

"This kid works for NOAA," Sara said. "He must be from the plane crash."

"What does that mean?"

"It means this kid knows a lot about these strange events," Sara said. "The only eyewitness. We have to get him back safely."

"There's a med center in Perishton," Mason said. "But it's at least an hour away. Did you find any water back there?"

"I'm looking for it."

"If you can get some water in him before we land," he followed, "he might not need any medical help. He just looks dehydrated, and he's a young kid, so he could snap out of it quickly."

"I don't know." She sifted through the back for the cooler.

"Look," Mason said. "He was walking and had no apparent injuries, so he should be all right."

"Found it," Sara said. "This thing is tiny."

"It's a plane," he replied.

"And the smell," she said, covering her nose and mouth. "When was the last time you used this?"

"Been a while."

"There are three bottles of water and two beers," she said. "At least they're unopened."

She pulled the water bottles out and quickly shut the lid.

"I have to wake him to get fluids into his system," Sara said.

She shook him and checked his eyes. No dilation. He was only asleep. She kept shaking him, shouting his name. He finally responded in a groggy voice.

"Where are we going?" he asked softly.

Sara could barely hear his voice and leaned her mouth to his ear. "Perishton," Sara said.

"Who … are you?" he murmured.

"NOAA," she replied.

His glazy eyes sharpened.

"Drink this," Sara said.

With the instinct of a starving man, Ethan grabbed the water bottle and tilted it to his mouth. Half went in, half rolled down his face. Sara grabbed another bottle. In minutes, there was color in his face and focus in his eyes.

"What were you doing out there?" Sara asked. "You're from the plane crash, aren't you?"

She could see the instant recall draw across his face. The crash, the fires.

"John," he cried. "Where's John?"

Sara shook her head. Then Ethan remembered the fiery crash and broke down as the horrific memory rushed in. Sara bowed her head and tried to console him, but Ethan could not stop sobbing. Mason could hear him from the cockpit.

"At least you're safe now," she consoled. "And that's a miracle."

***

Gauges on the console spun and flashed erratic readings. GPS tracking was offline. Mason kept flying, hoping the situation would resolve itself. The threatening skies were worsening.

"Hey," Mason shouted. "Things are getting pretty bad up here."

Sara climbed up front and saw brilliant Auroras glowing bright, even in the daytime sun. Ethan regrouped and crawled up between them, his pilot's eyes staring at the swirling gauges.

"Are you flying blind?" he asked.

"Ha, welcome aboard," Mason boasted.

"You can't keep going this direction," Ethan said. "I'm a pilot, and I've been tracking this phenomenon. Trust me, you don't want to keep moving in this direction."

"Well, how else are we going to get to Perishton?" Mason asked.

"You're heading east, right?"

"Best I can tell."

"Then turn and head north to the coast," Ethan said. "You can follow the coastline to the bay."

"Why do that?" Sara asked.

"Because it's been tracking east-southeast for days," Ethan said. "So, if we head north to the coast, we'll stay out of its path."

"Stay out of what's path?" Mason asked.

Ethan turned away in hesitation. His work was not common knowledge to the public. Even his superiors at NOAA had not thoroughly analyzed the data, nor did they have the new data stored in Ethan's computer or water-logged cell phone.

"Look, I saw your ID lanyard. We're on the same team," Sara said. "I'm Sara Gathers with NOAA. We're investigating these fires and are heading to NOAA—Perishton. Any information you can share would be helpful."

"Wait, did you say, Sara Gathers?" he asked.

"Yes, why?"

"Any relation to Julia Gathers?"

"Her daughter."

"Seriously?" he asked. Julia's name was on every NOAA letterhead. "OK, that's legit. So, you're up here to investigate the fires? Do you know what started them?"

"Yes," Sara said. "Methane gas leaching from the soil. We picked up soil samples for testing. Stored right behind you."

"OK, but do you know what started them?" he asked. "The heat source?"

"No," she said. "But we heard about these strange atmospheric disturbances. The same as we're seeing now. Maybe, it was a lightning strike."

"Ha, no," he said. "It wasn't."

He looked away again. Mason and Sara exchanged confused glances.

"Hey," Sara said. "I know you've been through something terrible. But we need your help here."

Ethan sighed.

"In real basic terms," he explained, "the Poles are moving. They're moving extremely fast."

Sara and Mason exchanged confused glances.

"I estimate at least 100 miles per day," he continued. "And it's a jerky movement. Starting and stopping again and again. The magnetic readings go wild when it happens. And when they move, they seem to interact with these excited Auroras.

"It makes a huge column of light that reaches from the ground to the stratosphere. A silent hurricane of light with tall vertical lines that change color.

"The first one left wilted grass, the second one stronger, mostly wilted ground vegetation. But some spots were dried and eventually ignited.

"The third one caught us by surprise. We were right on it before I could … Anyway, we had erratic gauge readings and control problems. But as we got closer, controls locked up, and the engine shut down."

"That's when you crashed?" Sara asked. "So, the other person on board didn't make it?"

Ethan swallowed, unable to answer.

"Was he NOAA, too?"

He nodded.

"So, whatever tracking information you had was lost as well?" she asked.

"No," Ethan said. "Not lost. It's right here."

Sara paused and turned. Ethan grabbed his satchel and checked his computer.

"OK," Sara said. "We're getting you back to NOAA."

She turned to Mason.

"This is huge," she remarked. "Let's follow the coastline. Get us there fast."

Mason acknowledged. The plane turned north under the Aurora-bright sky.

Sara tried her cell phone, but no service. She turned and looked down at the young man, still lying on the floorboard next to her. *What is all this?* Nothing had been the same since she got that call for the whale stranding. And now this.

"Birds," Ethan remembered. "I forgot about the birds."

"What about the birds?" Sara asked.

"They were everywhere," Ethan said. "They came out of no-where, thousands of them. They landed at the second site, but only around the perimeter of the dead grasses. They seemed lost and didn't notice us walking right through them.

"Then we saw them again, at the third site, circling the tower of light. And the caribou, they stampeded toward it."

Sara could not tell whether he was exhausted or dreaming. She reached down and patted his shoulder.

"Get some rest," she said. "We'll be there soon."

Chapter 14
Another Storm Brewing

Magnetic Field Tracking Facility
Perishton, AK

T he plane flew on as Sara thought about Ethan's story, and the thousands of lost seabirds circling the tempest. Regular bird migration follows magnetic field lines. Could sperm whales use magnetic field lines for navigation? Nothing proven. Could these strange phenomena have grounded them?

Soon they reached the north coast and flew out over the Arctic Ocean. The shoreline of the cold, steel-blue sea led them eastward. The Auroras slowly faded, and onboard instruments began functioning again.

"We're not far now," Mason said. "Is the kid asleep?"

"I believe so," Sara answered.

"Good, now his batteries can recharge," Mason said. "Hey, did that stuff he said about birds make any sense to you?"

"I'm not sure," she replied. "But it's got me thinking. This polar movement Ethan described is something completely new, affecting everything from people to plants and animals. I'm starting to think it's what stranded the whales in Clovis."

"This is all crazy," Mason said. "If it keeps up, and the Pole really is moving, it will ground commercial flights all around the world."

"That's right," Sara said. "Look what it's done to the instruments on this plane. And its confusing thousands of seabirds, so migratory patterns have been affected."

"Whatever is going on will eventually stop, right?" Mason asked.

Sara thought for a moment. "Honestly? I have no idea."

***

The plane approached Prudhoe Bay and Elliott Island, a manufactured outpost in the sea littered with towering oil-processing structures. Flashing lights on the tall stacks were an easy mark to spot from miles out. Mason made a slow circle around the island, then turned south toward Perishton, about ten miles from the coast.

Mason took a few minutes to convince Perishton Control that he had clearance to be in the air, but they eventually granted him permission to land. Ethan was still asleep, they had trouble waking him, but he finally came around. Mason called ahead to see if one of his buddies could pick them up, but no answer, so they took an airport shuttle to the NOAA facility.

"This is it?" Sara asked. "It's tiny, I mean, the radio towers are a dead giveaway, but the building is so small."

"Yeah, only a couple guys," Ethan returned. "But it's jammed with high-tech equipment."

They hopped out of the shuttle; Ethan ran up and pounded his fist on the door. The shuttle driver followed behind with the soil samples.

"You would think with all this technology," Sara observed, "they would have a doorbell."

Seconds later, David Thomas opened the door, and his jaw dropped before he rushed out and hugged Ethan.

"We thought you were killed," he sighed, wiping tears from his cheek.

Paul Moore burst through the door and hugged them both.

"I guess we're at the right place," Mason whispered in Sara's ear.

"These two came along and rescued me," Ethan said. "Otherwise, I might not have made it."

"And John?" David asked.

Ethan's head dropped, then Paul and David sobbed. Sara and Mason turned away.

Once inside, Paul and David took their usual seats. Ethan pulled up a chair, Mason sat on a table in the center of the room while Sara impatiently paced around it.

"Gentlemen," Sara said. "My name is Sara Gathers. I'm with NOAA."

"Sara Gathers," David interrupted. "As in Julia Gathers?"

"Yeah, she's legit," Ethan said.

Paul and David sat up in their chairs.

"I'm up here for two reasons," she said. "One, to confirm methane content in the natural soils. And two, to find out what information this young man can shed on these wildfires. Evidently, his computer has stored data from the plane's instrumentation that you are not yet aware of but can analyze."

"Your computer survived the crash?" Paul asked.

"Yep," Ethan said, pulling the satchel to his lap. "And this, too, but it's saturated."

He tossed his cell phone on the table.

"David," Paul said.

"I'm on it," David replied. He grabbed the phone and satchel.

He had the computer powering up in minutes, and the cell phone disassembled. The computer streamed information that paralleled what they charted at NOAA. The magnetic and electrical field changes were too immense to measure on their instruments, but the patterns were identical.

"This is about what I expected," Paul confirmed. "It confirms our assumptions, but it also shows our equipment needs to be modified to read much higher values."

"Can you do that?" Sara asked.

"We're working on it," David said.

"I also have video," Ethan offered. "We recorded the tower of light and the ground fires, too."

"The what?" Paul asked.

"It moves quickly, then suddenly stops," Ethan said. "Like it's alive and stalking something. When it moves, the magnetic readings explode, and it interacts with the Auroras."

Paul arched his brow and looked to the others to gauge their response.

"There's a column of light that flickers and changes color. It has a hurricane shape, but no wind and is at least a mile in diameter. It goes clear up to the Auroras and doesn't make a sound.

"It came out of nowhere, caught us by surprise. Extreme magnetism. The controls locked up, and the engine shut down."

Paul looked away in contemplation, then turned to David.

"David, can you get that phone working?" Paul asked.

"I'll see what I can do."

"Miss Gathers," Paul queried. "You mentioned something about methane content in the natural soils. Your mother recently told me the same thing. So, she sent you up here?"

"That's right," Sara acknowledged. "We have samples sitting outside the door."

"Soil samples?" Paul asked. "As you can see, we have no such testing equipment in this facility. I wonder why she sent you here?"

"Because she also knows," Mason interrupted, "that the Prudhoe Bay area is all about oil drilling. And where there is oil drilling, there is soil sampling. I'm a mud logger, and our labs are not far from here."

Mason's response relieved Sara. Paul acknowledged with a nod, then redirected.

"Ethan," Paul said. "It might interest you to know that it's moving again. The Pole has jumped to the southern coast of Alaska near the Canadian border, on or near the glaciers."

"What?" Ethan said. "That's 1,000 miles or more since I last saw it."

"About 700 miles," Paul corrected. "And it's not slowing down."

"Do you know what's happening?" Ethan asked.

"It's hard to speculate," Paul said, with the eyes of the group on him. "It could be an adjustment, some kind of natural correction. But we've never seen this rapid movement or high magnetic readings before. Not in recorded history. I recently told the Director this could be the start of a core flip."

A somber expression washed over Ethan's face.

"What does that mean?" Sara asked.

"It means the North Pole and the South Pole are about to switch places," Mason said.

"That's essentially correct," Paul said.

"Well, what will that do to us?" Sara asked.

"We're not sure." Paul grimaced. "Hopefully nothing, but there hasn't been a core flip in nearly a million years, so we really don't know."

"If it is a core flip, then it's certainly not a passive event. Cave dwellers, hunters, and gatherers might not have noticed. But today, our automated, electronic world will literally be turned upside down."

"There was the Laschamp event during the last ice age," David offered.

"That's true," Paul said. "But that was more of a weakening than a flip. The core did rotate partially and allowed more radiation to penetrate the atmosphere. But what we're seeing now is definitely not a weakening."

"Still, the core is a violent thing, and exactly how it works is unknown. But even another event like Laschamp would be devastating."

Ethan thought about it.

"I need to get back out there," Ethan said. "To keep tracking it."

"Good luck on foot," David pointed out. "Our plane is gone, and besides, no flights are allowed in or out of here."

Ethan smiled.

"Wrong on both counts," Mason said. "I have an aircraft and No-Fly Zone access. But first thing's first, kid. Let's get these soils tested."

"Agreed," Sara confirmed. "We'll head out to do that. You guys get your instruments adjusted and get that cell phone working."

***

Soon the shuttle bus returned with the same driver. They made their way to the materials testing labs near the coastline. Several metal buildings filled a campus, all for the purpose of testing oil, water, soil, rock, and anything else pulled up from drill rigs. Detention ponds and water-processing tanks flanked the buildings.

113

They pulled up to a building clad with several oil company logos. No doubt sharing information and finances for secondary operations was standard practice. Mason and Ethan toted the sample buckets through the entry door, down a short corridor that led to a check-in window where a balding man looked curiously at Mason.

"Hahn?" he asked. "What are you doing here? Aren't you a winter guy?"

"We have some special samples here that need testing," Mason said. "It's for the Federal Government."

"OK," he responded curiously. "And who are they?"

"We're both with NOAA." Sara pulled a card from her coat pocket. She tapped Ethan on the chest, he pulled out the lanyard around his neck.

The security guard shook his head. "What do I do with this?" he asked.

"Look," Mason said. "All you have to do is—"

"Have you lost power lately?" Sara cut in. "And seen any strange lights up in the sky?"

The guard nodded.

"Then let us in."

He pressed the access button, and the door opened.

"Much obliged," Mason said as they quickly passed and made their way down the hall.

"This way," Mason directed. "My office is right around the corner. And the labs right after that. Should be an engineer on duty that can help us out."

They passed into an enormous room with several lab tables. Offices bordered the room on two sides. Mason pointed to an office door with his name on it.

The other two sides had glass separation walls looking into rooms with racks of cylindrical soil samples, testing machines, incubators, spectral equipment, and compressors. Experiments were in process, mainly petroleum, but some soil and rock samples also sat on tabletops intermingled with wash sinks, gas piping, clamping apparatus, and test tubes.

A young man wearing a white lab coat pushed through a swinging door, studying the screen of a laptop and unaware of the visitors standing nearby.

"Ben," Mason said.

"Mason?" he replied. "What are you doing here?" He saw Sara and Ethan next to Mason, then dropped his computer on the countertop and ran across the room in disbelief.

"Ethan!" he shouted. "You're alive!" He grabbed Ethan and hugged him. "We heard about the plane crash and assumed the worst. Where's John?"

Ben Hadley looked anxiously around the room. Ethan dropped his head. Ben fell away, took a seat, and rubbed his eyes.

"Look," Ethan said, consoling him. "It was awful, but it's a miracle that I'm even here. If these two hadn't come along, who knows."

Mason did not realize all these young men knew each other. Sara pushed herself up on a lab table next to Ethan and Ben.

"I can only imagine what you must be feeling right now," she said. "But we need your help. We need to figure some things out."

Ben's gaze remained fixed and distant, fighting back the tears.

"Did you hear me?" she asked. "I'm with NOAA. We're here to have these soil samples analyzed for methane content."

Ben took a deep breath, then turned to the buckets of soil and smiled. "Well, those aren't going to do you any good," he said.

"What?"

"For one thing, you need to sample soils In-Situ," he clarified. "You need undisturbed soil. And even then, you would be using outdated technology."

"So, we didn't need to dig up these samples?" Sara scoffed.

"No, they might make good planters," Ben replied.

Mason gave him a look.

"But you did come to the right place. Follow me." Ben pushed himself up and walked over to a side office. "What branch of NOAA are you with?" Ben asked.

"I'm a cetacean biologist," Sara responded.

"Then why are you interested in methane emissions?" Ben asked.

"I'm not, but others in the organization are," she said.

"As Mason will tell you," Ben said. "These facilities are only for oil industry use. But technically, I developed this application on my own, and no one has reviewed it, so I can show it to you."

Sara restrained a deep sigh. Ben entered the room and sat down on a swivel chair with dual computer monitors.

"Scientists have been measuring methane emissions for decades," Ben continued. "Swamps, wetlands, peat bogs, rice paddies, and tundra. But it's always been small areas from small laboratory tests up to field-size with aircraft. But what I've developed has a global reach.

"Both NASA and the military have taken satellite images of the Earth's surface for decades. Now there is public access to a photographic history of the planet dating back to the 1960s. As the years go by and technology improves, we get more and more pictures taken more often and with more detail. I've spent months downloading everything I could find.

"Because what I realized is you can break photographs down to

116

see anything you want to see. By using spectral analysis to analyze the satellite imagery, I can detect methane fluxes anywhere on the planet, down to the square yard."

"You do this as a hobby?" Sara asked.

"I've been reading a lot about increased methane emissions in recent years," he explained, "and it got me thinking about a better way to quantify it. We use spectrometers here in the lab for many test procedures, so I'm familiar with the technique. I just had to get creative with the concept.

"Anyway, it is something that interests and concerns me about our planet."

"We're trying to find out if there is enough methane gas naturally leaching out of the soils to fuel those large fires," Sara said.

"Naturally? No," Ben replied. "But in the era of Climate Change? It's possible."

Ben pulled up a screenshot of northern Alaska and Canadian tundra's, color-coded with multiple layers laid out topographically from light yellow to red. He toggled through monthly images of the same area, the colors and limits continually changed. The red zone engulfed the entire permafrost region from western Alaska to central Canada at mid-summer, then relaxed down in the winter months.

"In case you haven't figured it out already," Ben said. "In the color-coding scale, red is bad."

"How bad?" Sara asked.

"The vertical axis indicates CH4/m2/d or methane in milli-liters per square meter per day," Ben said. "As a source (releasing methane into the atmosphere) or a sink (absorbing into the soil)."

"So, above the zero line is releasing," Sara said, pointing to the horizontal line on the graph. "And below is absorbing."

"That's right," Ben said. "Or put another way; it releases in the summer and absorbs in the winter. Only now, the winter absorption months are shorter, and the summer release months are much longer and much more severe."

"Look here," he offered. "Here is the same table ten years ago. The shape of the chart is similar but look at the width of the release months and the rates."

The group stared at the numbers side by side. The CO2 release months had more than doubled, increasing the peak from less than ten to over 500.

"So, the release rates have gone up fifty-fold in ten years," Sara said. "Am I reading that right?"

"You're reading it exactly right."

"How does this cycle get reversed?"

"Huh, it doesn't." Ben sighed.

"There has to be something."

"The world has to stop burning fossil fuels," Ben said. "How do you stop that? With a magic wand?"

Silence hung in the room as each contemplated the enormity of the problem.

"Decayed vegetation and animal materials have lain frozen in the tundra for millennia," Ben continued. "Now it's thawing out due to elevated temperatures worldwide, releasing methane at higher and higher rates."

"How do I compare this baseline to something else?" Sara asked. "You mentioned swamps."

"That's right," Ben returned. "Swamps and rice paddies typically release more methane than any other source. But this is more than double that rate."

Sara knew this was more than Julia hoped to find, but devastating news, nonetheless.

"I need color copies of everything you just showed us," Sara said. "Can you do that?"

Ben sighed. "What exactly will NOAA do with this information?" he asked.

"Distribute it to members of Congress and the U.S. Military at a closed session in Washington, D.C.," Sara replied.

"Seriously?" Ben asked.

"Don't mess with her, kid," Mason said. "I don't think she's in the mood."

Sara gave Mason one of those looks.

"OK, it's probably best to send the images electronically," he said. "All I need is your cell number."

***

Paul Moore and David Thomas watched intently as Ethan's cell phone video streamed across a viewscreen mounted on the wall. The tower of light shone in magnificent detail. Its vertical, colored linework reached up to the glistening Aurora. Background noise from the engine and confused chatter between Ethan and John added to the eerie intensity. Caught up in the replay, they did not notice Sara, Mason, and Ethan enter the room.

"You fixed it," a voice came from behind.

Paul and David turned.

"I have a way with electronics," David paused the video.

All eyes focused on the viewscreen.

"I didn't believe you, kid," Paul conceded. "I'm sorry. We've run through all the footage a couple times. It goes till you lose control of instrumentation and start spiraling down."

"No need to apologize," Ethan said. "Who could believe that?"

Sara and Mason wore expressions of total shock. David started the video feed again.

"Hey, wait," Ethan said. "Stop."

David paused the video.

Ethan approached the view screen and pointed to a small dark cloud near the lower left-hand side.

"Birds," he pointed out. "Start again and watch that blurry gray cloud."

David re-started.

"See," Ethan said, with his finger on the cloud. "Watch them move. They're orbiting the light tower."

"Can you zoom in?"

"I'm on it." David paused again. The still picture went granular as it zoomed in closer, and soon, seabirds came into view. Then David hit play again, and there they were, thousands of them orbiting the glowing phenomenon.

Ethan turned to Sara. "Told ya."

"This is unbelievable," she said.

"It's some kind of interaction between Earth's magnetic field," Paul said, "and this recent solar activity. That's all it can be. There can't be any other explanation."

"We need to get this footage to the Director," Sara said. "ASAP."

"She'll have it within the hour," Paul acknowledged.

"And what about those magnetic readings?" she asked. "The ones too large to read."

"Nothing yet," Paul said. "From what we can tell, the strength is very localized and very concentrated. Even stronger than fields generated by electromagnets if you can believe that."

"I don't know physics," Sara said. "But it appears you'll be searching for answers for quite some time."

"I'll have a hard time convincing your mother," he said. "But it's all we have right now."

Sara deliberated. "Ethan, on the plane, you mentioned something about Caribou," Sara asked. "Do you remember that?"

"Sure," he said. "At the third site, Caribou were stampeding toward the light tower as we flew over them. Then after the crash, I ran away from the fire and saw them up on a ridge. All standing there staring at the light, thousands of them. I remember thinking, 'I have to move,' hoping they kept their distance."

Sara studied his face. There was no speck of doubt, no eyes turning away or looking down. He knew what he saw, and now she believed everything he said.

What have I gotten myself into? I'm a biologist; nothing I've ever done prepared me for something like this. Should she cut ties and move on? She had tracked down all the information Julia requested and more. Wasn't that enough? She thought for a minute with all eyes on her. She was exhausted.

"I need to think and get some rest," she said. "Paul, you guys get that footage pulled together. Mason, is there a place around here we can get some sleep?"

Paul nodded.

"Barracks are right up the road," Mason said.

"We're going to get a few hours' rest," Sara said. "We'll come back here and regroup on the next steps."

∗∗∗

The Barracks room was smaller than Mason's apartment and had a single window that looked out to the refinery buildings. Not the most romantic setting, but that is not what they were there for. Sara peeked out the window.

"So, you spend the entire winter up here?" she asked.

"That's right," Mason said. "View's even better then."

Sara laughed, then crossed the room and checked out the bathroom.

"I need a shower in the worst way," she said.

"Be my guest," Mason said. "Should be towels and soap in there."

"Got it," Sara said and shut the door.

Mason flopped on the bed and was out in seconds. He awoke with Sara laying on her back next to him, wrapped in a towel, staring at the ceiling. He rolled on his side.

"How long was I asleep?" he asked.

"About six hours, I think."

"I'm sorry," he said. "You should have woken me."

"Don't worry about it," she replied. "I've been thinking."

"For six hours?"

"Mostly," she said. "The power flickered a few times, so the clocks are wrong. I must have left my phone at NOAA, so I'm not sure exactly what time it is now. But I've come to a few conclusions."

Mason sat up.

"There's never been a sperm whale stranding in Alaska," she explained. "Never been magnetic towers of light, with birds and animals chasing them. There's no doubt it's all tied together. We only lack the scientific model to prove it. Paul Moore also mentioned a potential core flip, right?"

"That's right."

"Then there's more information he has that I need," she said.

"Let's head back over there."

***

Paul Moore nervously typed away at his keyboard as David Thomas looked on. Ethan sat curled up in a chair, asleep, when Sara and Mason knocked on the door.

"Hey, kid, go get the door," David said. "Ethan!"

Ethan awoke and looked up.

"Someone at the door," David said then turned back to his computer screen.

When Ethan opened the door, Sara and Mason stepped inside to see two men that did not acknowledge their presence.

"I'm starting to dread emails from these guys," Paul Moore stated.

"What guys?" Sara asked. Paul turned to see Sara.

"Oh, good morning," he said. "How did you sleep?"

"Great," Mason said.

"Didn't," Sara said. "What guys?"

"Solar guys," Paul said. "We've had another coronal mass ejection from the sun. About eight hours ago, and it's from the same epicenter on the sun as the previous events, so it's headed our way and will hit us in about eighteen hours."

"What does that mean?" Sara asked.

"This is the largest one yet," Paul declared, still typing away. "Normally, it can cause satellite and communication disruption. But when the last two hit the magnetosphere, they interacted with that magnetic phenomenon and created those walls of light. This time we may have a similar, if not larger event, right there."

He pointed to a spot on the computer screen that showed the magnetic polar tracking lines.

"Have you shared this with the director?" Sara asked.

"Yes," Paul said. "The earlier two events. I'm sure Colorado has already informed her of this one."

"You also told her about the potential core flip?" Sara asked. "So, she's aware that the moving core and the coronal mass ejections are interacting?"

"That's correct."

"What else?"

"The timing of the solar and magnetic events seems to be the key to triggering these towers of light," he divulged. "When the Pole jumps to a new location, it releases extreme magnetic energy. If it interacts with all that energy from the solar wind, bang!"

"And the data."

"As we've told you, Miss Gathers," Paul said. "We can't yet retrieve the data; it's all empirical."

Paul pointed to the tower of light photo still shown on the main view screen.

"Defining that mathematically," he continued, "will take years, maybe decades."

Sara paused.

"What about the imagery," Sara said. "Did you send that to the Director?"

"Yes, about four hours ago," he replied.

"Thank you," she said. "And this potentially new event, do you think there will be another light tower and fire?"

"Very well could be," Paul replied. "This one is bigger than the others. We could get power outages and communication loss across the lower forty-eight. However, the Pole would have to sit there and be highly magnetic for eighteen hours for it to interact with the energy blast, and so far, it doesn't seem to stay in one place that long."

"The truth is …" Paul turned in his swivel chair to face Sara. "We don't know what is going to happen, but this location needs to be investigated."

Sara pulled Mason and Ethan aside. "Ethan," she said. "Do you still want to go out there and track this thing?"

Ethan brushed a hand through his hair with an approving nod.

"If what Paul told us is true," she continued. "Then there could be another major fire near the south Alaskan coast."

Ethan sighed.

"You fuel up," he said. "While I load some equipment."

"I'm on it." Mason started toward the door.

Sara made eye contact with Ethan and squeezed his shoulder. "Don't worry, we're going to be OK," she said.

Ethan nodded and headed to the storage area. Then Sara remembered the data Ben was supposed to send and looked around for her phone.

"My phone," she panicked. "Is it here somewhere?"

"Yes, it is," David said. "You left it over on that table. I figured you were tired and forgot. Battery was running low, so I plugged it in."

"Thanks again."

She checked for messages, and there it was, the methane imagery from Ben. Over twenty pages and all labeled.

"Good boy," she murmured. She scanned through the file and sent it to Julia. Now she had sent all requested data, including the incredible pictures of the light tower.

"Don't forget," Paul Moore said. "If there is another phenomenon, we'll need all the footage we can get."

Chapter 15

The Second Incident

Southeast, AK

When she arrived at the tiny Perishton airport, Sara saw a pile of stuff next to Mason's Cessna. He cleared out the back to lighten the load for the flight and make room for Ethan's equipment.

"Ethan, you help him load up," Sara said. "I need to make a call."

Sara stepped inside the terminal where no one was in earshot. She found a chair, sat down, and hit the "Mom" button. Nothing, the call canceled instantly. She hit it again, nothing again. Frustrated, she stepped outside, hoping for better reception. Nothing again, then she remembered Paul mentioned satellite disruption, so she tried a text and thought eventually, it would get through:

"Hope you received the information from Paul Moore and the pics I sent earlier. Another event is brewing on the south Alaskan coast. I'm flying out to investigate. Be in touch soon. Love you, Sara."

She crossed the tarmac toward the Cessna. Mason threw a pair of snow skis on the stack of odds and ends.

"Was all this in the back of your plane?" Sara joked.

"Hey, I like to be prepared," Mason replied, miffed by the lack of support for his hard work. "Anyway, there's plenty of room now for the kid's gear."

"All I really have is my computer, magnetometer, and a compass," Ethan said, holding up his backpack.

"That's it?" Mason asked.

Sara rolled her eyes and stepped onto the plane.

A man pulled up in a pick-up truck, dropped off a few cases of water and a box of essentials, then threw Mason's stuff in the truck bed.

"Hmm," Ethan said, fishing through the backpack. "Extra batteries and granola bars."

"OK," Mason said. "Hop on board."

They all strapped in, adjusted headphones, and throttled down the tarmac. They cleared the Perishton runway and headed south toward the Brooks Range.

"What do you think we'll see out there, kid?" Mason asked.

"Not sure," Ethan answered. "But this is a big one. So be prepared for the worst."

"What's our ETA?" Sara asked through headphone static.

"Hard to say since it's a moving target," Mason replied. "But five to six hours, plus or minus, is my best guess. We'll need a fuel stop in Fairbanks. It will probably be a No-Fly Zone, too, so there could be issues the closer we get."

The hop over the mountains did not do Sara's stomach any favors. When they dropped into a small municipal airport in Fairbanks, she considered calling Colonel Jackson for better transport over the Alaskan Range but decided that Dramamine would be quicker.

She felt fine now whether due to the Dramamine or the flat terrain north of the mountains, with no dizziness and no nausea.

Three hours into the second leg of the flight, they cleared the South Alaska Mountain Range and were in sight of the ice fields. Cockpit gauges flickered, and the compass started to spin. Mason checked the GPS, but its coordinates did not make sense.

"Flying blind," he said and continued to make gauge adjustments.

"So, we keep heading this direction, and we'll reach the coast?" Sara asked, remembering the flight into Perishton.

"Hopefully," Mason returned. "This is a south-southeast flight, so we're heading that way."

"We're still going the right way," Ethan said as he leaned up between them. "See, the field strength is increasing, so we're following it."

"Good thinking," Mason said. "I was starting to get nervous."

They cruised along, not knowing their distance, altitude, or location, led only by a handheld magnetometer. Mason commented that they might be in Canada since he did not recognize any landmarks. Thirty minutes later, the magnetometer went crazy.

"Hey guys, we're getting very close," Ethan said. "Readings are spiked again."

"I don't see anything," Sara said.

"That's good," Ethan said. "The event hasn't happened yet. According to Paul's time estimate, we have about ten hours to wait."

Ethan crawled up from the back and angled between them, his eyes fixed. A water line lay ahead, an inlet to the sea fed by an enormous glacier pushing down from a mountain pass. The bay forked in two directions with a forest in the center and dotted islands leading out to sea. The land on the approach side was flat but forested, as if ancient glaciers had spent millennia rubbing it down. Small icebergs and chunks of ice floated down the eastern inlet, but the western side was ice-free.

"We need to be very careful on our approach," Ethan said. "The Pole appears to be up beyond that fork to the left, in the foothills near that glacier. You should make the first pass from a few miles out. We'll see how the plane handles, then approach and find a landing spot."

"Not sure I want to get that close," Mason mumbled.

"Let's take this slow, guys," Sara ordered. "No chances."

"Take all the videos you can," Ethan said.

"Oh, what was I thinking," Sara said. She hurriedly pulled up her cell phone and aimed out in the distance.

"Mason," Ethan said. "I think we should make for a water landing and tie off to shore here on the west side. That way, we can get out quickly if we need to."

"I can't disagree, kid," Mason responded.

Mason pulled the plane down to 1,000 feet for the first approach. The cockpit filled with buzzing and whining noises as they drew nearer the epicenter. An old paper clip levitated from the aluminum floorboard. It floated at eye level for a few seconds, then snapped with a click to the steel control stick clutched tight in Mason's hand.

"That's a first," Ethan murmured through the headset. The expressions on Sara's and Mason's faces spoke for themselves.

They made a slow circle around the assumed epicenter. All appeared clear at this time, no fire, no scorched timber, and no dead vegetation. The casual observer would have no idea what lay in wait as mother nature plotted its next move.

"That's a good spot," Mason said. "We'll land there on the next pass."

"Where's a good spot?" Sara shouted.

"Basically, the inlet with no floating ice," Mason answered.

Sara gasped.

"How's it handling?" Ethan asked.

"No problems," Mason said. "Only issues are the gauges."

Ethan nodded. That was good, but not what he'd experienced or expected. It must only happen when the light tower is active.

"Hey, look down there," Ethan said. "Birds."

Tens of thousands of seabirds circled the epicenter, some higher, some lower, and some already on the ground.

"So, they are following it," Sara said. "They're totally lost." Sara's thoughts went back to the stranded whales. There had to be a connection.

"What does your magnetometer say?" she asked.

"Too high to read," Ethan showed.

An eerie feeling came over Sara.

It was moonrise when the Cessna splashed in for a landing on the western shore of the forked inlet. Ghostly Auroras reflected off the glacier in the distance as Mason tied the plane off to trees on the water's edge. Sara stood on the gravelly bank, reminiscent of a similar image she'd seen when she first met Mason. He top-checked the knots Ethan tied and gave a nod of approval.

"What now?" he asked Sara.

She turned to Ethan.

"We wait about ten hours," he replied.

"What a desolate place," Mason said.

"Except for that," Sara said, pointing across the inlet toward two small white structures tucked up on the hill. "What are they?"

"Hard to say." Ethan squinted.

Mason walked back toward the plane, hopped on the pontoons, and reached inside. He fumbled around for a few seconds, then appeared with blankets thrown over his shoulder and a pair of binoculars around his neck.

"Whatever they are"—he peered through the binoculars— "they look abandoned." He handed the binoculars to Sara.

"It's dark in the hill shadow," Sara said. "But I think there's an old chain-link fence around it. It's definitely abandoned, maybe an old military installation."

"That's possible," Ethan conceded. "Alaska has quite a few World War II-era outposts on the coast."

"OK," Sara said. "If something does happen here, it's not likely that anyone else will see it."

The Auroras crackled and brightened. They looked up as if expecting a firework show to begin. Then it died back down, and all took a breath.

"Ethan," Sara said, handing him the binoculars. "I need you to stay on top of the magnetic readings. Let me know if anything unusual happens."

"You mean the way it has been for the past week or so?" he sarcastically responded and got a sharp gaze from Sara.

"Really?" Mason burst out. "Here, kid," he tossed Ethan a blanket. "Gonna get nippy tonight."

Mason put an arm around Sara. "Let's take a walk."

Ethan found a boulder to sit on, pulled out the magnetometer and a granola bar, and stared at the sky. He lifted the binoculars to his eyes to focus on the swarming seabirds as more flocks flew in from the coast. The anomaly was a few miles out, but the cackling and cawing of the multitude drowned out all other sounds of nature.

Sara and Mason walked down the tight gravelly beach away from the plane. Some of the cobbles were large, slick, and made for a tricky way to go. So, they turned up the beachhead toward the tree line where the gravel thinned down to the sand.

"There we go," Mason said. "Much better."

Sara took his hand. The sandy pathway led up and curved back into a small estuary with a magnificent view of the hills leading away from the landing site. The twilight cast moon shadows in front of them as they walked. They decided to take a break and throw down blankets.

"I noticed it on our approach," Sara said. "And up close, it's even more obvious, even in the twilight, the drought is affecting the pines. They look thin, and their bases have more needles than ever."

Mason knelt and sifted his fingers through the thick layer of dead, brown needles.

"Drought's lasted two years now," he said.

"It won't take much to start a major fire here." Sara grimaced, staring out across the hills.

"Hey," Mason said. "There's nothing we can do about it."

Sara sighed.

"But we have some time to kill," Mason said and reached for her hand.

"That's original," she said.

"Better than nothing," he said.

***

Sara awoke to bright light, still warm under the blankets. She stood up, panicked in the chilly air. It was daylight again, but the

Auroras were more brilliant than the sky. Veins of lightning sparkled through and below them. She shook Mason, who grumbled up to his feet.

"What is it," he asked, squinting and rubbing his neck. Then a rumble of thunder rolled down from the sky. It echoed through the hillside. They both stood in awe. "How long were we asleep?"

"At least a couple hours," Sara said. They pulled their clothes on and brushed sand away as they went. "Let's get back to the plane."

They hurried down and around the beachhead. They spotted the plane but did not see Ethan. As they got nearer, they could see him asleep under a blanket, propped up against a large boulder.

"Hey, get up," Sara shouted.

Ethan awoke, shaking his head. "Where've you two been?" he asked. He saw by Sara's expression he was out of line again.

"Look," she said. "And listen."

Ethan pulled himself up and focused his tired eyes. His jaw dropped. He quickly checked his phone for the time.

"It's three hours ahead of schedule," he said. "This shouldn't be happening now."

"Unfortunately, it is," she said. "Is this how it looked before the light tower started?"

"With thunder?" he asked. "I don't remember hearing thunder."

"Maybe you couldn't hear it over the engine's sound," Mason said.

"Or maybe this one is stronger," Ethan fretted. "See those lightning bolts? They're way below the Auroras, not in the stratosphere. They're below ... and there are no clouds ..." Caught up in thought, he trailed off.

"OK, what does that mean?" Sara asked.

"Lightning is basically a result of friction from colliding ice particles inside thunderheads," Ethan said. "An electrical charge builds up and boom! But on a clear day, it shouldn't happen."

Pacing stopped.

"Unless there is an enormous surge of energy interacting with that magnetic field," he whispered. All senses heightened. The swarming seabirds disappeared in silence as they dove into the tree line.

More thunder claps. They all looked up to see lightning bolts striking the ground at or near the center of the magnetic anomaly. The sound was deafening. The ground shook from the rumble that roared through the valley of the inlet. Ethan instinctively ran for the boulder and hid behind it.

"Ethan!" Sara shouted. "What are you doing? We are three or four miles from those lightning strikes."

"That's not what worries me!" he volleyed back.

"What then?"

Suddenly the entire inlet lit up like a nuclear explosion.

"That!" Ethan shouted.

All turned away and covered their eyes. Sara and Mason made for the rock and pushed in beside Ethan.

"Get down!" Mason shouted.

"We need to take video!" Ethan shouted. He pulled out his cell phone and handed it to Sara. As he got another look, he noticed his magnetometer could not register anything. He smacked it a few times but no change. Then, as quickly as the blinding light came, it settled back down to a quiet, bright glow.

They all looked up from the rock to see the fantastic, rainbow-colored tower of light that Ethan had described. Contrasting vertical striations of light dancing around a circular core. Was this the stuff that inspired the ancients? Had this happened thousands of years ago, before written language? Was this where gods were born? Ethan stood with a thousand thoughts in his head and courageously walked out from behind the rock to face his monster. He ran a few steps across the beach, then stopped. A promontory before breaking waves, he stood shaking from adrenaline rush but not afraid anymore, even though it had killed John and almost killed him. What was it? It was magnificent, not Medusa.

Sara approached behind and took his trembling hand as tears streamed down his face.

"Are you OK?" she asked.

"It's more fantastic than I remembered," he said. He turned to see her consoling eyes, and fortunately, she was still shooting video with the other hand, so he did not have to ask.

"We need to get closer," he said. "We need to take the plane up this inlet to the eastern shore to get a better view of the base."

Ethan seemed confident. Sara looked over at Mason.

"We might have to taxi across the water," he said. "Not sure we can safely get up in the air."

"We're also going to need our sunglasses," Sara said.

A few minutes later, they tied off to a new shore. It had a clear view of the entire light tower. They were less than a mile out and could walk there along the beach line. But the walk might get tricky since they would have to step through countless birds perched on the beach. Some floated in the water, some scurried near the forest edge, and the trees seemed to change color and shape, weighted down with frightened, lost, migratory seabirds.

They disembarked onto a sandy beach. From this distance, the light at the base was brighter and flickered.

"Who has the binoculars?" Ethan asked.

"I thought you did," Sara said.

Mason climbed back on board and found them in the Cessna, in the pile of beach blankets. He tossed them to Ethan's waiting hands.

When Ethan lifted them to his eyes, he saw what appeared to be new layers of light inside the circular tower. Illuminated by rising mist from the ground, it fanned out in bright, changing colors shooting up from the earth. He pulled the binoculars away from his face, focused on the same spot, frowned, and pushed the binoculars back up to his eyes.

"What in the world?" he said softly. "A fan of jumping rainbow light is shooting up from the ground. It goes up a few hundred yards, then dies out."

He handed the binoculars to Sara.

"I see it," she said. "But it doesn't cross the entire base of light. And it's all different colors than the perimeter light."

She handed the binoculars back to Ethan and continued taking video. Mason felt a little left out.

"It doesn't make sense," Ethan said. "The main light tower is generated by the interaction of a solar energy burst with high magnetism in the upper atmosphere. But this light appears to be coming up from the earth."

He pulled the binoculars back up to his eyes and focused on the light fan. It did change colors, but as Sara mentioned, different from the surrounding light tower. And its colors were sharper and more defined.

Ethan could see the old military installation on the hillside beyond as he peered through this natural kaleidoscope.

Then something flickered and caught his attention. A tall tree went in and out of sight. He pulled the binoculars away from his eyes to gauge the effect in normal vision, then lifted them up to his eyes again. It appeared and disappeared, appeared, and disappeared, appeared, and disappeared. What was going on? He pulled the binoculars down again, then realized it happened as the kaleidoscope effect flickered back and forth. In fact, it happened as the color changed from red to orange. He quickly checked again, and again, and again.

"Look at this," Ethan said, handing the binoculars to Mason. "Focus on the old military buildings and look slightly to their left."

"What am I looking for?" Mason asked.

"Do you see that tall tree?" Ethan pointed. "It pops in and out of view."

"Not a tree," Mason said. "I think it's a radio tower."

"It's there in the red light," Ethan said. "But not in the orange."

Mason focused for a few cycles.

"That's the strangest thing," he said. "How did you even notice it?"

Sara grabbed the binoculars. There it was, nothing red, tower orange, nothing red, tower orange, nothing red, tower orange.

"Guys, it's probably a natural light effect," she said. "Like when heat rises from a hot road in the summertime." She handed the binoculars back to Ethan. "You have a youthful imagination," she mocked.

As the words left her mouth, something else caught her eye. The tops of the tall pines seemed to be moving, not all but some.

"Wait a minute," she said. "I see movement in the trees."

"Movement?" Mason asked. "You mean an earthquake?"

"No," Ethan said. "This is something else."

Then, a rumbling sound emanated from the same direction as the light tower. Tree movement increased, and smoke started rising from the area of the light fan. Then another sound came from that direction, but more like an animal sound. The rumbling increased.

"Over there!" Mason shouted.

A group of DC-10 tankers at high altitude appeared over the hills from the northwest, flying toward the light anomaly.

"Oh my God," Sara said. At the same time, the smoke burst into flames. It instantly engulfed the tall pines and spread with a rage across the entire footprint of light.

A group of four squadrons, in winged formation, took a wide southward pass around the anomaly.

"They're staying clear of it," Ethan said. "Till it dies down."

"This is going to get interesting really quick," Mason said.

The raging fire crossed the light line and reached the beachhead in seconds. Countless seabirds lifted to the sky and headed southward. Underbrush shook and crackled as deer and tinier creatures raced for safety. Yet another explosive and roaring sound drowned out all other noises. They all ran for the Cessna. Sara and Mason unclasped the tie-off ropes as Ethan hopped up on pontoons and dove into the cockpit. By the time he crawled into the back, Sara and Mason had already buckled into the cockpit seats. He flipped the starter switch and backed the floatplane away from shore. In seconds they were airborne, lifting high and away from the growing smoke cloud.

After heading south down the inlet, Mason made a slow southeast turn toward the bay of the icebergs. They saw a gigantic wave rolling out to sea followed by a city-sized iceberg that had broken away from the glacier.

"Must be heat from that fire or the energy blast," Mason shouted.

Then, suddenly the light tower vanished. As quickly as it came, it disappeared.

"Whoa," Mason said. "Did you see that?"

The others were speechless. Gauge readings on the cockpit console returned to normal.

"OK, this is good," Mason barked through the headset. "Electronics are back."

Mason continued his turn to get a view of the tanker planes. He went south of the growing smoke plume at a lower altitude than the tankers but could easily see them approach in attack formation.

Twenty DC-10's dropped in low from the southeast toward the cloud. Four sets of five planes in winged formation dove into the black smoke cloud and released their red-chemical payloads. In seconds they cleared the backside of the smoke tower, lifted to higher altitude, and headed back northwest from where they came. The dark black smoke cloud slowly turned white, and the fires at their base dimmed.

Then another squadron approached, tactically from the opposite direction. Twenty more tankers smashed through the white, billowy cloud, crisscrossing the entire area with more red fire-retardant liquid. The fire was out, and the smoke began to dissipate.

Mason made for the old landing spot as the second fleet pulled away and taxied up to shore. He throttled hard to get it up on the bank where the tie-off ropes still lay. The plane stopped at the lake's edge. They jumped out and re-clasped the ropes to the pontoons. Smoke and a chemical odor filled the air. They cautiously walked up the beach line toward the smoldering ashes and charred trees.

Chapter 16

Aftermath

Remember, no chances," Sara said.

Thousands of seabirds returned, filling the forest and beach near the dead zone, and as before, they paid no attention to the humans who carefully stepped between them. The once dark smoke that gave way to the thinner white had changed to smoldering steam whisking about in the breeze. They slowly stepped into the red, mushy ashes as the mist thickened to a fog. They noticed a scent in the air, something not expected. They heard a moaning sound, like the sound of an injured animal. Sara instinctively ran forward.

"Hey, what about no chances?" Mason shouted.

He and Ethan followed her quickly into the fog. It was hard to navigate their way through the sloppy red mush and fallen trees. Images seemed to appear and disappear. Up in the sky, Carrion birds circled, some swooping down and landing. Sara continued to follow the moaning sound. Strange shapes took form ahead, hooked spears moving in the breeze. Maybe a native tree or shrub stripped of its leaves in the fire.

Nothing could have prepared her for what happened next.

A hooked spear above the mist moved as Sara approached. It lifted up, then dropped back down, then she heard another moaning gasp. A light wind picked up, the clearing in front of them became visible. Sara stopped dead in her tracks as Mason and Ethan approached. In front of them, in the field of red and black ash, lay dozens of dead or dying woolly mammoths. Carrion birds were already dropping down on their carcasses.

A red gel covered the animals, who suffered horrific burns, some burnt beyond recognition. Most of their large manes and long hair that carpeted them for warmth had burned away. The stench was overwhelming. A large bull that lay twenty feet from Sara rolled its head and moaned again. She ran to its aid, not knowing what she could do to help.

"Stay clear!" Mason shouted, following her. "He's in pain and frightened."

Then the large bull raised his head again and let out a terrifying roar. His head dropped to the mud, and the gigantic, curved tusks slammed into the red mush one last time. It was over. He was dead; they were all dead. The only sounds left were carrion birds feasting on carcasses and grounded seabirds cawing at the great red spot.

"My God," Sara gasped. "These are woolly mammoths. They're not supposed to be here."

She handed her cell phone to Ethan. "Video everything you see and everything I say."

She stepped in to examine the eyes and teeth of the giant beast. "What's going on?" she wondered. "How is this possible?"

"Maybe they came out from the mountains," Mason said. "From a deep cave."

"Seriously?" Sara returned.

"Look, the kid said the Caribou were following it," Mason said. "So maybe it drew them out from hiding."

"These creatures have been extinct for 10,000 years!" Sara exclaimed. "And suddenly they end up in the middle of this ... whatever this is we're standing in the middle of, they couldn't get out and were burned alive."

A distant sound of woofing helicopters caught their attention. It picked up and approached from the northwest. Two Chinooks dropped inside the red perimeter, throttled down their engines, and landed. Wind gusts from the rotor blades cleared out the steam in front of them, revealing Sara, Mason, Ethan, and the herd of mammoths. Soldiers jumped from the first helicopter and rushed across the red and black surface. In seconds, a dozen heavily armed soldiers clad in black surrounded them. Ethan instinctively raised his hands. Mason reached out and tapped him across the ribs. Embarrassed, Ethan dropped his arms. Officers from the second Chinook soon followed.

"Stand down!" a voice shouted. "Stand down!"

"Colonel Jackson," Sara extended her hand. "I have to admit, it's a relief to see you and your men out here."

"Miss Gathers," Jackson responded. "I didn't expect to see you here. Aren't you supposed to be in Perishton?"

The colonel took in the devastation. "What in God's name is all this?" he asked.

Ethan was speechless. She really was legit.

"I'm not sure," she replied.

"Well, I never thought I'd live to see the day when someone with the last name Gathers uttered those words," the colonel replied. "Young lady, are these creatures what I think they are?"

"Yes, they are," she said.

"And I assume you don't know how they got here?" he asked.

"That's correct."

Jackson knelt next to the dead bull, like a big game hunter looking over his kill, then he stood and sighed. "Well, I can't fault you for that," he said. "This is an entire herd."

"I'm not sure how to deal with this situation," Sara said. "But until we understand more, it should stay under wraps. I'll brief my mother, so you can talk intelligently about this in Washington. I assume they'll want you down there after this."

"They've already called," the colonel said. "With everything else going on down there, I'm almost in violation of orders by being here."

"What do you mean?" Sara asked. "What else is going on?"

Jackson looked confused. "Where have you all been since this thing hit?" he asked.

"Up here without power or communication," she replied.

"Yeah, you and everyone else," Jackson said. "Three-fourths of the lower forty-eight have the same problem. The biggest coronal mass ejection ever recorded hit us in multiple waves. This one caused the most damage. It smashed power grids and blacked out the eastern and western seaboards. It even took out some military satellites. Washington D.C. is running on emergency power. I have a briefing with Congress in twelve hours."

"My God," Sara said, absorbing it. "Colonel, I suggest you leave armed soldiers here in the meantime. If possible, these creatures should be air-lifted ASAP to a military installation tonight. Do you have a freezer facility?"

"Let me see," the colonel said. "We still have power in Fairbanks, and that's a good thing. I'd have to pull some strings, move things

143

around, but I can probably make it happen."

"Also," she said, wiping her hands of red chemicals. "I'm not sure what effect this red chemical will have on their bodies. Is it possible to get them hosed off before storage?"

"Yes, Ma'am," Colonel Jackson said. "I'll bring in a couple clean water drops. Will that work?"

Sara nodded, then panned around, studying the military men.

"This event is unprecedented, Colonel," Sara replied. "Please tell your men not to discuss this with anyone. No photos, no selfies, no texts, no discussion. If what you're telling me is true, there is likely a national panic. We don't need to add fuel to the fire."

"Agreed," the colonel followed. "Do you need anything before we depart?"

Sara looked to Mason.

"We're good," he said.

"That should do it," Sara said. They shook hands. Colonel Jackson nodded to Mason.

The colonel pulled a business card from his pocket and scribbled something on the back. "If you need anything else," he said. "You can reach me at this number any time."

"Thank you," Sara replied.

With that, the colonel made a swirling motion with his finger. The officers gave quick nods to Sara then headed back to the helicopter. Colonel Jackson huddled with the armed soldiers.

Sara, Mason, and Ethan walked back toward the floatplane. Sara turned back to the unbelievable site and took a pano-shot of the scene. Mason stood next to her.

"How will you write this in your report?" he asked.

"I have no idea," she said.

"I hear ya," he said. "Let's hop on board and get back to Perishton."

They turned to see Ethan standing, motionless, looking toward the anomaly site. Sara walked over to him.

"Ethan," Sara whispered.

No response.

"What are you staring at?" she asked.

"That old military installation." He pointed.

They turned to the two old white buildings in the distance surrounded by chain link fencing.

"There's no radio tower," Ethan softly said.

The hair on the backs of their necks stood on end.

In disbelief, Sara's eyes checked the smoldering field of dead mammoths, but the charred trees did not reach the white buildings. No fire there. *There's no way it could have just been damaged*, she thought.

"This doesn't make sense," she murmured.

"I don't think it's heat from the road," Mason mocked.

"And check this out," Ethan followed, holding out his magnetometer. "Maybe we shouldn't go back to Perishton."

Chapter 17

The Secret Meeting

Washington, D.C.

"Men argue. Nature acts."
Voltaire

Strategic importance of the Arctic region heightened to levels not seen since the cold war with the greening of lands above the Arctic Circle. This unexpected twist from climate change gave access to mineral resources previously unobtainable in the frozen wastelands of Siberia, Canada, Greenland, and Alaska. Sinkhole craters dotted a melting landscape as Arctic temperatures spiked to ten degrees above normal averages. Shipping lanes cut through an Arctic Ocean, once traversed only by ice breakers, now ice-free most of the year. Methane release is now unstoppable.

***

The blackout lasted two days. The city was under martial law, as were most major cities on the eastern seaboard. Once-vibrant streets were eerily vacant; police cars and military vehicles patrolled slowly through neighborhoods. National guardsmen posted at most major intersections wore riot gear. The sun was setting when five unmarked black vehicles pulled up to the curb in front of Julia Gathers' townhouse.

All doors opened in unison as soldiers in full tactical gear took positions around the vehicles. Others scattered right and left of the gated townhouse entry. One black suit opened the front passenger door of the center car, and Colonel Jackson stepped out with a cell phone to his ear. As he approached the gate, it clicked open. Four armed soldiers rushed through the gate into defensive positions. Colonel Jackson scaled the steps to the front door, flanked by two black suits.

The door opened as they reached the porch. Julia stood calmly in her usual dress, long sweater, and beret-style hat with a computer bag sitting next to her on the floor.

"Colonel Jackson," she said, extending her hand.

"Dr. Gathers," Jackson said. "So nice to see you again. We're in kind of a hurry. We have an armed escort to the Capitol Building. Are you ready?"

Julia nodded. "When your man knocked at the door this morning, I didn't know what to think," she replied.

One black suit grabbed her bag, the other took her hand and escorted her down the steps to the motorcade. Colonel Jackson walked beside them.

"We have power to the Capitol Building," he said. "But this meeting will be in Senator O'Connell's private office."

The aide opened the door and helped Julia inside. The colonel sat next to her as a crowd of curious onlookers gathered in the park across the street.

"The Chiefs put us at Def-Con 4," the colonel said. "The whole country is in a panic. Martial law is hard enough to orchestrate and support, but now we have that, too."

The motorcade hurried down Pennsylvania Avenue. Angry crowds seemed to be outside every store, pharmacy, bar, and restaurant.

"They're starting to get restless" the colonel said. "We have to get those grids up tomorrow, or we'll have a real panic on our hands. We should have communication satellites back online tonight, so at least people can talk to each other again."

"So, was this another solar flare?" Julia asked.

"Have you had any contact with your daughter recently?" Colonel Jackson asked.

"She texted me a few days ago," Julia replied. "She was flying to southern Alaska to investigate another incident."

"That she did," the colonel said. "We ran into her and her companions up there. I'll tell you what I told her. Most of the nation is without power and communication. A large coronal mass ejection smashed out power grids that blacked out the eastern and western seaboards. D.C. and the UN are running on emergency power."

"And can you get it all restored soon?" Julia asked.

"Most of it," Colonel Jackson replied. "Might take years to get all of it."

Jackson pulled papers from his briefcase and handed the stack to Julia. She flipped through black and white pictures of the carnage at the last incident near the glacier.

"I see Sara in some of these pictures," she said.

"Yes, she was there first," the colonel said.

"This is unbelievable." She peered over her reading glasses. "Am I seeing what I think I'm seeing?"

"Your daughter said the same thing," he replied. "She ordered us to have them transported immediately to deep freeze."

"She ordered you?" Julia asked, brow raised.

"Her last name is Gathers; you know." He chuckled. "I don't question a Gathers."

Julia smiled.

Out the window, more crowds and desperate stares at the motorcade moving toward the Capitol building. Jackson could sense the fear emanating from the faces along the street.

"Julia, do you ever wish that we had done something different, you and I?" the colonel asked. "I mean, could we have pushed more change; could we have prevented all this?"

Still studying the photographs of her daughter and the woolly mammoths, she said, "Maybe, that's wishful thinking. The world would've had to change so much to prevent what's happening. The wheels of the industrial machine of our modern world were set in motion more than a century ago. It's not easy to turn back the momentum of a train running down the tracks. These machinations are powerful. Their momentum can't be stopped overnight. Certainly not by two people."

"Now you seem pessimistic," the colonel said.

"Would you have me lay down on the tracks?" Julia sighed.

The motorcade stopped at the steps of the Capitol Building. Julia and the colonel made it to Senator O'Connell's private office escorted by heavy guard.

His office was enormous, walls clad in black walnut and high, arched ceilings with layered insets trimmed in gold. O'Connell stood with an empty glass in hand, silently staring out a large casement window at dark streets fanning out across the city. The orange afterglow of sunset lit the horizon. O'Connell had his back to the door as Julia and Colonel Jackson entered the room.

"The capitol of the most powerful nation the world has ever known is without electricity," O'Connell said. "Can you explain that?"

"Well, Sir," Colonel Jackson replied. "There was the sizeable coronal mass eject—"

"I know that!" O'Connell shouted, cutting him off. "But how did **this** happen!" O'Connell motioned out the window. "We've had fail-safe protocols here since 9-11! And you're telling me we weren't prepared for this?!"

"Sir."

O'Connell flipped latches on the window jamb and pushed it open. "Do you hear that?" he asked.

"Hear what?"

"That's right," O'Connell responded. "Nothing. No sound. We've been sent back to the stone age!"

"Sir, we'll have power to D.C. within forty-eight hours," Jackson said. "The rest of the east coast soon after."

"I have credible sources that say we don't have enough transformers stockpiled to jump-start the grid," O'Connell argued.

"That assumes all transformers were blown out," the colonel replied. "But there are backup systems in place to prevent that. They are efforting damage and repair procedures as we speak. These guys are working around the clock to get the grid up and running again. And so far, no one has reported that level of damage."

O'Connell turned to his desk, a large oaken masterpiece with hand-carved trim and a green leather top. He reached for a half-empty bottle of Irish whiskey centered on the desktop and poured a jigger. He quickly slugged it down and paced around the desk in contemplation.

"Last night," he said in a calmer voice, "I looked out this window and watched the Milky Way march slowly across the sky. The last U.S. President to see that from the White House was Teddy Roosevelt in 1909."

"Senator O'Connell," Jackson said, but the Senator cut him off again.

"Don't get me wrong," the Senator said as he filled another jigger. "I like the Milky Way, I really do, but I don't ever want to see it again in this city."

A poetic, if not cryptic, description of the state of the modern world. Julia considered saying something but decided to wait for a quieter moment.

"Rumor has it," the senator continued, "Most people in this town don't even know what it is. An apocalyptic sign, they say, or some such nonsense."

O'Connell turned back to the window. Julia and Colonel Jackson exchanged concerned glances.

"The chiefs and the president are away in a safe place," O'Connell said. "At least we got that right."

"Sir," Colonel Jackson said. "I know this is extremely difficult, but we have an agenda to discuss. We also have some interesting information for you."

O'Connell raised an eyebrow, took a seat, and motioned for Julia and the colonel to do the same. Jackson passed a large manila envelope across the desk. O'Connell opened it and pulled out photos of the dead mammoths. He stood and flipped through the photos as he paced behind his desk. He shot bewildered glances at Julia and the colonel.

"This can't be real," he probed. "Can it? Where were these pictures taken?"

"Southern Alaska, near Valdez," Jackson responded.

"When?"

"Yesterday."

O'Connell continued pacing, flipping through pictures and gathering his thoughts. "They're all burned," he said. "Was this at the recent fire event?"

"That's correct."

"And who are these people?"

"The young woman is Sara Gathers."

O'Connell raised an eyebrow.

"I sent my daughter to assess the methane situation near the two northern fires," Julia said. "That led them to this fire."

O'Connell returned his focus to the pictures. "OK, back up for a minute," he snapped. "These are extinct animals. How did these animals get there?"

"Unknown," Colonel Jackson responded.

"I've heard that giant sinkholes are forming in the Arctic," O'Connell said. "Is it possible the fire melted away all the surface ice and exposed them?"

"Miss Gathers said some were alive when she got there," the colonel said.

"Alive?" O'Connell asked. "How is that possible?"

"We don't know," Jackson replied. "They are being airlifted to Patterson as we speak. They'll be stored in deep freeze until a necropsy can be performed."

"We need answers to this quickly," O'Connell said. "Before the story leaks out."

"Sir," the colonel said. "My men are sworn to secrecy on this situation."

"Same as the Overland Project?" O'Connell critiqued, then continued. "So you and your men did not see them alive?"

"That's correct, but—"

The senator interrupted and raised his hand. "Since we are honestly in the dark on how they got there, we will say they were exposed by glacial ice melt if asked."

Julia felt an eerie cloud settling down around her. "And Sara?" Julia asked. "What is she supposed to say?"

"I assume your daughter knows the significance of this find," O'Connell said. "And will want definitive answers before releasing information to the public. You will inform her of that, correct?"

Julia began to feel as if she were in a cage. "Of course," she replied in masked confidence. "I'll make sure she knows."

O'Connell accepted her answer but was not convinced by her eyes. He paced the floor again, sipping on whiskey. "You mentioned that Sara went up to investigate methane emissions," O'Connell said. "What did she find out?"

"It is as I suspected," Julia replied, reaching for papers in her satchel bag. "And even worse."

She pulled out color prints of images Sara sent from Ben Hadley, showing increased methane release around the globe, specifically in the Arctic regions. The color-coded changes were easy to translate.

"So, what do I do with this?" O'Connell muttered.

"Ha." Julia sighed. "I'm not sure there is anything you can do. This is simply the state of where we are, what we've done."

O'Connell had an expression of frustration and confusion.

"Sir, we need to fix what we can," Jackson said, picking up the color graphs. "Today, we have to deal with the blackout. Tomorrow, maybe this."

"You know," O'Connell said. "I hoped you two would bring tidings of good news in here today. I've had more stuff thrown at me this week than I can deal with, and the pile is getting deeper."

Julia and Jackson sighed.

O'Connell caught their eyes while pouring another glass. He carefully responded. "So, we have confirmation of the methane issue," he said. "The mammoth situation—I'm not too concerned about. Anything else?"

Colonel Jackson looked away.

Julia cleared her throat. "We have reason to believe core movement might become an issue," she said. "Our latest data show the Magnetic North Pole is moving south along the west coast toward the U.S. border."

O'Connell sighed, sat on the corner of his desk, and threw back the glass of whiskey.

Chapter 18

The Freezer

Fort Patterson, AK

No freezers at Fort Patterson could house woolly mammoths as Colonel Jackson had promised Sara. But his base did have exclusive access to nearby tracts of government-owned land that extended into the foothills of the Denali Wilderness. Many caves lay inset in these foothills, well hidden from the public and off-limits to hikers, a perfect hiding place for a couple dozen extinct mammoths. The good colonel also knew he could pull strings with a local HVAC contractor who maintained their heating and cooling equipment. They sealed the entrance to the vast cave with metal framing and a large overhead door. Followed by heavy refrigeration tanks, generators, and evaporators on flatbed trailers.

Hours later, a freezing cloud of water vapor pumped its way into the room.

Under cover of darkness, Chinook helicopters carrying the mammoths dropped in one by one. The beasts' burned bodies were wrapped and strapped with a heavy tarp. The straps came up to a single lifting point with two large steel rings for hook attachment. Their unwrapped heads and curved tusks hung down from shoulder straps, and they hit with a mechanical clang as they dropped onto flatbed trucks. The trucks drove into the cave, where long stalactites hung from the top of an enormous arched cavern. Beyond the cavern, tunnels leading farther into the mountain were sealed off to hold the ever-lowering temperature. The trucks paraded in and out of the cave. Inside, a military-grade tow truck hooked and hoisted the mammoths off the ground.

After the load out, two military guards surveyed the area. They checked doors and barricades for air leaks. Then made a final headcount of the mammoths and took in a few last breaths of the frigid acrid air.

"I'm guessing that Jackson wasn't out big game hunting," one guard commented to another. "That's why we aren't talking about this."

"Where'd they find these things?" the other guard asked.

"This place smells like a frozen bonfire. Did they melt out of a glacier?"

"No, look, they're all burned up," the other guard commented. "Anyway, a perfect place to hide prehistoric monsters."

They studied the grim scene, surrounded by ancient carcasses.

"I hear this place will get down to twenty below," the first man said. "We stand guard outside and keep the generators running."

Then a warning horn blasted, a spinning red light illuminated the cave, and the overhead door started rolling up. Two black-clad armed soldiers stepped across the threshold and motioned for the two guards to leave.

"Time to lock it down," one black-clad soldier declared.

The two guards quickly stepped outside. An armed soldier tapped a red button on the outside security panel, and the large overhead door slowly coiled downward.

"Rules are no one opens this door without permission from Colonel Jackson," the soldier said. "Understood?

"Yes, sir."

They stepped over to a control board.

"When this red light turns green," the soldier said. "That means the inside air has reached its optimum temperature."

"Yes, sir."

"You stand guard and check fuel levels," the soldier said. "We expect daily reports of any unusual activity."

"Yes, sir."

"If that light ever goes red," he ordered, "call us immediately."

"Yes, sir."

PART 3

Core rotation – British Columbia, Canada near the 45th parallel

As the axis of the core rotates, it leads to even brighter Auroras and more radiation swirling down through the atmosphere.

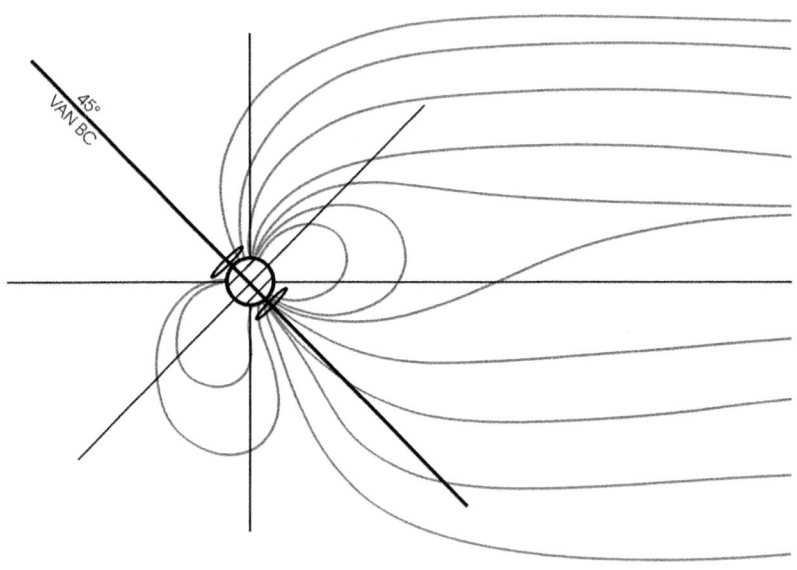

Chapter 19
Big Jump

Alaska's Southern Leg

R eadings on the magnetometer in Ethan's hand suddenly dropped to normal levels, around 60,000 nT, but something looked odd. He shook the device a couple of times to re-set it, but it returned to the same readings. He checked the direction of the setting sun, then looked off in the distance, speechless and confused.

"What is it?" Sara asked.

"It's jumped again," Ethan said, pointing south. "Now that direction is north."

Mason frowned and grabbed the magnetometer from his hand, he shook it, but it did the same thing. As he did, thousands of silent seabirds suddenly took to the sky and flew in the new north direction. Already airborne, Jackson's fleet of Chinooks seemed to lead them toward the horizon. The helicopters eventually veered back northwest (the new southeast) into Alaska, but a cloud of ten thousand seabirds stayed their course.

"I'm guessing we'll follow the birds," Mason said.

"You bet your ass we will," Sara replied.

The crew buckled in and adjusted their headphones. The plane lifted off and followed the dark cloud. Ethan flipped open the magnetometer, still 60,000 nT (+/-) and the arrow pointing north-northwest. Gauge readings on the plane console were also back to normal.

"We'll head down the coastline toward Sitka," Mason said. "That's where I usually fuel up. In the meantime, find us a backup airfield. We might need one."

"I've been down here before," Ethan said, opening his satchel. "I have radio frequencies to a few small airfields. But in the meantime, I have to send the video of the last event to Paul."

Ethan directed them to an airfield on a coastal town within in eyeshot of massive glacier fields an hour into the flight. They disembarked, fueled up, and asked for directions to the nearest restaurant. Mason requested a shuttle ride, but one of the station attendants was heading into town and gave them a lift.

"This little diner has everything from breakfast to dinner," the man said. "Where are you all in from?"

"Fairbanks," Mason responded. "We really appreciate you driving us out here."

"So, you flew in from up north?" the man asked.

"That's right."

"Did you see that bright light? Been crazy here lately," the man said. "Not sure what's going on, but I saw Auroras earlier this morning brighter than ever. People stood out on the streets, staring at it. The power was out. These things quit working, too." Holding his cell phone. "Not sure what it is, but I hope it ends soon."

"Yeah, we—" Mason said, then hesitated. "We're hoping for the same."

"You all hear about the beached whales down here?" he asked.

Sara popped up from the back seat. "No," she replied. "Where?"

"Not far," the man said. "Whales, dolphins, seals. You name it, they're beached."

She gave Mason a concerned look.

"Well," Mason said. "I *was* hungry."

"Can you take us there?" she asked and tapped his shoulder.

"Well, yeah," the man answered. "But what good can you do?"

"Just take us there," Mason asked. "Trust me."

A few minutes later, they were beachside. It was hard to navigate through pick-up trucks and cars to find a drop-off spot. But when they stepped out of the car, hundreds of people and even more stranded sea creatures lined a long, narrow beach. Sara at once hurried down a sandy path.

"What are we doing?" Ethan asked.

Mason pulled out his wallet.

"No, sir," the man said. "I don't want payment. I was happy to bring you out here."

"This isn't payment," Mason replied. "We need something to eat. Can you go back into town and bring supplies? We need food and water. Lots of water. Cases and cases of water."

He handed the man a credit card. "All you can get."

"Yes, sir," the man said.

Mason headed down the pathway. The man opened the door and shouted in Mason's direction. "Who are you people anyway?"

Sara was, well, Sara. She saw herds of stranded seals and dolphins shepherded into the water. Some went on; some returned. Seals were not a big concern to her since they spent most of their time on land. Some dolphins were resistant, thrashing and dying.

Bystanders at the beach's edge stood taking video and doing the same a few hundred yards away near a pod of white beluga whales.

A sadness came over her as she looked out at this scene of grief and confusion. This was the new reality. Core movement had caused these cetacean strandings. *So, they do navigate via magnetic field lines.* Why was nature making these creatures pay such a price? And what about the mammoths? Where did they fit into all this? Her frustration burst.

"Hey!" she stopped and shouted. "Do you people want to help or stand there and watch these creatures die?"

"Here we go again," Mason murmured.

"You want to make yourselves useful!" she continued to shout. "Go into town and get supplies. We need tarps, buckets, shovels, and water. Lots of water."

Mason walked up next to her. "Rope," Mason added.

"And rope," she shouted. "Strong, sturdy rope!"

People looked confused.

"What are you waiting for?" she shouted. "Get moving!"

The crowd quickly hurried up the hill.

Ethan approached. "Should I go with them?" he asked.

Sara rolled her eyes. "You're coming with us," she said.

Sara headed down the beach toward the dolphin pod.

"What about the stranded seals?" Ethan asked.

"Harbor seals don't need saving," Sara said. "But cetaceans can't live on land. We have to get them back in the water." She approached a group of people, still standing at attention.

"My name is Sara Gathers," she barked out, holding her ID badge. "I'm with NOAA. I specialize in aquatic strandings."

The crowd seemed to understand and exchanged reassured glances. Ethan pulled out his lanyard. Mason shook his head.

"A lot of effort is required to save these creatures," she followed. "I am not keen on the press, or anyone assumed to be. It's going to take hours to save these animals. So, if anyone is not up to the task, you should pack up now."

No one moved.

"Good," she said. "Is anyone here a rescue specialist? Firefighter, police, ambulance?"

"Lots of us," a man replied, stepping out from the crowd. "That's why we're here."

"Thank god," Sara said. *This won't be another Clovis*, she thought.

"Any of you fishermen?" Mason asked. "We'll need boats to pull the whales out to sea."

"Most of us are," one man replied. "It's Alaska."

"Any Gillnet boats?" Mason asked. "With reels?"

"Oh, yeah," came a positive response from many nodding heads.

Mason looked at Sara and grinned.

"We got this," he said.

A line of pick-up trucks soon brought in food and supplies. Hundreds of people swarmed the beach to help. Half of the town showed up with shirt sleeves rolled up. Sara was beside herself.

The belugas were much smaller than the giant sperm whales from Clovis, not much larger than porpoises. With proper boats, supplies, tools, and direction from Sara, all whales were back in the water in a short time. Most of the dolphins made it, too, except for a few improperly handled before her arrival.

With the creatures safely out to sea, Sara took a moment to regroup her thoughts. This core movement was causing catastrophic damage. Everywhere they turned, there was another example of the reach of this phenomenon. She was like a butterfly chasing a thunderstorm. What is next? Where were they going? Where is the core going? And what about the mammoths? Where did they come from?

"Ethan," Sara said. "We know the core has jumped. Your magnetometer points the direction. But how far has it jumped?"

"I'm not sure," he said. "Maybe hundreds of miles."

"The last jump was 700 miles," she said. "So how do you know this one hasn't done the same or more?"

"I guess I don't."

"Maybe we shouldn't keep going in this direction," she said. "Gather more information."

"Good point," Ethan said. "I'll follow up with Paul about the video and see what else he can tell us."

Ethan turned and walked away, typing into his phone. The line of the rescue workers shook hands and made their way up the sandy paths. Sara and Mason looked out over the ocean, keeping vigil on the empty beachhead and hoping it stayed that way.

"Is this a wild goose chase?" Sara asked. "I mean, what we're doing here?"

"Hey, guys!" Ethan shouted. "I have him."

Ethan hurried over to Mason and Sara, holding out his phone with Paul Moore on video.

"Paul," Ethan cut him off. "Here's Sara and Mason. Start over and tell them what you just told me."

"OK," Paul said with a harsh voice. "We've been studying the footage you sent, and what we found is almost impossible to describe. The first thing is this was stronger, way stronger than the earlier events as if fueled by another source. That light shooting out from the ground was hard to figure out. At first, we thought it might be a reflection from glaciers, but when we overlaid the exact location, we saw it was something entirely different. It's directly over a fault line, *the* fault line, the Ring of Fire that defines the Pacific Rim."

"That's right," Ethan realized. "That's exactly right. It just never occurred to me."

"What do you mean?" Sara asked. "How could you know that?"

"Lots of things float around up here," Ethan tapped his head. "I downloaded the entire NOAA database of natural disasters, from earthquakes to space weather. It's something like ten gigs. But that template, the Ring of Fire, really stuck in my brain."

"Seriously?"

"OK, Paul," Sara said. "What does all that mean?"

"We're not exactly sure," Paul continued. "But the joint between tectonic plates could be a fissure that allowed magnetic energy to vent up like a natural smokestack. That light fan was not only a half-mile long, but it also ran the full colors of the visible light spectrum.

"And here's the other thing: that change in light color you saw between red and orange when the radio tower appeared and disappeared? It also happened at the other end of the light fan. We saw the woolly mammoths appear, disappear, and re-appear between the green and blue light."

Silence and confused glances dominated the room.

"You know, ROY G BIV," Paul said. "The colors of the rainbow that you learned in science class. Red, Orange, Yellow, Green, Blue, Indigo, and Violet. Obviously, something is going on with the color changes related to what's visible."

He paused.

"I don't want to speculate any further, but those are the facts."

They exchanged concerned glances, then Sara took a breath.

"OK, what can you tell us about the recent core jump?" she asked. "We know it's going south, or new north, whatever. But has it stopped moving again? Do you know where it is?"

"That's the other interesting part," Paul said. "I believe we can now say we are experiencing a core flip. It has jumped about 900 miles south toward the U.S./Canadian border, roughly 100 miles west of Vancouver Island in the Pacific. Oddly enough, it's holding position directly over a jog in the same fault line, where it hooks and goes down to California."

Determined glances passed among the group.

"Mason," Sara said. "We can't get there safely with your plane. I'll contact Colonel Jackson for better transport."

"Paul," she turned back and spoke. "We're heading up to Fairbanks and will check in with you when we arrive. Stay on top of this thing. I want you to 'speculate further' when we get there."

"Yes, ma'am," he replied, and the phone went dark.

"All right, Mason," Sara said. "Let's get back to the airport."

Chapter 20
The Mammoths

Fort Patterson, AK

After hitching a ride to the airport, Mason and Ethan readied the plane for take-off. Sara pulled Colonel Jackson's business card and typed in his direct line. It picked up on the first ring.

"Jackson here," the voice said.

"Colonel," Sara said. "Sara Gathers."

"Good afternoon, young lady," the colonel responded. "How can I help you?"

"Since our last meeting," she replied, "we've been tracking core movement. We started down the Alaska coastline but found that it's jumped about 900 miles south into the Pacific Ocean, near the U.S./Canadian border."

"Excuse me?" Colonel Jackson asked. "Did you say 900 miles?"

"That's correct," she said. "We need to stay on top of it, but our floatplane is not up to the task."

"You can say that again," he said, a brief pause. "I'll arrange for a transport plane to shuttle you up to Ft. Patterson. Can you get to Sitka in two hours?"

"I'll make it happen," Sara responded.

"Good," he said. "I'll call ahead for clearance. I'm still in Washington but will be back in Fairbanks tomorrow morning. In the meantime, I'll find us transport to that new location."

"Thank you," Sara said. "I'll see you tomorrow."

"So, what did he say?" Mason asked.

"We're flying to Sitka," Sara said.

"Sitka?" Mason asked. "It's about an hour away."

"Good," she said, beaming with relief. "And we're hopping on a big plane." She was finally getting a smoother and safer ride.

The flight down to Sitka went smoothly. Mason nervously prepped for landing at another military base but was more confident about Sara's clearance this time around. Sitka had fewer buildings than Patterson, and from the approach angle, it made the runways appear longer. As they made for one of the shorter runways, a giant Cargo plane, a C-17 Globemaster, lifted off the main runway and headed out in the opposite direction.

"It's hard to believe something that big can get in the air," Mason commented.

The floatplane taxied down a runway, guided by multiple ground crew flagging them to a stop. The plane pulled in amid scores of military personnel, some armed, some in formal dress, some in black suits.

"Are they expecting the president?" Ethan asked, crawling up from the back.

"No, kid, they're not," Mason replied. "But I bet Sara gets a personal escort."

Sara pulled off her headset and unbuckled. Mason turned off the engine. Two black suits approached the passenger side and offered hands to Sara as she stepped onto the tarmac.

"Told ya," Mason said and opened his own door. "And we walk behind her."

"Wow," Ethan said. "Talk about legit."

Sara and the black suits approached the line of officers in formal dress.

"Miss Gathers," an officer stepped up and spoke. "We are here to assist you with anything you may need, from personnel to supplies. We have C-17 transport ready to take you and your group to Ft. Patterson anytime. The plane, runway, and all facilities are at your disposal."

Sara was honored, Mason was relieved. Ethan stood there with his mouth hanging open.

"Thank you," she said. "But we don't have the luxury of time. We need to board that transport as soon as possible."

Mason tapped her on the shoulder.

"Oh, yes," she continued. "And we do need to eat something."

"Yes, ma'am." He motioned to another officer.

An SUV pulled up momentarily, the black suits ushered Sara, Mason, and Ethan into the middle seat. Two black suits sat in front and three officers in the back.

"There is a great national concern," the captain related to Sara, "about this phenomenon, the power and communication outages. Colonel Jackson tells us you are key to solving this problem."

She turned to see the man's face and knew it was not a statement or an order. There was genuine concern and confusion in his eyes.

"We're with NOAA," she said.

All eyes were on her, even the driver peering into the rearview mirror. She felt anxious as she turned her gaze to Ethan and back to the captain.

"We've been chasing this problem for weeks now," she continued, measuring her words. "And we're getting to the bottom of it."

The SUV pulled up to the dining hall. After a quick meal, Ethan grabbed granola bars and a large bag of potato chips for the flight. Minutes later, they boarded the gigantic C-17 and taxied down a long runway. The cargo plane was mainly a big, loud open hull, but upfront was a comfortable seating cabin isolated from the clanging sounds in the rear. There were two sets of four seats facing each other and flat screens over each seat. No loud, Cessna prop-motor was getting on Sara's nerves, only the distant hum of turbine engines. Once the plane lifted to the sky, Sara quickly fell asleep.

Ethan's mind traveled back to the strange happenings of the second incident. How did the radio tower flicker in and out of sight? Was Sara right? Was it only a mirage? Paul Moore said the mammoths also flickered in and out of sight, but they were real. How could the change in light color explain both these phenomena?

Mason pulled a blanket down from an overhead compartment and draped it over Sara. He sat directly across from Ethan, whose eyes were fixed in thought.

"What are you thinking about, kid?" Mason asked.

His question was met with silence.

"Hey," Mason asked again, waving his hand.

Ethan popped to attention.

"Everything we saw at the last incident," Ethan said, crunching a handful of potato chips. "The radio tower, the mammoths ..."

"Freaky stuff," Mason said and motioned for the bag of chips. "All this is. Everything since I met her."

"But how did that tower disappear?" Ethan asked. "And how did the mammoths appear?"

"Maybe the tower was never there," Mason replied, with a chip in his mouth.

Ethan focused on the pictures again.

"And the mammoths?" Ethan returned his attention.

"Who knows, kid," Mason said. "The professor told us the light came up from between tectonic plates. Maybe they did, too."

Ethan shook his head and looked out the window.

They soon fell asleep and did not awaken till the wheels touched down at Ft. Patterson two hours later.

At Fort Patterson, a government vehicle waited for them on the tarmac. A group of officers stepped out of the car as Sara walked down the boarding stairs.

"Hello, I'm Sara Gathers," Sara said, extending her hand. "I believe we met the last time I visited."

"Yes, ma'am. Captain Ronald Marcus at your service," he replied.

"When will Colonel Jackson arrive?" Sara asked.

"He lands at 0900 hours tomorrow," he replied. "We can escort you to your quarters if you'd like."

"That would be fine," she said. "Thank you."

As the vehicle passed the campus of buildings, Sara's waking mind thought of something. "Captain," she said, "can you take us to the freezer building?"

"Ma'am?" he asked.

"You do have a freezer on-site?" she asked.

He nodded and motioned for the driver to veer off the other way. They soon found themselves walking through the mess hall. They pushed through a set of swinging doors and approached a large metal door with a latch. He pulled it open, and Sara stepped inside. The food freezer was no more than ten feet in each direction with shelving on all walls, loaded with boxes of frozen foods.

"This is it," he commented matter-of-factly.

"No," Sara said. "I mean the freezer building. The really big one."

The captain looked confused.

"This is the only freezer we have, ma'am," he said.

Now Sara looked confused. Ethan peeked inside and frowned.

"Hmm," she mumbled. She made eye contact with Mason, who also looked perplexed.

"I guess I'm a little tired," she said. "If you can, please show us to our quarters."

"This way, ma'am," the captain said.

They were taken to the officer's residences, where separate condo spaces were prepared for all three. Sara and Mason took the first one and dropped their bags. Clearly exhausted from their journey, Sara lay back in the bed next to Mason and kicked off her shoes.

"What was that all about?" Mason asked.

"I'm not sure," Sara said. "But that officer really didn't know what was going on; maybe that's a good thing. We'll find out in the morning when Colonel Jackson arrives."

They received a wake-up call at 0800 hours. The colonel arrived early and requested they meet him for breakfast. He had a private room prepared.

"I hope the flight up here was comfortable," the colonel said.

"Yes," Sara replied. "Thank you. I slept the whole way."

"And your quarters?" he asked.

"Couldn't be better," she said. Mason and Ethan had their faces buried in plates of food.

"And the grub?" the colonel asked.

Sara kneed Mason.

"Fantastic!" Mason said. "I didn't know eggs could be prepared this way."

"Maybe not at the King Crab," Sara commented.

"Colonel," Sara said. "As we discussed before, the core has jumped too far for a small plane to reach."

"Yes," he replied. "I have it all arranged. We fly out of here in four hours and catch a ..." He paused. "Are you OK with boats, young lady?"

"Uh, sure," she muttered. "I guess."

"I don't think it's safe to get near that thing with any aircraft, certainly not over water," the colonel continued. "So, I made some calls and found better transport. An amphibious assault ship leaving Anchorage can take us out to the anomaly. It's an aircraft carrier for helicopters, and it's about to disembark for Hawaii. We'll board a Chinook here at 1300 hours and rendezvous with the carrier at 1630 hours.

"The only hitch is it will still take ten hours to reach the anomaly after touching down on the carrier. And that assumes it doesn't move again."

Sara considered the idea. Gauged Mason and Ethan's faces since both had stopped eating and were speechless.

"I guess it's our best option," she said. "And a safe one, too. Thank you for setting this up."

"My pleasure," the colonel said, sipping his coffee.

"Colonel, I haven't heard from my mother recently," Sara said. "How did things go in Washington?"

"Well." The colonel gathered his thoughts. "Senator O'Connell was not too happy with anything we had to say. Especially about the mammoths. But he's under an incredible amount of pressure, so I guess I wasn't too surprised."

"What did he say about the mammoths?" she asked.

"Couldn't wrap his head around it," the colonel replied. "Officially, they melted out from the permafrost during the fire."

"What?!" Sara popped out.

"Until we can prove different," he said. "They don't want this leaking to the public."

"Colonel," she calmed down. "Where, exactly, are the mammoths being stored? I asked your men to take me to the freezer, and they took me over there."

The colonel chuckled. "He actually took you into the kitchen. Can't fault him for doing his duty. But this is top secret, as you and I discussed. I have them stored off-site in a deep mountain cave.

"Young lady," he continued, sipping more coffee. "I've never been a big fan of O'Connell; that's common knowledge. If you could somehow prove where they came from, that they were alive when you first found them, that would go a long way toward regaining his trust in our abilities to solve this whole situation and give me a longer rope to work with."

Sara thought about it, then checked the clock on the wall. "Colonel," she said. "Can you get me to that mountain and back before we hop on the helicopter?"

He stood, pulled a phone to his ear, and spoke softly for a few seconds.

"Special Op's escort will be out front in five minutes," he said.

Soon they were in a caravan of SUVs on an hour-long drive to the mountain cave. Sara thought about the autopsy procedure. What was essential, what single item, what single piece to the puzzle could help her figure out how and when they died. Then it hit her. All she needed was a fecal sample. If they were modern animals, they would have modern bacteria in their bellies and skin and hair. That was it; that was all she needed. It was also quick and easy. It could not have been a better solution with time of the essence.

And then another thought popped into her spinning mind.

"Carno-ply," Sara said. Her concentrated gaze softened as she turned to Colonel Jackson. "That's the key."

"Excuse me?" the colonel asked.

"All waters of the mammoth era contained *carnobacterium pleistocenium*," Sara explained. "It's from Paleo-biology. Pleistocene era waters had these tiny microorganisms floating around everywhere. So, if these mammoths melted out of ice, we could easily verify it with tissue samples. Carno-ply bacteria would be abundant. But if there are no carno-ply bacteria on them, they are modern animals."

"All right, then," the colonel said. "Sounds like you know what you're looking for."

The paved road eventually turned to gravel and made a winding pass through the heavily wooded foothills of the Denali Range. Finally, they approached a guard gate sided by chain-link fencing that ran off in both directions. The caravan slowed, the lead car driver held out a badge, and a security gate slowly rolled open. Minutes later, they pulled to a stop in front of a giant steel wall. Two guards approached the caravan as all car doors swung open.

"Colonel," the guards stopped and saluted.

"At ease, gentlemen," the colonel said. "We need access to the freezer."

Freezer, Sara suddenly thought. *It might be 20 below in there, and I am wearing a sweater.* When she turned to say something, the black suits were already pulling special low-temp gear from the trunks.

"You need to put this on, ma'am," one said, handing her insulated white overalls. "There is also a hood with a face mask. We all need to be geared up before going inside."

Ethan was noticeably nervous. Mason pulled the suit on as if he had done it a hundred times before.

"We need cutting tools," Sara said. "Preferably scalpels, a sharp knife, a first aid kit, and a cooler."

One black suit pulled a knife from his coat. Another found a first aid kit in the trunk.

"We have these, ma'am," he said.

"I guess that will have to do," Sara said. "Thank you."

"Hey," one of the guards ran up. "You can use my lunch cooler."

Sara opened it and looked inside.

"Clean enough," she said. "Thank you."

The guards flipped a switch, and the giant coiling door slowly rolled open. A rush of icy smoke rolled out from underneath, and the troop of white-garbed investigators stepped inside. Sara peered through plastic goggles into the dark cave. There was a 'thwack' sound as a guard lifted the main switch; a few seconds later, the frozen lights began to turn on. First, they flickered, then dim light cast a hazy glow across the room. As the glow started to grow, it slowly lit the entire cave.

Gigantic mammoths lay frozen in the icy fog, their tusks sticking above the cloud. An eerie memory for Sara from when she first saw them fall in smoldering ashes.

"We have twenty minutes," the guard said and flipped the switch to lower the door. "Then we have to step outside to warm up."

Sara spotted the large bull right away. She'd seen him die, so maybe his tissues could help her find some answers with a bit of luck.

"Mason," she said. "Need some help over here."

Everyone followed her through the mist toward the giant beast. Sara knelt in her white, low-temp suit and fanned mist away from its feet. She rubbed his frozen skin, looking for the right place to cut, but the burnt hair was rock-hard and matted with red fire retardant.

"Too much red chemical here," she murmured, as frozen vapor puffed through an oval-shaped mouth screen with every syllable. "I need more light."

She focused on its belly, fanned away more mist, and studied his underside, hopefully, shaded from the chemical drop. As she hoped, the area between his gigantic legs had no red coloring. Flashlight beams zoomed in, following her hands. She reached in with the knife but could not get penetration, so she handed it to Mason. He scraped hard and was able to remove enough material to fill a plastic bandage holder from the first aid kit. It was so hard that Mason could not tell whether he was scraping away skin or bone.

"This is good," Sara said. "Now, we need to get a fecal sample."

"You're kidding," Mason groaned.

"No," Sara said, pointing to mid-thorax. "We have to make a deep incision into the belly."

"You ever try to carve a frozen turkey?" Mason asked.

"It's a bitch," the colonel chuckled. "We need to drill."

"Maybe chainsaw," Mason followed.

"Maybe, but we can't get it done now," the colonel said. "Miss Gathers, where do you intend to send these samples?"

"Up to the labs in Perishton," Sara responded.

The colonel considered his options.

179

"We can head back to the base," the colonel offered. "I'll dispatch those samples today before we head south. In the meantime, I'll send a crew down here to dig out the other sample you need. Does that fit the bill?"

"That will do," Sara said. "Thank you."

The colonel redirected.

"Gentlemen," he said. "In case any of you need a reminder: Miss Gathers excavated these extinct creatures from glacial ice down near Sitka, and this was the only facility available to store them. No one talks about this, not even to your wives. Any questions?"

Straight faces, no response.

The caravan made its way back to Ft. Patterson and readied for the long helicopter ride. The colonel dispatched the cooler of tissue samples to the Perishton Lab with a note from Sara Gathers to specifically search all samples for evidence of *carnobacterium pleistocenium*, attention Ben Hadley. They returned to their rooms, packed, and showered. Soon, Sara stood in the waiting room outside Colonel Jackson's office.

The room was basic military with tile floors and drab green walls. There were paintings of mountains and some enlarged photos of the base on the walls. Sara impatiently paced the floor while Mason calmly watched her. Ethan checked his phone for the latest news stories.

One photo caught Sara's eye as the colonel stepped out to greet her.

"Are we ready?" the colonel politely asked.

"Yes, I believe so," Sara replied, still focused on the photo of the base. "Is this an old photo of Ft. Patterson?"

"Yes," the colonel replied. "Circa World War II, I believe."

She continued looking at the photo.

"Why do you ask?" he said. This got both Mason's and Ethan's attention.

"So much has changed," she said. "I hardly recognize it."

"Got a whole room full of them over here," the colonel said, pointing to another door in the waiting room. They walked into a room wallpapered with framed pictures of every base in Alaska. Old photos, new photos, some in color, some black and white.

"Quite a collection," she said, walking next to the colonel.

The colonel had stories about each picture and everything in them. Sara was amazed by the detail and organization. Each image had a brass label with the name of the base and the year of the photo. The colonel could have talked for hours if they had the time. They made a complete pass around the room, but Ethan stood by the door, focused on pictures from one base.

"What is it, son?" the colonel asked.

"Colonel, where is this facility?" Ethan asked.

"Fort Andrews?" the colonel pondered. "Let me see. I believe it's down on the southeast coast, abandoned for years now. As a matter of fact, it's not far from where you found those mammoths."

Just as Ethan thought.

"Sara, look," Ethan whispered, his heart racing. "Look at the dates on the labels."

"Yeah," she replied. "1942 and 1982, so, what?"

"Look closely at the buildings," he said. "Then back and forth between them. We've seen this before. A tall radio tower in 1942 and no radio tower in 1982."

"How is this possible?" Sara asked. Chills shot up her spine.

"It's *definitely* not heat from the road," Mason said.

"The tower was re-located when they built the pipeline in the '70s," the colonel said. "Why are you folks so interested in that tower?"

Chapter 21

Heading South (or North)

The Carrier, North Pacific Ocean

The Chinook ride to Wright Air Force Base in Anchorage was much smoother than the ride Sara remembered on Mason's Cessna. They stopped only for fuel and quickly lifted off for the carrier. Soon, they were over the crisp blue of the North Pacific, speeding out toward the carrier. Military personnel seated themselves on one side of the unfinished cabin. Colonel Jackson, Sara, and the others sat opposite, flanked by armed soldiers in black army garb.

"Orders were sent to the captain of the carrier," the colonel barked over a headset. "To re-route the vessel to the coordinates of the anomaly after we rendezvous. We should reach the ship as scheduled at 1630 hours."

Sara hoped the Dramamine did its thing. Mason could not wait to land on a carrier at sea. Ethan had only seen Chinooks in pictures, but now he was riding in one. *This chick really is legit*, he thought, *but I got to quit saying it.*

The double-propped helicopter charged out into open water, and soon, hills from the coastline disappeared. It was difficult to sense airspeed at high altitudes, but the Chinook flew low across the ocean, barely above water. Sara could make out every detail in the waves and trailing spray that pushed out from spinning rotor blades as they raced out into the Pacific.

Ethan nervously checked his magnetometer that showed they were still on course. He sensed the black suit watching over his shoulder next to him, so he quickly put it away.

"Fifteen minutes to the carrier," a voice came over cabin headsets.

"We all stay seated on touch-down," Colonel Jackson shouted through the headset. "Wait 'till the guards hop out to determine if it's safe and motion for us."

Minutes later, the Chinook hovered over a circular landing spot on the ship's deck. Its rotor blades slowed down and it landed. Colonel Jackson, Sara, and the others appeared with guards walking behind. The ship's officers stood waiting nearby.

"Captain." Colonel Jackson saluted.

"Colonel," the captain responded dryly, also saluting. "Captain Ethan Wales. These are my officers."

"Gentlemen," Jackson returned.

"Colonel," he said. "I must say that I've never been re-routed from a planned destination before. But the orders came from the top."

"It is an unusual circumstance," Jackson said.

Captain Wales's eyes quickly scanned the civilian attire of Colonel Jackson's companions. "Maybe we should discuss this situation in private," he said.

"Are you having trouble with navigation these days?" the colonel asked.

"Excuse me?" he responded. Not appreciating the colonel's comment.

"These people are with NOAA," the colonel said. "They've been tracking this thing for weeks now. They're the best in their field, and Washington wants them here. That's why I'm here, too."

The captain adjusted his posture.

"This is a national crisis," Jackson continued. "It's their job to figure out what's going on. And we need to get them down to the designated coordinates to investigate the situation."

"I have some pretty smart personnel on board, myself," the captain retorted. "And they tell me those coordinates are at the heart of something very unusual and dangerous. Extreme magnetism and high energy bursts."

Ethan's and Sara's eyes sharpened, and Wales picked up on it.

"I will not place this vessel in a dangerous situation," he continued, as captains always do to protect their ship. "Despite what Washington orders."

"And I wouldn't ask you to," the colonel said. "We've already lost one man to this thing, so we know we can't get too close to it."

Wales saw Ethan's head drop. "I'm sorry to hear that," he offered. "So, what's your plan?"

"You get us to a safe distance from the anomaly," the colonel said. "Then we'll hop on the big bird from there."

The two men stared at each other for a moment, straight-faced.

"Lieutenant," the captain barked. "See our guests to their quarters and give them directions to the galley."

Captain Wales turned back to Colonel Jackson.

"We're scheduled to reach the Anomaly, as you call it, at 0430 hours tomorrow," he said. "In the meantime, I have scheduled a de-briefing at 1800 hours. We need to know more about what we're getting ourselves into."

"Thank you, Captain," Jackson said.

"The lieutenant can also direct you to communications," he said. "Where you will have Internet and cellular access."

"Thank you," Sara said.

The captain signaled the crew to secure and tie-off the Chinook for the overnight journey. The group crossed the flight deck and entered a large hanger that led to a corridor running the ship's length. Sara, Mason, and Ethan brought up the rear.

"Once we get to communications," Sara directed to Ethan, "contact Perishton. We need updates on the anomaly's location."

"I'm on it," Ethan replied.

"Oh, and also get a hold of your friend Ben," she said. "I want to know when those tissue samples arrive."

The debriefing room was small and uncomfortable, with a rectangular table in its center, rimmed with a dozen folding chairs. The only decoration on the gray metal walls was an old-style clock, complete with hour, minute, and second hands. The Navy men sat on one side: Colonel Jackson, Sara, and the others on the opposite side. Most of the colonel's staff stood behind him. Both sides wore formal dress. Sara, Mason, and Ethan did not.

Captain Wales sized up the group opposite him with cold laser vision. Clearly, he was unhappy about this mission and certainly not happy about escorting civilians around the Pacific basin. This was painfully obvious to Sara, but Colonel Jackson expected it.

"Captain Wales," Sara broke the silence. "Before we start, I want to apologize for our appearance because we mean no disrespect. We've been out for weeks now, chasing this anomaly, with little rest or food. By foot, by boat, by plane, it has been non-stop. This young man is a pilot, and his plane crashed at an anomaly site up in the Yukon where he lost a crewmate."

Ethan's head bowed again.

"We are exhausted and committed but not exactly dressed for the occasion."

"I appreciate that, Miss?" Wales asked.

"Sara Gathers," she said, sliding her credentials across the table.

"I've seen that name in the news lately," he said, studying the badge.

"My mother is the Director of NOAA," Sara said. "She's been at all the hearings in Washington."

"And some that aren't," Colonel Jackson cut in, grabbing the attention of the room.

"I'll cut to the chase," the colonel continued. "And all this is for your ears only. Nothing goes outside this room. The bottom line is, we believe Earth is undergoing a core flip."

"A core flip?" Wales asked, thinking about it. "Do you mean the North and South Poles switching places?"

"That's correct," the colonel answered.

"I didn't hear that on the news." Wales shot a glance at Sara.

"And you won't either," the colonel said.

"Is that why one of my brightest young navigators has been trying to convince me the North Pole is sitting off the coast of Seattle, Washington?" Wales asked and raised an eyebrow at the man sitting next to him.

The man beamed a confident smile.

"That's exactly right," the colonel replied.

"And you're heading out to investigate," captain said.

"Correct."

The captain paused again.

"The location of Seattle, Washington," he said, "does not exactly define a complete flip."

"It's jumping," Ethan Sites cut in.

Captain Wales flashed a look in his direction, as if reminding him that children do not speak at the dinner table.

"It's never been completely stable," Ethan continued. "As I'm sure mariners already know. But for the past few weeks, it has been moving extremely fast, and when it does, when it jumps hundreds of miles per day, it releases large amounts of magnetic energy. The most recent jump, the location we're heading to, was a southward jump of 900 miles. The largest one so far. Uh … Sir."

Wales smiled. Ethan (and Mason) were relieved.

"Then perhaps you and my navigator should work together on this thing," he said to many exchanged glances and nods of agreement.

After the de-briefing, Sara and Mason returned to their room to regroup. The room reminded her of the debriefing room, painted navy gray. It had a bed bolted to the floor and a tiny closet next to the bathroom. A single light hung over the bed.

Sara and Mason tried to sleep, but the light shining through the porthole window filled the room. They decided to take a walk and soon found themselves on the flight deck. The Auroras shone with supernatural illumination against the first dark sky she'd seen in a long time, evidence of how far south they had traveled. The Auroras emanated from the south, not from Alaska, even more supernatural.

"This is both beautiful and frightening," Sara said, hands grasping a handrail. "What is the world coming to?"

Faint crackles of light rippled through the brightness. Mason wrapped his coat around Sara and put an arm over her shoulder.

"I'm not too happy," she fretted. "About facing this thing over water."

"We're on a big boat," Mason said. "And we'll be on a big, safe aircraft."

Sara nodded.

"And Ethan won't be at the controls," he followed.

She broke a smile.

"These guys don't take risks," he said. "They'll keep a safe distance."

"Mind if I join you?" a voice came from behind.

"Captain Wales," Sara turned. "Of course. We were taking in the view. Is it OK if we're out here?"

"Seas are calm," he said, holding out life jackets. "But you should still be wearing these."

They quickly pulled them on and fastened them up.

"Care for a drink?" he asked. He pulled a metal flask and two jigger-sized glasses from his coat pocket.

Sara curiously accepted.

"I saw you from the bridge deck," he continued. "You're casting long shadows in this light."

Captain filled their glasses. "I keep this handy for special occasions," he continued. "I get this stuff in San Francisco and keep a stock of it. Best bourbon on the planet."

Sara took a healthy sip. "Smooth," she complimented. "Thank you."

Not really a test, but he was curious about her.

"Hmm," Mason said. "That is good stuff."

Captain Wales took a sip from the metal flask.

"What's this thing going to look like," he asked. "When we reach it?'

Sara took another sip.

"We've seen it in two forms," she replied. "In its natural state, it's benign, highly magnetic, and invisible, except for those." She pointed up to the Auroras. "But when it interacts with solar energy, and there's been a lot of that recently, it explodes into a hurricane-sized structure."

Wales frowned in disbelief.

"I know," Sara said. "Sounds crazy, right?"

Wales did not speak but took another sip.

"When we saw it explode over the southern coast of Alaska a few days ago," she said. "I thought we were all dead. Only a half-mile from the epicenter. Fortunately, we were on foot and behind big rocks."

"So, we keep our distance," he commented.

Sara threw back the rest of the glass. The captain refilled.

"Captain," she said. "I'm a cetacean biologist, not a storm chaser. But this phenomenon is affecting everything on our planet, even wildlife. It's changing the world so rapidly. Someone must keep track of it, keep a journal of these strange events. And my mother has assigned me that duty."

Wales took another sip. "So, the world is turning upside down," he said.

No response. Only concerned faces.

"You two should get some rest," he followed. "Tomorrow's going to be a long day."

Sara finished writing the day's events, then lay in bed, eyes on the ceiling. Mason watched her for a moment, then walked over to the porthole with no blind. He studied it for a minute, fished through the closet for a coat hanger, fit around the porthole, and hung his coat over it. This caught Sara's attention.

"Good thinking," she said.

Mason jumped in bed and curled up around her.

"Now you can get some sleep," he replied.

"Not quite yet," she said, reaching up for the light, then wrapped her arm around him.

At 0300 hours, Sara and Mason made their way to communications, where they found Ethan at a makeshift station, pecking away at his laptop. Two young military men sat nearby with headsets, studying images on a large flat screen.

"Good morning," Ethan said. "Sleep well?"

He got another stare.

"Any contact with Paul Moore?" Sara asked.

"Yes," Ethan said. "The magnetic Pole is holding the same position, and no solar activity in the forecast. So, we should be OK on our approach."

"All right," Sara said. "That's a relief." She noticed a small electronic device next to Ethan's fingertips on the table. "What's this?" she asked.

"My counterpart here," Ethan replied, pointing to the crewman next to him. "Couldn't believe the 'ancient contraption' I used to measure magnetic fields. So, he let me borrow this military-grade model for the expedition."

"He can keep it," the crewman said. "We'll send his old one to the Smithsonian."

"Look." Ethan pointed. "It's digital, higher resolution, waterproof, and has rechargeable batteries that last for weeks."

Indeed, a boy with a new toy. Sara patted him on the shoulder, then panned the room. It was much smaller than she imagined, their presence still unnoticed by other military technicians. She pulled out her cell phone and saw it had a great signal.

"Is there any place I can make a private call?" she asked.

Ethan pointed to a door on the opposite end of the room.

"Excuse me," Sara said and walked that way.

Mason pulled up a chair next to Ethan.

Sara seated herself in a closet-sized room and hit the 'mom' button. She heard static, then extended access time, no doubt since she was calling from a ship at sea, but she eventually made a connection.

"Sara, darling," Julia Gathers said. "Is that you?"

"Yes, Mother," Sara replied. "It's good to hear your voice. How are things in Washington?"

"Conferences, meetings, and hearings," Julia said. "Now that they've restored power and communication to most of the country, everyone has questions and wants answers. And it seems, they all think I have the solutions. I've never been thrown into the spotlight before."

"Hmm." Sara chuckled. "I'm sure you'll manage it."

"So long as I keep giving them answers," Julia said.

"Have you been in contact with Colonel Jackson?" Sara asked. "We're on an aircraft carrier in the North Pacific, en route to the current core location. We should be there in a few hours."

"Excuse me?" Julia asked.

"There's more you need to know," Sara replied. "I assume the colonel told you about the mammoths."

"Yes, he did," Julia said. "He mentioned you found some of them alive."

"That's right," Sara said. "We pulled tissue samples for testing. Hopefully, the results can prove where (or when) they came from."

"I don't follow," Julia said.

Sara paused.

"We saw some things on the South Alaskan coast that we can't explain," she replied. "That incident was more powerful than the others, and we were close enough to see something strange. Images of things that, we have since confirmed, are from a past time, for instance, the mammoths. My best explanation for their presence here is that they were somehow transported through time."

The phone crackled before Julia answered. "How many people know about this?" Julia asked.

"Only those of us who saw it," Sara replied.

"And Jackson?"

"No," Sara said. "We are having a hard time figuring it out, so we don't want to spread rumors."

"And who are we?" Julia asked.

"The NOAA team from Perishton," Sara said. "Paul Moore's team is studying the footage as we speak."

"Do you have footage?"

"Yes, actual video."

"With everything going on in Washington," Julia explained, "the last thing I need is another unexplainable issue. O'Connell scoffed at those photographs, so we need time to work out answers. Meanwhile, one step at a time, stay on the tissue sample testing and contact me when you get results. I'll contact Paul on the urgency for answers and the need for secrecy."

"I have to tell you that I'm nervous about this voyage," Sara said. "We arrive at the core, or whatever you call it, in a couple hours."

"Sara, darling," Julia said. "Have Jackson and his staff go out to investigate. I would feel better if you did."

Another pause.

"We stared the last one down point-blank," Sara said. "And it was a bad one, but this one is over water, so retreat is more difficult if something goes wrong. But I'm up to the task. I trust this captain and his ship."

"No chances?" Julia asked.

"No chances."

Sara thought for a moment. "I have to say, Mother," she said. "I am intrigued about this assignment. This thing affects all wildlife, especially those that navigate through magnetic field lines. Who knows what we'll find out there?"

"The world doesn't know about this yet," Julia said. "Find out all you can before we have to tell them."

Chapter 22

Sea Monsters

The carrier cut through a calm sea at high speed, Captain Wales steadily peered through binoculars toward the horizon. As bright as ever, the Auroras rimmed a giant arc around a central point yet seen. As with the invisible black hole, this immense tempest, only an hour away, would not reveal itself.

Colonel Jackson approached Captain Wales on the bridge.

"Your team ready?" Wales asked.

"Just give the word," Colonel Jackson said. "We can be ready and assembled on deck in ten minutes."

In short order, Jackson's team huddled up next to the Chinook. The pilot, geared with helmet and goggles, signaled crew members to pull open the side panel door. Jackson's team boarded the helicopter and buckled up as the dual rotor blades started turning. The whining sound rose to a heavy thumping, and the Chinook lifted off the flight deck. It leaned forward, the engines throttled up, and soon the Carrier was behind them as they headed out into the open sea.

"I gave the pilot orders," Colonel Jackson said through a headset, "to get us ten miles from the anomaly and follow a circular pattern around it. Once we determine the safety level, we can decide if a closer approach is possible."

Sara struggled with the idea of what may lie ahead but rationalized this could not be the scale of the last event. She hoped and prayed this strange phenomenon would spare the world from more consequences.

Minutes later, a bright flash, and the darkness on the horizon lit up. All onboard looked in the direction of the cockpit.

Sara turned to Ethan. "No solar activity predicted, right?"

"That's what Paul told me," Ethan said. "This has to be something else."

The Chinook throttled down to a stop and hovered. The pilot rotated the craft ninety degrees, so the passengers had a straight-on view of the light.

"It's shooting up from below," Ethan pointed out. "Same as last time."

"What does that mean?" Colonel Jackson asked. "I thought it was an enormous tower shooting down from the sky."

"The light tower is from the sky," Ethan said. "An extension of the Auroras down to ground level, but this is entirely different. According to Paul Moore, it's positioned over a fault line. Extreme magnetic energy is spewing up from that fissure."

"So, how is it lighting up?" Sara asked.

"We're not sure," Ethan replied. "It could be that low fog over the water provides a background for visual appearance. It's the same pattern as before, fluctuating up and down, side to side, matching the colors of the rainbow."

"But is it stable?" Colonel Jackson asked. "Is this all it does?"

"All I can tell you is," Ethan said, "this is all that happened last time, then it disappeared in a flash."

Sara unbuckled and looked for a better view across the aisleway but tripped as the helicopter rocked. She fell into the outside row of seats, where soldiers caught her and helped her up. She had an unobstructed view of the light fan, and with the early morning glow from the approaching sun, she saw a dark cloud around the bright light.

"Come look at this," she said.

Ethan and Mason popped up to see. The Chinook rocked again with the unbalanced weight. Soldiers at once shifted positions to compensate.

"Like clockwork," Ethan said. "They show up at every event."

More seabirds than they had ever seen, circling in multi-layers up a thousand feet. The sea below churned in an unnatural way, not with typical wave patterns but something else.

"Why are they circling these Polar anomalies?" Sara asked. "Seabirds don't normally circle the Poles."

"Must have something to do with high magnetism," Ethan reasoned. "Their traditional field lines are gone or changed so drastically they don't know what to do."

Made sense, what she suspected, and a good enough explanation for now.

Sara turned to Jackson. "Can we get closer?" she asked.

The colonel made his way up next to her and peered through the porthole.

"Commander," he shouted through the helmet mouthpiece. "Let's move to one mile from the anomaly and hold that position."

"Hang on!" the pilot shouted.

The Chinook leaned forward and flew toward the light fan. Momentarily they were on top of it, the giant helicopter resumed a hovering position. The light fan was awe-inspiring from that distance, at least a mile long and just as deep. More than a line as it appeared in southern Alaska, a thin ring shape took form with light hopping and sparkling around the perimeter. But Sara's eyes caught something else.

The sea around the oval-shaped light fan swirled and churned as seabirds raced around it. Sara saw whales leaping from the water and porpoises following in chorus. As she studied closer, schools of jumping fish hurried in the same direction, all following the same pattern around the core. The whirlpool effect left no doubt in her mind about what caused the strandings. These creatures were completely confused, like the birds.

Then, as quickly as it came, it vanished. The light fan disappeared, but seabirds overhead and the swirling sea continued.

"Are you taking video?" Sara asked. No answer to her concerned tone. Ethan held the cell phone tight, focused on the view screen.

The water went flat when she turned back, and marine life disappeared. The seabirds in the sky thinned out and seemed to move toward the coast. A moment of silence took hold inside the Chinook.

"Is it over?" Mason finally asked.

Ethan reached for his new digital, high-res magnetometer.

"I think so," he responded. "And it might have jumped south again. Hard to tell."

Seconds later, the ocean exploded where the light fan once was. A giant sea creature burst through the surface. A creature, whale-sized and humpbacked with green skin, mottled with patches of black, had an enormous jaw and a mouthful of sharp teeth. It came down, jaws wide open, and smacked the water with a gigantic splash. Seconds later, it exploded to the surface, with what appeared to be a porpoise in its mouth. Then it hit the water again.

"It's heading our way!" Colonel Jackson shouted. "We need altitude!"

The pilot throttled up the rotors, lifting the helicopter quickly skyward. The beast leaped from the water again, a few feet below the Chinook, then disappeared in the deep.

"He would have gone right through us!" one soldier shouted.

"What the hell was that thing?" Jackson shouted, turning to Sara.

She acknowledged his concern but looked away. He sensed she knew something, and it terrified her. Sara and Ethan made uneasy eye contact, then their gazes dropped.

A long pause, a long stare. Jackson did not know what to think.

"Son, did you say the magnetic field has dropped away?" Jackson asked Ethan.

"Yes, sir," Ethan acknowledged. "Everything back to normal."

"But you mentioned another jump," the colonel followed.

"I think so," Ethan said. "But we have to get shipside to confirm."

The colonel gave a swirling motion with his finger. With that, the pilot turned the helicopter back toward the Carrier.

On the return flight, crew members jawed about the monster they saw while Sara reflected on the event. They made a routine landing on the red target of the flight deck, then disembarked to re-group.

While the Chinook re-fueled, Ethan sat in the control room confirming his assumptions. The core had made another big jump to southern Oregon, in the Cascade Mountain Range. Sara discussed with Julia the strange events she witnessed at sea. And again, her orders were to keep it under wraps until she found a plausible scientific explanation. So, when the Chinook lifted off, it carried a lot of concerned faces and unanswered questions. News of the Auroras hovering over the western seaboard filled the Internet, news stations, and political talk. Senator O'Connell summoned Colonel Jackson and Julia to another meeting.

Hours later, the Chinook landed at the Sitka Military Base, where Mason's floatplane sat fueled and ready on the tarmac. Sara was still processing the last event and the giant sea creature. She could find no logical explanation for what she saw; a Jurassic-looking animal, not a sea monster, clearly not from our time. She would have to study archives to figure out the era of its existence. Twice now, living pre-historic creatures have appeared. *But this one is millions of years old, not thousands. Time travel? Is it possible?*

When they dis-embarked, Jackson pulled Sara off to the side.

"Your mother and I have been called to another meeting in Washington," he said. His concerned expression did not go unnoticed. "Look, I've been around a long time, and I can tell when a person is troubled. Something is going on, something your scientific mind can't figure out. Something you're holding back on."

Sara looked down and searched for words like a kid who had broken a window.

"We have seen pre-historic creatures," she said, "at two sites now. How does anyone explain that?"

"Do you think *you* have an explanation?" Jackson asked with fatherly concern.

Sara paused. "If I told you what I thought," she said, "you wouldn't believe me."

"Does it frighten you?" he asked. "You seem uneasy and edgy."

Sara thought about it.

"You're right." She sighed. "Maybe I need more time to digest this information. Once we get those lab results back, it will shed more light on the problem."

Venting those ideas, that quick interaction, let her mind re-focus.

"Colonel, one other thing," she said. "That creature has to be hunted down and killed at once. Can you 'pull any strings' to make that happen?"

"Why would we hunt it down?"

Sara took a deep breath. "Because it's not from our time," she said.

There were two ways to interpret that statement: either it is a living relic from the past, or … well … the other possibility did not make any sense.

Jackson played along. "How would we hunt it down?"

"With big ships and lots of blood," she grimaced. "Coastguard should be able to do it."

"But I can't just—"

"We can't take this lightly," Sara interrupted. "If it is pre-historic, its appetite could be voracious, and we know nothing of its reproductive abilities. Imagine if it started reproducing?"

She started down the tarmac toward Mason's plane.

"If it's pre-historic," the colonel shouted. "Then it's been down there for a long time, reproducing."

Sara stopped.

"Or are you suggesting the magnetic event simply conjured up this monster?" Jackson asked.

Sara quickly turned; her eyes snapped with intense focus.

Jackson was a logical, common-sense man who had traveled the globe countless times, served in two military campaigns, and seen things most civilians cannot even imagine. But for the first time in his life, the word *supernatural* suddenly became a genuine concept, and it showed on his bewildered face.

Sara continued across the tarmac.

The Cessna throttled up and pulled away from the hanger. Colonel Jackson watched it roll toward the runway, still digesting his discussion with Sara.

An officer approached.

"Colonel," he said. "Any orders?"

"Is my plane ready for Washington?" the colonel asked.

"Yes, Sir."

The colonel paused and watched the Cessna lift off the runway.

"I need to speak with the navy," he said. "Get me in touch with the captain of that carrier."

Chapter 23

Another Secret Meeting

Washington, D.C.

Julia and Colonel Jackson sat patiently in a small waiting room outside Senator O'Connell's office. It had been nearly an hour since his assistant announced them.

"He's doing this on purpose," Jackson whispered.

Julia patiently flipped through documents. They heard a buzz a few minutes later, and the assistant picked up the phone.

"Yes, sir, thank you," she said, then turned to them.

"Senator O'Connell will see you now." She rose and escorted them to his office.

The Senator sat behind his desk, reading some papers. Julia was relieved to see no sign of whiskey bottles. She and the colonel seated themselves in two chairs opposite his desk.

"I remember when the planes hit the towers," Senator O'Connell said. He leaned back, pulled off his glasses, and rubbed his eyes. "A big national panic hit. Back then, we hadn't dealt with a national crisis since the assassinations in the '60s, so people were shocked and frightened. Our callousness had worn off.

People forgot about real crises. Then came the wars in Iraq and Afghanistan, and we were tough again. But we fell back quickly, so we had panic in the streets again when Covid hit a few years later."

He stood and paced.

"But this," he said. "This is entirely different. We're under siege by the forces of nature and haven't the slightest idea how to deal with the situation. Where does it go next?"

He picked up a remote and aimed at a flat screen on the wall. A giant image came to life with dramatic nighttime footage of the fiery Auroras over California.

"Look at it," the senator said, flipping through channels. "I've never seen anything like it. On every station. People are scared to death, and I have to admit, I'm a bit nervous myself."

He paced around the table.

"I've been on naval vessels up in the Arctic and seen the Northern Lights," the senator continued. "But they're not like this. Why are these so bright?"

"Senator," Julia said.

He cut her off. "Hospitals out there," he said, "are treating people for severe sunburn and dehydration. We are considering lockdown orders for the west coast, but you know what Americans think about that idea."

O'Connell paced his way back to his chair and took a seat.

"Guidance systems have gone haywire," he said. "We had to stop all commercial air transportation for the western United States. No flights west of Denver."

"Senator," Julia said. "The last time we spoke, I mentioned our latest data confirmed core rotation, and the core was moving south toward the U.S. border. Yesterday, it jumped again, down near the California-Oregon border."

"So, the North Pole is in Oregon?" the senator scoffed.

"Unfortunately, for now, that's correct," Julia said. "Our Solar Group also informed me that magnetic field lines naturally shift with this movement, which explains the Auroras. As the magnetic axis rotates downward, more solar radiation enters the field vortex, causing brighter than normal Auroras and UV radiation."

"I assume it will continue to move," O'Connell said.

"Probably so," Julia replied.

O'Connell paused. There seemed to be no quick solution, no button to push. And he was a button-pusher, instant gratification through power; tell people to do something and they did it, fear was a big motivator, but now the shoe was on the other foot.

"Senator," Colonel Jackson said. "Regarding power and communication. We have eighty percent power restored to the east coast as far as the Mississippi, fifty percent from there to the Rockies. The west coast is a different story, but we're working on it.

"Communications are getting better by the day. Military satellites have performed far better than civilians' due to superior shielding, so we allocated half of them for civilian use. Next week, we are launching a dozen new satellites with even better shielding.

"Watchdog groups are already barking about violation of privacy, claiming the military is trying to spy on private citizens."

O'Connell shook his head. "Better than no communication at all," he said. "Or did they consider that?"

O'Connell pulled a half-empty bottle of whiskey from a desk drawer, sat it on the desktop, and stared at it. Then stood and paced again.

"At least we are getting the basics under control," he said. "I've been thinking a lot lately about what you told me. About the methane and the mammoths, now this."

No noticeable concern appeared on Julia's face, but she had spent decades perfecting a poker face. Not naturally her style, but a required tool in a corporate world. She wanted to discuss the time travel issue but now was not the right time. O'Connell was walking an emotional tightrope, and he did not need another shot from left field.

"Senator," Julia said. "Methane release has been going on for decades, an issue the world has caused. It is not only us; it is the whole world. The mammoths are, most likely, a by-product of that situation, and we will have answers on where they came from soon."

"And what do I tell the president," O'Connell redirected. "About the North Pole in Oregon?"

"My best guess is it won't be there long," Julia replied.

"How long?"

Julia shook her head. "Senator, I have no tricks up my sleeves nor rabbits in my hat," she said. "There's no way to tell when the next jump will occur. But it will occur."

PART 4

Core rotation – Approaching the 30th parallel.

As the angle of rotation decreases, field lines drop back and expose the planet to extreme radiation and powerful Auroras. An ozone hole opens up and bombards the lower latitudes with large doses of UV radiation.

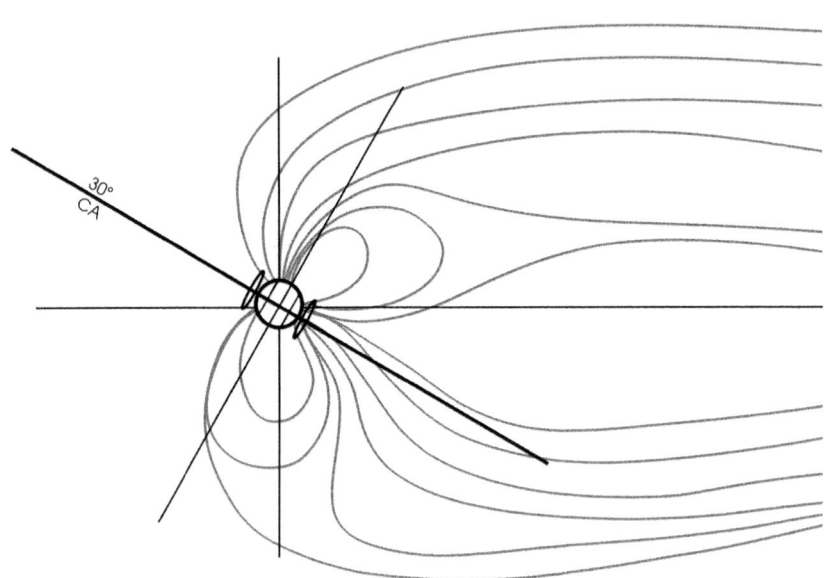

Chapter 24

Brain Storming

Going to California

O nce airborne, Sara pulled out her phone and searched for pre-historic sea creatures. She started with archival records of vertebrate animals from the University library using her (still active) student ID and password. Sara quickly found that the Triassic-period Sea life was too primitive. Some giant beasts but nothing with the skeletal development and mottled skin textures of the creature she saw from the helicopter. When she switched over to Jurassic-period Sea creatures, it did not take long to track down the culprit. There it was it shocked her to see the jaws of a Pliosaurus. Its colors from an artist's rendering were nothing like the real monster, but the shape of its head and jawline were unmistakable. She was convinced she had seen an actual sea creature, one that had been extinct for 150 million years. *Can these things be popping through time portals created by electromagnetic interactions? Is it possible?*

Mother wants to keep this under wraps, Sara thought, *until we reach a definitive solution.* Sara considered her options. How could she solve the time-travel puzzle? How could it be tested? She circled back to the reality that she was not qualified to research the topic. It would take teams of scientists' years to figure it out, so she had to keep it under wraps. And hopefully, the phenomenon will simply not happen again.

"Hey," Ethan said, crawling up from the rear. "I got something! Live stream with Ben from Perishton."

"You are kind of breaking up," a voice came through Ethan's phone. "Check your signal."

"I'm in an airplane, man," Ethan shouted. "Just deal with it."

"Oh, OK," Ben said.

"You have to speak up," Ethan shouted. "The cockpit is pretty noisy."

"Is that hot chick still with you?" Ben asked.

Mason laughed out loud. Ethan's head dropped.

"Yes, I'm still here," Sara said.

A nervous silence followed. Ben cleared his throat.

"OK," he said. "This what I've come up with, so far. As you asked, I looked up record files for microbes called *Carnobacterium pleistocenium*. Took a while to find. It was buried in the paleobiology database."

Then a crackle, sound cut in and out.

"And?" Sara asked.

"Perfect match," Ben replied.

"Excuse me?" Sara questioned.

"*Carnobacterium pleistocenium* filled the slides under the microscope," Ben said. "Some are still moving around. I checked twenty samples to be sure."

Sara's heart dropped. How could they be there? Surely not, because the mammoths were alive. Living animals from present time when Carno-ply bacteria did not exist. It started to set in that she might be wrong.

"What does that mean?" Mason asked.

"It means they're ancient," Sara replied. "Not from our time."

Mason looked confused.

"I must admit," Sara continued. "I was both excited and nervous about the results. But this doesn't help my hypothesis."

"I don't understand," Mason said. "It was alive. We saw it."

Sara stared at the console.

"Why can't you carbon date them?" Mason asked. "Isn't that what scientists do with ancient things?"

"No, we can't carbon date them," Sara said. "It will show them to have died a few days ago."

Engine roar and distant crackling sounds filled the headsets. Then Sara thought of something. That was what she needed. A Carbon-14 date would prove an animal previously believed extinct had recently died. Washington could not say they melted from the ice with that evidence.

"On second thought, that's good thinking, Mason," she said. "It will prove the animal died a few days ago."

"It also proves something else," Ethan said. "Remember the radio towers?"

"I'm lost," Ben said. "What about the radio towers?"

Ethan got that look from Sara.

"Ben," Sara redirected. "Track down the closest university lab that does carbon dating and send them a few samples. Make it a priority. We need results quickly."

"Uh, that sounds expensive," Ben said.

"Probably is, but I'll cover it," Sara replied.

"I'm not sure where to start," Ben said.

"I have confidence you can do this," Sara stated. "Get online and dig into it. We land in a few hours, and I'll be in touch then."

Sara motioned for Ethan to cut the call.

"Remember, guys," Sara said. "This time travel business doesn't go beyond this cockpit.

"But consider," she continued. "Carno-ply dates the mammoths to ancient times, but it does not rule out they died eons ago, because if they moved through time, the Carno-ply would still be there."

"And that sea monster," Ethan said. "The one you've been researching. Do you think it also moved through time?"

"Have you been looking over my shoulder?" Sara asked.

Ethan shied away.

The Cessna flew along the southern Alaskan coastline toward Canada. On the horizon, the sun dipped below the Pacific Ocean rim. The darkening sky did not last as a new light in the sky took hold. The Auroras were dazzling, immense, and clearly emanating from a southerly location.

Mason found a small airport near the border for refueling. They made their way into a tiny terminal for food and water but found only three vending machines: soft drinks, candy, and cold pre-packaged sandwiches.

"Any good?" Mason asked the attendant.

"Not bad," he replied. "If you're in a hurry."

Mason turned to Sara. Her shoulders shrugged, so he swiped a credit card and started hitting buttons. The attendant brought over a cardboard box, and Mason loaded it up with cans and bags that slowly dropped into dispensers. While Mason focused on the mechanical churning and clanking of vending machines, Sara and Ethan stepped toward the counter where a screen on the wall had a live newscast from Seattle. A woman holding a microphone stood behind a large crowd of on-lookers gazing skyward.

"For yet another night," she began, "we are witnessing the most unusual phenomenon ever seen in the skies over Seattle. These Auroras stretch horizon to horizon. And we're told they are this bright in LA. People are frightened, panicked, and searching for answers. Cases of severe sunburn are filling hospitals along the west coast. Reports of unusually high UV levels have led to predictions that an ozone hole has opened up over western skies.

"Washington has been very secretive about this situation," she continued. "But rumor has it a statement from the White House and NOAA will be released soon."

Sara was concerned about her mother and wondered if calling her would do any good. Ethan was overcome by the naivete of the masses.

"I wish I were one of them," he said. "I think it's harder to know everything we know than to know nothing."

Sara noticed his watery eyes. "Hey," she said. "We still have work to do. We don't know all the answers yet. Let's get back on the plane."

By the time they reached Oregon, the core had jumped again. But this time, the movement was hard to track. The core wobbled with the motion of a gyroscope losing momentum, careening downward in random, chaotic motion. Multiple Poles formed on the east and west sides of the globe. Both NOAA and NASA tracked their locations hourly. Commercial flight groundings worldwide created more panic, and communications were available but unreliable.

***

An elderly couple sat on the front porch of their farmhouse near the foothills of the El Dorado National Forest. They had owned the property for forty years and could never get enough of the panoramic view of California's Sacramento Valley. But this evening, and many recent evenings, the scene took on a whole new atmosphere.

"Martin," Becky said. "I'm afraid."

"Oh, you know," Martin replied. "They always exaggerate this stuff in the news. They only show pictures of the crazies in the city."

"But this is real," Becky said, raising a hand to the sky.

The Auroras filled the evening sky with glittering color and movement. They had never appeared in the night skies over California before, and rumors ran rampant. Some heard it was outgassing from Mount Saint Helens or the result of failed military experiments to control CO_2 levels or pollution floating across the Pacific from China. There was even a crazy rumor about the North Pole moving.

Martin stood up and stretched.

"How's your back?" Becky asked and reached up to rub his lower back.

"Getting older," Martin returned. "Along with the rest of me."

He stepped off the porch, then craned his neck to survey the property.

"I saw Jerry in town this morning," Martin said. "He stays in contact with some of the fellas up in Prudhoe Bay. Evidently, there are no more Auroras up there."

"What does that mean?" Becky asked.

"I don't know," Martin said. Realizing it upset her, he quickly followed up. "It could be a rumor."

She fidgeted in her chair and gazed, uncomfortably, at the peculiar lights in the sky.

"I'm going walk around back," he said. "Check on the gardens and water the horses."

Martin and Becky were conservative people. They kept a large garden in the summer, canned in the fall, grew their own grapes, and made their own wine. Cibolo-area vineyards produce some of the best grapes and outstanding wines, with years of practice.

Next to their 1980s, ranch-style house stood two barns. The pole barn housed a tractor, farm implements, and Martin's Cessna aircraft. It had large rolling doors that opened to a grass runway cutting through gently sloping natural grasses and coyote brush fields. The other barn was older and more conventional with a hayloft, perfect for their two horses.

Martin inspected the gardens, checked leaf growth, vegetable sizes, and moisture in the soil. Tomatoes, cucumbers, many varieties of peppers, avocados, strawberries, and everything else in the garden looked healthy. He walked the fence surrounding the garden and vineyard, looking for evidence of wildlife intrusion, then top-checked the electrical connections and display readouts on the sprinkler display panel. He was proud of his new and improved sprinkler system that had worked well since he spent $10,000 on new controls and a deeper well to feed it. He was buddies with a local well driller, who, without a permit, drilled him a new well more than twice as deep as the old one.

He stopped in the horse barn to check on Champ and Bonney. Champ was an old Walking horse Martin inherited from a neighbor who moved away. Bonney was a painted horse Becky bought to ride through the hills. He checked their stalls, brought them fresh water, and let them out to walk the fence line.

He started toward the vineyard but felt an unusual sting on his gloveless hands. He rubbed them and looked up at the Aurora-filled sky. Concerned about the ozone hole rumors, he decided to wait 'till evening to walk the vineyard, so he returned to the covered porch where Becky sat with a glass of water.

"When do you think he'll be here?" Becky asked.

"He called yesterday," Martin replied. "And told me it would be this morning. But with him it could be next week."

"Well." Becky sighed. "It's nearly dinner time. Why don't we go inside and prepare something to eat?"

***

Another hour passed; the setting sun neared a choppy range of hills across the Sacramento Valley. Table wiped down and dishes bussed, they stood in their wine cellar, debating about the perfect bottle for the evening. That's what they called it, though in reality the *cellar* was a makeshift closet Martin built inside a converted garage. The rest of the garage was committed to wine production, complete with a grape smasher, oaken kegs, fermenting basin, and corking machine. They moved the car into the pole barn with the plane.

After dinner, they sat on the front porch to share a glass of red Barbera wine, and soon Becky's ears perked.

"Martin," she said. "Do you hear that?"

Martin stood, panning the valley. "There he is," he said with a proud smile.

A white Cessna floatplane with unmistakable blue striping flew in from the north. Its wings made a customary stuntman wobble as if to say hello. The Hahns both waved as the plane turned in for a landing on their grass runway.

"Boy better keep that nose up," Martin said, totally focused on the plane's descent.

"Martin, he knows what he's doing," Becky said, in a tone that made it clear they'd had this conversation before.

The plane straightened up, extended wheels and adjusted flaps for the approach, then slowly dropped toward the runway.

"Runway looks good," Mason said. "I think Dad just cut the grass."

"What?" Sara asked. "Where's the runway?"

"It's grass," Mason replied. "Did I mention that before?"

Sara grabbed the overhead straps with both hands. Ethan crawled up from the back, eyes wide open.

"This might be a little different than you're used to," Mason said.

Sara gave him one look. Seconds later, the plane made as soft a landing as Mason could manage, but he still noticed both Sara and Ethan bounce noticeably. From the corner of his eye, he caught a glimpse of Sara's face, looking as if she were on a roller-coaster.

He throttled the engine back and taxied to a stop near the barn doors. Becky anxiously ran toward the plane. Martin held back, curiously taking note of the unexpected passengers in his son's plane. While Sara caught her breath, Mason unbuckled and hopped out to greet his mother.

"Honey," she said, embracing Mason with a warm hug. "You made it. I'm so glad to see you. And you look so …" Becky was so excited to see him she had not noticed his shaven face.

"Oh, my," she said, caressing his stubbly cheeks. "I haven't seen this face in so long. It's been covered by that ridiculous beard."

Then a clanky *thud*. Becky turned to see Ethan trip out the pilot side door, slip on the pontoon, and land flat on his back. Mason chuckled. Martin hurried over to help. The passenger-side door swung open; Becky's craned her neck curiously. Mason darted away, leaving a confused expression on Becky's face. He reached out to help Sara to the ground.

"Sorry about that," he said. "I forgot to mention the runway. Are you OK?"

"I'm fine," Sara returned, gaining her composure.

Martin had Ethan on his feet, wiping the dust off his back. Mason escorted Sara around the plane. He had not brought a girl home since high school. Both parents stood expressionless.

"Mom, Dad," Mason said nervously. "I'd like you to meet Sara."

"Hello," she said, extending her hand. "I'm Sara Gathers. Nice to meet you both. Your ranch is breathtaking."

"My god, you're beautiful!" Becky blurted out. "And not a stitch of make-up."

Sara blushed. "You're too kind."

"Welcome," Martin said.

"After flying in that thing for so long, you must be exhausted," Becky said. She was obviously excited to have another female on the farm since, well, ever. She put an arm around Sara and walked her up to the porch.

"You OK, young man?" Martin asked.

"Yes, sir, I just lost my balance," Ethan replied. "I'm Ethan Sites. Nice to meet you."

Martin nodded.

"I've seen better landings," Martin voiced in Mason's direction. "And I bet they have, too."

"Fighting a little crosswind," Mason said. "You know how it is."

Martin sighed and headed toward the porch. He saw Becky proudly pointing across the valley and Sara politely following along. He passed them on his way to the front door.

"Did she tell you about the earthquake of '89?" he asked. "Right after we bought the place."

He smiled and kept walking. Mason shook his head and followed his dad through the door. It was the only bad story about the place, except for the occasional bear visit, but Martin loved to pass it along to newcomers.

"Oh my god," Becky said. "This was before any of you were born. It was unbelievable. The ground in the valley rolled up and down like a wave in the ocean. Dust spouts popped up everywhere. Then rocks came rolling down from the hills. We were lucky none of them hit the house."

"Let's hope that doesn't happen again soon," Sara said. "I still have sea legs from that flight."

Becky laughed out loud. "I think we'll be OK, sweetie," she said. "Let's go inside and help the boys round up something for you to eat."

"I need to sit for a few minutes," Sara said. "I'll see you inside."

The sun eventually set below the distant Cascades, leaving only the Auroras to light the sky. Martin and Mason grilled a customary wood-smoked brisket for his 'first night back' dinner. They sipped on red Barbera from Martin's latest batch, talked about the vineyard, horses, and local gossip. Ethan enjoyed the discussion but did not want to intrude on their reunion, so he stepped away to the vineyard.

Becky prepped salad and vegetables in the kitchen. She checked on Sara and found her asleep on the porch swing. She dropped a roll-down shade, then quietly went back into the house.

The guys returned to the kitchen with perfectly grilled brisket, washed up, and grabbed seats at the table. Two bottles of red Barbera were open and ready. Martin poured Becky the first glass and handed the bottle to Mason. Becky told them to keep their voices down as Sara was napping.

"So, are you a fisherman, too?" Martin asked. Judging by Ethan's soft hands, he already knew the answer but was understandably curious. Neither Ethan nor Sara were the kind of friends Mason had ever brought home to dinner.

There was hesitation in Ethan's response, almost waiting for Mason to respond first.

"Well, I work up in Perishton," he offered, taking a sip. "This is really good, and you make this?"

Martin lifted an eye. The re-direction did not work.

"Long haul to Bristol Bay," Martin said. "Mason, I didn't know you went up to Prudhoe this summer?"

"Yes, we do," Becky said to Ethan and shot Martin a look. "I'm glad you are enjoying the wine. Martin spends countless hours out there perfecting the blend."

"I hadn't planned on it," Mason returned to Martin. Becky huffed. "But things kind of worked out that way."

Martin did not speak and let Mason cut away at the brisket.

A trick Mason had seen for years. It meant Martin knew there was more to it than Mason had given. Mason cleared his throat with a sip of wine.

"I met Sara on a rescue in Bristol," he said.

"A rescue?" Martin prodded.

"Beached, uh, stranded whales," Mason said. "It's what she does. I heard about the problem and flew out to help. It took days to get them back out to sea, fighting off wolves and coyotes, but we finally managed it."

"I heard the whole story," Ethan said. "It's very cool."

Becky sat at attention; Martin was not so impressed.

"Why Prudhoe?" he asked. "And this kid?" He pointed a fork at Ethan.

Mason took another sip of wine.

"Sara works for the government, so does he," Mason said. He'd found over the years that it was best to streamline information for his dad, short version only. No lies, that always backfired. But leaving out a few facts usually got him past the gate. "I took her up to the tundra to investigate wildfires. That's where we found him."

"Oh, OK," Martin said, digesting this new information.

"What do you mean, OK?" Becky said. "There's a lot he's not saying."

"Mr. and Mrs. Hahn," Ethan interjected. "I was there. They rescued me …"

"Sorry, I fell asleep out there," Sara said, stepping into the kitchen. "I felt so exhausted after that flight."

"I'm going to grab you something to eat," Becky popped up.

Ethan picked up his plate and went over to the countertop to make space for Sara, who took the open seat.

"Dad asked about how we met," Mason said. "And how we came across this guy."

Becky placed a cold glass of water in front of Sara.

"Thank you," she said.

Sara took a long drink. "And?" she asked.

"I was about to tell them," Ethan said.

"Young lady," Martin interrupted. He was going to ask a question but stopped short as another thought crossed his mind. "Who do you work for?"

"NOAA. Why do you ask?" she asked.

"And that stands for?" Martin replied.

"National Oceanographic and Atmospheric Administration," she said.

"Martin," Becky interrupted, placing a plate of brisket and veggies in front of Sara. "You're being rude."

"I'm sorry," he said. "But your name sounds familiar."

Sara's eyes caught Mason's, then Ethan's. She knew Martin was prodding them about why they were here, and clearly, they had stepped lightly on the topic.

"My mother has been in the news lately," Sara said, cutting to the chase.

"The lady in Washington," Becky said, with an expression of surprise and understanding. "I see the resemblance." Along with most Americans, the Hahns kept the television on all day lately. And recent newscasts featured a voice of reason in Julia Gathers, who rose from anonymity to a crucial national figure in a few short weeks.

"And you've been sent out to investigate these odd goings-on?" Martin asked. He threw back the remaining wine in his glass and reached for the other bottle. "So, why with these two guys? Why not a team of scientists?"

Before Sara could answer, her cell phone vibrated on the table. An uneasy tension filled the room.

"Excuse me, I have to take this," Sara said and stepped out on the back porch.

"Sara Gathers," she answered in a professional voice. In earshot of the kitchen window, she continued toward the vineyard.

"Ben Hadley here," the voice said. "I have some information for you."

"Go ahead."

"I overnighted a sample of mammoth tissue to a carbon dating lab in Washington," Ben replied. "I found an old college buddy through a web search; he works at the university, testing labs. He tested the sample after-hours since I'm an unauthorized source. He told me the rate of decay of carbon-14 can't be accurately measured."

"What does that mean?" Sara asked.

"It means the tissue sample is from a recently deceased animal," Ben said. "It's not ancient. Even though *Carnobacterium pleistocenium* organisms are present, the animal recently died."

A strange adrenal rush came over her. A feeling of awe and vindication consumed her. Now she had the proof she needed. An animal previously believed extinct that died before her eyes had ancient bacteria on its skin. It was not a modern-day leftover. There could only be one explanation, no doubt in her mind that it moved through time. Somehow it moved through time.

"Maybe it came up from a deep cave," Ben continued, sensing what he thought was her disappointment. "You know, I saw a special on the Science Channel about these deep, undiscovered caves in Siberia."

"It's OK," Sara cut him off. "This helps. Really it does. Can you send me the results? I need the documentation."

"Sure," Ben said. "I'll text you the file."

"Thank you so much for your help," Sara said. "Also, let us know the cost involved."

Sara returned to the kitchen amid the ongoing discussion. She heard Ethan say *light tower* and cast him a look. The Hahns' bewildered faces told of a story Sara didn't yet believe they should share.

"Many unusual things are happening on our planet, right now," she said. "And no one completely understands them yet. They are happening so fast we can't keep up. We are a scout team, gathering facts on the front lines."

"I don't doubt your credentials," Martin said. "But why isn't there an organized government effort to do the research?"

"They are organizing," Sara replied. "But in the meantime, someone needs to keep track of these strange events that unfold and change daily. We are working with many branches of NOAA and the military."

Mason and Ethan nodded in agreement.

"Soon, our effort will be over," Sara said. "My mother is under the gun and needs someone she can trust to do this work that hopefully wraps up soon."

Martin re-filled the glasses around the table. "Would you like something else?" he asked.

"No, thank you," Sara said. "By the way, and I'm not just being polite, this Barbera is a very good blend."

Martin gave an appreciative nod before he asked a final question. "What can you tell us about this?" he asked and pointed toward the sky.

"Only that if I were you," Sara replied. "I'd try to stay inside most of the time."

Becky sighed and hung her head.

"Hey." Sara touched her hand. "This is a passing thing. And I really believe it will not be this way for long. But I can't talk about it."

Chapter 25

Western Lights

El Dorado, CA

After dinner, Mason and Martin inspected the floatplane. Martin grumbled more than anything, complaining that Mason treated the plane the same as the old Jeep from his high school days. Mason played along, knowing he should not compare four-wheeling to flying at 3,000 feet. He always kept up with service on his plane, but nothing ever met Martin's standards.

"How's it looking?" Sara asked as she walked up.

Martin and Mason turned to see a freshly showered Sara holding a glass of wine.

"It's looked better," Martin said. "We're going to push it in the barn and service it."

Mason could not take his eyes off Sara. Martin could not help but notice.

"You ride?" Mason asked.

Sara looked at the horse barn. "Horses?" she asked. "I grew up with them."

"Why am I not surprised," Mason said.

"They haven't been out yet today," Martin said, giving up on the service discussion.

They prepped the horses for a ride. Sara be-friended Bonney instantly and saddled her up without a problem. Martin was impressed. Mason took it in stride. *This girl can do anything*, he thought, and not for the first time. Becky hurried out from the house.

"You should wear these hats and gloves to protect yourselves from the UV," she said.

Sara thanked her, donned the flat-brimmed Spanish-style hat, and shook the reins. Soon, they crossed the fence line and started up the slopes.

"Do you always ride with a Winchester rifle?" Sara asked. He'd stashed it in a leather sheath before they mounted.

"For long rides, yeah," he answered. "You never know what's up there at night."

"Hmm," Sara said, an unexpected reality.

They rode the horses up in the hills by Aurora light.

"See that ridge?" Mason asked. "Up there, that outcropping of rock. You can see the whole valley from there."

Sara studied the terrain and saw where the grasses met the tree line and the craggy rocks. "So, we stay on this path," she said, "until we get to those trees. Then cut through them, up and around?"

"That's right," Mason replied. "You up for it?"

"Are you?" Sara asked.

Mason grinned, made a double click sound, and snapped the reins. Before long, they were ducking tree branches and sidestepping boulders but moving at a steady pace. The horses followed a seemingly memorized path through the woods. In minutes they broke out to a clearing of flat, exposed rock. The unobstructed view of the valley was more than Sara expected. The ranch below appeared tiny by comparison to the outstretched valley.

"It's amazing," Sara said. "I've never seen a view quite like this."

Then a soft crackle, a shimmer of faint lightning, and the heavens flashed briefly. A sad reminder of why they were here in the first place. Sara sighed. They dismounted the horses and tied them off to a nearby tree.

"Do you think this will ever end?" Mason asked. "I mean, in our lifetime."

"I have no idea," Sara replied. "But I hope so. Is that a good enough answer?"

"For now," he said.

Mason put his arm around her. Their gaze continued, eventually the crackling died down, and the Aurora resumed its typical luminescence.

"Hey, I got something for you," he said and pulled a compass from his pocket. "Just found it in my old room. The leather chain is still good, too."

"What's this for?" Sara asked.

"Are you kidding?" he replied. "It's hard to tell our ups from our downs anymore. It might come in handy one of these days. And if things don't straighten out in our lifetimes, then it will become a museum piece."

"Thanks." Sara laughed and hung it around her neck.

Sara's gaze turned to the flora surrounding the open flat rock.

"These wildflowers are everywhere," she commented. "I noticed them on the ride up. What are they?"

"Milkweeds," Mason said. "They're all over in the valley foothills. The horses love 'em."

Sara looked over, and sure enough, Bonney and Champ were both chewing on the white flowers.

"I took a call from Ben Hadley earlier," Sara redirected.

"Carbon dating?" Mason asked.

"Yes," Sara replied. "It showed they recently died, not eons ago. We have an enigma since we know ancient bacteria is present on their skin."

"Wait a minute," Mason said. "How can they both be true?"

A confident expression came across Sara's face. She was brimming, then Mason followed his own question with a question.

"Are you telling me," He followed, "that we're down to one possibility?"

"We saw it in the radio towers," she replied. "And I think we saw it in that Jurassic-era Sea creature, too."

"They moved through time?" Mason puzzled. His mind wandered. He studied the Aurora, mystified.

"I know," Sara said. "This is way over my head, but at this point, it's the only logical explanation. From our perspective, it truly is supernatural. It will take years, if ever, for the scientific community to explain it. But we saw it. We have seen it twice now. Will it happen again? Who knows?"

"So, what next?" Mason asked. Sara shrugged.

The evening left the Auroras and a crescent moon to cast light on the valley and surrounding foothills. Mason gathered some nearby sticks and branches for a fire, then pulled out a couple blankets from the saddlebag.

"How many girls have you brought up here?" Sara asked.

Mason did not respond. He found a flat spot nearby, kicked away a few rocks, and unfurled a blanket. He busily rolled it out, patted the edges, and then used the other for a pillow. A cross-armed Sara patiently watched with a long-suffering expression on her face. But she considered this was an improvement from the night they lay naked on a cold Alaskan beach before coming face to face with the mammoths.

Mason stood, satisfied with his handiwork.

"One," he said. He could feel Sara looking even before their eyes met.

He turned back, assembled the wood, and had a fire blazing in minutes.

Sara had given up on men. She loved her work and the ongoing contact it brought with her mother. Their relationship had grown during Sara's time at the NOAA. She found fulfillment in being a frontline rescue worker for creatures in the wild. Honestly, she never imagined looking at, or having feelings for, another man again. But this was unexpected, different than anything she'd imagined. Mason had an honest, straightforward nature that she had not seen in a man before. She was falling in love again.

They spent the whole night on the blanket below the flickering sky. The supernatural light in the sky was fantastic, but Sara worried about its unnatural effects on the ecosystem.

They made plans, talked about their future, even if the world turned upside down. The hours passed, the colorful Aurora continued its dance, and Sara began to drift off.

"You know, I've been thinking," Mason said. "If they stay down here in California, we can't call them the Northern Lights anymore. We own them now, not the Arctic. We should rename them the Western Lights."

Sara smiled, curled up next to him, and fell asleep.

★★★

She woke up with tingling fingertips. A Monarch butterfly was perched on the back of her hand; she had not seen one in years. She watched it gently flap its wings in a morning stretch. She studied it for a few minutes until it finally flew off. It moved directly toward the milkweed patch next to the flat rock where Sara lay. When her eyes focused, she realized the green stems and white flowery tops of the milkweeds had turned orange, covered with Monarch Butterflies.

She sat up and looked around. Monarch Butterflies filled the flat rock fields, tens of thousands of them. Their multitude stretched down the trail into the woods. She had never seen anything like it. She stood and walked to the edge of the exposed flat rock, then knelt to look at them closer. Dozens of butterflies to a single milkweed stalk, they clung unmoving, drawn to the nectar.

At the edge of the outcropped rock formation, Sara peered down the hillside. A sea of red and orange rolled down into the valley. Millions of Monarch butterflies filled a valley that had none the night before.

Mason rolled over and sat up. "Good morning," he said.

"Do you see this?" she asked, with unfurled arms. "It's amazing."

Mason rubbed his eyes and took note of Sara's discovery. Sara had a child-like moment and wanted to run through the milkweed.

"It's your lucky day," Mason said and knelt over to inspect milkweed. "We don't see them every year on their migration."

Then something clicked, and a sad expression rolled down Sara's face. Monarch butterflies were an insect species that migrated, and they did it in the fall, not summer. Core movement and changing magnetic field lines had caused this to happen. The insects, the seabirds, and whales were all victims of the unfolding phenomenon.

Sara peered up at the early morning sky, beaming with Aurora background light. She picked up her hat and gloves and checked on the horses.

"Everything all right?" Mason asked.

"Yeah," Sara sighed.

"You sure?"

She regrouped.

"I wish these things were not happening to the natural world," she said. "It makes me sad to see so many things literally hanging in the balance, or imbalance, depending on how you interpret core rotation."

She continued to saddle up Bonney. "Truth is," she continued. "Without our relationship, I'd be lost, too."

She turned and hugged Mason. "Everything will work out," he said.

"I truly hope so," Sara replied.

∗∗∗

They made their way down the hills and stalled the horses. From the barn, Mason could smell bacon frying. They cut through the back door to the kitchen where Becky prepped breakfast.

"Good morning!" Becky happily said.

"Good morning," they replied.

Mason stepped through the hallway into the living room, looking for Ethan, but there was no sign of him. He started toward the bedroom and his eye caught something out the bay window. Ethan's foot hung out from the front porch swing. Mason shrugged and went back to the kitchen.

"That boy sleeps a lot," Becky said.

"Riding on a Cessna floorboard," Mason answered, "is not doing his back any good."

"Oh." Martin chuckled. "That would put me in the hospital."

"How far?" Becky asked.

"Total?" Mason grinned. "Or just this leg?"

"Total!" Becky exclaimed.

"Since Perishton." Sara shot a look at Mason.

"And before that?" Martin asked. "You found him wandering in the tundra?"

"He's young," Mason said. "He can take it."

Soon, Ethan stumbled into the kitchen, turning heads as he made his way to the coffee maker. All he could muster through his heavy eyelids was, "Smells like coffee and bacon."

"You sit down, young man," Becky ordered. "And I'll fix you a big plate. You take cream and sugar?"

"No, thank you," Ethan said. "Just black."

"And how do you want your eggs?" she asked.

"Anyway, is fine. Do you need some help?"

"You sit right there and be comfortable," Becky said and placed a cup of coffee in front of him.

Ethan nodded and cast a gaze in Sara's direction.

"I got a call last night," he said, taking a sip of coffee.

Sara's concerned gaze caught the attention of all in the room. "And?" she asked.

Ethan panned the room, then fixed weary eyes on Sara.

"It's all right," she said. "What did Ben say?" The Hahns were good people, and Sara knew it. She saw it in their eyes and already knew it in their son.

Ethan took a deep breath.

"It's finally converging," he said. "The multi-poles merged into a singular polarity. Somewhere in the desert of southern California, near a town called Paso Robles."

Chapter 26

Sea Hunt

North Pacific Ocean

The Coast Guard Cutter *Tenacity* received a distress call from a fishing vessel off the Oregon coast. Per navy orders, the legend-class ship was searching for a large, predatory sea creature menacing waters near the Canadian border. The call came late in the afternoon, and the location was more than an hour away. *Tenacity* pushed through choppy seas at twenty-five knots toward a flashing GPS locator signal. The sleek 400-foot ship, painted Coast Guard white with traditional red and blue banners, had armament and gunnery atypical for Coast Guard vessels but more common in the post 9-11 world.

"Any further communication?" the captain asked.

"Nothing," a voice replied.

"Another wild goose chase," he grumbled.

Spotters shouted as they closed on the signal. "Off starboard!" the man shouted. "It's listing."

The boat floated silently on its side with no flashing beacons, no waving sailors, and no lights. At more than a football field in length and perched forty feet above the water, the *Tenacity* maneuvered close to the half-sunken fishing boat and lit it up with high-powered floodlights.

"Thing's been wrecked," the captain murmured. "Part of the aft hull is ripped off."

"Orders?" the lieutenant asked.

"Dispatch the drone," the captain said. "Let's get a closer look."

Minutes later, a small drone whizzed like a hummingbird to the shipwreck. All eyes focused on a video screen as the drone circled the boat. Scars were ripped along the aft hull, leaving long pieces of tangled aluminum hanging away. The drone flew toward the cabin, where it found access through a broken window. It darted inside and instantly lit the dark cabin. But a 360-degree panoramic video found no signs of crew members or operating equipment.

Captain turned his gaze from the screen to the lit-up shipwreck.

"Pull it out," he said. "Little hummingbird has done all it can." He studied the floating carcass of a boat that was minutes from dropping to the ocean floor.

"Shall we tow it in, Captain?" one man asked.

The captain studied the scene with binoculars, half curious, half angered.

"Not yet," he said. "Let's keep our distance. If the thing we're looking for wrecked this vessel, then maybe it's still around."

Young shipmates cleared their throats.

"Aim two floodlights straight down in the water," he ordered. "And keep the others on the boat."

Two men ran out on the bridge deck and lit up the ocean in front of the giant cutter.

"Why do you think it attacked a fishing boat?" a mate asked.

The captain did not respond at first, then pulled away his binoculars.

"It might have been attracted to motion in the water," he said. "Or fish blood leaching over the hull, or both."

That gave him an idea.

"Swirl those deep floods around," Captain said. "In a circular motion."

Tension grew as the captain patiently stared down into the deep. The lights had attracted countless fish and squid, darting through the beaming light.

"Lieutenant," the captain shouted. "Get someone up on that 35-millimeter gun,"

"Excuse me?" the young, confused voice responded.

Captain flashed a stern look.

"Yes, sir." The lieutenant hurried off. Coast Guard training focused on search and rescue. The use of force was a chapter in a book rarely used.

Captain pulled the binoculars back to his eyes and returned a cool gaze to the fishing boat. He had never seen a vessel wrecked that way. Had it been hit by another ship? He dropped the binoculars and stepped out onto deck. Two crew members were busy prepping the big gun.

"It's still in lock position!" the captain shouted. "Get that thing ready!"

Panicked crew members doubled their efforts.

The captain returned to the bridge, rubbed his face, and sighed. He picked up the binoculars and continued to survey the situation. Something was different. He dropped the binoculars from his face, then lifted them again. They were gone; the schools of fish darting through the light were all gone. Then something dark obstructed the view, passing from one light to another. He raced from the bridge onto the main deck.

"Stop those lights," he shouted. "Move them together and hold them in one spot."

The bright lights pointed deep and laser-sharp into the dark waters, no marine life, nothing moving. Choppy water pushed the wrecked fishing boat like a rubber duck in a bathtub while the same waves broke against the iron hull of the *Tenacity*. Then it came again. A dark shadow broke the artificial light.

"Is that gun ready?" Captain shouted.

"Manned and ready," a crew member motioned, thumbs up.

Moments later, a giant, boney dorsal fin lurched up and swam slowly across the patch of light.

"What in the hell is that?" a voice cried out from the main deck.

"Commence fire!"

Chapter 27

The Third Incident

Paso Robles, CA

Soon, climate change will reach a tipping point. In ten years, one-third of all plant and animal species living in the nineteenth century will be gone.

The Industrial Revolution took 150 years to bring the biosphere to its knees. But natural phenomena can be a more significant threat. We think all the predictables are on the horizon until something unexpected creeps up and surprises us. The next something could be catastrophic, or it could save us from ourselves.

***

The town of Paso Robles is at the heart of a wine-growing region in south-central California. Nestled in the rolling Cholame Hills, it is about 200 miles southwest of the Hahns' ranch. A few miles east of town, the hills level out to a flat, desolate valley where temperatures reach 120 degrees in summer.

"How much farther?" Sara asked through the headset.

It startled Mason since she had been asleep for a while. Her growing fear of UV radiation had her donning the hat and gloves she received from Becky.

"According to my sketchy flight readouts," Mason said, "we have less than thirty minutes."

Ethan lay rolled up in a blanket on the floorboard. Mason reached back and tapped him on the head, but no response.

"Why don't you wake him?" Mason asked. "Have him check magnetic readings."

Sara rubbed her eyes. "Red wine does not agree with me," she said. "But that Barbera, your parents make, is good stuff."

Mason saw she was noticeably out of sorts. He tapped Ethan a couple more times on the head. Ethan mumbled a few words and rolled over.

"Where are we?" he asked. "I have a headache."

Sara massaged her temples and sighed.

"Homemade batches take some getting used to." Mason smirked. "You're both dehydrated. Should be water in the cooler."

Ethan sat up to look for it.

"I need to know where we are," Mason said. "Pull out your machine and see what it says."

Ethan passed water upfront, then flipped the power switch on his new digital magnetometer. He studied readouts in the new format showing they were slightly off course. The anomaly was due south, but they were heading southwest.

"We should be heading south," Ethan replied, leaning between Mason and slumping Sara. "Not southwest."

"South puts us in the desert," Mason said. He already had a plan. "We're heading southwest to Paso Robles. We'll stay there for the night."

No arguments.

"I think it's best we visit the anomaly at night," he said. "That desert gets up to 120 degrees in the daytime but drops forty degrees at night."

Sara curled back under her sombrero. Ethan wanted no part of this discussion, so he flopped back into his sleeping bag.

***

They found a bed and breakfast a stone's throw away from a winery overlooking teddy bear-brown hillsides and vineyards. At midday they checked into the flop and lay down for a nap.

By late afternoon, Mason felt restless and did not want to disturb Sara's sleep, so he found his way to a tasting room. Under cover of shade, he found a seat at the bar not far from two middle-aged couples chattering away. He discreetly motioned for the lady behind the bar so he would not interrupt the ongoing conversation. He ordered a glass of Syrah; she handed it to him along with a cold water, and he reached for the wine. Mason thought about tomorrow's flight and hoped the heat in the valley would drop to a tolerable level before they landed. Images of the light tower raced through his mind.

Mason needed a break from recent events to let his head unwind. But the conversation a few feet away seemed to get louder by the minute and centered around the Auroras and UV radiation. He sniffed, swirled, and sipped the wine. Not what he'd expected, not as good as home, so he pushed it aside and drank the water. The atmosphere not being what he'd hoped for, he paid for the drink and turned to leave.

He noticed a figure seated on the other side of the bar area under the shade of a giant eucalyptus tree. Quiet, unmoving, and staring in Mason's direction. Startled, he made eye contact with the man, then walked away. Mason thought he had seen the man before but could not remember where. Something was not right about the man, maybe the shadow or the dark business suit. Nobody in California wore a business suit to a wine-tasting, especially not in 100-degree weather. Mason turned to leave; he made no acknowledgment of the man.

He decided to catch a ride out to the airfield to check on the plane and ensure it was ready for tomorrow's flight. Minutes later, he was talking to a service manager, but the conversation had nothing to do with service.

"So, you're telling me we might be grounded here?" Mason asked.

"Might be," the man said. "Situation changes hourly with all these atmospheric goings-on."

A loud whoofing sound picked up, distant but getting closer. Mason walked to the window.

"For two days now," the man said. "Military aircraft of all kinds been heading out to the valley."

Mason shook his head and approached the counter.

"Did you hear about the compasses?" the man asked. "In Seattle, they point north, but their aim is south. In LA, they point north the way they should, and here in Paso, they just spin."

"What about my plane?" Mason asked. "Is it ready if they clear us to go?"

"We got you fueled up," the man said.

"Yeah, thanks," Mason replied. He had to let Sara know what was going on.

***

The airport shuttle dropped him off at the B & B. Mason cautiously panned the area for inconspicuous figures reading newspapers or standing on street corners, but all looked good. He found his way back to the room where Sara was on the phone, wearing a shower robe. She mouthed to Mason that her mother was on the call, so he stepped out onto the patio and closed the sliding door behind him.

"We plan on heading out there tomorrow night," she said.

A pause.

"Mother?" Sara asked.

"I'm sorry, I have a lot on my mind," Julia replied. "It's dark here now, and the National Guard are starting to patrol. I would like to move out of the city with everything going on. Go stay with my sister."

Another pause.

"Just a pipe dream," Julia continued. "They need me here, and they always want answers from my crystal ball."

"Maybe you should take a break," Sara said. "None of this is your doing."

"Can't run away from a good fight," Julia followed, then regrouped. "So, you're investigating the new core location tomorrow, and little danger since no solar activity is predicted?"

"That's right," Sara said. "There is something else. We received results from the lab that carbon dated the mammoth tissue. Tests show they recently died, not eons ago. It proves what I already told you. It's the smoking gun. They moved through time."

"Sweetheart," Julia sighed, knowing unwelcome ears could be listening. "The powers that be will want more proof, and with all that is going on, they don't need another issue to panic the masses."

That response made Sara pull the phone from her ear and stare at it. But she guessed what Julia guessed and played along.

"Maybe you're right," she said. "This whole thing is wearing me down, too. I've run myself ragged, and now I'm chasing ghosts. We'll get out there tomorrow and continue tracking the anomaly. Good night, Mother."

"Good night, sweetheart."

***

Mason took Sara's hand as they crossed the street to an Italian bistro with Ethan in tow. The ordinarily dark desert sky, illuminated by Auroras, cast long shadows as they walked. They found seats outside in a courtyard overlooking the valley and laid their phones on the table. Ethan plopped the magnetometer on the table with a *thud*. He got a reproachful look from Sara. They asked for water and sifted through menus.

"I went out to check on the plane this afternoon," Mason said. "Flight clearance might be an issue."

"We'll drive if we have to," Sara said. "How far is it?"

Ethan flipped on the magnetometer.

The server brought out a bottle of water with three glasses. Ethan paid no attention, pecking away at buttons on his new machine. This caught the server's attention.

"Thank you," Mason said. "And don't worry about him. He takes some getting used to."

The server grinned and walked away.

"The polar position is holding," Ethan said. "Same as this morning, and we are about fifty miles west of it."

"We could drive," Sara said, gauging Mason's face.

A man approached from the bar; his steps caught Mason's attention. The same man he'd seen earlier at the tasting room. Three more men in military dress seemed to come out of nowhere and stood at his flank.

"Sara Gathers?" the suited man asked.

Taken by surprise and assessing Mason's eyes, she offered. "Gentlemen, how can I help you?"

"Ma'am, we are here on orders from Colonel Matthew Jackson," the suited man followed. "We were told the two of you are acquainted."

"We are," Sara replied cautiously.

Mason took a sigh of relief. Ethan was impressed.

"We were also told that you will be traveling out," the man paused, panning the onlooking crowd. "For an expedition into the valley tomorrow night."

Sara, remembering her conversation with Julia, answered tactically. "Currently, yes," she replied. "Why do you ask?"

"Ma'am, all commercial and private civilian air traffic were grounded effectively at," he said, checking his watch, "1800 hours today. Are you aware of this new development?"

"I've heard something of it," Sara replied.

"The colonel recommends we escort you," the suited man paused again. Onlooking faces turned away. "To the site."

Sara considered the offer. Mason raised an eyebrow with a nod of approval.

"He also recommends that you modify plans and fly out tonight," the suited man continued. "Due to the unstable condition of the anomaly."

Sara did not respond but lifted her cell phone to check the time.

"We will have vehicles at your hotel at 2100 hours," the suited man said. "That will deliver you to Fort Collins for helicopter transport to the site. Is there anything you need from us for the expedition?"

Sara thought about it. "A digital video camera," Sara replied. "With infrared capabilities."

The suited man seemed confused.

"Do you think you can handle that?" Sara asked.

"Yes, ma'am," he answered.

"Here we go again," Mason critiqued.

The military men excused themselves. Sara's bewildered eyes drifted as if seeing a story yet to be told.

***

A fleet of black SUVs pulled up curbside at 2100 hours on the dot. Sara, Mason, and Ethan hurried into the rear vehicle, and the motorcade pulled away. They were cruising low over the desert in a Chinook helicopter within the hour. Ethan had his magnetometer in hand, studying the readouts.

Sara was really feeling it this time. Twice now, she had seen extreme magnetism and energy episodes that gave rise to unexplainable supernatural events. She had no idea what to expect and wished she had one more night to prepare herself for what was to come.

"You look nervous, ma'am," said the suited man who took a seat across from her. "Have you been briefed on what's out there?"

Mason chuckled. Sara looked away. The suited man and flanking soldiers in tactical gear seemed amused by her timid reaction.

"No one knows better than her, what's going to happen out there," Ethan shouted defensively through the headset. "She's the only reason any of us are here."

"Calm down, kid," Mason said.

"What do you mean?" the suited man asked. "What's going to happen?"

"Have *you* been briefed?" Mason asked the suited man who shied away.

"We're going to measure magnetic strength and positioning," the suited man said. The soldier's ears perked.

"And look at the pretty Auroras?" Mason followed. "That would make for a nice evening."

"I don't understand," the suited man grunted.

"Stay on your toes, gentlemen," Sara sternly spoke. "Keep your wits about you and firearms at your side."

The suited man half-laughed, the soldiers rolled their eyes. Sara did not appreciate their lack of respect.

"Let me put it to you another way," she said. "Why do you think Colonel Jackson went out of his way to provide armed escort for three civilians into a parched valley?"

"It's standard procedure—"

"Standard procedure!" Sara cut him off. "I'm sure you're carrying a side-arm in your jacket, and these men are all carrying semi-automatic weapons as we fly by a cover of darkness into the middle of nowhere. Doesn't that seem odd to you?"

"Not to mention that we didn't even ask for your help. You had to covertly seek us out."

"And we appreciate that," Mason offered.

Sara continued, "We were with Colonel Jackson on two previous occasions," she said. "When this thing locked into position and unleashed its fury."

"Quiet!" Ethan shouted, studying his magnetometer. "Readings jumped again."

"What does that mean?" the suited man asked.

"That usually means," Sara said, craning her neck to see out the window. "Something is about to happen."

"The core is spinning and gaining energy for the next jump," Ethan said. "And right before that jump, unusual things can and have happened."

"Like what, for instance?" the suited man asked.

He looked to Sara for answers, but her gaze remained fixed in anticipation. She had a weariness in her eyes that only came from experience, first-hand experience with dreadful situations. The suited man had only seen this look in PTSD cases with war veterans. A glimpse of knowing and living through things that most people do not know or even think about. He settled back in his seat and peered out the window, looking for what Sara already knew was out there.

The Chinook pressed along through thin desert air. The pilot's voice crackled through headsets, "Destination—five minutes." Thumping chopper blades throttled away. Nervous tension filled the cabin while Sara's unmoving eyes studied the dimly lit horizon like a night owl stalking its prey. She calmly pulled out a pair of sunglasses. The suited man looked confused.

"Damn." Mason thumped his leg. "I forgot mine."

Then a bright flash lit up the cabin. The explosive brightness startled the soldiers to arms. The suited man turned in awe to see bright, dancing rainbow colors shooting up from the valley floor. A wall of light warped and shifted like a dust devil darting across the land. He turned back to see statuesque Sara had not moved a centimeter. Her eyes were not surprised by the wonder in the distance she had seen many times before.

"No closer than one mile," she said to the suited man. "Inform the pilot."

The suited man quickly relayed the message, and soon the Chinook settled down for a soft landing, its chopper blades churning up dust. The exploding lights were a mile away but looked as if you could reach out and touch them. Cooling engines were still winding down when the team disembarked. Sara panned the terrain.

"Two men stay with the Chopper," she ordered. "The rest of you follow me."

"Excuse me," the suited man said. "This is a military operation. You can't—"

"This is our only way out of here," Sara cut him off, pointing to the Chinook. "It's our stronghold. It must be protected."

Many confused faces, but no other comments.

Sara Gathers walked defiantly toward the magnetically charged anomaly. What would happen this time—monsters from the past or spaceships from the future? Why was she even doing this? Something drew her on toward the light. She had to know what it was. Could this be the last time she would ever see it, last chance to figure it out? Mason and Ethan followed while three armed men flanked them closely.

The lit-up landscape seemed to move around them. Reptiles, snakes, coyotes, you name it, all moving away from the light. There were rustling sounds in the brush all around. One soldier almost tripped over a side-winding rattler that did not rattle or hiss as it raced past.

The light up-shooting formed a perimeter more than a mile in circumference, mere tracer rounds of the great power churning below. The distinctive color pattern from red to violet matched the layout of the two earlier incidents. The team marched cautiously toward the magnetic light fan and stopped a hundred yards from its edge.

"Stay sharp, gentlemen," Sara said. "And ready your weapons."

The metallic sound of cocking guns rang out. The suited man felt a lump in his throat. Sara looked over her shoulder toward the helicopter, then tapped her headset.

"Are we still in contact with the chopper?" she asked.

"Yes, ma'am," a voice came over the headset. The pilot motioned thumbs up.

Sara took a deep breath and started toward the bright lights.

"Is anyone filming?" she asked, with an expression that said they'd better be. The suited man lifted the camera to his eye.

"What am I filming?" he asked.

"Anything inside there that moves," Sara said.

"Like what, snakes, reptiles?"

"Nothing that small," she said to a chorus of nervous chills.

"How are the readings, Ethan?" Sara asked.

"Too high to register," Ethan said.

The light band seemed to grow and hum, dwarfing the human figures as they approached.

"Sara," Ethan said. "I think we should move off-center toward the red end of the spectrum."

She paused and considered the situation.

"Good idea," she answered, remembering that everything ancient emerged from the green and blue light.

The team started in that direction. All but the suited man, who stood holding his camera. This did not go unnoticed by one soldier.

"Excuse me," the soldier said.

All turned and huddled around the suited man, squinting in the direction of his camera's aim.

"What is it?" Sara asked. "I don't see anything but bright flickering light."

"There's something in there," he said. He lowered the camera, then put it back to his eyes.

The soldiers readied their weapons.

"I see why you asked for infrared," the suited man said. "It's only visible in the infrared."

He handed the camera to Sara.

"It appears to be a campfire," she said, walking as she spoke. "Wait, there's a figure sitting nearby."

Then as quickly as it appeared, the gigantic fan of light instantly disappeared. The startled team stepped back, motionless. A couple hundred yards away, a small light remained, not Aurora-like, but common in color, tiny and glowing.

"Ethan," Sara said. "What are the readings now?"

Ethan sifted through his satchel. He first grabbed the laptop, then deeper in, he found the magnetometer. He pulled it out and flicked some switches.

"All normal," he said, his eyes scanning all readouts. "Yes, everything back to normal."

"OK," Sara sighed. "Here we go."

The team slowly stepped through the bleached, sandy terrain littered with brush. Ethan's eyes were relieved to see no signs of smoke or scent of ash. The solar interaction must have been the catalyst all along. Could only magnetism have created the light this time?

Halfway there, and no change in the light. Definitely a campfire, but no sign yet of the figure Sara spoke about.

"Spread out, gentlemen," Sara said. "There's someone, or something, near that fire."

The soldiers dispersed. The suited man dropped in line behind Sara and Mason. Sara continued cautiously, eyes fixed on the fire, watching for any movement. The soldiers ran into flanking positions and reached the fire with weapons pointed toward the ground when Sara reached the encampment.

She saw something as unexpected as the mammoths in Alaska. Three figures lay on the ground in fetal positions, backs to the campfire, and heads curled under their arms. All were naked, a male, a female, and a child. Not human, their faces were boney and Neanderthal in appearance. Covered in hair from head to foot, the hair on the male's head was black and matted. They made whimpering sounds, scared out of their minds. Clearly, Sara's team frightened them. She motioned for the soldiers to move back behind the campfire. Now she stood alone between these people and the light of the fire. She could not think of the best way to attract their attention, but with the light fan gone, they slowly sat up, thinking they had weathered the storm.

Sara tried to gauge their lineage by appearance: Homo erectus? No, too long ago and not native to the Americas. They had to be and appeared to be Neanderthal, which would make them at least 40,000 years old. No one uttered a sound. They studied her as she studied them. Sara decided that a crouched position would be less intimidating, so she knelt, showed the palms of her hands, and smiled. This had the intended effect, and soon they crawled toward her.

The male stopped in front of her, reached out, and felt the material of her shirt sleeve and pants. Still fascinated, he reached up and touched her soft, smooth hair. Something that resembled a smile broke out on his face. Then concerned soldiers rushed up from behind the campfire.

The ancient people rolled back from fear into the brush. The soldiers continued to form a perimeter. Cries rang out from the bush.

"Stop!" Sara shouted. "You're scaring them!"

Prehistoric ears had never heard an enunciated word or seen such alien creatures before. The male stood in amazement. The female grabbed her child and ran off into the darkness. Sara instinctively went after her.

"Stay with him!" she shouted. Armed soldiers closed their circle. Mason and Ethan followed Sara.

Arms flailing as he ran, Ethan noticed something flicker. Readouts on the magnetometer strapped over his shoulder flickered. He slowed down to look. On, off. On, off. On, off. On, off.

"Hey!" he shouted. "Hey, this isn't good!"

Sara was in full sprint, with Mason not far behind.

"Something is happening!"

An explosion of light burst around them. A light fan shot up from the ground, forming its familiar perimeter, but this time, and for the first time, people from the current place in time were inside it. Sara stopped dead in her tracks. Mason and Ethan raced past, not seeing her stop. Sara could see stars above but nothing outside the wall of light. She looked for Mason and Ethan.

A low thump shook the ground, and a new, brighter light appeared. Sara's ears popped as a tube of white light engulfed her. Inside the light fan, and running its length, a magnetically charged tube of light had appeared. Like a flux tube on the sun, its twisting shape warped and writhed, with the entire team of soldiers and civilians scattered along its length.

Sara's eyes adjusted to the light, then saw Mason and Ethan had run past her.

"What's happening?" she asked. No response, but the fear in their eyes told a story.

Then in a flash, Sara Gathers vanished.

PART 5

Chapter 28
The Other Side

Mercy Hospital

"If time travel is possible, where are the tourists from the future?"
Stephen Hawking

Sightings of bright lights bursting through the distant valley sky filled local newspaper headlines. No explosive noise went with the light that lasted only a few minutes. No official investigation followed, and locals found no evidence of the incident. A week later, two men stumbled out of the desert.

***

The hospital room was simple, olive-colored wallpaper, yellow floor tile, and acoustic ceilings, one bed occupied, one not. The unconscious man lying in bed had been there for two days. An IV bottle hung from a metallic tree stand, dripping clear liquid into his veins.

A nurse entered the room with a new IV bottle in hand. The man moved slightly and moaned. His eyes opened and shut a couple times. "How are you feeling?" she asked, placing a hand on his forehead. No response, only a confused expression.

"Are you hungry?" she asked.

The man shook his head.

"OK, I'll go get the doctor."

Minutes later, a middle-aged man with a clipboard entered the room.

"So, how are we today?" the doctor asked.

No response. The doctor flipped through a chart as the nurse changed the bottle.

"It seems your friend has abandoned us," the doctor said. "Do you know where he went?"

The man shook his head.

"You suffered extreme dehydration and exposure," the Doctor said. "What were you doing in the valley?"

The man suddenly had a flash of memory. He shifted nervously. The doctor held out a laminated lanyard: Ethan Sites, NOAA.

"Is this where you work? A government agency?" he asked.

Ethan mumbled.

"And this device was in your satchel," the doctor held out Ethan's cell phone. "What is it?"

Ethan sat up quickly and grabbed the phone. The startled doctor backed away from the bed.

"It's turned off," Ethan said. "Have you turned it on?"

Both doctor and nurse looked confused and frightened. Ethan held a thumb on the right side of the phone.

"Ethan Sites," he said, and the screen came to life.

The doctor and nurse stepped closer on either side of the bed.

"I have no signal here," Ethan said. "What's your Wi-Fi password?"

No response. The doctor curiously stared at the cell phone, his head inches from Ethan's.

"Is that a miniature TV?" he asked. "The picture is incredible."

It was Ethan's screen saver of waves crashing on a rocky coastline. Ethan quickly turned it off, then studied the Doctor's appearance; his haircut and sideburns seemed out of place. The stethoscope around his neck seemed archaic and the nurse had long, curled hair and wore heavy make-up.

Ethan felt a resurgence of energy flowing through his veins. He was suddenly awake, aware, and confused about his circumstances.

"Doctor," Ethan redirected. "You mentioned another man was here. What did he look like? Was he tall with dark hair?"

"Yes, he was," the Doctor replied. "But no identification. Did he work with you?"

When they woke up in the desert, Mason and Ethan found no signs of magnetic disturbances, Sara, the soldiers, or the Chinook. After a few days' walk, and not knowing where they were, or when they were, they decided to bury their identification. Because if they had emerged in another time that information could get them in trouble.

"And he's gone?" Ethan asked.

"Yes, he left this morning," the nurse retorted. "Without permission."

"I have to get out of here," Ethan said. "I need to find him."

"Son, you are in no condition to go anywhere," the doctor said. "You still need fluids, and you're sunburnt."

"Are those my clothes hanging on the wall?" Ethan asked.

"Yes, next to your satchel," the doctor replied. "That has other devices we can't identify."

A laptop. They can't identify a laptop computer, Ethan thought. *What kind of hospital is this?*

"How do I check out?" Ethan asked.

The doctor sighed.

"Just sign this," he said. "No charges due. Someone paid the bill."

Ethan swung his feet over the side of the bed.

"We'll step out while you get dressed," the doctor said. "And one other thing, there is an envelope for you in the satchel."

Ethan got dressed, grabbed his satchel, and started for the door but stopped short and opened it. The yellow manilla envelope had nothing written on it. He opened it and found a note stapled to newspaper clippings.

'Call me at 805 223-1934.'

'Careful what you say.'

He also found one hundred dollars in cash at the bottom of the envelope.

Ethan made his way down the elevator to the main lobby. He was surprised to find his doctor standing by the revolving exit door.

"Son," he asked. "Can we talk for a minute?"

Ethan paused, then nodded.

"Let's forget the fact that you are in no condition to walk out that door." The doctor gestured. "Let's also forget the fact that you walked out of the desert a week after everyone in this town saw those mysterious lights in the sky. How about the fact you had no identification in your wallet and an unknown source paid your hospital bills? You have high-tech devices that I've never seen before, and I'm a pretty smart guy. And your clothing looks European."

Ethan looked away, his eyes watered.

"Son," the doctor continued. "You don't have to leave. It's safe here. Why leave?"

Ethan paused.

"I didn't know 'till just now," Ethan said and pushed his way through the revolving door.

257

Chapter 29

Stepping Out

Paso Robles, CA

Ethan walked out onto the street and looked in both directions. The town did not look the same, a shadow of its former self. The restaurants, office buildings, even the streets were different. He felt a rush of panic. Cars passing by were vintage, but not vintage. Out-dated models, rusty and beat up. Where were the shiny new Mercedes Benzes, Ferraris, and Porsches? These were old Chevys and Fords; the kind locals drove. And the doctor had never seen a cell phone. He started to lose his breath. Was this really happening?

Light-purple evening clouds lifted over the mountains when Ethan Sites crossed the street in the direction of a telephone booth. He had never used one and did not know he needed a dime to place a call. He lifted a frustrated gaze to the cityscape and saw a restaurant-bar a couple blocks away.

Ethan walked down a dusty sidewalk lined with dusty cars. Then he recalled something from his mind's eye—all the plates were blue. The license plates were all blue like they used to be in the 1970s and '80s. Was this where they'd ended up? He needed time to regroup and think about it.

He approached a tiny restaurant and stepped inside. He panned the dining area decked out with dark wooden chairs, tables, and old Spanish tile. The room was crowded, and the bar at the back of the room had a body in every seat.

No wait staff greeted him, so he walked up to the bar to ask for change. He found a vacant stool, where an empty whiskey glass with a ten-dollar bill inside lay on the counter.

"Can I get a menu and a glass of water?" Ethan asked.

"Sure," the bartender replied. "Here you go."

Ethan took a long cool drink and picked up the menu, then someone slapped him on the shoulder.

"I was about to go check on you," a voice said.

Ethan turned to see Mason looking down at him, smiling. Ethan jumped to his feet and bear-hugged him.

"I can't believe you're here," Ethan blurted. "How did we get to the hospital? Where is everyone else?"

A grim expression of realization rolled down Mason's face. Ethan fell away in disbelief, reaching for the barstool.

"They're all gone, kid," Mason said. "And we're stuck here."

Suddenly, blocked memories of the long walk back returned. Memories that dehydration had temporarily burned away. First a look of recognition, then sobbing.

"She's gone, kid," Mason said. "I can't find her."

"This isn't real," Ethan murmured. "This isn't happening."

"The best I can tell," Mason said. "It's the late 1980s, judging by cars and haircuts."

"That's impossible." Ethan grimaced.

Two men sitting next to them at the bar with curious ears sipped slowly at their drinks.

"You said it yourself, kid," Mason said. "Don't you remember? We all disappeared into different 'colors of the spectrum.'"

A look of recognition.

"We're all in different times," Ethan whispered.

"That's right," Mason replied. "At least we're familiar with this one. And the whiskey tastes the same."

"So, what can I get you?" the bartender asked.

Ethan did not respond, his mind processing the situation.

"Two cheeseburgers," Mason interjected. "And more water, please."

The cold water had Ethan feeling better by the minute. His eye caught pink and blue watermarks on the ten-dollar bill next to the whiskey glass. If they were in the twentieth century, then the ten from Mason's wallet would look counterfeit. He slowly reached out, grabbed it, shuffled through his satchel, pulled a ten out of the envelope, and placed it on the counter.

"Where did you get that, kid?" Mason asked.

A pair of curious eyes noticed the exchange.

"Thought I'd cover your drink," Ethan said, knowing someone was watching. "Thanks for coming back to get me." His nervous appearance did not go unnoticed.

"I've been coming in here for ten years now," a big man next to Mason said. "And I've never seen you two before. And what's that smell? When was the last time you two bathed?"

His comment received a nasty frown from Mason.

"You're the two that walked out of the valley, aren't you?" the big man asked.

After a long, straight-faced stare, Mason said, "Excuse me." And turned back to Ethan.

"I see they bandaged you up," Mason said. "You took a nasty fall out there."

Ethan did not say a word. He felt like all eyes in the room were on him.

"You're still not thinking right," Mason said.

The bartender laid a serving tray on the countertop. "Two cheeseburgers!" he shouted.

Ethan had already snatched one up before Mason could say 'to go.'

"After this, we'll go check on the plane," Mason said.

That did not make sense. Ethan paused for a second, then continued wolfing down the burger.

"What plane?" the big man asked. "I work at the airport. There are only seven planes there now, and none of them are yours."

Mason ignored the comment and started eating. Ethan dropped a ten on the bar and picked up the half-eaten burger.

"Maybe we should go," Ethan said.

Mason pushed a hand down on Ethan's shoulder to re-seat him.

"Let's finish eating," Mason said. "Bartender, another whiskey."

Mason had learned a few things in the cold Alaska winters: never flinch at the first sign of a threat, try to be patient with bullies, and more whiskey never hurts.

"You never answered the question," the big man said.

A nervous bartender pushed a glass in front of Mason; he slugged it down.

"You already answered your own question," Mason replied. "It's not at the airport."

Mason continued eating the cheeseburger.

A tap on the shoulder. "Then where is it?"

Mason pointed to the bartender and the empty glass. Ethan pulled out a couple bucks. Mason slugged down another shot.

"You answered that one, too," Mason said and patted him on the cheek. "It's out in the valley."

Mason reached for a cheeseburger when the big man took a swing at him. Mason ducked, elbowed him in the gut, and decked him with a right cross. His buddy charged at Mason, who stepped back, tripped the man, and shoved him to the ground. Ethan panicked, grabbed his cheeseburger and satchel, and darted away from the bar. Then something hit him from behind.

Chapter 30

The Lockup

Paso Robles, CA

The next morning Ethan woke up with a sore neck and back. His neck had taken a cheap shot from a chair. His back spent the night on the rock-hard floor of a jail cell while Mason snored away in the opposite corner. Ethan sat up, cross-legged, and rubbed his neck. The guard on duty approached.

"Do you need anything?" he asked.

"A glass of water," Ethan moaned.

The guard walked to the water dispenser and brought him a cup.

"Thank you."

"Hey, kid," the guard said. "We know this wasn't your fault. Even your buddy there just defended himself, according to witnesses. You should be out of here soon."

"Thank you." Ethan's eye caught a glimpse of his satchel hanging on the wall.

"Excuse me," he said. "Is it possible to get my satchel hanging over there?"

"Can't do that," the guard replied and turned away.

"Wait," Ethan followed. "There's a manilla envelope inside. It has research papers I need to review."

The guard sighed, then found the envelope.

"Looks harmless enough," he said and handed it to Ethan.

"Thank you," Ethan replied.

Ethan quickly pulled out the newspaper clippings and cash. The dates on the remaining twenties were 1979, 1986, and a crispy 1988. He felt a rush come over him. This was real. Then he sifted through his pockets as the curious guard watched. He pulled out the 2028 ten-dollar bill he'd snatched from the bar. He nervously folded all four and stuffed them in his pants pocket.

He grabbed the newspaper clippings and the note 'careful what you say', then sighed, remembering last night's fiasco.

"Good job," he mumbled.

He flipped through the stack of clippings. He focused on dates and headlines. 'Mysterious lights in the eastern sky,' 'UFOs or Military tests,' 'Two strangers walk out of the desert,' all dated April 1989. His heart raced the more he read. He'd assumed all along that the envelope was from Mason, but all he'd paid attention to before was the note and the cash. All this information came from someone else, someone from the past. Someone from the past?

"Hey, kid," a voice grumbled, startling Ethan from deep thought.

"Mason!" Ethan shouted and jumped up. "You're OK!"

"Yeah," Mason said, getting to his feet. "What do you expect? I've been lying here all night."

"OK, your paperwork came through," the guard interrupted. "Bail was posted."

Ethan beamed a boyishly hopeful look, countered by Mason's confusion.

"You two work for the lady on the hill?" the guard asked and turned a skeleton key.

Ethan's beam flattened.

"Weekends," Mason dryly offered.

"Your stuff is hanging over there," the guard said. "You sign-out up front."

He led them through gray corridors to the front desk. Mason grabbed Ethan's arm tightly, shook his head, and put a finger to his mouth. Ethan acknowledged. He started to realize that something unbelievable was on the horizon. Who was communicating with them? Was this good, or bad?

The front desk officer handed Mason a clipboard with a document of three-leaf paper.

"John Doe 1 and John Doe 2," he said.

Mason flashed a gaze and scribbled his name on the bottom. Ethan did the same.

"You two should stay clear of the Mexicali," the guard said. He walked them to the front door. "And stay up there on the hill for a while."

They stepped out to a bright sunny morning. Mason and Ethan both covered their eyes from the glare.

"What do we—" Ethan started to ask.

Mason cut him off. "Not now, kid," Mason said. "We need to get somewhere and think."

The jail was tiny, like the town. They stepped out onto the sidewalk and looked down a dusty road with cars parked on both sides. The Mexicali was only two doors away from jail.

"Well, that was convenient," Mason murmured.

Ethan was lost in thought. *Talk about coming to a crossroads in your life—where do we go, north or south? What did the guard mean by 'the lady on the hill'? What hill? Hills are all around. If all this is real, I'm not even born yet; who can I possibly know? Maybe we have familiar faces. But someone bailed us out. We have a few bucks in our pockets; we can at least check into a hotel and shower.*

Ethan fumbled through his backpack; everything was still there, nothing scratched or broken. Mason's eyes caught a familiar sight, something from an old memory. He stopped, grabbed Ethan's arm, and pointed.

"Look," he said.

"At what?"

"Over there," Mason said. "Across the street."

Ethan's gaze caught an old rag-top Jeep, olive green with no side-doors. Someone wearing sunglasses sat behind a dirty windshield. Both men stopped momentarily with total focus. Then Mason broke into a sprint. He ran so fast that he slid, rear first, over the hood of a parked car. He raced across the street to the Jeep and stopped a few feet away.

Like something out of a dream, he threw a hand across his face and cried.

"You're alive!" Mason fell to his knees. "You're alive!"

Chapter 31

Sara Gathers

Reprise

Ethan ran up behind Mason, mouth hanging open. Sara calmly stepped out of the Jeep and held out a hand to Mason. He got to his feet and hugged her long and hard.

"I was sure I'd never see you again," he blurted out.

"You were sure," she responded. Her confident tone brought a smile to Mason's face. "A bar fight, seriously?"

"You made him smile," Ethan said. "He hasn't smiled since you disappeared. Wait a minute, you disappeared, we saw it. You disappeared, so how—"

"Then you disappeared, too," Sara pointed out. "Or we wouldn't be standing here, would we?"

"So, how?" Ethan asked.

"My god, you two reek," she said, and walked back to the Jeep. "We need to get moving, and you're both riding in the back."

Sara cranked the ignition a few times. The smell of gasoline filled the air, the old muffler popped, and the engine thundered to life. She turned the wheel and headed down the road. In minutes, they were out of town in the teddy bear-brown hills of the Cholame. Mason could not take his eyes off her. He could not believe what had just happened. She'd saved them, and Mason knew it. And she was as confident and attractive as the first time he'd seen her on that remote beach in Alaska.

"How long have you been here?" Mason shouted over the wind and motor.

Sara glanced over her shoulder. "Two years," she replied.

Her gaze and response were that of fact, not expression. Mason could tell she had been through something other than the extraordinary events they had both experienced. A bit of anxiety came over him, but he let it go.

"And you still live here?" he asked.

Sara nodded.

They curved through winding roads up and out from town for half an hour. Soon, they were in the midst of vineyards. They passed row after row, acre after acre, field after field, and ranch after ranch until they reached a nondescript sign reading 'Second Chance Ranch' where Sara made a tight left onto a dirt road that pushed Ethan over into Mason's seat.

"That move was familiar," Mason said.

Sara smiled. She slowed down on the dirt road, but a cloud of dust followed as they made their way up winding terrain through more and more vineyards. Workers waved and raised their hats to Sara as the Jeep passed droves of ripened vines. In the distance, a chalet, maybe a destination, came into view.

Mason looked over at Ethan. Neither had words. Where was Sara taking them? What was going on? They pulled up to a Spanish-style house, not a modern replica made to look old, but old with a sagging porch framed with round posts and beams. Two big dogs ran up to greet Sara, who bent down to pet them.

Mason hopped out of the Jeep onto the dry, dusty soil. The view was terrific; vineyards all around, reaching down and through the hills. He walked around the Jeep to Sara, who was petting the dogs.

"Are you the lady on the hill?" he asked.

"Excuse me?" she asked and stood up. The two retrievers at her feet looked abandoned.

"The guard back there," Mason said. "Asked if we worked for 'the lady on the hill.'"

"Some people call me that," she said and snapped her fingers. The retrievers hurried off. "Let's go inside. Get out of the sun."

The house was clean, well kept, and simple, with tile floors and stucco walls. They made their way into the kitchen, where Sara reached for glasses in the cupboard.

"There was some trouble out here, at first," she said. "I bought the ranch in an auction after the business went under. The previous owner inherited the property but had no idea how to operate a vineyard or run a winery."

Sara turned the faucet handle to fill the glasses and noticed that Mason and Ethan seemed mesmerized by running water.

"Anyway," Sara continued and handed them each a glass. "With the house abandoned, locals took over. So, I had to call on the sheriff a few times before they finally got the hint."

Mason and Ethan slugged down their water.

"Then I made a few contacts, found good workers, a couple of distribution sources, and an excellent winemaker. I turned the place around quickly. It was a community effort up here, so I guess they gave me a nickname."

Sara pointed to a couple of bags on the living room couch.

"I bought you guys some new clothes," she said, sipping on water. "What you're wearing can't be washed enough to use again. Besides, you stand out from the crowd in twenty-first-century clothing. You need to look like guys from the 1980s."

She directed them down the hall.

"You'll find two showers that way," Sara said. "And one of them is in my bedroom, so keep it clean."

Within the hour, a week of grime and facial hair was gone. Both men found their way back to the kitchen, but no Sara. They heard music coming from the backyard and stepped out under a shaded canopy where Sara sat with a glass of wine in hand and two dogs at her feet. A small coffee table had a spread of cheese, crackers, and three bottles of red wine.

"I've sat out here for days, weeks," Sara said. "Staring into the hills, contemplating everything: why I'm here, how I'm here, I'm not even born yet. You name it, I've thought about it."

Mason took a seat and reached for a bottle.

"One thing I've concluded is I don't fit in this time," Sara said. "I don't belong here; I know so much about it. When something happens in the news, it's like, oh yes, I've heard of that."

Ethan also took a seat and reached for the crackers.

"So, I decided to do something about it," Sara said.

"So, you bought this ranch?" Mason asked.

"Huh, no." Sara chuckled and took a sip. "I bought this property because I needed somewhere to work, think in solitude, and wait for you two. I'm glad you appeared when you did, or I would have acted alone."

Mason was confused.

"Acted on what?" he asked. "And how did you ever afford to buy this vineyard?"

Sara chuckled again. "Horses," she replied. "Remember our horse ride? I told you I grew up with them. My mother took me to the tracks to watch races. We watched them on television—read books about them, too. By the time I was thirteen, the winner of every major race since Secretariat was committed to memory, and I have a good memory."

"Why Secretariat?"

"My mother's favorite horse," she said. "And the greatest ever. But eventually, I lost interest and moved on to other things."

"So, now you buy and sell horses?" Mason asked.

"No, not at all," she replied. "But I keep two in the stable over there."

Mason sipped from his glass with a curious look.

"Last year, I went to the casinos in Las Vegas," Sara said. "It was easy. I won more than enough to buy this ranch. But I haven't been back; I don't want to raise too many eyebrows."

"Good thinking," Mason said. "But wait a minute, to buy this ranch and win big in Vegas requires identification. Uncle Sam wants to know who you are."

Ethan's curiosity piqued.

"OK, all this is really cool stuff," Ethan said. "Especially since you saved us. I mean, I didn't think we would make it back alive. But how did you know? How did you know we would ever get here?"

"Well, I wasn't certain," Sara replied. "But you told me yourself, and I've had a long time to think about it. The colors of the spectrum, remember? A rainbow lens, the light changes were a lens for looking or traveling through time. We saw the towers in red light, and the mammoths appeared from the green light. The closer you are to the end of the red light, the closer you are to your own time.

"I was a few feet behind both of you when it happened to me. That meant you were closer to the end of the red color spectrum, so if it transported you through time, you would arrive after me."

"So, you waited all this time?" Mason asked.

"When I appeared in the desert alone, I waited a few hours for both of you. But nothing happened, so I found my way to the highway and hitched a ride back to Paso Robles."

"You hitched a ride?"

"Forget about it, kid," Mason said. "Back to the ID thing."

"Oh yeah, I needed money, so I found a part-time job," Sara said. "One of the girls working there noticed I didn't have a driver's license. She thought I was on the run and wanted to help out, so she gave me a name in LA. I drove down there one weekend and came back with a driver's license, birth certificate, the works."

"Good thinking," Mason said.

"Ever since then, I've read all the daily newspapers in the valley," Sara said. "Searching for articles about strangers from the desert. I even went back fifty years on micro-film just in case you went the other way."

"And if we didn't appear?"

Sara spun her wine glass and reached for a cracker.

"You want to go for a ride?" she asked. The retrievers jumped to attention and ran for the stable.

"I guess they know what that means," Mason said.

"Would you like to come along?" Sara asked Ethan. "Check out the barn?"

"No thanks," he replied. "I want to check on my computer and phone, power them up."

***

The stable was small but meticulously crafted with Douglass fir siding and timbers. Rolling doors at each end made for easy access and good airflow for the horses.

Opposite the stable stood another barn of similar design with a sign mounted high up near the gabled peak that read, 'Second Chance Ranch Winery.' Gravel parking lots wrapped it on three sides. A dozen or so cars and trucks sat parked at the backside.

"Is that the production facility?" Mason asked.

"Yes, it is," Sara replied. "I'll take you on a tour later."

When they reached the stable, the retrievers were racing circles through and around the hand-built structure.

"What are their names?" Mason asked.

"Gertie and Max," Sara replied. "Max is a great guard dog. Nothing comes near this place that I don't hear about."

Once inside the stable, the impressive rafter construction and hayloft caught Mason's eye.

"Definitely not pole barn construction," he said. "This is nicer than the house."

"I hired a specialty crew," Sara said. "They worked long hours for nearly two months to complete the job."

The horses snorted, shook their heads, and pawed their hooves in anticipation of Sara's approach.

"Here, grab a handful," she said. "They like sunflower seeds, kind of a treat."

"And what are *their* names?" Mason asked, holding a bucket to the big horse's mouth.

"This one is Winning Colors," Sara said. "And yours is Risen Star. Big winners last year."

Mason smiled.

"Don't give him too much of that," Sara said.

After a treat, they saddled the horses and headed out into the hills. Mason panned the countryside.

"How big is this ranch?" he asked.

"Five thousand acres," Sara replied.

Mason turned his head.

"But mostly forested hills. If it were all vineyard, I couldn't afford it."

"How much did you win?"

Sara laughed and bumped her heels. Both horses started up a dirt trail, past the vineyards through open, grassy hills. They raced alongside as if challenging each other to the finish line. Sara bent over to take the wind; Mason just hung on. When they reached the tree line, the trail thinned to a path; the horses slowed down and moved into a single file line. Winning Colors took the lead with Sara.

"What was it like," Mason asked from Risen Star's saddle, "When you found out where you were?"

"I was in shock," Sara replied. "Reality had re-formed around me. I cried a lot, then I realized some of the group might have suffered a worse fate, sent back to pre-historic times, and died horrible deaths. Suddenly, the 1980s didn't seem so bad after all, so I snapped out of my depression and took advantage of it."

"So, the other guys caught up in the light," Mason said. "You think they went that far back in time?

"Hopefully not, but if they moved through time," Sara replied, "they went back, way back. Consider their location in the light fan."

"At least they had weapons to defend themselves," Mason said. "For a while."

"I thought about that, too," Sara said. "If they did travel across time with those weapons, they could have changed history had they arrived at any time in the civilized era, but that didn't happen. They either buried them or went so far back in time the weapons don't exist anymore."

The trail wound up through wooded hills and spilled out to a grassy flat with craggy rocks.

"This is my favorite view," Sara said and dismounted her horse.

Mason got off Risen Star and held the reins.

"They don't have to be tied off," Sara said. "They like it up here. They'll eat grass all day."

She unstrapped two rolled-up saddle blankets and walked toward a small cluster of outcropped rocks.

"These make for good seats," she said and patted them in place on two rocks. "I've sat here for hours on end. Thinking about the future."

"What about the future?" Mason asked and sat down on a rock.

Sara thought about it for a moment. "I found my mother," she said.

"Excuse me?"

"I didn't actually meet her," Sara followed. "I'm not sure what kind of metaphysical laws that would break. But I had to know if she was alive and working at the university. It would somehow prove to me all this was real. So, I took a trip to campus and found her picture on a wall with all the other faculty members. That was a happy day for me, and it turned things around. That's when I decided what to do."

"And what's that?"

"Follow in her footsteps," Sara replied. "And reverse the effects of climate change."

"OK," Mason said. "And how do we do that?"

Sara paused.

"What do you know about the *Valdez*?" Sara asked. "The *Exxon Valdez*?"

"The oil spill?" Mason responded. "Everyone knows about that."

"Right," Sara said. "It horrified Mother. It happened years before I was born, but she still talked about it. I couldn't remember the exact date or time, but I knew it was in '89.

"Last month, I traveled up to Alaska and sought out the ship's captain. That tanker was gigantic, and I stood dockside, looking at it for the longest time. Knowing its fate was like staring down the Titanic.

"Anyway, very few well-dressed women walk industrial boat docks, so when a crew member approached me, I told him I was a reporter looking for the captain. He said I wouldn't be allowed on the ship but knew where the captain dined every night."

"And you went to the restaurant?" Mason asked. "How did you know who he was?"

"Research. I found his picture from micro-film at the library, so I knew who to look for, and luckily for me, he was dining alone that night. I sat at the bar for a while and watched him. I was curious about his nature, his personality, since the stories after the accident painted him as a carousing drunkard. But there sat a well-dressed man, napkin on his lap, slowly cutting a steak and sipping on a small glass of whiskey that he didn't finish, content in his own company.

"I approached him and introduced myself as a big-oil engineer. He motioned for me to take a seat. I asked if he was the captain of the

Valdez, he nodded. I told him I was concerned about seafloor shifts from the 1986 earthquake as it related to Prince William Sound.

"He countered that the '86 earthquake was way out in the Aleutian Islands. He answered so quickly it caught me off-guard. I responded that the same fault line runs along the entire south Alaskan coast, and updated studies are not complete regarding upheaval and underwater landslides, especially near shorelines.

"He paused and asked if I was an environmentalist, to which I answered no. I continued that I was concerned with ships of that size navigating these waters without updated nautical maps. I asked him to stay in the center with no deviation when moving through the bay, stay in deep water. He smiled and said he had complete confidence in the current charts. I begged him to reconsider. He said he'd think about it, then politely excused himself.

"After the conversation," she continued. "I thought that planting the seed might be enough to keep him on guard during the next voyage. But nothing changed, and a few weeks later, the ship ran aground on a reef. I felt worse than my mother could have imagined. I should have tried harder, should have done something more but had no idea what that might be, except resorting to violence."

Sara wiped her eyes, stood, and paced.

"So, you tried to stop the *Exxon Valdez* disaster?" Mason asked. "Wow, I mean, wow."

"Maybe history is an immovable object," Sara said. "Who knows, even if I were successful, would the same thing have happened somewhere else?"

Mason considered the possibility.

"You know," he said. "All super-tankers were re-designed after that accident to a double hull specification. That way, a breach in the outside hull won't damage the oil storage tank inside."

"So, you're saying it took a disaster to create improved ship design?" Sara asked.

"That's right," Mason responded. "You shouldn't feel bad; this was not your fault."

"I've read that after every earthquake," Sara said, "new structural improvements are made to buildings and bridges. So, we learn from our mistakes."

Mason nodded.

Sara continued pacing.

"We have to convince the world that catastrophic effects from climate change are on the horizon," she said. "Not let it break before it's too late to fix, and we can't do it ourselves. We need someone in a higher position, someone respected in the field, like my mother."

"But how do we reach out to Julia?" Mason asked.

"She has to know where we came from," Sara said. "I've thought about this for a long time, and now it makes more sense than ever. We've got to jump-start it next month. I have a plan if you want to help."

"Of course," Mason said. "I'm in."

Sara stopped pacing. "Then we need some information from Ethan's computer."

Chapter 32
The Plan

D r. Julia Gathers wrapped up a morning lecture about the effects of CO_2 emissions on global warming, then made her way down a terrazzo floor hallway to her office. She pulled up a chair at her desk and flipped through a stack of mail. A large white envelope caught her attention; it had green flagged edges and a registered mail receipt:

Ethan Sites
Asst. Mgr. – Operations
NOAA – (NCEI) Magnetic Field Tracking Facility
Perishton, AK

She was familiar with NOAA but not Ethan Sites and had never heard of Perishton, Alaska. She checked her watch, then opened the letter. It held a single piece of paper with a typed note.

April 21, 1989

Professor Gathers,

I will be brief: catastrophic natural disasters are on the horizon, some this year. We need your expertise to guide us, the nation, and the world through a web of events unfolding that will undermine the planet's future. You must believe me. Do not throw this letter away, and do not tell anyone about it. I will contact you again soon.

Ethan Sites

P.S. Race results at Churchill Downs next month
   Win - Sunday Silence
   Place - Easy Goer
   Show - Awe Inspiring

Was this a student prank or a deluded admirer? Should she contact the campus police? She rechecked her watch, placed the envelope in a desk drawer, and moved on to her next lecture.

***

"You're sure this is the right approach?" Ethan asked. "She will receive the letter soon, if not already."

"Yes, I'm sure," Sara replied, sipping coffee. "She watches every race with great anticipation."

Sara, Ethan, and Mason sat huddled in the kitchen, now referred to as the War Room.

"The Loma Prieta earthquake occurred in October," Sara said. "Your computer told us that. If we haven't won her confidence by then, the earthquake will surely convince her."

Ethan did not buy into the plan but did not see a downside either. He was concerned about his laptop. Specifically, the battery life that would eventually give out. He had a power cable, but something inside could break—too many variables. Nothing is designed to last forever. It would eventually go dark, and the information stored on the hard drive would lay dormant for decades.

"Sara, I've got the laptop up and running," Ethan said. "But I need to find a way to download or print out the most critical data before we have a problem. Without backup, I'm afraid of a hard drive crash or several other problems that can't be fixed. And if none of that happens, eventually, the battery will die. Portable computers of this era can't process a five-gig data file, so I need access to a mainframe."

Sara thought about it.

"Next week," Sara said, "we'll enroll you in a university as a computer science major."

"Excuse me?" Ethan asked. "Even in the 1980s, universities require grade transcripts, and I don't exist."

"You're a foreign exchange student who has lost everything," Sara replied. "And since I will pay all expenses upfront, they'll let you in."

"Still." Ethan struggled with the idea. "What if their computer can't process a file this size?"

"Last year, I read in a newspaper article," Sara continued, "that Lawrence Livermore National Laboratory upgraded their super-computer and gifted the old one to Berkeley, who now has the most computing power of any school on the west coast."

"Hmm." Ethan sighed. "Then it might be possible, but gaining access to that machine is not going to be easy, especially for an undergrad, and communication between that machine and my laptop—I'm not sure if—"

"I'm sure you'll figure it out," Sara said confidently.

"OK." Ethan thought about it. "It might work. I could set it up here. I need a modem and a login password to communicate with the mainframe. But the rate of transmission will be tortoise speed, at best."

"No!" Sara popped out.

Mason and Ethan looked up from their coffee.

"We can't do that. No transmissions from this house."

"Is there a problem?" Mason asked.

Sara did not respond.

Chapter 33

Berkeley

The next day Sara drove Ethan up the coast to the bay area. They wound through San Jose, then up the east side of San Francisco Bay to Berkeley campus for an appointment in the admissions building. They met with Charles Whitaker, an admissions officer in his early fifties; he had thinning hair and wire-rimmed glasses.

Sara introduced herself and Ethan. She explained Ethan's situation, then sat expressionless, awaiting a response. Ethan nervously watched with fingers crossed.

Whitaker cleared his throat and sat up in his chair. "Ma'am," he said. "This is a prestigious university with the highest admission standards. We turn away more valedictorians than most schools accept."

"And that's why we're here, sir," Sara followed. "I want him at the best school."

"Acceptance is based on many other factors," Whitaker pointed out.

"Hardship cases, for instance?" Sara asked with a tone. "This boy's parents were killed last year during an uprising in South Africa where they worked as missionaries. Technically, he's with me as a foreign exchange student, even though he's still an American citizen."

"Miss Gathers." Whitaker sighed. "Do you have papers confirming that?" There was a hint of a willingness to bargain in his voice.

"No, we're working on it," she said, her eyes dropped. "But it takes time. Ethan's parents were friends of the family. When he returned to the states, he looked me up."

"All that's well and good," Whitaker said. "And, Ethan, I'm sorry for your loss, but I can't just—"

"I can go on and on with this," Sara said. "But at the end of the day, he can pass any admittance exams and definitely test out of all computer science classes."

"Again, Miss—"

She raised her checkbook. "And I will pay all expenses upfront for the first year. Just give him a chance. That's all I'm asking."

"Look," Whitaker said. "There are many community colleges in the bay area he could attend. Enroll in one of those schools."

"He deserves better than that!" Sara thundered.

Something came over her. Even though she was lying through her teeth, it was justified in her mind. Ethan had lost his friends, family, life, and world. In a sense, he had lost much more than the boy she described, and she had, too. And this was not some kind of prank; they were trying to save the world for chrissakes.

"You have one of the best computer science programs in the country," she said.

"*The* best," Whitaker interrupted.

Sara received that comment with a smile.

"Then throw your best at him," she said. "If he doesn't ace all exams and offer innovative ideas that raise eyebrows, we walk away."

Whitaker turned in his chair and looked out his office window. An office with a window that took years of service and seniority to obtain. Service based on decisions both thorough and exact. He thought about admittance requirements, how he had never strayed from that fine line and his duty to enforce them. Were the rigid guidelines too rigid? Had they lost something he had never considered before? Should he take a chance? He thought about it for a long silent moment, then spun in his chair.

"Put your money where your mouth is," he said.

Sara laid her checkbook on his desk.

Whitaker took a long look at Ethan; did he see confidence or despair? His eyes panned between Sara and Ethan, then he turned again and looked out across campus through his office window.

"Over there." He pointed. "Do you recognize that building?"

"Yes, sir," Ethan said. "The computer science building."

Whitaker cautiously stared Ethan down, strumming his fingers on the desktop.

"Some of the brightest minds of the computer age spent years of their life in that building," Whitaker said. "And I know quite a few of them."

He sighed again.

"I'll make you a deal," he offered. "And it's because I don't want Miss Gathers to risk her money. There is a computer revolution going on down in the valley. I can get you an internship there at one of the largest companies. Prove your mettle, and they'll send me a recommendation that we can all hang our hats on."

Ethan sat up in his seat. *Sunnyvale,* he thought, *Silicon Valley! What was I thinking? Oh yeah, I wasn't because I've been time traveling. It's here, right here in California! And I will have cutting-edge computer technology at my fingertips.*

Whitaker stood and extended his hand, "Deal?"

"Yes, sir!" Ethan agreed with a firm handshake.

Chapter 34

The War Room

Whitaker kept his word and arranged for an internship in the valley. The following week they found Ethan an apartment in Sunnyvale. Sara looked up the I.D. man from L.A. and got the ball rolling on detailed identification for Ethan and Mason.

"All right," Sara said. "I'm excited about this. We have a plan and a busy two weeks ahead of us."

"Yeah," Ethan said. "Except you guys have the easy part. You just go to Vegas and gamble."

Sara flashed a look that made Ethan realize he had crossed a line (of some kind). Sara pushed the conversation back on track.

"So, you drive up there this week," she said. "And get your apartment set up. You can use one of the cars parked behind the winery for commuting back and forth to work. And no phone calls to this house. Every Sunday at five I'll be at a different telephone booth. Here are the numbers with dates for each one. You call me with weekly updates."

She handed him a slip of paper.

"Why all the cloak and dagger?" Ethan asked and got another laser look. He made an apologetic hand wave.

"Imagine what would happen to you," Sara asked, "if you got caught with your laptop in Silicon Valley. A machine forty years ahead of its time. And those people up there will know what they're looking at; they're not novices. Those microchips are not invented yet. Feds, military, everyone will come down on you and whoever you're 'working with.' Who knows what they could do to all of us? Do you understand?"

Ethan nodded his head.

"Your equipment stays here until you have a working plan on how to access and print that information," she said. "Make sense?"

Another nod. "Hey, back to the cars," Ethan said. "Can I take the black '71 Chevelle? I love those side pipes."

"Uh, no," Sara replied, with an arched brow.

Mason broke out laughing.

"That's my baby. You can take the Impala."

Ethan sighed.

"OK then, the next step will be the race. You must call me the day after the Derby," she continued. "This Sunday. Then we'll decide about our next communication with my mother."

⋆⋆⋆

That night Sara lay in bed going over everything in her mind, each step she'd laid out over the past week. Mason lay next to her.

"You're staring at the ceiling again," he said.

"I think I should go alone," Sara replied.

"Go alone?"

"To Las Vegas."

"Why?"

"Because I need to lose money out there," Sara replied.

Mason propped himself up on his shoulder. "Excuse me?"

Sara hopped out of bed and walked to the window. It was a perfectly still and cloudless night. Her moon shadow crossed the room. Mason's eyes caught the lines of her perfectly shaped body silhouetted through her nightgown.

"I think someone is following me," she spoke softly.

Mason jumped up and ran to her side, his heart racing. "What do you mean?" he asked.

"It started a few months ago," she said. "A car followed me from town. There was a man at the restaurant who followed me out here. He kept his distance, then stopped for a few minutes out by the mailbox.

"Eventually, he drove on. But ever since, I catch strangers out of the corner of my eye that shouldn't be there. They never approach, just watch."

"Are you sure you're no—"

"This is real," she cut him off. "Not imagination. I even saw him once in Las Vegas. He was sitting at a bar while I was playing blackjack but left before I could confront him."

"OK, this is creepy," Mason said. "Maybe I should step in the next time we see him."

"I don't think it's *him* I'm seeing," she said. "Just his tentacles, but I think you're right."

Mason looked confused.

"I'm going for the serpent's head," she said.

Chapter 35

Vegas

On Friday night, the eve of the Kentucky Derby, an elegant lady wearing a black cocktail dress and heels stepped out of a stretch limousine in front of Caesar's Palace. The driver offered a hand that she graciously accepted, cradling a coin purse in the other hand. All eyes in the porte-cochere turned to watch this splendid lady walk to the main entrance where bellmen hurried to open doors and followed with her bags. She crossed the threshold to a sea of eyes casting a gaze her way, one face with a reminiscent smile.

She checked in, then made her way to a betting booth and stood in a long line of gamblers waiting to place derby bets. Momentarily, a man dressed in a casino uniform appeared next to her but did not say anything. The lady seemed puzzled at first, but then a voice came from behind.

"Miss Prada, I presume," another man said.

Sara turned to see a middle-aged man wearing an Armani suit.

"I hope you had a nice flight. When you made the reservation, I thought transportation from the airport was the least we could do."

"Mr. Angeli," Sara replied. "So nice to see you again. I did appreciate the ride. Thank you."

"You're quite welcome," Mr. Angeli said. "I've also arranged the new presidential suite for you, complimentary."

"For a woman who takes you for millions?" Sara returned.

Mr. Angeli smiled. "It seemed that way at first," he said. "But after your departure last year, this place was packed full of sightseers and gamblers, spending money and hoping for a glimpse of Sara Prada."

Sara raised a curious eyebrow. She hoped she would get a chance to speak with Mr. Angeli, but this was all unexpected.

"This way." He politely gestured.

Sara turned to see a new booth open up, and a smiling face was awaiting her.

"May I help you?" the bookmaker asked.

"I see you had $250,000 placed into a reserve account," Mr. Angeli said. "What is your pleasure?"

Sara smiled at Mr. Angeli, then turned to the bookmaker. "$100,000 on Easy Goer to win."

The bookmaker flashed a grimacing stare at Mr. Angeli, who confidently nodded.

"He's the favorite," Mr. Angeli said. "Most people will take that bet. Four to five odds, I believe."

Sara acknowledged with a nod. The bookmaker took a few minutes to access her account and transfer funds. In time, he completed the transaction and handed Sara a ticket. She and Mr. Angeli walked through the lobby toward the main casino.

They reached the casino floor to multiple camera flashes that quickly turned into a photo-op. Hollywood's finest would have been jealous. This was more unexpected by Sara than the limo ride but obviously planned by Angeli.

Sara leaned toward his ear. "Did you know I placed a losing bet?"

"With a hundred thousand dollars?" he replied, furrowing his brow. "You're joking, right?"

They continued to smile and wave at a cheering crowd.

"No." she leaned back to his ear. "Easy Goer will place, not win."

Another puzzled look came over Angeli. "How do you know that?" he asked.

No answer.

"So, what are you up to now?"

"Maybe I'm finished with all this, maybe not," she replied. "But I just gave you some valuable information."

"Hmm, we'll see."

Mr. Angeli motioned with an appreciative hand, and the cheering stopped. He shook hands with a few essential guests. Sara did the same but did not know any of them. Eventually, the crowd and onlookers moved on. Sara thanked Mr. Angeli for his hospitality, then he escorted her up to her room.

***

The presidential suite was, well, a presidential suite. An automated entry door opened to a grand foyer that led to a two-story great room with full-height glass looking out over the Las Vegas strip and the mountains beyond. On the far side of the room, beyond a sunken floor rimmed with white leather couches, a bartender waited patiently behind a white marble bar with bottles on mirrored shelves stacked to the ceiling. A rushing noise from behind caught Sara's ear; she turned to see a faux stone waterfall scale to a second-floor balcony.

"You've got to be kidding me," she said. "Is there an actual bedroom somewhere in here?"

Mr. Angeli smiled.

"You also have a private exercise facility," he said and started across the room. "5,000 square feet with anything you need day or night, 24/7." They reached a hallway that led to an equally impressive space.

"This is a bedroom?" Sara asked.

"Your bags are on the footboard," Mr. Angeli said.

Sara panned the room, delighted with everything. Especially his hospitality.

"Mr. Angeli," Sara said. "This is too much. I don't know what to say."

"Dinner tonight?" he asked.

Sara knew something was up. He either genuinely appreciated her newfound celebrity, which brought him money, or he wanted to jump her bones, or both. Was he trying to get information from her? Trying to figure out her secret to winning? Whatever the reason, she had his undivided attention and much more. And Sara needed to talk with him about the stalkers, but this was not the time. She was not ready; she needed more time to think it through.

"Thank you," Sara answered. "But I'm exhausted from a long week and travel. How about tomorrow night, after the race?"

"Your pleasure." Angeli nodded, then dismissed himself.

***

Sara unpacked, walked the suite, and saw the bartender was also gone. She found a crystal glass behind the bar and poured herself a bourbon and soda, then stood by the tall window and looked out across the sea of lights. Sara eventually made her way to the leather couch and sat in thought, sipping on the drink. She wondered if she was being watched. Didn't matter.

It would be good to have this man on her side. Stuck in the past and trying to make a difference in the world was dangerous. Someone was already stalking her, and who knew what else could happen. He didn't seem sinister, so why would his people be watching her? Was he that good at playing his hand, or was he genuinely appreciative of her presence? This would take time to figure out. If he could be a trusted ally, she might have to up the ante to keep him on her side. But jumping in bed with him was the last thing she wanted. Sara was still in love with Mason, and even though two years apart left a void inside her, the gap was closing.

Her deliberation continued. She thought about the fact that Mr. Angeli owned a casino and realized what would genuinely interest him. She went back behind the bar, opened a few drawers, found a pen and paper, and sat on a barstool. Sara went over in her mind, again and again, reaching back to childhood, remembering all the finishers for every Triple Crown race. She wrote down the top three finishers for all races from '89 to '95 to visualize and reassure herself. She wrote, scratched out, and re-wrote until the list of finishers finally congealed in her mind and made sense.

That was it, what she needed, five years should do it. With this information in hand, Mr. Angeli could assure the Casino's future, and Sara would stay inconspicuously in the background with a powerful ally for life. But she still had to play her cards right; the timing was everything, if she played them at all.

***

The next day was race day. The Casino was alive with activity as the preliminary races streamed on closed-circuit screens everywhere. By late afternoon, just minutes from the starter's gun, Sara sat alone at a high-stakes table playing blackjack. Mr. Angeli approached and sat next to her with one eye on the screen across the room.

"Not interested in the race?" he asked.

"No, not really," Sara said. "Sunday Silence, Easy Goer, and Awe-Inspiring, in that order. Like an old re-run."

She tapped for another card that quickly slid across the velvet tabletop. Angeli looked at the stack of chips then leaned in to see her cards.

"I already have the house against me," Sara said. "Now, the master of the house, too?"

Angeli grinned. "Just interested in what you do next," he said.

Sara paused, then tapped again, got another card, and motioned to stop. The dealer turned up a king that broke his hand.

"Nice job," Angeli said.

Sara concurred as the dealer pushed more chips her way.

"Excuse me," Angeli said. "I need to step away and watch the run."

The dealer moved the stack of game cards aside and re-loaded the dealer's shoe. Sara motioned for the cocktail server and ordered a drink.

Sara continued to play, ignoring the race. The crowd noise seemed to drift like a rolling tide toward a bank of television screens. She was slightly nervous about the race and what Angeli would think when the results were exactly as she predicted. Didn't really matter now; the race was on. And she was intrigued, like taking a new car out for a spin; this would be the first time her knowledge of the future would be revealed to another person, hopefully, one she could trust.

She sipped on her drink as the dealer dealt out another round of cards. Her mind drifted away from the card game to the greater game she set in motion with Angeli. When would she, or should she, reveal the list kept tightly in her purse? This was unexpected, definitely a gamble, and she was on her own with this one. Her decision and hers alone.

"Ma'am?" the dealer asked.

Sara snapped out of it. She started to respond when Mr. Angeli returned to the table. He motioned for the dealer to step away, then sat next to Sara. He was noticeably confused but kept his composure.

"I guess," Mr. Angeli said, searching for words. "I want to ask you something."

Sara kept her eyes downcast.

Angeli looked away, then back, his dark eyes focused on her concerned face.

"How did you know what would happen?" he asked. "How have you ever known any of this? And why did you throw away $100,000?"

Sara didn't move, then softly responded. "Are there eyes in the sky?" she asked. "Hidden microphones?" She pointed up to cameras and over to the pit boss.

Angeli motioned them away. Sara felt an adrenaline rush come over her.

"It's just you and me," he said.

Sara paused.

"Did you have hobbies as a little boy?" she asked.

"I don't understand," he replied.

"You know," she said. "Collect baseball cards, have a favorite team or player?"

Angeli let out a frustrated sigh.

"I'm trying to explain," Sara said.

"OK," Angeli replied, then pushed out a smile. "The Yankees. I liked Micky Mantle as a kid. But my father, who took me to all the games, always said Joe DiMaggio was the greatest ever; he even gave me a signed baseball."

The tension level dropped.

"He talked about him so much," he continued. "I thought I knew the guy."

"My mother loved horses," Sara said. "Everything about them. She thought they were so pristine, so magnificent, and so innocent. So, I grew up with them, too. Mother always told me about Secretariat. She was even there when he won the Kentucky Derby in '73. At first, it didn't interest me because it happened decades before I was born."

Angeli did some quick math in his head and furrowed his brow. "But eventually," she continued. "I became fascinated with the races, so I memorized the results for all races starting with Secretariat. You know, the way kids do, I made charts, drew portraits of the horses, everything. I cataloged over three decades of race results, always hoping for the next Secretariat, but he never came along, so I lost interest."

More quick math.

"Did you know Secretariat's heart was twice the size of any horse ever?" she said with drifting eyes and sipped her drink.

"Then I grew up and lost interest," she said. "I went off to college, started a life."

Angeli studied her face; she wasn't making this up.

"But when you're young, your mind is like a steel trap," she finished. "And a lot of those memories are ironed into your subconscious. So, it doesn't take much to reconstitute them."

Angeli shook his head in thought.

Sara caught herself, afraid she had said too much. Another rush came over her; she lost her breath. She pushed her stack of chips away, then stood to excuse herself. Angeli leaned back, startled.

"Another donation," she said.

"You seem upset," Angeli said. "Still on for dinner tonight?"

"Sure," Sara replied. "I'll meet you here in an hour."

"At the blackjack table?"

Sara nodded and walked away.

He watched her walk briefly, contemplating their discussion, then motioned to the pit boss. "To the house," he said, pointing to the chips.

Angeli reached for the drink Sara left at the table, sniffed it, took a sip, and sat, statuesque, staring into space.

Chapter 36

Dinner

Sara didn't have long to regroup. Just enough time to make another drink (that she really needed), call down to reserve the same high-stakes table, and change clothes. Sara touched up her face and pulled out an evening dress only worn at casinos. Minutes later, drink in hand, she relaxed on the leather couch to gather her thoughts and take in the incredible view.

In time she reached for the telephone, but heard an unexpected ring, more like a gong, a repeating gong that echoed through the suite. She looked around for a grandfather clock but didn't see one. Then she realized it was a doorbell, the presidential suite had a doorbell, of course, and someone must be ringing it.

She crossed the great room, down the hall, and through the foyer to the entry, where she touched a speaker button on the wall. "Who is it, please?" she asked.

"Guest services," a familiar voice responded.

Sara pushed the 'door open' button, and the large entry door slowly rolled open to reveal Mr. Angeli in a black tuxedo.

"I thought we were meeting in the casino?" Sara questioned.

"Agreed, but then I realized," Angeli said, "when you're in the presidential suite, the casino comes to you."

He made a bowing motion, stepped back, and a team of casino workers paraded through the door with a blackjack table on a rolling cart, followed by a food line of salads, entrées, and desserts. They set the blackjack table in front of the waterfall and a dinner table by the glass wall. After setup, all workers quickly dismissed themselves except for the chef. Sara scanned the spectacle.

"Impressive," she said. "But where's the bartender?"

She was impressed but, at the same time, did not really care. Not her thing and not why she was there.

"You're looking at him," Angeli said. He walked behind the bar, held up a key, and leaned over to unlock a cabinet. "You've been drinking the cheap stuff. How about some 100-year-old bourbon?"

She approached the bar and took a seat. "How did you find 100-year-old bourbon?"

He cracked open the bottle and reached for a shot glass.

"Connections."

He placed the shot in front of her. She reached for it but stopped short. A flashback came to her from the other side when Captain Wales handed her a shot glass on the deck of the assault carrier.

"Something wrong?"

"No." Sara sniffed the bourbon and sipped it. "Very smooth."

"Nothing better," Angeli said.

Sara threw back the shot. Angeli raised an eyebrow.

"On the rocks," she said. "It would be a shame to mix this with anything."

"You don't look like a meat-eater," he said. "So, I have the chef preparing sea bass." Angeli reached for a crystal glass. "You also don't look like a girl that shoots bourbon."

"Is that a question?" Sara asked.

"Maybe."

"I told you I grew up with horses," she said. "Where there are horses, there are bourbon drinkers."

"Where did you grow up?"

Sara heard a flash of fire and turned to see the chef tossing chopped vegetables in a wok. A nice distraction from twenty questions.

"This looks interesting," she said. "Never had sea bass from a wok before."

Snubbed, Angeli offered, "Maybe, we should step over to the dinner table."

They sat at a white cloth table in front of the high bay window. Sara felt pressure mounting but knew she had the upper hand. The chef finished preparing dinner and excused himself. So, it was down to one table, two glasses of bourbon, and two people sitting across from each other with many questions. Angeli took a quick gaze at the city lights, then turned his dark eyes back to Sara.

"You're the most attractive woman I've ever seen," he said. "You're very insightful; you never flinch. But now something's wrong."

Sara calmly sifted chopsticks through her entrée.

"Earlier today, you told me the mind is a steel trap," Angeli said. "Mine is when it comes to numbers. Otherwise, I couldn't run a casino."

Sara reached for her glass.

"I've been going over the numbers in my head, and based on everything you told me this afternoon, it means you were born five to ten years from now."

No answer.

"And obviously, that's impossible, or you wouldn't be sitting here."

No answer.

"I'm waiting."

She took a drink.

"The race results today," Sara said. "Were they exactly as I said they would be? And was I right last summer on all three races?"

No answer. Frustration bubbled up inside Angeli at her evasiveness.

"You know," she said. "I'm really not that hungry." She stood up and walked over to the card table. "Where did the dealer go?" she asked.

A confused Angeli shook his head and followed. "The bartender is the dealer," he replied politely.

Sara pulled up a seat at the blackjack table where $100,000 in chips lay stacked. The dealer's shoe was already filled.

"I assume this is the balance of my reserve account?" Sara asked. "To cover room charges, correct?"

"Only if you lose," he said.

She pulled out two $500 chips for her first bet.

Standing in an unfamiliar position, Mr. Angeli, 'the dealer,' pulled cards from the shoe and dealt out the first round.

Two kings to Sara, and the seven of spades turned up for the dealer.

"Hmm," she said. "I'll split."

She moved the cards side by side, then pushed half her stack of chips in front of one card and the rest in front of the other. Angeli looked puzzled.

"Might be a short night," he said. "Do you want to lose another $100,000?"

"We'll see."

He pulled the five of hearts for the first hand and the two of diamonds for the second.

Sara tapped for another card and got an eight of hearts for the first hand: bust. The next card out was another king: bust.

Mr. Angeli sighed and shook his head.

"I still don't understand why you came back here," he asked. "Why you're throwing money away, and now this?"

"I don't care about money," she replied, took another sip, and stared at her cards. "I need information."

Angeli was taken aback. "What kind of information?"

Sara looked nervous and fidgeted in her seat. "I'm being followed," she said. "Once in a while, I see men in black suits following me. Do you know why they would do that?"

"That's not me," Angeli was stung by the accusation.

Sara smirked.

"No, seriously, that's not me."

Sara paused. "Then we're even?"

"Well, not even," Angeli said, staring at the pile of chips on the dealer's side. "But the wound is healing."

Sara took another drink.

"You know what I think?" Angeli said. "Maybe it's the Feds."

"The Feds?" Sara frowned.

"Maybe they think you didn't pay all your taxes," Angeli said. "You're not into anything else, are you? I mean, you seem like a high-class lady, always have."

Sara felt chills. This was not expected. If not the casino, then who? Big Oil? The Feds? The military? Another time traveler? Now things were worse.

A long silence followed, with each studying the other's face. *Has she really been telling me the truth?* Angeli wondered. *Can she really be from the future?*

I know he's a casino owner, Sara thought, *but he is a straight shooter, probably since I'm a casino celebrity, whatever that means? Why would he lie when he clearly makes money from my presence? I think I can trust him; I need to trust him.*

She took a deep breath, reached for her purse, pulled out a folded piece of paper, and slid it across the table.

"These are the last ones I can remember," Sara said. "After that, it gets fuzzy."

Angeli stared down the paper before picking it up, then gazed at Sara as he reached for it. He studied the unfolded paper, then looked back at her.

"Hmm, '95, as in 1995?" he asked. "Six years from now?"

Sara nodded.

"How can you know these results?" Angeli asked. "Even the names, when the horses aren't alive yet?"

"You can't always play those horses," Sara replied. "Sometimes you have to lose, or people will get suspicious."

He looked back at the paper. "So, you saw these races?"

"No, they all happened before I was born." Sara grimaced. "Kind of like you and DiMaggio."

"This is just not possible, and you expect me to believe this?" Angeli snapped, then paused. He was a businessman in a world where everything had to stack up and make sense. "OK, I believe something has happened to you, maybe not time travel, but something has happened to you, and it's a gift. A hard knock on the head would be easier for me to believe, so I'll stick with that."

More silence. Angeli paced for a bit, then sat on a rock by the faux waterfall.

"Why did you give me this?" he asked, holding up the paper.

Sara's eyes drifted, then turned back to Angeli. "If there ever comes a time when I need help," she replied. "Would you help me?"

Angeli couched his response. "Depends," he said.

"On what?"

"I'm not sure," he said. "I guess it depends on what kind of trouble you're in."

Sara dropped her head.

"But if there is something I can do," he said. "Then sure, absolutely."

That was reassuring, a sort of foundation, like the rock he sat on. Angeli committed to something that lifted her spirits. When she'd come to Las Vegas, Sara was sure he was the man watching her, but now she knew he was not, and he had her back if she needed it.

She broke out a smile. "Thank you."

Angeli excused himself and walked to the entry.

"You know," Sara followed. "I wasn't sure what to expect when I came out here. But I'm glad I did."

Angeli turned as he reached the door. "You were looking for answers," he said. "And you found some. Maybe not the ones you wanted. But consider this, now that you have lost, the public will see you differently. All the fanfare will die out, and maybe the men following you will, too."

"You're a good man," she said. "I thought you would be the kind that wanted something else."

Angeli looked at her, "Even I could not violate an angel sent from heaven." He tapped the 'open door' button.

She hugged him before he walked away.

***

The following day, Sara called for a cab and made her way to the lobby, bags in tow. Mr. Angeli, greeting a busload of tourists, did a double take when he saw her heading toward the exit. He quickly snapped his fingers and pointed the bellmen her way. Before she made it to the door, they reached for her bags. She graciously accepted and followed them out to the porte cochère.

"Is this how you normally dress?" Mr. Angeli asked.

Sara turned. "This is it," she replied with lifted arms, wearing jeans, a brown suede jacket, and hair pulled back in a ponytail. "And it really feels good to cut through a crowd around here unnoticed since I'm not a celebrity anymore."

"Only to some," Angeli said. "Looks like you're ready to ride off into the sunset."

"Maybe not yet," she said. "But a short ride at sunset might be in order."

"So, you do have horses?"

"Oh, yes."

"Did you call down for transportation?"

"A cab is on the way."

Mr. Angeli furrowed his brow and snapped his fingers. "The lady needs a ride," he said to the bellman. "To the airport?"

"Right."

"Ladies don't ride in cabs," Angeli pointed out.

Sara beamed. "Thank you for everything."

"No," Angeli said. "Thank you. It was truly, my pleasure."

The limousine pulled up, the bellmen took her bags, and Mr. Angeli helped her inside.

"Come see us again," Angeli said. He double tapped the top of the limo and watched her pull away as his mind drifted.

"Anything else, sir?" the bellman asked.

Angeli re-grouped. "No," he said. "Everything's fine."

Chapter 37

The Winemaker

A chartered Learjet made a smooth landing on the Paso Robles runway and taxied up to an open hanger. The pilot opened the exit door, and a drop-down stair unfolded. Sara stepped out, looking for Mason; at first, she looked toward the terminal but didn't see him. An anxious feeling came over her, then someone cleared his throat, and there, Mason stood below with one hand on the ladder. He offered a hand and helped her down the steps. She was so relieved to be back, and her face showed it. The pilot followed with her bags as Sara and Mason embraced.

"How did it go?" Mason asked.

"We'll talk about it in the car," Sara said as they walked toward a one-story masonry block terminal. "By the way, how did you get out here? I thought only pilots and passengers were allowed on the tarmac."

"I just made a waving motion and walked out the door," Mason replied. "The attendant started to say something, but he recognized me and stopped short."

"How did he recognize you?"

Mason nervously scratched his head. "Remember that bar fight I got into?"

"Yes."

"He lost."

Sara suddenly felt surprised and embarrassed since she always got special favors from the airport. Whenever she needed a plane, it was available. And the man with a bandaged nose, staring out the window at her, was responsible.

Mason reached for the door; Sara stepped across the threshold and felt an uneasy tension. She stopped and turned to the attendant. "I would like to apologize," she said. "For my friend starting a fight with you."

The attendant was speechless. Mason kept moving.

"Mason, stop!" she let out. "I want you to apologize to this man for what you just told me."

Mason shrugged with a boyishly defeated look.

"Now!" she shouted.

"Ma'am, that's not necessary," the attendant said. He was more worried about losing a premier client and getting fired. "It was my fault anyway."

"Yes, it is necessary," Sara said. "You two shake hands and make-up."

The pilot, holding the bags, did not know what to think.

Mason reluctantly reached a hand across the counter, and the attendant did the same. They exchanged apologies.

"I hope you both meant that," Sara said. "Sometimes, I just can't understand male ego."

Both men nodded. The pilot still looked confused.

"No more whiskey and no more bar fights," Sara ordered and walked off.

Mason grabbed her bags from the pilot and hurried away.

A disgusted Sara hopped into the Jeep. Mason threw her bags in the back.

"Would it help to know he started the fight?" Mason asked and turned the ignition.

"No, it would not," Sara replied. "This place has always taken care of me. If I need a plane, it's there. But now, who knows?"

Mason pulled away. "At the time, I didn't even know you were alive," he said. "My world had crashed, and I had more to think about than ruining a business relationship."

Sara was still ticked off but realized she had lost sight of that one. She had been here for so long it seemed forever, but Mason had just arrived. She calmed down. "That's still no excuse," she said.

"I understand," Mason said, "and I'm sorry."

***

They wound through the Cholame Hills in the bright midday sun. The conversation turned to Las Vegas, how she intentionally lost on the horses and found an ally in Mr. Angeli.

"Damn," Mason said. "Wish I could have seen that presidential suite."

"Is that all you have to say?" Sara asked.

"No, not all," Mason replied, then thought about it. "So, you really think you can trust that guy?"

"Yes, I do," she said. "He believes I can predict race results. And after the Preakness and Belmont, there will be no doubt."

Mason sighed.

"I'm just not sure how this plays out," he said. "I hope you made the right decision."

"Me too."

∗∗∗

They came up to the 'Second Chance Ranch' sign and turned on the dirt road. When they reached the top of the first rise, a flash of light caught Sara's eye.

"Did you see that?" she asked. The Jeep continued down the hill.

"See what?"

"A flash of light," Sara replied. "You can't see it now, just wait till the next rise."

Eventually, a helicopter came into view, sitting next to Sara's house. Obviously, it had landed some time ago since there was no dust in the air. It was definitely not a government issue; it had a more elegant appearance, painted shiny black with blue stripes. Two guards in uniform stood next to it, definitely civilian, probably corporate.

They pulled to a stop in front of the house. Sara hopped out and stared down at the guards, who paid no attention to her. She quickly made for the house, pulling a key from a coat pocket. Sara turned the deadbolt and hurried inside. She cut through the living room, then down the hallway to the bedrooms and back out—no one there. Mason was peering out the back window when she made her way to the kitchen. She walked up next to him and saw a man sitting at the backyard table under the umbrella drinking wine, her wine from her cupboard; she recognized the bottle. In his late thirties or early forties, he was well dressed, with dark, combed-back hair. His gaze focused on the wine barn, away from the house.

"Is this the serpent?" Mason asked, below his breath. "The one you've been spooked about?"

Something inside Sara exploded. She bolted to the door, swung it back, and threw open the screen. Two retrievers sprang from hiding in the horse barn and ran to Sara's side. No reaction from the stranger.

"Who are you?" she demanded. "And why are you here?"

Still no reaction.

"Good wine," he slowly let out. He remained undistracted by Sara's presence, focused on the wine barn. "You should try it."

No reaction from Sara.

"Please, have a seat." He motioned toward the chair opposite him.

"My wine," Sara said. "My label. Of course, I've tried it."

"Not this one," the man replied. "It's made just for me."

Sara grabbed a bottle and studied the label. All bottles on the table, with different vintages, had the same 'Special Reserve' label across the top.

"Where did you get these?" She turned to the wine barn. "Henri would never go behind my back."

"Please." The man gestured again. "Have a seat."

Sara grabbed a chair, retrievers at her feet, and studied the man's stoic face. Mason approached; his gaze fixed on the two guards.

"You first caught my attention with the trifecta bet in last year's Kentucky Derby," the man calmly said. "My curiosity was piqued when you picked more winners at the Preakness and Belmont. At Belmont, you had the audacity to pick another trifecta."

Sara didn't move.

"All in all," the man continued, swirling his wine. "You took in $12,242,123 from four different casinos under the alias, Sara Prada. At least you spread their losses. Although Caesar's did dole out the lion's share."

He sniffed the wine and took a sip. "But it was nice of you to give some back yesterday."

Sara said nothing.

"And all this from a woman with no past," he queried. "And no identity. Well, no real identity."

The man swirled glass and sniffed the wine.

"You came from nowhere, with no money, made a fortune, then hid away in these beautiful hills," he said. "But now you reach out to lose money."

He thought about it.

"To ensure your anonymity?" he asked.

Sara was getting nervous.

"And then two more accomplices magically appear; from the desert, no less," he continued. "You and the others all have fake but remarkably impressive identifications. And the young one has very high-tech devices."

"How do you know that?" Sara asked. Ethan was up in the valley, and fortunately, his cell phone and laptop were not with him. So, she knew he did not have them. Hopefully, they had not gotten to Ethan. She would find out at five today.

"Is that how you manipulate betting?" the man asked. "What shall I call them, 'Enigma Machines?'"

"They're not Nazi code breaking machines," Sara scoffed. "But you act like a Nazi."

The man didn't acknowledge that comment, still in process.

"Why does she continue to wield this power?" he asked, speaking to himself. "And this time to shoot herself in the foot."

Sara started to say something.

"I'm sorry, I've been very impolite," the man said. He stood and adjusted his jacket. "I should introduce myself. My name is Arthur Melton, owner, and steward, of Hearst Castle."

Sara shook her head. "So, why are you here?" Sara asked. "Why all the cloak and dagger? And why are your men following me?"

"Information," Melton replied. "One does not obtain wealth and stature by doing things the usual way. Cutting edge ideas, bold moves, pushing oneself to the limit—that's how it's always done. Timing and a little luck along the way help, too. And, of course, there are always random lottery winners that do nothing and one day stumble into a fortune. But you, my dear, you are of an entirely different ilk."

Sara knew he was on to her, but he didn't have all the information he was looking for, so she let him go on.

"Being a successful man myself," he said. "I study other men's careers to learn their secrets, how they get to be where they are and what pushed them to get there. And it always follows a similar curve… until you. You, Sara, have re-defined the curve."

His concentrated eyes turned to Sara, she knew he had finished speaking and wanted some answers, but she refused to bend to his pressure.

"Why did Henri go behind my back and make these bottles?" she asked.

"You are of a strong will, Sara," Melton said. "No matter." He took another sip. "He works for me."

"For you?"

"Yes," Melton replied. "When you posted a large ad in local newspapers for a winemaker, I thought 'this is it.' I have one of the best in the business at Hearst Castle, so I inserted him. Not as a spy, because Henri is an honest man and would never stoop so low as espionage. Just to listen and report if he heard anything unusual."

Sara leaned up in her chair. "And what did he report?"

"Nothing," Melton replied. "Until him." He pointed to Mason. "Until he arrived, I was losing interest. In fact, I had lost all interest and was ready to pull Henri from your employ. But the events of the last few weeks have changed everything."

Sara took some time to respond. Melton poured her a glass of reserve.

"Look," she said. "If Henri told you anything about me or my character, you know another thing for your curve. It's that I'm an honest, genuine person. I'm not a witch or a conjuror of magical powers." She wiggled her fingers in the air with that.

"But my circumstances are unique, and those machines you mentioned have nothing to do with it. They're just machines."

Melton swirled his glass.

"I can't tell you how I know the things I know," she sighed. "But I can tell you I'll never place another bet. My financial future is all that you see around you. It's all in the vines."

Melton considered her words.

"We're both still relatively young," he said. "A lot of things can change on life's journey. And you still have a power, whether magical or mechanical, I do not know."

He took a last sip of wine and stood to excuse himself. "Take care of yourself, Sara," Melton said. "Come visit me at the Castle sometime if you'd like a tour."

Sara felt relief and confusion, all at the same time. "So, how did you acquire Hearst Castle?" she asked.

"Many people in high places owe me favors," Melton replied. "I purchased it from the state a few years ago at a reasonable price."

Melton made his way toward the helicopter but stopped short and turned back to Sara. "*Valdez!*" he shouted above churning helicopter blades. "Why did you go to *Valdez*? No casino there."

No response.

He and Sara stood in a fixed, speechless gaze.

Then he turned back to the helicopter and swirled his finger. The sleek chopper lifted to the sky and headed west. Sara watched it clear the tree line.

"The wine cellar!" she shouted.

Mason ran for the wine barn, then heard the kitchen screen door slam shut. He stopped and realized Sara had gone the other way. He ran back to the house and saw Sara moving chairs away from the kitchen table.

"Help me with this," she said.

They lifted the table, moved it aside, then rolled up the rug below.

"A trap door?" Mason asked, half-joking.

"Hey, don't laugh," Sara replied. "It's been here for a hundred years. Dirt floor and all."

Mason lifted an inset handle and pulled the door open. Sara grabbed a broom hung from the pantry door, quickly descended a tight staircase, and drew an overhead light string at the bottom.

"No footprints," she said, scanning the room. "He didn't find it."

"Dirt floor comes in handy," Mason said. "A built-in surveillance system."

"I don't come down here often," she said. "But I always broom the dirt as I back out to cover my tracks."

The basement was sizable for an old cellar. Complete with wine racks, an old safe, and a chopping-block table.

"There's no way they got some of this stuff down that staircase," Mason said. "Probably hoisted them down before the floor was finished."

Sara studied the bottles in the racks; nothing touched there. Then opened the safe.

"Deeds, titles, a stack of cash, and my Colt .45, all here," she said. She bent over, pulled a box from the bottom shelf, and flipped it open. "Ethan's computer, cell phone, and power cords are all here. He didn't find the safe. If he was even looking for it."

"So, what now?" Mason asked.

"We have a secure hiding place for Ethan's computer," Sara said. "But we're being watched, and Ethan's probably being watched, so he needs to get back here to go over what's happened."

Sara checked her watch—three o'clock.

"He is supposed to call me at five," she said. "Let's head into town, grab a bite to eat, and wait for his call."

First Angeli and now Melton. What have I gotten myself into?

PART 6

Chapter 38
The Next Step

Sunday afternoon, Ethan sat on a couch in his apartment, studying Sara's scratched-out note. *How did we ever get into this?* He checked the time—half-past four. He looked at the touch-tone phone, hanging on the wall with its long, coiled cord. He'd ordered pizza last night, but he thought about trying a payphone today, like Sara. He had never used a payphone before, but it gave them complete anonymity.

He grabbed a handful of change, stuffed it into his pocket, and headed out. A few minutes before five, when he got to the phone booth, he checked his new wristwatch and waited. The last thing he wanted was to call early, or late, and hear it from Sara, who had a big sister way with him. He didn't want to screw up.

Mason and Sara pulled into a local sandwich shop and grabbed a couple subs, then parked at the grocery store within earshot of the phone booth.

"What time is it?" Mason asked.

"Almost five," Sara said, checking her watch. "I still can't get used to wearing this on my wrist."

"Yeah, but it is kind of cool," Mason admitted. "I need to get one, too."

A few bites later, they heard the phone ring. Sara hopped out of the car. Mason sat with a sandwich in hand.

"Hello?" She picked up the phone.

"Sara?" Ethan tested.

"Did you get your apartment set up?"

"Yes, all good."

"What about your job?" Sara asked. "Did you get started at Integral Technologies yet?"

"Yes, Thursday and Friday," Ethan said. "They showed me around the first day, described what I'd be working on, and took me to see the mainframe. It's a Cray. It's nothing like the machine in Perishton, but hopefully, I can work with it. Nice people at Integral Technologies, so I think I'll blend in easily."

"So, what do you think? Sara asked.

"I'm starting out at ground level," he replied. "So, I'm kind of working on the periphery. Eventually, I will get some level of access to the Cray."

He paused.

"But the thing is, Sara, this will take time, a long time to figure out. I think I should come back next weekend and ..."

"Hey," Sara nervously cut him off. "You need to come back this evening."

"Excuse me?"

"There are a few things we need to go over," she said. "Some new developments."

***

Julia Gathers sipped tea at her home in the hills overlooking the San Francisco Bay. The letter from Ethan Sites lay on a coffee table in front of her. A letter she had reread time after time. The sun was setting on the day after the Kentucky Derby as she pondered the double meaning in the letter. She panned across the bay, and from one end to the other. Visibility was as good as ever, but it was Sunday, no pollution from commuter traffic.

The mysterious letter had suddenly taken on a new light with Saturday's shocking race results. Julia had been caught in a web of confusion ever since the horses crossed the line and the results appeared on television. She couldn't shake the eerie feeling. Was it real, not a prank? And now she wondered if, and when, Ethan Sites would contact her again.

***

It was dark when Sara heard the Impala crunching up the gravel driveway. Its headlights veered around the house and found their way to the wine barn. The car parked, its engine turned off, and Ethan appeared from a settling dust cloud, satchel and all.

Sara pushed open the kitchen door and stepped out with a bottle of wine. Mason followed with a bowl of spaghetti.

"OK, I'm here," Ethan said as two retrievers ran up to his feet. "So, what's the big deal?"

"The car looks a little dirty," she observed.

"And?"

Mason chuckled; the retrievers ran to Sara.

"So, what's up?" Ethan repeated.

"Right now, dinner," Sara replied. "Go inside and wash up, then grab plates and silverware. We'll talk later."

"Oh, OK." Ethan went into the kitchen but stopped short. The table and chairs were pushed aside, and a large trap door propped open. Confused, Ethan peered down inside. He thought about it momentarily, then re-grouped and reached for the silverware.

Sara had poured the wine when Ethan returned with plates in hand. He turned and pointed to the kitchen.

"I'm hungry, kid," Mason said and grabbed the plates.

"I assume," Ethan asked. "The creepy basement in there has something to do with why I'm back here."

"When I returned from the airport this morning," Sara replied. "A helicopter was parked in the side yard, and a man was seated at this table, and he knew a lot about us. Me, you two walking out of the desert, and your computer. And it turns out Henri worked for him."

"The winemaker?" Ethan asked. He reached for a piece of bread and took a scoop of spaghetti.

"He's an eccentric who has interest in me," Sara continued. "And what I'm up to."

Ethan put his fork down.

"This is a game-changer," Sara said. "With eyes on us like this, I think we should pull you back from your job and lay low for a while. Stay here and write down the critical information we need for the next few months."

"Makes sense," Ethan said. "By the way, direct access to plug the laptop into a mainframe is way above my paygrade. The only way until then is to use a telephone-line hook-up. I ran some numbers, and it will take years to download and print a five-gig file using telephone lines.

"This is just going to take more time than I first thought. We jumped into this like it was super-critical, but we do have some time to work this out."

"Like after the October earthquake?" Sara asked.

"Exactly," Ethan responded. "In the meantime, I'll transfer data from the laptop to the cell phone, so we have it in two sources."

"Good thinking, and we need to separate them," Sara said. "Until you have access to that mainframe."

"OK, so the helicopter guy," Ethan said. "What else did he say?"

"We'll talk about it after dinner," Sara replied.

They re-grouped in the kitchen and took Ethan down to the cellar. Sara showed him the vault, computer and all. Ethan was concerned about moisture in the basement affecting his equipment. Still, he found no signs of water infiltration, no mold on the wood framing, no calcium deposits on the walls, and the dusty dirt floor was another good sign. Afterward, they put the kitchen back together and sat down to discuss.

"We have three things to work out," Sara said. "What we do in the fall, how we do it, and the next contact with my mother. So, flip open your computer and look at that data file on natural disasters."

Ethan had the file open in no time and accessed the year 1989. It listed a handful of events, but most importantly, he found the October earthquake Sara was spooked about:

> Loma Prieta EQ
> Location: Nisene Marks State Park, CA
> Santa Cruz section of the San Andreas Fault
> Date: October 17, 1989, at 5:04 pm

Magnitude: 6.9
Duration: 8-15 seconds
Peak Acceleration: 0.65g
Type: Oblique-slip reverse
Estimated Damage: $6.0B
Injuries: 3,757
Deaths: 63

Sections of a 1.25-mile stretch of the double-decker Cypress Street Viaduct in Oakland collapsed, killing 42. The photographs were frightening.

A map of the collapse study showed the old double-deck bridge pathway that extended from 6th Street in the south to the MacArthur Maze in the north. The study had an overlay listing from the original 1950's engineering documents showing the bridge as individual bents (or sections). It described the collapsed length of the bridge from bent 63 at 16th Street up to bent 112 at 34th Street.

Cypress Street Viaduct

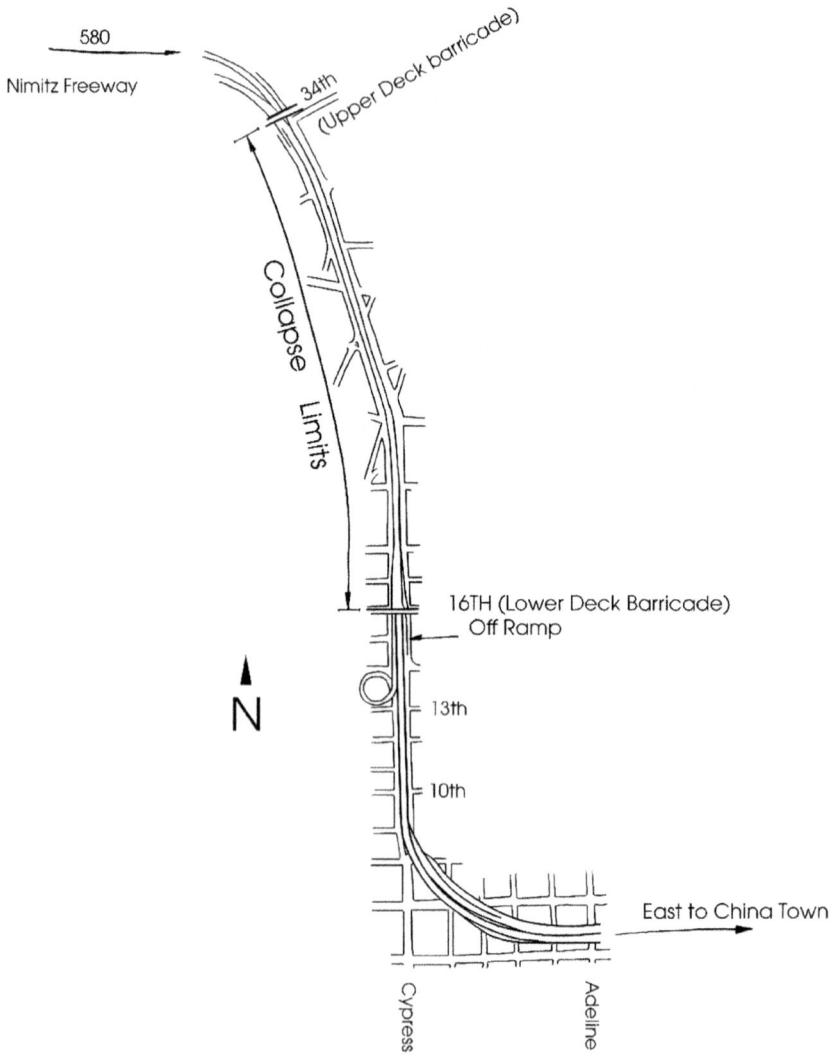

"I've only heard stories about this," Mason said. "How people in nearby businesses and neighborhoods brought out ladders, trucks, you name it, to search for survivors. They got drivers off the upper deck, but cars below were smashed. Nothing they could do."

"Look." Sara pointed to the map. "It's the Mandela Parkway. This bridge used to be there."

Ethan pulled up collapse pictures of crumbled columns and folded bridge decks. Cars pinched in half like mud under the boot, one end flattened, and the other sprouted up. Panic ladders lined the wrecked structure for miles while smoke billowed out between the pancaked concrete layers.

"People were in those cars," Sara said.

"Ain't no way to die," Mason murmured.

They panned through picture after picture, taking in the enormity of the disaster. The scene was a war zone.

"We're going to stop this," Sara said.

Ethan turned to Sara.

"How?"

"Cars," she answered. "Lots of cars."

Mason and Ethan leaned back in their chairs, wheels turning.

"Ethan, can you go back to the plans again?" Sara asked. "The drawing of the bridge. We need to know how to access it, on and off-ramps, how traffic flows, and how many lanes."

Ethan flipped back to the document and zoomed in on the bridge plan. The upper deck had directional arrows pointing south toward China Town, arrows on the lower deck pointed north toward the MacArthur Maze.

"Here we go," Ethan said. "The upper deck is one way south, all four lanes. And the lower deck is four lanes, too, but one way north. It looks like we can enter the south ramp at 16th Street, just two blocks from bent 63."

"Where the collapse begins," Sara said.

"That's right," Ethan replied. "And from the north, you come into the upper deck from Interstate 580."

"So, the upper deck is accessed from the MacArthur Freeway," Sara said. "And spills out in China Town. The lower deck is accessed at 14th Street and drops off at the MacArthur Maze."

"So, where are you going with this?" Mason asked.

"Now we know exactly when this bridge collapses," she replied. "And the extent of the collapse."

She studied the bridge plan on the computer screen.

"We will stop traffic on both decks," she said. "Minutes before the earthquake, so no one gets hurt."

"Don't we need permission for that?" Ethan asked. "It sounds dangerous. I mean, isn't there another way?"

"I learned the hard way," Sara said. "You can't reason with people and hope they make the better choice. You have to take action."

"We'll need at least four cars on each deck to stop traffic. This happens during rush hour, so we can't mess up the timing. We also need lead vehicles to get off the bridge. That means a minimum of ten drivers, all committed to the cause, and we have three here, so seven more."

Ethan looked scared.

"That's a fleet," Mason said. "We'll have to rent them."

"Or buy them," Sara followed. "That way, I can use cash. We go to used car lots or buy from individuals, so there is no paper trail. Then strip the registration numbers."

"What about license plates?" Mason asked.

"We pull them after we stop on the freeway," she said. "And take them with us, along with the keys."

"How long have you been planning this?" Mason asked.

"A long time," Sara replied. "The lead vehicle will have to be sizable, so four people can jump in easily," she continued.

"OK," Ethan said. "Then who are the other seven drivers?"

"The guys working here in the fields," Sara answered. "They'll do anything I ask, especially if it's for a good cause."

"Do they know about this yet?"

"No, not yet."

"Hey, look," Ethan said. "It says here the quake hit just before a World Series game at Candlestick Park between the Giants and the A's, so the game was canceled, no one hurt. But on the Bay Bridge, one section of the upper deck on the eastern side collapsed, resulting in one death."

"Let me see that," Sara said. She panned down through the picture file, and there it was, an upper section of the bridge dropped down onto the lower deck at a support tower for the first trestle bridge.

"We need more cars." Sara sighed.

"And drivers," Ethan said.

***

Julia pulled Ethan's letter from a desk drawer and set it aside. There was no move she could make; that letter was a prod, an introduction. The incredible race results proved it was no prank, so she would hear from him again.

She stared down a stack of exams to grade on one side of her desk and a pile of unopened mail on the other. She flipped through the mail, sorted bills and official letters, then tossed the junk. Something in her mind hoped for another letter from Ethan, but no such luck.

She started to reach for the exams when something caught her eye, a light on her desktop phone. She hit the message button.

"Dr. Gathers," the voice said. "Arnie Wilmore here with NOAA. I'm familiar with your work and would like to speak with you about coming on board with us. Our organization has a very bright future, and we're looking for people like yourself to help us expand. We're opening up a new division, studying the effects of climate change, and I think it's right up your alley.

"Anyway, I recently mailed you a letter with information about us and my direct line. Please reach out with any questions you may have. Hope to hear from you soon."

NOAA? Someone else from NOAA reaching out? How odd. She flipped through the stack of mail and found it. The return label was nothing like the letter from Ethan Sites, so it hadn't caught her eye at first.

Julia knew the organization only on the surface, had no personal contacts, and never read their work. The letter described their operations based out of Boulder, Colorado. The National Oceanic and Atmospheric Administration studied space weather and Auroras, measured sea level rise, tracked hurricanes, and checked a wide range of marine activities and climate studies.

She remembered her work with the EPA, how they'd reached out for help and how volatile a political issue it became. What she'd expected to be a research project for the public good turned out to be a battle, indeed a battle, between her and the U.S. military. The experience left her exhausted and grateful for her position at the university, where she gladly returned. But eventually, she felt something was missing, and the life of academia, though rewarding, had its limitations.

Maybe it was time for a change. Julia looked at the stack of exams on her desk, then leaned back in her chair and thought about it.

Why two completely unrelated letters from NOAA? One with supernatural overtones and the other from a head-hunter. Coincidence?

***

The Bay Bridge was five lanes wide top and bottom, so they needed ten cars and two lead cars for that one. Now Sara had to find twenty-two drivers to pull it off. She considered the options; was there another way to stop traffic quickly and safely? They read on.

"Wait a minute, it says here, the bay bridge death happened after the earthquake," Sara said. "A confused driver didn't see the collapsed section and drove off the upper deck."

"And?" Mason asked.

"So, we only have to block the upper deck," Ethan replied. "Six more drivers."

Sara thought about it. "Unless we try something different," she said.

"Like what?"

"Look." Sara paced. "The Cypress Street Viaduct collapse killed forty-two people during the earthquake, so it must be blocked off completely. But the Bay Bridge is something different, one death after the earthquake and from the upper deck. Couldn't we just block it off with one semi-trailer? Then, we only need two more drivers, one in the semi and one in the lead car."

"Why not use semis for both bridges?" Mason asked.

"That seems too dangerous, less reliable," Sara replied. "The viaduct is curvy and more congested. Maneuvering a semi-trailer on that freeway could be tricky, and we have no room for error. But the Bay Bridge is straight, so it just makes more sense we could do it."

"Who's going to drive it?"

Sara stopped and thought about it. "It's still five months away," she said. "We have plenty of time to work on the details."

"What about other deaths from the earthquake that didn't happen on bridges?" Ethan asked.

"Two-thirds of the deaths were on the Cypress Street Viaduct," Sara said. "You can do your research, but you'll probably find that collapsed residential buildings caused the balance."

"So, all we have to do is ..."

"Warn them?" Sara interrupted. "Tell anyone in California about an earthquake tomorrow, and all you'll get 'What else is new.' They just won't believe you."

"And by the way, we can't get caught, we can't go around telling everyone about future events. We have to focus on the bigger picture."

Ethan hung his head.

"Only my mother," Sara said. "And possibly a couple others will know in advance."

"In the meantime, Mason, I need you to start buying used cars."

Sara blew the dust off an old bottle of Cabernet she found in the cellar and reached for a corkscrew.

"The man that landed in the side yard was Arthur Melton," she told Ethan. "The self-proclaimed 'Steward of Hearst Castle.' He's very eccentric, egotistical, and wealthy. And for some reason, he's interested in me and what we're up to. I'd be more concerned if we were still in the Internet age and your cell phone actually worked. But since we're not and our communications are somewhat muted, we just go about our business and watch our backs.

"He knew about my trip to Las Vegas last year. How much I won at each casino, including this weekend. He seems most interested in how I acquire wealth."

"And what if he keeps nosing around?" Mason asked.

"He's not with the government," Sara said. "He has no legal or police powers, so he can't really do anything. Not to mention we're not doing anything illegal. So, again, I say we stay the course but keep a cautious eye.

"Ethan, did you notice anyone up in Sunnyvale watching you near your apartment or work?"

"I wasn't looking for that," he said. "But nothing suspicious. Even the pizza delivery guy was a high school kid, and he was in a hurry.

"Maybe this Melton guy doesn't know about my job. If you didn't tell him, then he might not know."

"We can't risk a noticeable connection between you and the high-tech world," Sara said. "I'm sure he'll track that sooner or later. But we can't mess up this plan, and the last thing we need is to give this guy more reason to keep snooping around."

Sara paused again before continuing. "On a different topic," she said. "We need to work on a second letter to my mother and then plan to meet with her. The Preakness is less than two weeks away. If we gave her race predictions and something else about future natural disasters, the hook might set in. See what else you can find in there."

Ethan flipped through the laptop data and found a September Hurricane.

Hurricane Hugo
Landfall: Sullivan's Island, SC
Date: September 22, 1989, at Midnight
Category: 5 (Saffir-Simpson scale)
Estimated Damage: $11 B
Deaths: 67

"So, one month before the earthquake, the east coast gets hit with a category five hurricane," Sara said. "OK then, we add that into the letter."

"And what about meeting her?" Ethan said. "Do I add that, too?"

"I don't think so."

Chapter 39

Believe it or not

A week before the Preakness, Julia received another letter from Ethan, and as she watched the race unfold, she wondered how this was possible. She was not excited about horse races for the first time in her life; now, she was spooked by them. And why did the letter mention a September hurricane?

Monday morning, she packed up and headed for campus. Mondays were good days for Julia. She liked walking on campus; it took her mind off things and brought her into focus. It was the last week of class, and she planned a refresher lecture for the students in her morning class, but she was not prepared after the distractions from Saturday's race. No worries, it was a first-year course on the importance of protecting the environment and the side effects of global warming, stuff she knew by heart.

The lecture went off as expected, and Julia followed with her customary comment that any questions could be brought up to the podium afterward.

Half a dozen kids approached her, most of them good students seeking more tidbits of information. In a few short minutes, they were on their way. Julia packed her suitcase, then noticed another student approaching.

"I'm sorry," Julia said. "But I don't recognize you. Are you part of my class?"

The man stood half-dazed before responding.

"I'm sorry, too," he replied, fumbling for words. "And no, I'm not part of your class."

Julia raised her eyebrows in anticipation, still no response.

"I have another class to teach," she said and started away.

"I'm Ethan," the man said and bashfully looked away. He didn't know what came over him, but Julia had a striking resemblance to Sara and was even more lovely.

Julia stopped in her tracks and turned. *This is a young boy*, she thought. *How could a young boy know the things he wrote about?* They studied each other.

"I'm so sorry to interrupt your life like this," Ethan offered. "Umm."

No response.

"Maybe," he suggested, "I can walk with you to your next class, and we can talk along the way?"

Julia thought about it and nodded.

They exited the lecture hall and walked out onto a grass-covered courtyard between buildings. Students with backpacks bustled between classes; some were sitting beneath trees and others reading on park benches.

"I guess I want to say, you first," Ethan said.

Julia contemplated. "No one can predict a Trifecta," Julia said. "And certainly not twice in one month."

She paused while a group of students passed.

"And simultaneously, you write about future environmental problems," she continued. "Hardly similar topics, so one is obviously a hook."

She looked at Ethan. "Your turn."

Ethan took a breath. "I need you to believe me," he said. "And yes, the races were a hook."

"So, what else do you know about the future?" Julia smirked. Her mocking tone stung Ethan.

"Unfortunately," he responded, "everything." He brushed a hand through his hair nervously.

"Are you willing to tell me how you know these things?" Julia asked.

Ethan sighed.

"Because that would seem to be an essential first step to gain my confidence."

Ethan locked up under pressure. He felt as unprepared as some of the sleeping students in Julia's lecture. He'd thought this would be easier, but Julia, like her daughter, was very inquisitive and to the point—intimidating.

"I can't tell you that," he said. "But I can tell you how I got here, and the reasons I'm here are way more unbelievable than simply picking two trifectas."

Julia redirected. "Your first letter seemed to say that you needed me to save the world," she said. "Save it from natural disasters or something like that."

Ethan nodded in agreement.

"So, how am I supposed to summon the future?" she asked.

Another reflective break.

"Because you're only twenty-nine years old right now," Ethan said. "And there's still a lot of time before ..."

A loud gong rang out across campus.

"I'm late," Julia said and started away.

"Can we meet again?" Ethan asked.

Julia checked her watch. "I wrap up today after lunch," Julia replied. "I can meet you here."

"Here, in the courtyard?" Ethan said. "OK, thank you."

***

Ethan paced around a park bench, sat for a bit, then stood, paced some more, and checked his watch against the clock tower. It was half past one, and no sign of Julia. He took a seat and waited.

"Sorry, I'm a bit past my time," a voice came from behind.

Ethan turned to see Julia sporting a beret and purse. "I was afraid you'd changed your mind," he said, beaming.

"Not at all," Julia said. "There's a café not far from here. It's never crowded and a good place for conversation."

"Sounds good."

"We can take my car," Julia said.

They made their way to a small place off-campus, away from the college crowd. The hostess seemed happy to see Julia and greeted her by name. The only other guests were seated outside, so Julia requested an inside table by the window.

"I can't help but notice," she said. "You keep staring at me."

"Oh, I'm sorry," Ethan answered, boyishly shy. "But you remind me of someone."

"It's all right," she said. "I get that a lot."

A server brought water and menus.

"According to your letterhead," Julia said. "You work for NOAA in Alaska."

"Is that a question?"

"This whole conversation is a question," Julia replied.

"Yes," Ethan said. "Until recently."

"And between recently and now?"

Ethan sighed.

"You said I was *only* twenty-nine years old," Julia asked. "How do you know that? And you also said there's still a lot of time."

Julia was searching for a connection between Ethan and Arnie Wilmore. Perhaps that could solidify the legitimacy of Ethan's unbelievable statements.

"If you can't be honest with me," she said. "Then how can I ever believe or trust you?"

Still nothing.

"I can see this is hard for you."

Ethan was still tight-lipped but re-grouped. "There are three of us," he said.

"OK?"

"And umm." He stalled out again.

"OK, let's talk about the easy part," Julia said. "How did you pick two trifectas?"

Ethan started to answer but felt a rush come over him like he was about to completely blow it. What would Sara say? And Mason? What if Julia thought he was a fraud and stomped out of the room? The fate of the entire project lay in the balance. He started to sweat and reached for a glass of water.

"Are you all right?" Julia asked.

Ethan pulled it together. "One of our group has a passion for horse racing," he offered. "Even for those in the past. And my computer has an entire library of natural disaster events that date back to this time."

He could feel his hands shaking, so he quickly dropped them below the table and looked away.

"*Back* to this time? So, you're saying that those races already happened from your perspective," Julia said. "Not predictions, just fact."

"That's right."

Julia could tell by the look in his eyes that he believed what he was telling her. He was in a confession, of sorts, and she was the vicar.

"Look," Ethan said. "We're not expecting you to jump in head-first over two horse races. Winning your confidence will be a slow process. But I'd like to think, at this point, you're willing to listen to us."

Julia took a sip of water.

"When you see the September hurricane, what they name it, when and where it makes landfall. Then you'll know because no one can know that. No one. Then you'll believe."

"Even if I do believe you," Julia said. "What if I decide not to follow and stay where I'm at?"

"You won't." His voice was suddenly strong, certain.

Caught off-guard by the swiftness of his reply, she asked, "How can you be so sure?"

"Because that's not you," Ethan said. "I can't believe that Julia Gathers would turn her back on the world. You're not wired that way."

A long pause. Ethan took a sip of water. "We don't need to talk again this summer," he said. "Unless you want tips on horse races."

Julia smiled.

"I'll contact you again in September, after the hurricane," Ethan said. "There will be another natural disaster in October, and by then, we're hoping you'll be on board."

Julia studied his face.

"Take the summer to think about it," he said.

Julia pondered the situation. This could not possibly have any connection with Arnie Wilmore. There was no rush to meet with him, but at the same time, working for NOAA would create a platform to affect the kind of change Ethan spoke about. The summer to think about it, definitely. Reaching out to Wilmore, probably.

Chapter 40

Hugo

The pieces were falling into place. Mason bought a fleet of eleven used cars from multiple sources and one rag-tag flatbed semi from an onion grower. He parked them all behind the wine barn. Everything's easy when you pay with cash. Mason spent the summer changing oil, tires, brake pads, batteries, and stripping off VIN numbers. He rigged the license plates with snap-off screws for quick removal on the bridges. He also installed CB radios in all vehicles, tuned to the same frequency.

Ethan had to quit his job and lay low but managed to transfer most computer files to his cell phone as a backup. No word from Julia as expected, and nothing from Melton as hoped.

Sara replaced Henri with a trusted employee. Miguel was a man who understood winemaking and oversaw vineyard maintenance and harvest. Sara also knew Miguel was a man she could trust, and he had the respect of the field hands. If she played her cards right, the fleet of vehicles would have drivers for the October earthquake.

When a tropical storm materialized off the African coast in early September, Sara and Ethan followed it with fearful anticipation. In many ways, it was worse than the upcoming earthquake since it took weeks to cross the Atlantic. When it was finally named Hugo and ripped through the Caribbean Islands, Sara was devastated. She could not sleep as the giant storm roared up the east coast toward South Carolina. As Ethan's computer predicted, the death toll was a grim reminder that knowing the future was more of a curse than a gift. But Sara's failure at *Valdez* would not repeat itself; she was committed now more than ever. Her plan for Loma Prieta had to work.

***

Sara and Mason prepped for dinner. Ethan stumbled into the kitchen, rubbing his neck.

"You were in that hammock for two hours," Mason said.

"A siesta life for me," Ethan said and sat down at a table with four place settings. A curious expression crossed his face, but the screen door swung open before he could comment.

"*Senorita*," Miguel said with a polite bow. "It smells wonderful in here."

"Welcome," Sara said. "Please, have a seat. Italian is the house specialty."

Mason placed bottles of white and red wine on the table.

"So, what's the occasion?" Ethan asked. He got a look from Sara as she lay down a cutting board of bread. Mason brought over salad and lasagna.

"How is everything going back there?" Sara asked.

Mason poured the glasses before sitting down.

"Going well," Miguel responded. "Production is on schedule. I expect to be in the fields picking in a few weeks."

Mason grabbed the lasagna and passed it around.

"And how many hands do we have now?" Sara asked. "Fields and Wine Barn included."

She needed twelve drivers to block the bridges, and four were at the table.

"It changes," Miguel said. "We have four full-time in the winery, but the field varies. With the harvest coming up soon, I'll bring in more than forty part-time workers."

"And how many of them are legal?" Sara asked.

Miguel lowered his eyes. "*Senorita*," he murmured.

"No," Sara said. "I'm not worried about that."

Miguel did not respond.

"I need to know how many you can trust," Sara said. "How many you actually know, and who would do anything for you."

Miguel panned the faces in the room.

"Without question," Sara followed.

"There are a few," Miguel said. "Why?"

***

Julia thought about it long enough: all these predictions were correct and to the letter. This was real. But yet, she had no way to contact Ethan, and sitting around waiting was frustrating. She decided to reach out to Arnie Wilmore to see if his letter was a random employee search or fate. Should she write, call, or just fly out to Boulder?

The next day Julia touched down in Denver. He'd cold-called her, so she would cold-visit him. She rented a car and headed up to Boulder. The ride out to the foothills of the Rockies only took an hour. Soon she saw a campus of white buildings surrounded by military-like fencing. She pulled up to a guard gate and rolled down the window.

"I'm here to see Arnie Wilmore," Julia said.

A portly gentleman wearing a green uniform stepped out of the guard shack and studied the car. "Do you have an appointment?" he asked.

"No, I do not," Julia replied. "Please tell him Dr. Julia Gathers is here to see him."

The guard cautiously stared down the beautiful Julia. Her eyes did not blink; her expression did not waver. He went back into the guard shack and picked up the phone. Moments later, he stepped back out.

"Building five," he said, pointing the way. "Just follow the road around. It's on the backside of campus."

Soon, she was at the entrance to non-descript Building Five. She stepped inside the lobby, where another man in a green suit greeted her and escorted her back to Arnie Wilmore's office.

"Dr. Gathers," Arnie said, extending a hand. "This is a pleasant surprise. Since I had not heard back, I assumed you were not interested." The middle-aged man had the usual reaction to seeing such a striking young woman but concealed it well.

"I thought that I should see the facilities," Julia said. "To give the offer serious consideration. I'm sorry to drop in unannounced. If someone else could show me around, that would be fine."

"I cleared my calendar for the morning when I heard you were at the gate," Arnie said and handed her a visitor's lanyard. "Where would you like to start first: Physical Sciences, Chemical Sciences, Global Monitoring, Weather Forecasting, Paleoclimatology?"

"No preference, but I'd like to see them all," Julia said.

They took a golf cart for an hour-long tour to four facilities and ended up at the Weather Forecasting Building. The place Julia was particularly interested in after the recent devastation of Hugo.

As they passed from reception to the hallways, Arnie shook hands with most of the staff. Julia was impressed with how many people he actually knew by name and how receptive they were to his presence. Mainly, an open and warm atmosphere, with no sense of pressure or urgency like she was accustomed to at the university.

They finally entered a large, open room with computer monitors and maps everywhere. Hand-marked charts tracking the route of Hugo remained on the walls. Some stacked two and three high reached the ceiling. There were multi-color scribbles and taped notes following daily, sometimes hourly, movement and intensity. Arnie cut straight through the room to the director's office. He turned to introduce Julia, but she was not there.

He and the director stepped out of the office to see Julia poring over tracking maps. By the time they crossed the room to introduce the director, Julia had climbed a rolling ladder and grabbed a note taped just next to Sullivan's Island.

"It got pretty intense in here," the director said. "Just before landfall."

"The accounts from the news media painted a picture of confusion," Julia followed from atop the ladder. "That you didn't know where it would make landfall."

"Hmm," the director scoffed. "They're pretty good at creating chaos."

"But the taped notes would support chaos," Julia pointed, holding the note from the map. "The closer it moved to shore, the more random the notes. Look at this one: 'Pressure dropping. Hope it doesn't stall and increase wind velocity.'"

She handed the note to the director. "Good thing they didn't see that one," she said.

The director sighed. Arnie could see Julia's eyes fixed on the director. He knew right away this was why he wanted her here. She was all about investigation, solution, and decision making, and he needed that drive to head up this branch.

The director backpedaled. "I'm sorry," he said. "I'm Ross White, Director of Operations."

"Julia Gathers," she said, extending a hand. She moved on to more wall charts. "This map has the most notes of all. Where it turned north, right?"

"When it reached Puerto Rico at Category Three, we expected it to head straight across the gulf into Mexico," White said. "But then it turned north."

He paused.

"We definitely need to improve our tracking systems and hurricane prediction models. But right now, that kind of technology doesn't exist. It hasn't even been imagined."

Julia arched her brow and continued to study the charts.

"Back here, it was upgraded to a tropical storm," she said. "In mid-Atlantic."

"That's right."

Julia flipped through taped notes.

"Why Hugo?" she asked.

"Coin toss, really," White answered. "Hugo or Humphrey."

Julia shot a look of dismay, layered with agitation and frustration. First, the disorganized notes and mapping, now the coin toss.

347

Indeed, they could do better than this. They needed better data: satellite imagery, GPS tracking down to the inch, aerial surveillance, and better water temperature sampling.

"This just isn't good enough," she said, almost to herself. "We can do better than this."

* * *

On the cart ride back to Building Five, Arnie offered Julia the director's position. Julia, of course, wanted to think it over for a few days. Arnie agreed; they exchanged good-byes in the parking lot. Julia started away then turned.

"One last thing," she said. "Have you ever heard the name Ethan Sites? Perhaps working here on campus?"

Wilmore shook his head.

"No, I haven't," he replied. "But I can check records if you like."

"I think he works in your Perishton office," Julia said.

"Perishton?"

"Yes, Alaska."

Wilmore furrowed his brow.

"You mean up on the pipeline?" he asked. "No facilities up there."

Julia tried not to react. "Thank you," she said.

"But we have tossed around the idea of a new facility there in a few years," Wilmore continued. "Study of Arctic climate is critical to our mission. That area used to be barren and hard to access, but now they even have an airport."

Julia nodded and excused herself.

The very idea of Perishton was in its infancy, yet Ethan said he worked there. Julia thought about it the entire drive back to the airport and on the plane ride.

Another piece to a puzzle of future events. *Is it possible?*

***

"I have a vital project," Sara said. "That involves all of us."

Miguel did not respond.

"I need twelve drivers that can handle a vehicle," she said. "Four are sitting here, so eight more."

Miguel saw in her eyes this was no joke. Mason and Ethan had the same look.

"And it could be a little dangerous," Sara said.

"Of course," Miguel said. "Whatever you ask, we'll do for you."

Tension dropped. Sara went around the kitchen and rolled down the blinds at each window. Mason and Ethan stood up and cleared the table.

"Are we not eating?" Miguel asked.

Mason and Ethan pulled chairs aside and picked up the table, leaving Miguel seated at the only remaining chair. He stared down his dinner on the countertop by the sink. Sara tapped him on the shoulder.

"It's OK," she said. "You can get up now. We'll eat in a bit."

Sara pulled his chair away. Mason rolled up the kitchen rug and lifted the trap door. A confused Miguel cautiously stared down into the cellar as Sara hurried down the staircase with a broom.

Mason motioned for Miguel to follow. When he reached the cellar, Sara had the safe opened. She pulled Ethan's computer and cell phone and laid them on the chopping block table. Ethan flipped open the laptop as Miguel looked on.

"What is that? A computer?" Miguel asked. He was confused; the only computer monitors he knew were the bulky type with cathode ray tubes of the 1980s.

"Yes, built in the '20s," Ethan said. "You probably don't recognize it, but it has enhanced graphic software and RAM greater than anything you've ever seen or heard of before."

"Wait, they didn't have computers in the 1920s."

No answer.

Miguel looked over at Sara.

No answer.

Ethan opened an Icon labeled 'Cypress.'

"Don't bother asking questions for a few minutes," Ethan said. "Just watch."

Full-screen footage popped up with a female reporter at a news desk. Behind her, an inset screen showed a collapsed bridge, smoke, fire, rescue vehicles, and ladders propped up against collapsed bridge decks. Panicked people milled around everywhere; some stood on sidewalks taking in the expanse of the disaster.

"Today marks the 20th anniversary of the tragic collapse of the Cypress Street Viaduct," the reporter said, "that killed forty-two people during the October 1989 earthquake. Memorial services are being held at the new Cypress Freeway Memorial Park on Mandela Parkway where the bridge once stood."

"Is this a movie?" Miguel asked. "I don't understand."

"No, this is actual historical footage stored on this computer," Ethan replied. "The Loma Prieta Earthquake occurs on Tuesday, October 17, 1989, at 5:04 P.M."

"*Maria.*" Miguel crossed himself. He felt faint and stepped back from the table.

Sara let it set in while Miguel absorbed what he had just seen.

"Where did this machine come from?" Miguel asked. "How do you know all this?"

"A supernatural phenomenon a few decades from now threw us back in time," Sara replied. "And all I can tell you is we're here to help. We will be on that bridge with a fleet of cars to stop all traffic from getting to those bridge decks, so no one dies. Will you help us?"

Miguel was a god-fearing man who focused on his life, work, and family. These supernatural events were way beyond anything he had ever experienced, and it showed on his frightened face.

"Do you really think we can stop that?" Miguel pointed to the screen.

"We can't stop the earthquake, and we can't keep bridges from collapsing," Sara said. "But we can keep people away from them."

Miguel took a weary breath. "Then, of course, I'll help," he said. "Whatever you ask."

"Thank you."

"So, that's why he's buying old cars and fixing them?"

"That's right," Sara replied.

"What about the big semi," Miguel said. "What's it for?"

Ethan pulled up the Bay Bridge collapse footage, where one section of the upper deck dropped onto the lower deck.

"More than one bridge collapsed," Sara said.

"How do I explain this to other people?" Miguel asked.

"You don't have to; I will," Sara replied. "So, the big question is, do you know eight people you can trust to help us keep it a secret?"

"I think so." Miguel confidently nodded.

"Good," Sara said. "We need them here a week before the others to go over the plan step by step. The earthquake is four weeks away, so I need them here in three. Can you do that?"

"*Senorita*," Miguel replied. "For you, I can have them here tomorrow."

"And also," Sara said, "knowledge of these machines never goes beyond this cellar."

***

Julia wrapped up her last lecture of the day and walked out to the parking lot, where Ethan waited next to her car. She stopped momentarily.

"You again," she said.

"If you're available," Ethan said, "I have more information I'd like to share."

Julia nodded. They took her car toward the same off-campus restaurant. On the drive, Julia started in with questions.

"Over the summer, I looked into some things," she said. "I checked out NOAA Perishton, and it does not exist."

"Not yet."

Julia accepted that and moved on.

"Hurricane Hugo," she said. "Every detail was just as you said it would be. That leaves me with only one possible explanation."

Tight-lipped, Ethan nodded his head in agreement.

"You told me there were three, including yourself," Julia said. "When do I meet the others?"

Ethan fidgeted with his satchel and took a deep breath.

"I have something to show you," he replied. "But we need to be in private. No one else can see this."

Julia peered at the pouch, thought about it, and turned the wheel. "OK," she said. "We'll go to my place."

A few minutes later, they were standing in Julia's home overlooking San Francisco Bay. She hung her sweater on the entry coat rack and dropped her book bag on the floor.

"So, what's in the bag?" Julia asked.

Ethan found a seat on the couch and pulled out his cell phone and laptop.

"This is a 21st century cell phone," he said and turned it on. A screen saver background appeared with scores of icons populating the display. "Way more advanced than the prototypes you might have seen. It has more computing power than NASA had for the Apollo missions and works by accessing satellites and the Internet. Unfortunately, neither advanced satellites nor high-speed Internet are available in this century."

Julia was taken aback by how casually he spoke about timelines.

"So, its use is limited to its stored memory," Ethan said. "Good thing is its stored memory rivals most super-computers today. Touch an icon and see what it does."

Julia tapped the calculator icon, and it instantly filled the screen. She was impressed with the clarity of everything. She tapped a few others and experienced the same feeling, like a child with a new toy. She tapped the calendar, and February appeared.

"Hmm." Ethan smirked. "No Internet access."

"What is this?" Julia asked. She pointed to 2028 in the top left corner.

"That was the year we moved through time," Ethan said softly.

A long silence.

"Here, look at these pics," Ethan said. He panned through his library of photo albums and found 'South Alaskan Shore.'

"We all decided it was important that you see this," he said. "You're about to see video footage of an unbelievable natural phenomenon that three of us witnessed first-hand."

Someone was running along a beach taking shaky video feed, camera in hand, approaching Ethan from behind. A bright towering light source beyond reached high in the sky. The camera turned momentarily to see Ethan's face streaming with tears. A female voice spoke to him. Then the camera turned back to the tower of light.

"What is that?" Julia asked.

Ethan panned forward and stopped where the group ran through the foggy aftermath of the fire.

"OK, this is really hard," he replied. "But you need to watch. I'm holding the camera now."

At first, nothing was visible, but smoke and voices were crying out. "Sara! Sara!"

Then moaning sounds and birds cawing. The smoke cleared to reveal Sara standing over a dead, burned mammoth. Julia covered her mouth and listened to Sara's explanation. Ethan stopped the footage.

"It wasn't long until we figured out these events: the bright light, energy, and magnetism opened up a time portal," Ethan said. "A few weeks later, we got caught up in one."

"Who was that woman in the video footage?" Julia asked, noting a clear resemblance.

Ethan measured his response. "Someone who saved me," he said, then redirected. "There's something else I need to show you. It's from NOAA archives on my computer."

He flipped open the laptop and turned it on. Julia had a thousand questions; Ethan rifled through a few of them, then cut to the chase. He played back the duplicate footage of the collapsed bridge that he showed Miguel. Julia was speechless.

"I hope you can see by now," he said. "That I'm not making up any of this. I'm here for two reasons: To gain your complete confidence in our knowledge of the future, and to convince you to work for NOAA and push legislation to limit CO_2 output. To pull us back from the brink. The phrase 'carbon neutral' must become your creed statement as you go head-to-head with Congress and the corporate world."

Julia had thought about this for months and always arrived at the same conclusion, but facing it was more shocking than she imagined. Part of her still believed this was all a hoax, but it was a new reality.

"So, do I work there in your future?" she asked.

"Yes, you do," Ethan answered. "I don't know when or why you make the switch from academia, but I'm sure it happens in this century."

"And you really think I can make this kind of change for the world?"

"Absolutely," Ethan said. "Especially when you're equipped with knowledge of future events. You'll be able to drive your point home with strategic accuracy."

Frustration set in. "Who was that girl in the video?" she repeated.

"I can't tell you that."

"What else can't you tell me about the future?" Julia demanded.

"There are so many things we'll discuss in time," Ethan said. "But for now, that's about it, except to say I will be on that bridge with the others, and no one will die this time. I'll contact you afterward, and we'll make further plans."

Julia stood and paced. "This is unbelievable," she said.

"I know it's a lot to take in," Ethan said. "But you need to think hard about this because we need you. The whole world needs you, Julia."

She let out a sarcastic sigh, shaking her head.

"One last thing," Ethan said. "You can't mention this to anyone, or it will put us all in grave danger."

Julia sat down in her armchair, took a deep breath, and looked out over San Francisco Bay.

Chapter 41
Organizing the Troops

Monday October 9

Sara and Mason were at the backyard table under the umbrella, sipping on red wine when the sound of crunching rock caught their ears. Moments later, the Second Chance delivery van pulled to a stop in front of the wine barn. Miguel and another man hopped out, walked to the van's rear, and opened the hatch doors. Many people of Hispanic descent unloaded from the van, seven in all, five men and two women.

"*Senorita,*" Miguel said. "You asked for eight, and here they are."

Miguel introduced them as his three brothers, two sisters, three cousins, and all very close since childhood. Delighted, Sara panned the crowd, stood, and greeted them all.

"Miguel has prepared sleeping quarters for all of you in the winery," Sara said. She noticed Miguel and the ladies whisper translations to the others.

"*Senorita,*" Miguel's brother Pedro stepped forward. "We are at your service."

"Thank you," Sara said. *At least three of the eight speak two lan-*

guages, she thought. *Good start.* "So, get freshened up, and we'll all meet back here for dinner."

Sara ordered pizzas and sent Ethan into town to pick them up. She instructed Miguel to keep the mission secret, and he was true to his word. Sara also heard through the rumor mill that every worker, field hands and all, knew about her unbelievable winnings in Vegas. So, in their minds, she was already a miracle worker with gifted insight, a visionary, a prophet of sorts. She hoped they were already on board with whatever she had to say.

After pizza on card tables in the backyard, they adjourned inside, where a set of drawings lay on the kitchen table. The old blueprints caught everyone's attention, but Sara did not mention them. Instead, she made her way through the room, talking as she went.

"Once again, I really appreciate your all being here," she said, with the room's undivided attention. "I've been very concerned lately about something that I want to share with you. This summer, I went up to Oakland to meet with a distributor," she said. "We had dinner in China Town afterward; I got lost and missed the exit for the freeway."

Ethan raised a curious eyebrow and made eye contact with Mason, who did not react. Miguel and the others listened with composed curiosity.

"It was near sunset, so I stopped and pulled a map from the glovebox," Sara continued. "I'm still not sure if it was sun rays cutting through trees, smog, my imagination, or a combination of the three. I had to raise my hand to shade the glare, but what I saw was unbelievable. The entire Cypress Street viaduct, the north-south section of elevated bridges leading to San Francisco Bay, collapsed in a plume of smoke and fire."

Miguel was conveniently standing behind the rest of the group and did not react. The others were intrigued.

"I know it sounds crazy," Sara said. "But a few days later, I was sitting outside listening to the radio. Then suddenly, there was a news alert about an earthquake at the start of World Series game three. I turned the radio down to listen and look for signs of ground motion, but nothing. I don't follow baseball, but I figured the earthquake had to be in LA or San Francisco, so maybe it didn't reach here. I went inside to check the TV, but nothing on any news station.

"The next day, I went into town and bought a newspaper. Nothing about an earthquake and articles in the sports section only talked about the baseball regular season. The world series was two months away."

She continued pacing.

"I am convinced this was divine intervention." She motioned a hand toward Mason, Ethan, and Miguel. "So, I told these guys we had to do something to keep people away from that bridge."

She pointed to the drawings on the table.

"And now we know the World Series is played in San Francisco," Sara continued. "Game three will be played on October 17th, next Tuesday."

This was followed by a moment of silence and turning heads. Sara did not care what Mason and Ethan thought about the deception. In fact, she thought it best just to dump it on them and avoid any debate. The last thing Sara wanted was to have anyone else know the absolute truth. She was protecting the innocent.

"OK, so I believe you," Miguel's older sister, Luisa said. "But what are we supposed to do about it?"

"I'm glad you asked," Sara replied.

Everyone stood and gathered around. She unrolled the set of blueprints on the table. She found them on microfilm at the library and had them reproduced up to full-scale sheets. The stack of engineering plans had all structural layouts and details from foundations to bridge decks, outlining steel reinforcing of every bent from 13th Street to 34th Street. The first drawing showed the overall layout of the system of bridges. Sara highlighted bents 63 and 112, the limits of the collapsed decks per the forensic report from Ethan's computer.

"As you know," Sara said. "It's not hard to stop traffic on a highway, especially during rush hour. A disabled car or an accident backs up traffic for miles. We must have our vehicles on that bridge at the right time and stop. It won't take long, just a few minutes, and no one will die."

Sara laid out the plan for the Cypress Street bridge blockade: five cars on the upper southbound deck, four-stop, pull plates, and run to the lead car. The same plan for the north-bound lower deck. All had to be done at five o'clock, on the dot. Miguel and Ethan would be the lead drivers. She did not mention the Bay Bridge since it was not part of her 'vision.' It would just happen without discussion. If anyone asked, the big rig would be there for backup or support if something went wrong.

Sara closed with a practice discussion. They all needed training, starting with test driving the vehicles to get a feel for their handling. And like any big operation, they needed a trial run on the bridges the day before the quake. Accessing the bridges from two directions in rush hour would be tricky and lining all cars at the precise moment would require practice.

"We're starting now," Sara said. "Everyone outside. All ten cars are parked behind the barn. Mason and Miguel will assign each person to one car. You'll start it up and drive it around the property to get a feel for how it handles. Any questions?"

No one said a word, no questions or arguments. Sara pointed to the screen door. The group jumped to attention and headed out across the lawn.

Sara breathed a hopeful sigh as they crossed the yard. Their heads turned in quiet discussion.

Sara reached for the last piece of pizza.

Chapter 42

Trial Run

Mason led the group behind the wine barn and approached the first vehicle. He knelt down and pulled the license plate.

"I rigged the plates with snap-off screws," he said. "Watch here. Grab the right side and give a good tug."

Mason pulled the plate off and flipped it over.

"You see this?" he asked. "The screws are set in plastic inserts and pop right out by applying pressure."

"But why do this?" Mariana asked.

"When we stop on the bridge," Mason said. "You'll get out of your car, run around back, pull the plate, then hop in the lead car. So, there will be four plates on the floorboard when the lead driver takes off."

"That way, police can't trace the cars, right?" Mariana followed.

"That's right," Mason said. "I stripped the VIN numbers, too."

Mason opened the driver's door, turned the key, and the engine in the white Chevy Impala roared to life. He tapped on the gas pedal a few times, listening to the clean sound of the carburetor, then flipped a switch on a device mounted atop the dashboard. It had a handheld microphone with a coiling cord attached to its side. Clearly not a factory-installed machine; it was a CB radio.

"I installed CBs in all vehicles," Mason said. "And set them to the same channel. Two cars will do all the talking, the others just listen."

"We're going up to Oakland Monday for a trial run," Miguel added. "The lead driver on the upper deck will have the call name High Flyer and the lower deck will be Low Rider. So, if you're on the upper deck, only listen to High Flyer, on the lower deck, Low Rider."

"That's me," Ethan said.

"And like Mason said," Miguel continued. "The CBs will already be turned on. Don't talk, just listen, or it will get confusing."

"That's right," Mason said. "So, now we hop in and drive the property for practice."

***

The practice sessions went well, no accidents, no cars careening off dirt roads into vineyards. But most importantly to Sara, in the days leading up to the trial run, no one questioned what they were doing. She worried about defectors in the ranks, but not a hint of anyone going AWOL. On the trial run, everyone was up early and ready for the trip north.

The cars headed down the crunchy gravel drive out to the main road just after lunch. They traveled in two groups of five vehicles, ten minutes apart, to be less conspicuous and practice CB protocol. Their destination was China Town, just east of the Cypress Street Viaduct, where they would meet and wait for rush hour traffic.

***

"High Flyer here." Miguel's voice rang out over crackling speakers. "Breaker for the Low Rider. What's your twenty?"

"About a mile back," a voice returned.

"10-4."

Miguel shrugged his shoulders and nodded.

"So far, so good," Mason said.

Sara and Mason both rode with Miguel and left the big rig behind. Sara described it to the group as a backup vehicle if something went wrong. Another deception, but not needed for the trial run.

The ride up the freeway to Oakland's China Town only took a few hours. They pulled into a supermarket parking lot mid-afternoon to regroup. Sara unrolled her map of the bridges on the trunk of Miguel's vehicle. Both teams huddled around as she pointed out strategies.

"Low Riders hop on the freeway here." Sara pointed to an on-ramp near Market Street. "And follow the signs to the lower deck where you must be grouped in formation when you reach 10th Street."

"You will drive side by side for a few blocks behind Ethan and prepare to stop. And this is where he'll stop tomorrow, at 16th Street. But today, he'll just slow down."

Sara lifted her gaze to confident eyes, acknowledging her instructions.

"High Flyers follow the signs to the upper deck," she said. "It leads out to the Nimitz Freeway. You'll have to head north toward Berkley."

She pointed to the map, north of Oakland. "There, you take the off-ramp and work your way to get back onto the bridge heading south. Once you get back to these interchanges, you drop off on the Cypress Street Viaduct, upper deck. And be prepared to stop right at 34th Street."

"That looks complicated," Luisa said.

"That's why Miguel leads the High Flyers," Sara agreed.

Ethan shrugged. Mason chuckled.

"And it will take a lot longer than the Low Riders," Mariana followed.

"That's right," Sara said. "So, today we time it. Low Riders from this parking lot. But High Flyers start timing from Berkley because that's where they'll line up tomorrow."

All nodded in agreement.

"Tomorrow, both teams must stop at the barricade lines by 5:00 P.M., no later," Sara said. "Today, we see how long it takes to get there from each starting point."

Sara checked her watch.

"It's about 3:30 P.M., so High Flyers should head out now. Low riders leave here at 4:40 P.M. High Flyers leave Berkley at 4:45 P.M. We'll meet across the street afterward for a bite to eat."

∗∗∗

The tiny Chinese restaurant barely had enough parking, but twelve cars managed to fit in with a few spaces to spare. They all gorged themselves at the buffet and snapped open fortune cookies after dinner.

"So, the Low Riders were five minutes early to 16th street?" Sara asked.

"Yes, exactly five minutes," Ethan said.

"And High Flyers were five minutes late?"

"Yes, ma'am," Miguel responded. "Traffic was snarled on that road. No quick way through."

"That's not good," Sara said.

"And there's another thing," Miguel said. "When we finally made it to the Cypress Street bridge, it was chaos in that spaghetti bowl. Cars cut us off everywhere. And we had to line up right there. Not easy."

"Did you get them in line?" Sara asked.

"Yes, but it was close."

"So, five minutes late and barely enough time to get lined up," Sara said. "There can be no mistakes. I want you to leave ten minutes earlier. You might have to wing it at the barricade if you get there too soon. Maybe open all the car doors to keep irritated drivers from cutting between cars."

"Good idea."

"Anything else?" Sara asked.

"We're all re-fueled," Mason replied. "And no mechanical problems."

"OK, we wrap up and drive back down to Paso," Sara said.

A patrolman had just finished his rounds and stopped into the same restaurant for carry-out. He backed in next to the last car in a packed parking lot and stepped out of his squad car. It must be a party; he had never ever seen more than a couple of vehicles in the lot. Something caught his curious eye as he passed the rear of the first car, an expired plate. He circled the car, studied the inside and checked the VIN number but it was missing. Curious, he checked plates and VINs on the next car, then another, and another. All the same.

The patrolman entered the restaurant and saw Sara's team bunched up at two tables. No one else in the restaurant but wait-staff. Mason noticed him approach the table and turned to face him.

"Excuse me," the officer said. "Are those your vehicles parked out front?"

"Yes," Mason said. "Those are all ours."

"I need to see your identification," the officer asked.

Mason and Sara handed him their driver's licenses.

"These look in order," he said and handed them back. "But those are un-registered vehicles sitting out there, and they will have to be impounded."

Mason at once stood up. Sara cut in front of him.

"Officer," she said. "These cars are in transit. We're taking them to a ranch near LA, where they will stay on that property. Not for road use."

"Doesn't matter," he said. "Any vehicle in the state of California must have proper registration."

Sara could sense this was going the wrong way and heard Mason's chair slam back against the table. Before she could respond, nearby sirens interrupted her. Squad cars and tow trucks poured into the parking lot. Policemen emptied out and hurried into the restaurant.

All cars were towed, Sara and her team were arrested.

**

The women were placed in a separate but adjoining cell from the men. It took some doing, but Sara got permission to make a call.

Then she paced the jail cell, her head spinning. *Not again.* She was so shaken up that she felt nauseous. *Valdez* all over again, but worse.

She stopped mid-stride. "I'm sorry," she said. "This was not supposed to happen. And look what I've done, to all of you."

Luisa jumped up to console her. "Lovely lady," she said, hugging her. "This is not your fault. Don't blame yourself. We all tried. You tried to save lives, and that's not a crime. It was a mission of hope. But sometimes things just go wrong, and you can't help it."

An exhausted Sara found her way to a hard steel bench. She lay back and closed her eyes as Mason reached through the cell bars and took her hand. But her mind was engrossed with the thought of failure.

Sara went through the mission in her head, over and over again. How had this happened? How could she clean up this mess? Sara wished she could talk to Julia for advice, but that door was locked.

Sara suddenly realized this was it, checkmate, no other choice, all would die tomorrow on the bridges. *Does a timeline reach out and correct itself like wounded tissue? Is it something I can't fight?* After long deliberation, she finally fell into a deep sleep.

***

Just after seven in the morning, the sounds of clanging metal doors filled the room. A dark figure stepped inside and flipped a light switch. Sara lifted her head, squinting through the light. Her heart leaped when she saw Mr. Angeli, dressed in his usual finely tailored suit. It was a miracle.

She sprang to her feet and approached the bars. Mariana and Luisa sat up in anticipation. Mason, Ethan, and Miguel scratched their heads and rubbed their eyes.

"Sara Prada," Angeli said without making eye contact. "Or is it Gathers?" He paced back and forth on the free side of the bars, his shiny shoes clicking on the concrete floor. "The lady who picked three trifectas and gave me five years' worth. A lady worth millions of dollars and who owns a successful vineyard."

Angeli shook his head with a pitiful smile. "The magnificent Sara Prada who should be courted by kings and princes is now behind bars in front of me for grand larceny."

She lifted her head to speak, he motioned her to silence with a hand.

"And they tell me," He continued. "That you don't even exist, and neither do some of these guys."

The pacing continued.

Sara's head dropped.

"And the thing is, I don't believe it's a hit on the head anymore. No one can know the things you know, so every move must be for a reason."

Sara held her tongue.

"Why steal cars?" Angeli asked in contemplation.

More pacing.

"They're not stolen," Sara said softly. "They were paid for in cash."

Angeli stopped and turned. "Then why strip all the VIN numbers?"

A long silence. Sara could not make eye contact.

"I'm waiting."

"We need those vehicles to save lives," Sara murmured. "Lots of lives. And if we can't get out of here by afternoon, it will be too late."

Angeli stopped in front of Sara, his cold, dark eyes cutting through her.

"If it were anyone else," he spoke forcefully. "I'd say you were crazy." He walked toward the door.

"You said you'd help me," Sara pleaded. "If I ever needed it."

He stopped.

"Can you get our vehicles out of impound?"

There was a long pause.

"Maybe," Angeli re-grouped. "The prosecutor owes me a favor or two. But why should I get you those vehicles?" Angeli approached the bars. "Are you going to look at me?"

Sara managed to lift her head. "If I die today," she said. "At least you'll know it was for a good cause."

"Not good enough," Angeli said. "NOT GOOD ENOUGH!"

Sara recoiled at his outburst and pursed her lips. "If we don't get out of here, something—" she said, shakily.

"Something, what?" Angeli asked.

"If you get us out of here," she sniffled. "I'll tell you everything."

Angeli's dark eyes cut through her with laser precision, but Sara held her ground this time. He could tell from her expression there was a reason for all this. Angeli snapped his fingers, and the door rolled open.

***

Half an hour later, Sara was escorted into a black limousine with Angeli. The others followed in a black SUV.

"I can only assume you called me," Angeli said, "because there's no one else in this century you can call for help. Other than the guys riding behind us." Angeli handed her a glass of aged bourbon.

"Thank you," Sara said and took a sip.

Angeli studied her face. Her gaze looking straight away, wheels turning, eyes welling up.

"It happened in the summer of '28," she said. "I work for NOAA. Earth's poles started shifting; north moved south and south to north. On top of that, there was intense solar activity. When solar flares hit the atmosphere, they somehow interacted with magnetic energy from Earth's core."

Angeli furrowed his brow.

"I saw it first-hand as it transported things from past to present in Alaska and from present to past in California. That's where it got me."

"What about them?" Angeli asked, pointing to the SUV.

"Two of them as well."

"How long have you been here?"

"Two and a half years," Sara said.

Angeli reached for his glass and took a sip. "So, what's all this about?" he asked. "Twelve cars and twelve people."

Sara took a big sip. "I'm only telling you this because I trust you," she replied.

Angeli's stoic face did not budge.

Sara sighed.

"Tomorrow at 5:04 P.M., there will be an earthquake in the bay area," Sara said. "A bridge in Oakland will collapse completely, killing forty-two people."

"And?"

"And we will stop traffic on two bridge decks," Sara said. "So that no one dies. That's why we need our cars back."

The businessman knew no one would make this stuff up, especially not Sara. He considered her words and their consequences. "There's a big problem with that," he said. "If you use automobiles that I had released from impound, I can be implicated."

Sara shook her head. "Then how do we do this?"

"*We* don't do anything," Angeli said. "But you have to change your plan."

"OK, how?"

"They returned all your personal belongings," Angeli said. "True?"

"Yes."

"Then surely you have a credit card in that purse."

Sara nodded.

"Then go out and rent twelve cars," Angeli said.

"But they can be traced back to me," Sara said.

Angeli chuckled. "Sara, you were just in jail for grand theft, auto," he pointed out. "Do you really think those impounded cars won't be traced back to you if they are on that bridge?"

Sara's heart lurched as she was hit with the realization. "Good point," she said. "But we also have CB radios and—"

Angeli raised his hand. "Improvise," he said. "Think on the fly."

Sara sipped the bourbon.

"You have another problem," Angeli said. "Two of the Hispanic people have outdated passports. That's federal, so it will take more time to get them out."

"How much more time?"

"Could be days," Angeli said. "Even the prosecutor can't pull strings with the Feds." Angeli could see she was really spinning on this one. He leaned over with a confident grin. "Improvise."

Chapter 43
Re-Grouping

Angeli's motorcade dropped them off at a local rental car company. An unusual sight for the store manager, mainly when the driver escorted Sara into the store. Ten rental cars later, Sara and the crew were off. They avoided Oakland altogether and drove east into the Berkley Foothills, where they found a wooded park to re-group.

It was almost nine in the morning when Sara laid her map out on a picnic table and weighed it down with a couple of rocks. She let everyone know they would have to pull this off with two fewer drivers than initially planned. She let them know that the two brothers would be released soon.

The group was waiting for Sara to talk about the dark-suited man, but it never came up. They did not want to pry, so no questions were asked.

"We also have to do this without CB radios," Sara said. "So, it's a game of Follow the Leader. But at least we had a dry run and know what we're up against."

"What about the plates?" Mason asked.

"Just leave them on," Sara said. "I'm totally exposed now, so it doesn't matter."

"Easy enough," Mason said. "And now we're two drivers short. I've been thinking about this, and I came up with the best way to leave the five High Flyers together since it's the trickiest approach. But we lost two Low Riders, so we drop the lead car, move Ethan back in line, and Sara drives the fourth."

Everyone seemed to agree.

"There's an on-ramp right next to our barricade line on the lower deck." Mason pointed. "When the Low Riders stop, grab your keys, and run down the ramp out into the neighborhoods.

"The earthquake might start as you're running down, but don't stop to look back; you might look suspicious. Just keep going. When the shaking begins, people won't really notice someone running scared.

"There is a city park at 16th and Adeline, just a few blocks from the bridge. That's where we meet up. Everyone can pile into Miguel's car since it's the biggest one."

"Won't we look suspicious?" Luisa asked. "With ten people jumping into one car?"

"No one will notice," Mason said. "Not during an earthquake."

"Makes sense, and I like your plan," Sara said. "Except for one thing."

"What's that?"

"I'm not driving a car."

"I saw you handle that Jeep on the beach," Mason countered. "I think you're more than qualified."

"Well, wait a minute," Miguel said. "We have ten people and ten cars. Both of you are driving, right?"

Sara and Mason's eyes locked.

"We are both driving," Sara replied.

"No, no," Mason stuttered. "You're not—"

"Yes, I am," Sara said. "This is a one-person operation now."

"I can handle this," Mason claimed.

"What are you guys talking about?" Luisa asked.

Memory recall struck, and Miguel let out a sigh.

Luisa turned to Miguel.

"What!?"

Sara broke eye contact with Mason. She did not really know what to say. Only a chosen few knew about the Bay Bridge collapse. No one else would believe her if she told them about another 'vision.' Besides, the others did not need to know if all went as planned. Sara and Mason would have simply been alternate lead cars in their minds.

The group was supposed to leave Paso Robles the morning of the earthquake. Sara would excuse herself and Mason to stay back and take care of something, then make up time on the freeway to catch up along the way. But she never got to play that card after landing in jail. So, this group would launch from here, the park.

She came up with something quick. "There's something I have to do," Sara said. "And I can't talk about it."

She pulled a key from her pocket and walked toward the rental cars.

"It's that man in the limousine," Luisa said. "Isn't it?"

Sara stopped momentarily. Luisa believed her.

"Who was he, and why did he help us?" Luisa asked.

Sara almost said something but kept walking.

***

Sara was on the freeway in minutes. There was still plenty of time for her to reach the Second Chance Ranch, fire up the flatbed truck, and get back to Oakland. But any problem on the highway could eat up that lead time.

It was half past noon when Sara climbed into the big rig. She had driven semi-trailers before, but all makes and models were different. It only took a few minutes to get oriented with gears and foot pedals. She checked gauge readings; oil pressure and fuel were good (all that really mattered for this trip). She had to adjust the seat since Mason's long legs pushed it too far back.

Minutes later, Sara headed down her gravel driveway with a cloud of dust trailing behind. She turned onto the paved road by the Second Chance Ranch sign, upshifted, and started north. She took a long look at that sign and wondered if she would ever see it again.

Two and a half hours later, she was on the outskirts of San Jose. She reached for the CB a couple times but realized no one would respond. It frustrated her that she had no contact with Mason or Miguel. What she wouldn't pay for a reliable cell phone.

She still had two hours before the earthquake and only one hour to the bridge. She would make it before rush hour traffic.

***

"All right, we have two hours," Mason said. "So, we need to get into positions. High Flyers follow Miguel and the rest follow me."

Miguel led his team out to the freeway and west toward San Francisco. Thirty minutes later, they reached the approach ramps to the Bay Bridge. Miguel's eyes caught sight of the first trestle, where the collapse would happen soon. He glanced south and caught a glimpse of his objective, the Cypress Street Expressway, where mild traffic flowed across the double-deck structure. He tried to focus on their goal, not the impending disaster.

He switched to the northbound freeway and wound his way up to the exit for the East Shore State Park. When the High Flyers pulled to a stop, Miguel checked his watch. It was 3:48 P.M., less than an hour 'till showtime.

***

Mason and the Low Riders patiently waited in DeFremery Park, where they would return on foot after the earthquake. He wondered where Sara was and how the flatbed was handling. He should have done it himself, but when Sara got a full head of steam, there was no stopping her. Mason checked his watch and strummed his fingers on the steering wheel.

***

Sara made it to Oakland and pulled off the highway onto Frontage Street near the old tracks, in clear view of the Bay Bridge. It was a couple of miles away, but her aim was in clear sight. She had to stop right before the first elevated trestle.

The Bay Bridge had two main sections, the east section from Oakland to Yerba Buena Island and the west section to San Francisco. Initially constructed in the 1930s, the east span was steel trestle-type construction. The open-latticed framework carried westbound traffic on its upper chord and eastbound traffic on the lower. The span that reached Yerba Buena Island blossomed up to giant trusses crossing deeper water.

Sara stepped down from the cab and walked out to study the situation. She checked her watch: 4:08 P.M. It would all be over in an hour. "*Improvise*," she mumbled and shook her head.

She thought about exactly where to stop. In her mind's eye, she visualized the collapse. Old photos of the deck collapse showed the fallen section at a major bridge expansion joint over a trussed abutment.

The east end of the collapsed section remained attached to the upper deck, but the west end fell to the lower deck. The oncoming upper deck traffic would slide down a steep ramp if they could not stop in time. The lower deck traffic would have a ramp drop right in front of them. But the fatality came sometime after the quake when a misdirected driver went the wrong way and drove off the buckled section. So, if she could stop just past the clean break in the upper deck, the driver would see her truck and stop. She had to stop west of the gap, on the San Francisco side, or all this would have been for nothing.

Sara considered the aftermath. She'd be stuck on a miles-long bridge with only one way off, west to San Francisco. No lead vehicle to drive away in, so she'd have to walk it, maybe find a concerned motorist to give her a lift. Most vehicles would stop when the shaking started, so maybe, she could hitch a ride. Or perhaps she could hang back to save the motorist going the wrong way.

Sara rechecked her watch. It was a quarter past four. Fifteen minutes to the toll booth plaza, ten minutes in line to pay, then five minutes to her destination at the trestle bridge. That gave her fifteen minutes to spare. She could pull over and wait on the roadside past the toll booths to get back on schedule. Perfect.

Sara climbed into the truck cab and reached for her purse. She fished through it and found the compass that Mason had given her. She studied it, rubbed it, then hung it from the rearview mirror.

Chapter 44
Carbon Neutral

Had the race predictions really convinced her? Julia wasn't so sure, but other things Ethan described had her believing. After all, why would someone go to such extremes? He'd used horse race results as a platform to discuss future ecological dilemmas.

Either way, it didn't matter now. If the earthquake happened this afternoon, there would be no doubt. She took the day off from teaching and prepared herself for whatever came. She spent the morning preparing, removing books from shelves, dishes from the pantry, and laid mirrors and picture frames on beds. Taking no chances, she placed her small TV set on the living room floor; if it fell off the wall shelf, she'd miss all news coverage. She put it in front of the sliding glass door, in view of San Francisco Bay. She used an extension cord for good measure in case it slid across the floor. Finally, she tossed a throw pillow in front of it, better than falling off a chair.

The anticipation was getting to her by mid-afternoon, so Julia poured a glass of wine and stepped out onto her porch overlooking the bay. She loved the smell of the air and the view of the bay.

Julia found a seat next to the glass tabletop and swept a few leaves away with her hand. From that perch, she considered some of the things Ethan described. Julia kept circling back to the phrase carbon neutral. *What exactly does that mean?* she wondered.

Will combustion engines and power plants be replaced with non-carbon producing counterparts? So, I push for electric cars and nuclear power plants? Yeah, right, in a world controlled by big oil and 'No Nuke' ecologists. He can't mean wind and solar; they are still in their infancy. What if it's a give-and-take situation? How would I do that?

Julia took a sip from the glass, spun it a few times, and took another sip. She looked over trees that reached down to the bay and up the slopes on the other side. The vast sea of green leaves was as inspiring as the blue water in between. She re-focused her attention to a big oak branch hanging overhead, and the dried leaf that fell to the ground.

Then something hit her: leaves absorb carbon dioxide. *Is that what Ethan means? Can nature absorb all human-made carbon emissions to balance in a neutral state? Is that possible? Only if we lower emission levels and replace the balance with clean energy. How would we legislate and track it? Or is it a combination of such technology and clean energy?*

Julia Gathers was on to something. She leaned back in her chair and took another sip of wine.

Chapter 45

Loma Prieta

Miguel checked his watch. It was 4:35. Time to go. He fired up the rental car, rolled down his window, and made a swirling motion with his finger. He listened to the other engines starting up, threw his car into gear, took a deep breath, and gently pulled away. He made his way out of the park and up the on-ramp to freeway 580-South. In minutes, the group was riding four cars wide behind Miguel's lead vehicle.

Tuesday traffic was about the same as Monday, going slow but with no significant back-ups. Miguel was relieved but knew more congestion lay ahead. He knew that soon they would be the cause of the congestion. He kept an eye on the trailing vehicles as they held formation.

Miguel had reasoned that the best way to pull this off was a slow approach and prolonged approach. He also knew that speeds picked up once cars cleared the primary freeway system and dropped onto Cypress. So, after his team stopped, the road in front of them would clear out in minutes.

Miguel rechecked his watch, only 4:46 and they were over half-way there. He had to slow down.

***

Mason thought about when to leave DeFremery Park. Their trial run had started in a supermarket parking lot a few minutes away. But today, they were a bit closer to the Market Street on-ramp. He turned the ignition a couple of minutes past their scheduled time.

His caravan met some unexpected issues with road construction on the main avenue leading to Market Street. When they reached the freeway, there were only ten minutes until the quake. Mason pushed along while Ethan and the others scrambled to keep up. Before Mason knew it, they were on the curved southern leg of the Cypress Street Viaduct turning north. Mason counted the side streets on either side of the bridge; they were closing in on the 13th Street on-ramp. Next would be the barricade line at the 16th Street off-ramp.

All vehicles were in formation, side by side, windows down. Mason had two cars to his left and one to the right. He tapped his horn once. Everyone made eye contact and motioned thumbs up.

***

Miguel slowed down enough that rush hour traffic pulled away from him, giving separation between the High Flyers. *Working as planned,* he thought, peering at the advancing taillights. He checked the rear-view mirror; all traffic was falling in line behind his team of vehicles.

Miguel saw the maze of concrete ramps and fly-over bridges where Oakland's east-west freeways mix together. The Bay Bridge was now in full view out to the west. He rechecked his watch, 4:55 P.M. Five minutes till they would make a complete stop, looked about right.

Miguel felt his heart pounding as they drew closer to the overpasses. Traffic was hundreds of yards out in front of him. The scattered sound of honking horns built up from behind.

He reached the maze of overpasses, underpasses, and changing lane signs. He flipped on the turn signal for the Cypress Street Viaduct and checked carefully as everyone followed in line. Miguel dropped down to 25 MPH when they reached the curving ramp that ducked under another one.

This was it. Miguel could see the stopping point about a quarter mile away. Just over a minute to the barricade. Only a handful of cars from the on-ramp made their way in front of him but moved ahead quickly. Less than a hundred yards now, Miguel raised an arm out the window and made a fist. Game time.

***

Mason tapped his horn twice, and the others turned on their emergency flashers. With the 16th Street ramp upon them, Mason slowed down. All vehicles slowly came to a stop. Mason checked his watch. It was 5:03 P.M., the shaking would start any second.

"Grab your keys!" Mason shouted. "Run!"

Luisa, Mariana, and Ethan hurried along behind Mason. They quickly reached the 16th Street on-ramp, took a tight right, and sprinted down the ramp. A few frustrated drivers stepped out of their cars and pumped angry fists at the fleeing group.

"Get back in your cars!" Mason shouted as he ran. "NOW!"

When they reached the base of the on-ramp, a vehicle was turning onto the ramp. Mason instinctively lifted a hand for it to stop.

He stood in front of the car, staring down the driver that wanted access to the bridge. Ethan and the others stopped.

"Keep going," Mason said.

It was just then that the trembling started.

The driver in the stopped car opened his door to confront Mason, but the shaking caught his attention.

"Run!" Mason shouted.

Fifty feet above, unknown to Mason, Miguel raced past on the upper deck going due south. He had barely cleared the danger zone. Miguel breathed a sigh of relief to see no vehicles in his rearview mirror.

***

Alone in a flatbed truck, Sara maneuvered her way through a sea of winding concrete bridges. She finally merged onto Interstate 80, which led out to the bay. She followed sign after sign until she cleared the maze of curving concrete chaos. Then the road straightened out to the approach ramps for the Bay Bridge. She veered up to the toll booth line of semis at 4:32 P.M., not bad, but how long was the line?

Sara paid the toll fifteen minutes later, pulled through the gate then pulled off to park. Her watch said 4:49 P.M. She had eleven minutes to reach the first trestle and come to a stop across five lanes of traffic. And there was a lot of traffic. She was getting a little nervous. She also knew the other teams were maneuvering into positions on Cypress. She prayed all was going well.

Sara studied the traffic. It was moving, not moving fast, but moving. Then she had an idea. She rechecked her watch, and at 4:54, she threw the big rig into gear and pulled out.

"They say fortune favors the brave," she murmured. "Here we go."

She quickly merged into traffic and signaled left. No one yielded. She leaned into the next lane to the sounds of honking horns. Then again, into the center lane. She could now see the first trestle about a mile away.

This was taking longer than she thought. It was right at five, and she was only halfway to the trestle when she started her plan. Sara was in the middle lane and started a serpentine maneuver, swaying the semi-trailer side to side. First, gently, then taking up two lanes, then three. Traffic pulled aside and behind, pumping fists and fingers but giving distance for this crazy driver. Soon she had all five lanes covered in this snake-like pathway.

The clock was ticking down. Less than a minute left. Sara realized this might be it for her, maybe the last thing she ever did.

Traffic pulled way back, not knowing what was going on. Cars in front of Sara pulled farther ahead, exactly what she wanted. She kept an eye out on the trestle approaching fast. It was time. She down-shifted, slammed on the brakes from the far-right lane, and cut the wheel as hard as possible. In her mind's eye, she hoped this would be as easy as the big turn on the beach when she ran off the coyotes, but this was a semi-trailer. The wheels lifted on the driver's side, skidding tires screeched, and black smoke billowed out from the rear axles. She finally got the truck to a stop at the end of a sideways turn. Sara took a deep breath, but to her horror, she was at the base of the trestle, directly over the expansion joint. She had stopped short of her mark, straddling the breaking point in the bridge.

Then it hit. The bridge shook along its entire length and waffled side to side, up and down. Sara was tossed into the passenger seat. People cried out as their cars were tossed like toys in a bathtub.

But the cries were soon muffled by an enormous crash as the giant trestle span next to Sara's truck dropped onto the bridge deck below. A cloud of smoke billowed out from both sides as twisted steel and crushed concrete smashed into its final resting place. Seconds later, Sara felt more movement in the cab and realized what was happening. The truck cab started to roll over the side of the broken bridge deck, pulling the flatbed down with it.

Sara scrambled back over to the driver's side seat and flung open the door, but the cab was already dropping off the side. The truck, cab, and all crashed down to the lower deck. Sara's mind raced with thoughts of death. Time blurred, then darkness.

Pain and coughing woke her from an unconscious state. Reality re-formed around her. She panned through the shattered windshield and instinctively reached for anything to help herself up and out of the cab. Moments later, she rolled out onto the side of the truck cab. She was bleeding and breathing hard when she got to her feet. She took in the wreckage, the truck cab broke loose from the flatbed frame, and somehow that frame was speared up above the top deck. She turned her gaze to the coastline and hills where puffs of smoke, scattered cries, and sirens filled the air.

She'd done it. This was not a repeat of *Valdez*. It almost killed her, but she'd done it. And it all happened like clockwork.

The shaking finally came to a stop. A dust cloud blew out across the bay, exposing the collapsed damage. Sara turned to see a confused crowd appear from their cars, looking down at her. She wondered how this would all work out. Was this her last stand, where it all ended, was this even real-life or an illusion? Would they think she set this all up? Would she spend years in prison for saving people?

There was no way to pick herself up and get away from the wreckage. She never predicted this possibility. She always hoped she'd stop the truck, hop out, run to Mason's car, and ride off to safety. But failure? She never considered failure. A tearful smile came across her face. She stood helpless and afraid in an uncontrollable adrenaline shake.

The crowd of curious onlookers grew on both sides of the fractured bridge deck. Nothing was said. Everyone stopped short and looked in awe at what had just happened.

Then the sound of chopper blades filled the air. A sleek black helicopter raced across the bay from the south. It pulled into a hovering position on the east side of the collapse as if studying the situation. Soon the helicopter made a slow descent onto the eastern bridge deck. The small crowd pulled back to their cars as the chopper touched down, blowing dust everywhere. A hooded figure appeared from the dust cloud, standing opposite the chasm of wreckage from Sara.

"Sara!" Arthur Melton shouted. "What are you doing here?"

No answer.

Melton studied the wrecked flatbed. The people across the crevasse backpedaled.

"How could you possibly know this would happen?" he asked.

More whoofing chopper blades as a TV news helicopter raced across the bay. Sara looked up to see the other helicopter take up a hovering position.

"I can get you out of here," Melton shouted.

Sara focused on the new helicopter, then back at Melton.

"But we have to go now, or it's too late," Melton shouted. "There is no other way off this bridge. I've been listening to police radio; they already know about the Cypress Street blockade."

Sara thought about it and nodded. Melton nodded back and hurried to the helicopter that lifted up and slowly reached the fallen bridge deck. Sara turned her head from the wind and dust; the crowd raced back to their cars. A rope ladder dropped from the black chopper. Sara grabbed hold with both hands and managed to get a foot on a rung. The chopper lifted to the sky with Sara hanging on as the ladder reeled its way in. She looked out on the sea of backed-up cars, none of which fell into the collapsed bridge deck. And the rear of the flatbed poking above the bridge deck stood as a makeshift warning beacon to anyone approaching.

No one would die here today.

Two dark-clad security types pulled her inside and quickly rolled the side door closed. They maneuvered Sara to a seat and strapped her in. The black chopper bulleted west across San Francisco Bay. The TV helicopter made chase but was no match. The black helicopter quickly crossed the bay, over the hills and out to the ocean. They flew low over the Pacific to avoid radar, speeding southwest.

"How did you find me?" Sara shouted through a headset, while one man bandaged her bleeding forehead and handed her a water bottle.

"My people found out you were jailed," Melton replied. "And the impounded vehicles, from police radio."

Sara adjusted the earmuffs and mouthpiece that seemed very 21st century to her.

"They traced your name back to the arrest last night," he said. "They know you rented those cars for the Cypress Street blockade."

"You know about that?" Sara asked. "Did it work? Were they successful?"

"It's only been a few minutes," Melton replied. "But so far, no fatalities. No injuries of any kind. News coverage from multiple helicopter views shows all traffic stopped on both sides of the collapse."

Sara felt a rush of relief.

"Where are we going?" Sara asked.

"We're getting you to safety," Melton said. "We'll rendezvous with one of my freighters in about forty-five minutes."

"But wait," Sara said. "I need to get to my team—"

"You can't do that," Melton cut her off. "Think about it. The police know who you are, and now the public will, too."

"How so?"

"I guarantee you," Melton said. "That TV helicopter has video footage of you being lifted into this helicopter. It will go national, probably already has by now."

"Then they can trace this helicopter, too," Sara said. "And you'll be implicated as well."

Melton smiled. "This helicopter can't be traced," he said. "No markings, no registration, and it's not even kept at my private airport. We also had the benefit of deception. Only local authorities have reacted since no one could foresee the earthquake—except you. The military will be called in later. So, this quick escape will not be tracked by radar."

Sara considered his words, but she was exhausted. The long day, and her injuries, caught up to her quickly. She leaned her head back and fell into a deep sleep.

The sleek chopper powered on.

***

Julia's house was situated near the top of a ridgeline where the road behind sat higher than her house. She reasoned that the road was safer than the house since nothing could fall on her. So, she walked out to the mailbox and checked her watch; it was 5:01. Three minutes until the earthquake. Was she crazy to believe all this? She would find out soon enough. She walked the lane with a constant eye on the bay and found a perfect vantage point between the tree line.

At 5:03, she stopped and turned complete attention to the bay. Julia listened intently, stood square, head up, and waited. It seemed to get quiet. She didn't hear or see any birds; she must be imagining that, like anticipating something in a scary movie. But then she did feel something. The ground did feel different.

At once, the ground shook. It started slow but grew in waves. Julia knelt to the ground and looked in awe as the landscape rolled up and down. Sounds she had never imagined filled the air as rocks rolled down the hillside, taking out trees as they moved. The ground waffled again; it knocked Julia to the ground, and her kitchen window exploded out of its frame. Her neighbor's stone chimney toppled over and crashed into rubble, just missing Julia's house.

Fifteen seconds of terror seemed like an eternity, and then silence. When something beyond human senses affects a person, it takes time to react. Julia slowly got to her feet. Smoke and dust filled the air. Across the bay, broken dust clouds rising from the treetops appeared to be forest fires.

Julia ran inside to check on the house. All seemed in order except for the kitchen window. Her TV set was still where she'd left it. Relieved there was no significant damage, she ran to her neighbor's house, where the chimney had fallen. Doris was elderly, and no doubt frightened about what had just happened.

By the time Julia made it out the front door, Doris was already standing in her front yard near the downed chimney.

"Honey," Doris said. "I don't know what I'm going to do about this."

"Let's get you inside," Julia replied. "I'll make us some tea."

The place was a mess, but nothing major other than the chimney. Julia got to the kitchen and found broken dishes from the cupboards on the floor and countertops. The refrigerator door hung open, with almost everything spilled out. She sighed and closed the refrigerator door.

"Let's go to my place," Julia said. "Not as much damage."

They walked next door, where Julia helped Doris to the living room couch. Julia went off to make tea while Doris relaxed. When Julia walked into the kitchen, she panicked. Everything from her cupboards and refrigerator was neatly packed into boxes and coolers. Her bathroom was the same, and wall hangings, clocks, books, and lamps were. What would Doris think about that?

Once Doris caught her breath, she noticed the TV set and throw- pillow on the floor by the sliding glass door. Wall hangings lay next to her on the couch, all nicely stacked. Julia quickly returned from the kitchen in hopes of keeping her preoccupied. She caught Doris looking while handing her tea.

"Honey," Doris said. "How did you clean up so quickly?"

Julia thought about it.

"I was actually re-arranging," she answered. "And cleaning when it hit."

Doris didn't look convinced.

"Why don't we turn on the news," Julia said. "To see what they say about the earthquake."

Every channel had the same coverage of the Cypress Street Blockades in Oakland. All traffic was safe from harm on both bridge decks, with four automobiles blocking access to the collapsed bridges. The same rhetoric from other news stations that four cars on each bridge deck came to a stop, and the drivers scattered away.

Julia covered her mouth in shock. Then another live feed cut into the broadcast. It was clearly helicopter footage of the Bay Bridge where another collapse had occurred. The camera focused on a semi-trailer that had dropped into a collapsed section of the bridge deck; smoke still billowed from the wreckage. Then, a black helicopter came into view, hovering over the destruction with a drop ladder. The camera zoomed in close to the drop point. The ladder pulled a woman from the wreckage, reeled her in, and soared off into the distance. The feed continued momentarily, but the black helicopter left from the opposite side of the trestle bridge and was quickly out of sight.

The station quickly cut to a split-screen: one side showed a newscaster trying to explain what she had just seen; the other was a zoomed-in still photo of an injured Sara Gathers hanging from a rope ladder.

"We have multiple eyewitness accounts," the reporter said. "That describes a truck swerving side to side, clearing traffic, and making a wild ninety-degree turn to a stop just before the earthquake hit. When the bridge deck collapsed, the truck was pulled down, too."

The backdrop was the buckled bridge deck, and the rear of the flatbed speared up behind her.

"When we arrived, our helicopter hovered over there." She pointed out away from the bridge. "There was an unknown helicopter where I'm standing now and a hooded man looking down into the wreckage. Then the helicopter slowly lifted, maneuvered into position over the tear in the bridge, and dropped a ladder. It rescued a lone individual, assumed to be the driver. The woman you see now on your screen.

"And there's one thing that rings true from each eyewitness account: If it weren't for that truck, many people would have died here today."

"Honey," Doris asked. "Is that you hanging from that ladder?"

Bewildered, Julia did not react, her face stoic and silent. She went over to the throw pillow and sat cross-legged in front of the TV set.

***

The newscast went viral. Coast to coast, local and national news stations could not get enough of this developing story.

Dinner was served in the cafeteria at Fort Patterson Air Force Base in Fairbanks, Alaska, when news broke of the California earthquake. All eyes were focused on the TV set mounted to the wall.

"Man, that chick is hot," a voice said.

"No kidding," another man said.

"Hey," a third voice added. "I know her."

A chorus of laughs burst out.

"No, I'm serious," he affirmed. "Well, I don't actually know her, but I know who she is."

The main doors swung open as Captain Matthew Jackson entered the room.

"Captain!" All voices stood and saluted.

"At ease, gentlemen," Jackson said. He made his way to the buffet line and filled a plate. On his way to the tables, Jackson noticed all eyes on the TV set. He stopped and turned, assuming they were watching a World Series game.

"Captain?" a voice asked. "Isn't that the lady who took us down in the VX trials?"

Jackson laid his plate down and approached the TV. "Gentlemen," he said. "What in the world is going on here?"

***

Miguel nervously waited in DeFremery Park with four drivers from the High Flyers team.

"I can't believe this actually happened," he said in Spanish. "I mean, I knew it was supposed to happen, but wow! And we did it. We did it!"

The whole group was so excited. Guys in the back seat patted him on the shoulder. Guys in the front seat hugged him.

"Where are those guys?" Miguel said, checking mirrors and gazing out across the park.

He only knew the park's rendezvous point, but it was a big park. Sirens and flashing lights filled the air. A sound that had scared him yesterday but not so much today. He was grateful for their change in fortune and tried not to think about the 'what if' they were still in jail.

Suddenly the passenger doors swung open. Mason shoved his way into the front seat, Luisa and Mariana dove into the back. Ethan jammed in there, too.

"Let's go!" Mason shouted.

"Where to?" Miguel asked and threw the car in gear.

"South on Adeline," Mason replied. "Till we reach the harbor, then loop west on Harbor Road. Shouldn't be too much traffic that way. We can see the Bay Bridge from there."

"How did everything go up there?"

"Perfect," Miguel replied. "Not one single car on the upper deck."

"Same below," Mason said. "We did it! We did it!" Mason let out a howl that could be heard across the park.

Twenty minutes later, they were at the shore of the Outer Harbor. Mason pulled out a pair of binoculars and focused on the bridge collapse. Helicopters hovered on both sides, and emergency vehicles packed the decks.

Sadly, he saw the upended semi-trailer, nose down in the wreckage. He dropped to his knees and handed the binoculars to Miguel. Miguel lifted the binoculars to his eyes, then hung his head low.

"What is it?" Luisa asked and grabbed the binoculars. "Is that our truck?" she asked. "Is that our truck?"

Neither Mason nor Miguel could respond.

"It's Sara, isn't it?" Luisa asked. "What did she do?"

***

Eventually, they packed into the car and drove south. The farther they went away from the city, the fewer signs of earthquake damage. They could all tell Mason's heart was ripped out. You could hear a pin drop in that car. After a couple hours, they stopped for gas. Mason did not move. Miguel worked the pump. Everyone got out to stretch their legs while Ethan and Luisa went inside for water and snacks.

The salesclerk had his back to Ethan and Luisa as they placed everything on the counter.

"Excuse me?" Ethan asked.

"Oh, I'm sorry," the salesclerk said, ringing up their stuff. "Can you believe this? I mean, I don't know what to think. But it looks like we got some local heroes or superheroes that saved a lot of people."

He turned back to the television. "Oh, there she is again."

Ethan and Luisa looked up in amazement at a freeze-frame of Sara on a rope ladder. Ethan fumbled for cash in his wallet. Luisa burst out the door and ran across the parking lot.

"She's OK!" she shouted. "She was rescued!"

Chapter 46

Hearst Castle

Sara opened her eyes and rubbed her forehead. Deep sleep rejuvenated her, and everything was coming back now, the jail cell, the flatbed truck, and falling into the collapsed bridge. She looked up to see Melton sitting across from her.

"There's our destination," Melton shouted over the headset. He pointed to a large ship with a setting sun as a backdrop. The oil tanker was heading south through calm Pacific waters. They pulled into a hovering position over a clearly marked helipad.

"It says *Melton* on the side," Sara sarcastically offered.

"Hang on," Melton said with a smile. "Crosswinds."

The helicopter touched down in the center of a red circle. The engines throttled down while two crewmen latched the helicopter in place. Sara started to unbuckle.

"Not yet," Melton said.

No sooner had the words left his mouth than Sara felt a mechanical movement jerk her seat.

The helipad was supported on scissor lifts extending downward into the ship's hull. In seconds Sara could see inside the gigantic tanker.

"It's retractable," Melton said. "In a few minutes, they'll roll it off the gantry. The pad goes back up, and no visible helicopter."

"So, you're in the oil business?" Sara asked.

"Yes," Melton replied. "In a big way. This ship is carrying crude from my oil fields in the Philippines. The Melton Oil & Refining company imports oil from all over the globe."

The helipad stopped with a *clang*. When the doors rolled open, two technicians greeted Melton and Sara. They escorted them across an immense metallic floor toward what appeared to be an elevator shaft. Sara could not help but notice 'Melton Oil' embroidered on the technicians' jumpsuits.

The elevator took them up ten floors to an outlook, atop the command bridge. A technician handed Sara a hooded windbreaker. They walked out into what would be a calm summer day, but for the stiff breeze.

"We're doing about twelve knots," Melton said. "I thought the windbreaker might be helpful."

"Thank you." Sara pulled it on. "And it even says Melton Oil."

Since Melton now had her undivided attention, he wanted answers. This curiosity standing next to him was unlike anything he had ever imagined. What was her secret, her special gift? How could he get that, too? Sara zipped up the jacket and took in the view from the giant ship. The sunset and open sea air seemed dreamlike compared to the nightmare she had just experienced.

"You are worth millions," Melton stated. "But with your knowledge, you could be worth billions. So, why are you blocking bridges instead of relaxing on a beach with servants fanning your half-naked body?"

"You don't know anything about me," Sara replied. "Just financial statistics."

"You're right," Melton said. "In fact, I'm not even sure your name is Sara Gathers. Your manufactured identification dates back two and a half years, but before that, nothing. I know you and your accomplices didn't exist until recently. And you have unnatural knowledge of the future."

Sara was not in the mood for this discussion, and Melton could sense it. She was worried about Mason and the rest of the team. Had they made it back all right? Were they arrested?

"I apologize for being so direct," Melton said. "I know you're tired, but we still have a few hours before reaching port. I'll show you to a cabin where you can rest up."

The elevator descended to the second level, crew quarters. Sara followed Melton to the end of a hallway, where he pulled a key and opened a door.

"This is my private cabin," Melton said. "But it's yours for the night. I'll be next door if you need anything."

Sara panned the room. Definitely an upscale hotel appearance and hardly used.

"I could use a nightcap after this day," Sara said. "Is there room service?"

"Right this way," Melton replied. He crossed the room and opened a cabinet above a bar sink. "What's your pleasure?"

"Bourbon on the rocks," Sara said.

"I'll make two," Melton said. He poured the drinks and started for the door but stopped short and turned. He remembered asking her a question when they first met but received no answer.

"Why did you go to Valdez?" he asked.

Sara flashed back and sipped her drink.

"You went there to try and prevent the spill," Melton said, puzzle pieces falling into place. "Didn't you?"

"These gigantic ships aren't safe," Sara replied.

Melton sipped his drink.

"That's not what I asked," he said. "The *Valdez* had design flaws. This one does not. Its double hull construction is unique, and it operates with a dozen isolated tanks, each tank separated by cofferdams. One tank is always empty as a backup in case of a leak. Fully loaded, we can carry 300,000 metric tons of crude oil."

"That translates to about 100,000 metric tons of CO_2 being thrown up into the atmosphere," Sara countered.

Melton cocked his head. He didn't think in those terms. "An interesting response," he said. "But that still doesn't answer the question."

"I'm not prepared to discuss this with you," Sara said.

"All of a sudden, your gambling fortune," Melton reasoned, "seems to be nothing but background noise. A step into a larger arena."

"Good night," Sara said softly.

"We'll discuss this tomorrow," Melton said.

***

Sara awoke to a tap on the door at 6:00 A.M.

"Ma'am." A man with a breakfast tray was at the door. "We will rendezvous with the *Exodus* soon. Would you like something to eat?"

"Please."

"Mr. Melton requested," he said, placing the tray on a coffee table, "that you be ready in sixty minutes. I will be here to escort you down to the docking level."

"Thank you," Sara replied. "I'll be ready."

***

The mighty tanker slowed to a stop and dropped its anchors. An ocean-worthy yacht gently pulled alongside and tied off while officers from the main deck of the tanker looked on. Inside the tanker, the crewman lifted latches and cranked open a small man door on the port side, just above the waterline.

Once secured, a metallic ramp dropped in from the yacht. Sara and Melton made their way up the ramp, and soon the *Exodus* headed out to open sea.

"We're fifty nautical miles to San Simeon," Melton said. "Should be docking within the hour."

Sara was not surprised by the over-the-top extravagance of the *Exodus*. Between Angeli and Melton, she was kind of getting used to it. She also knew that, at some point, Melton would corner her for more answers. However, it was a pleasant cruise, and to her delight, complete with fancy drinks. Melton captained the boat from a shaded deck and told sea stories the whole time. Once they made the sight of land, Melton handed Sara a large sunhat and scarf. "Put these on," Melton said.

"What's this for?" she asked.

"And make sure it covers your face," he replied, "so no one recognizes you."

He turned the wheel and checked depth gauges. "Up ahead is my private harbor," Melton said while dropping the big yacht to idle speed. "It was part of the deal."

"Deal?" Sara asked.

"When I purchased Hearst Castle from the state of California," he said. "The harbor came along with it."

"If it's private," Sara asked, "why the disguise?"

"Sometimes paparazzi camp out over there on San Simeon Pier," Melton replied. "It's still public, but the harbor up ahead is mine."

Melton tenderly pulled the yacht up to the pier. Crewmen with tie-off ropes jumped out and stretched their lines. Melton turned the key to shut down the engines. A limousine waited at the dock while the crew tied off the boat. Sara and Melton exited down a fabric-covered ramp.

"Here at last," Melton said as the limo pulled away. "We'll be at the Castle shortly."

Sara was still not convinced that Melton's actions were genuine. She believed, without a doubt, that he was only interested in her knowledge of future events. But at this point, it didn't matter; he'd pulled her off that bridge when Sara had lost all hope. Now she just had to play along and see where this was going.

She thought about Mason and the others. How did they fare? Did they make it back to the Second Chance Ranch? Then she considered what Melton said. Would her exposure lead the authorities to the ranch? Could everyone already be arrested? Should she try calling the house? All these things she would keep in play until she found out what Melton was up to.

***

Glorious Hearst Castle was just as Sara imagined it would be. She had never been there but heard stories and seen pictures since childhood. Melton hadn't changed anything; the furnishings and tapestries were all still there.

"It costs a fortune in maintenance and restoration," he quipped. "I can't afford to change any of it."

Melton stopped short of a full tour since he knew Sara might not be up to it. He directed staff members to show her to her room.

"They'll take your clothes and wash them," he said.

"What I'm wearing is fine," Sara replied.

"No," Melton said. "Yesterday, you crashed a truck and were pulled from a smoke plume in those clothes."

Sara shrugged.

"Even the sea air could not blow away the odor emanating from them," Melton followed. "In the meantime, we will find you something more appropriate to wear."

Sara grudgingly conceded.

"We'll have brunch by the pool," Melton said. "'Till then, I have business issues to deal with."

***

To Sara's relief, the clothes laid out on the bed were very conservative. At exactly 11:00 A.M., she heard a knock on her door and was escorted poolside, where Melton was already seated. He sat alone, facing the famous Romanesque columns and a backdrop of foothills. As Sara approached the table, she was reminded of their first meeting at her ranch.

"This is my favorite view of the property," Melton said.

"I can see why," Sara said.

Melton stood while a waiter pulled out a chair for Sara. He laid out lunch entrees and placed two bottles of her Special Reserve on the table.

"Seriously?" Sara asked.

"It's a good wine," Melton replied. "Would you like some?" And on cue, Henri appeared at the table and opened a bottle.

"Good morning, Madam," he said and poured her a glass.

"Good morning to you," Sara replied. "Although I'm not sure I'm happy to see you."

"I'm sorry, Madam," Henri offered.

"We did not intend to upset you," Melton said. "Henri, please have a seat."

"You're not upsetting me," Sara said. "I'm just confused by all this."

"Henri's employ involves more than just winemaking," Melton said.

"Like what, for instance?" Sara asked. "Does he rescue damsels in distress, like you?"

Melton laughed.

"Am I supposed to live up in one of these fancy towers?" Sara followed. "Guarded by two knights in shining armor?"

"No," Melton replied, still chuckling. "Just the opposite." He sipped his wine. "After brunch, I'd like to show you something."

***

They stepped into an elevator, where Melton touched the LL button.

"This takes us to the lower level," Melton said. "Where they used to store food and beverages."

"And the wine cellar," Henri added with a smile.

Momentarily, the elevator stopped, and the door rolled back; they stepped out into a dark room. Melton flipped a light switch to reveal a large room with empty shelving lined against concrete walls.

"When I bought the place, there was still food stacked here," Melton said. "I had it all cleared and cleaned out."

They proceeded across the room to an opening with no door where Melton flipped another switch.

"This is the wine room," he said.

The room stretched like a library stack with shelves lining the walls and rows of central shelving with tight aisleways.

"There must be thousands of bottles here," Sara said.

"Tens of thousands," Melton clarified. "Mostly Henri's work that we distribute. Others have been here for more than fifty years. But that's not the best part. Step over here, please."

They walked over to a rack centered on an outside wall. It was slightly different from the rest, and it had a gap between it and the next shelf. The only gap between any rack in the wine cellar. Melton nodded to Henri, who reached into the opening, pulled something, and the frame moved like it was dislodged.

"Step back," Henri said.

"You've got to be kidding me," Sara said, sarcastically.

Henri pulled on the rack. It rotated about one end and swung open to reveal a large cavity. Henri stepped forward, pulled down a lever, and a vast catacomb lit up. Sara stepped inside to a jaw-dropping moment.

"They must have discovered it during excavation for this basement," Melton said. "But no public or private records of the caves exist. Henri found them by chance while restoring the wine cellar. This is the best part of the castle to me, like finding a priceless painting in the attic of an old house.

"The main area in front of us was built and furnished by Hearst," Melton said. He pointed to a cave across the way curving out of sight. "That run extends down into a vast open cave structure."

They walked into the heart of the complex. Hearst's private library. The Newspaper Mogul devoted one area entirely to press issues. Glass-cased shelves and storage units displayed the most important headlines of Hearst's day. A wooden bar positioned in one corner was elaborately carved and detailed, vintage bottles still lined its shelves.

"This is amazing," Sara said. "And it all looks new."

"This cave is free of stalactites," Melton said. "And as dry as a salt mine. Nothing ages here."

As with the castle above, Melton hadn't changed any of Hearst's work, partly because it was a piece of living history and partly because he didn't want workers down there. It became his own private study.

"All it needed was a little dusting," Melton pointed to a tributary cave. "As I mentioned, these forks extend out into the foothills."

Melton flipped another switch, and they lit up. All caves lined with high-tech equipment built carefully into them, a high-tech extension of Hearst's vision.

"You two have been busy," Sara said.

"Weekend projects," Melton said. "One extends to a house on the property a half-mile away. We found a hand-built shaft cut up through the top of the cave."

"There was an old round, rusty lid at the top," Henri added. "When we cranked it open, we couldn't push it up. Something was holding it down."

"It took a few days," Melton said. "But we finally found it in the garage of an old house on the property, carefully covered with a wood-burning stove. We had the lid restored to good working order and rolled the stove back over it to maintain secrecy."

Melton took Sara to the castle, but why show her this? A secret cave that only a few people ever knew about. Sara began to realize that Melton was not the Nazi he thought he was.

"OK," Sara said. "So, why am I here, and why are you showing me all this?"

Melton responded cautiously.

"Because this could be your new base of operations," he offered. "The castle facilities would make a better workplace for you, completely hidden from the world; you could work in anonymity."

"I am completely hidden," Sara said.

"Not anymore," Melton said. "Follow me." He grabbed a remote and clicked on the television. "This footage has gone nationwide. Someone in Paso Robles will recognize you, and the authorities will come calling if they haven't already.

"But I can put a team of people at your fingertips," Melton continued. "Vehicles, boats, helicopters, an entire tactical security team at your disposal."

"I don't need that type of help," Sara said. She turned her gaze to the Hearst media center. "My days of rescuing are over."

"*Valdez*, yesterday's earthquake, and many others, I'm sure," Melton said. "You see things before they happen, Sara. But now you say that in the future, you'll sit back and watch catastrophic events unfold, watch people die, and do nothing to stop it?

"Look at them," Melton said, standing at Sara's side. "Newspaper articles from days gone by, yet mostly about disaster, war, and tragedy of all kinds. Humanity is caught up in it, then, now, and in the future."

Sara could not pull her eyes away from the yellowed headlines.

"What future did you come from?"

Sara hesitated. "One on the brink," she whispered. "One of impending disaster, caused by people like you."

"Because I throw millions of metric tons of CO_2 into the atmosphere?" Melton asked mockingly.

Sara looked away. "I've seen enough for one day."

"I'm sorry," Melton tendered.

"I'm going back to my room," Sara said.

✳ ✳ ✳

Sara thought about it all afternoon. Her meetings with Melton could not all be by random chance. Were the forces of nature pulling them in the same direction? Or was it that the higher you move up the ladder, the fewer people populate each level, where people like Angeli and Melton reside. This was an open door, and she should consider the invitation.

But this man stood for the industries she was fighting to stop. She couldn't possibly ally with him. On the other hand, he had perfect resources for her, but he didn't really know about her mission. If this were to have any chance of working, Sara would have to tell Melton everything, and he had to buy in.

The sun hung low in the western sky when Sara seated herself at a poolside table. Momentarily, a shadow crossed her and stopped.

"I thought you might like some refreshments, Madam," Henri greeted her and laid down a Charcuterie plate and a pitcher of lemonade.

"Henri," Sara said, a brief smile came to her face. "Thank you, I'm starving."

"And I know what you like," Henri replied. He handed her a napkin and sat across from her. "I must apologize for the deceptive manner in which we first knew each other. It was not my choice, and I was uncomfortable with it."

"I believe you," Sara said. "Thank you."

"The vineyards here are vast," Henri said. "Maybe one day we can walk them together and sample grapes."

"I'd like that," Sara replied.

Henri stood and patted her on the shoulder. "I'll leave you to your dinner," he said.

Sara assumed Melton would make an appearance sooner or later. She enjoyed the offerings from Henri and watched the sunset. Eventually, Melton walked up and sat at the table. Sara kept to herself.

"I've had more boring conversations with myself," Melton said, breaking the silence.

No response.

"Sara, whatever burden you carry must be released," Melton said.

"You have no idea," she smirked.

"What was it like?" Melton asked. "In your future on the brink."

Sara got up and walked toward the Roman pergola; Melton followed.

"Wildfires in the Alaskan tundra," she said. "Methane bubbling out of arctic lakes. The north pole was centered where we are now, with an ozone hole streaming in UV radiation. And frightening auroras along the whole west coast."

She reached out and touched an ancient stone column.

"Hmm," she whimpered. "They were nicknamed the Western Lights. Some called them Aurora Cancerous because the pole was closing on the tropic of Cancer, and so many suffered from severe sunburns."

Melton paced and thought about it. "And how did you get here?" he asked. "Into this time period."

"It's hard to explain," Sara said. "It was an accident, a natural phenomenon. It had to do with the core movement that we were tracking. But I'm stuck here, and I can't go back. So, I decided to do something about it. To make people aware of what's coming, both man-made and natural, and hopefully turn the tide."

"So, to prove your story is legitimate and effect change," Melton said. "You tried to stop the *Valdez* and then saved many people from dying in an earthquake."

"Prove it to just one person," Sara said. "Because she can change the world, not me."

"Who?"

"I can't tell you that," Sara said. "Not now anyway."

"These are the first steps," Melton reasoned. "You're laying a foundation to start a movement against pollution, greenhouse gasses specifically."

There was a growing fear inside Sara that Melton was too dug in. She hoped she could convince him to be a leader and move away from oil to alternate fuel sources. But when she really thought about it, she realized it was impossible. Melton owned a fleet of oil tankers, Hearst Castle, and who knew what else. A billionaire in his thirties who would be an old man before any future disasters would occur.

Her mind tripped back to a more immediate problem. She had to warn Mason and Ethan about the police and the only way was to drive to the ranch.

"I need to borrow a car," Sara said.

"Excuse me?"

"I have to get to the ranch," Sara replied. "To warn Mason."

"Sara, that could be dangerous," Melton said. "The authorities could already be there. I can send in specialists so that neither you nor I are implicated."

"And how long will it take to round up those guys?" Sara asked.

Melton arched his brow.

"It's only an hour from here," Sara said. "I can be there by nightfall."

"No."

"What?"

"*We* can be there by nightfall," Melton replied. "But you should change clothes first. Back into what you wore yesterday. They should be clean by now."

In short order, they left the castle in an off-road 4WD vehicle. Melton knew the curving roads through the foothills and made good time. When they reached the outskirts of Paso Robles, Sara gave directions, and soon they crept slowly up a gravel road.

The property was dark, there were no lights in the house. Only an old barn light illuminated the area behind the house. They pulled up and parked near the barn.

"This doesn't look like your property," Melton said.

"It's a big ranch," Sara said. "This is the south house. I don't use it for much of anything, but we keep equipment in the barn."

"So, why are we here?"

"Turn the lights off," Sara said.

Melton turned the key and pressed the light button.

"The house I live in is over that ridge, about a half-mile from here."

Sara started walking; Melton followed.

"So, we have the element of surprise," Melton said. "In case some-one is there."

"That's right," Sara said. "No chances. From that ridge up ahead, we'll be able to see the house and the wine barn."

They cut between rows of vineyards and saw a growing light beyond the ridge. Sara bent over and eventually knelt between the vines as they drew closer. The house and wine barn were in full view.

The house was surrounded by emergency vehicles, police cars, ambulances, and unmarked vehicles. Men in tactical gear moved in and out of the barns, the house, and around the immediate property.

"I guess they're interested in me," Sara whispered. "I hope Mason and the others were not there. I don't see their vehicle, so that's good. Let's go." Sara tugged at his jacket.

When they got back to the vehicle, two figures leaned against it. Sara stopped dead in her tracks, heart pounding. Not again, she thought. Then a voice broke the silence.

"Nice ride," the familiar voice said. "Would have made a great getaway car."

"Mason!" Sara cried. She ran over and hugged him.

"Ethan!" she said. "I'm so glad to see you."

"I thought we lost you on the bridge," Mason said. "Then we finally saw the rescue on TV."

He turned his gaze to Melton. "Do we have you to thank for that?" Mason asked.

Melton nodded. "I don't really want to break up this reunion," Melton replied. "But we should be going."

"We'll be all right," Sara said. "This lane goes away from the house. They were separate properties till I bought them up. Just go slow. No lights."

Melton pulled away, and the four-wheel-drive disappeared into the darkness.

"Question," Melton asked. "Could the authorities have confiscated your secret devices?"

"Not a chance," Sara replied.

"Because they're in a hidden basement," Mason said.

"No," Sara said. "They're not."

"What?" All voices said at the same time.

"I had a long time to think about it on the ride down from Oakland," Sara said. "What if something went wrong and the authorities showed up? Like they are now. So, I took them from the cellar, went to the bank, and placed them in a safety deposit box."

"That's brilliant, Sara," Melton said.

"We need to get there first thing in the morning," she said.

Melton came to the end of the gravel lane and cautiously looked around. He flipped on the headlights and turned onto the main road.

"Maybe you shouldn't go," Melton said. "I can send Henri. No one will recognize him."

Sara did not respond.

"Sara, I think it's best," he repeated. "But I'll leave that up to you."

Melton kept his eyes open for anything suspicious off the side of the road. "And you realize now," he said. "There's no going back to that ranch ever again."

She finally offered. "I'll think about it."

Melton downshifted and pushed his way through the winding hills.

"Wait," Sara asked. "Where's Miguel?"

"He took the others down to LA," Mason replied.

"Thank god."

Ethan pointed at Melton and turned to Sara. "So, are we on the same team now?" he asked.

Melton chuckled.

✳✳✳

The castle shone like a beacon at night, visible for miles in the darkness. Mason remembered Melton talking about Hearst Castle, but it seemed surreal when they reached the entry gates. He looked over at Sara to gauge her response but saw none.

A brief tour took them directly to the cavern where Melton laid out the plan for future covert operations. How they could all work and live in the castle, totally hidden from the public?

"We really get to work here?" Ethan asked.

"And live here?" Mason added.

"I'm not so sure yet," Sara said.

"What more proof do you need?" Melton asked. "Then what we just saw at your ranch."

"In time they will …"

"Will what? You'll be chastised by the press," Melton said and lifted a hand to the glass cases of Hearst headlines. "You will be grilled for months, or years, by governmental agencies, military, and police.

"And they won't let up, Sara, ever. You and your two companions must be disguised in public from now on. Tactical gear, hair color, you name it.

"As previously mentioned, I can put a team of people at your fingertips," Melton continued. "Vehicles, boats, helicopters, an entire tactical security team at your disposal."

Mason raised an eyebrow.

"One other thing," Melton said. "Eventually, you'll need someone in the military you trust to source out information, covertly."

Sara turned in frustration.

"Anyone putting together the puzzle," Melton said, "as I did, will learn about your enormous winnings, *Valdez*, and now the earthquake. They won't just forget, not about you."

"Really," Sara said. "And what about you? A man who stands for everything we are fighting against. Am I supposed to be a turncoat who sides with the enemy?"

Melton reached for a remote. From the techno side of the cavern, he pulled up a video showing his oil fields and fleet of tankers. Then he clicked on another screen of wind farms and vast solar arrays.

"These are mine, too," Melton said. "I've made enough money to last ten lifetimes, so I'm mothballing the fleet and converting to renewable energy sources. There are many governmental subsidies on infrastructure build-up, so, low start-up costs. Once up and running, they get you hooked into the power grid. The power companies must accept and pay for your contribution to the grid. I'm even considering electric cars, but battery development is not there yet."

"It will be," Ethan said.

Melton picked up a thick binder from a worktable and handed it to Sara. "These are bills of sale for the oil tankers," he said. "The ledgers are quite lengthy, but you're welcome to study them."

Sara flipped through the ledgers with intent eyes.

"You don't know me," Melton said. "I don't want to be an old man who realizes I could have had a hand in preventing your dismal future."

Sara looked around the facility, wheels turning in her head. "What if we put out a decoy?" she asked.

"Excuse me?" Melton asked.

"A few minutes ago, you said that we had to be disguised in public," Sara replied. "But what if the public thought someone else drove that flatbed and was lifted into your helicopter?"

"Like whom?" Melton asked.

Sara made eye contact with Ethan.

"Julia?"

Chapter 47
Julia Gathers

I t had been weeks since the earthquake. The For Sale sign posted in the front yard said everything. Julia contacted Arnie Wilmore and accepted the NOAA position in Colorado. She felt like the anonymity of the Boulder campus would be a perfect fit for her, especially now.

The house was in boxes when she received a call from Ethan. He wanted to stop by to wish her luck and fill her in on the latest news. She packed the car with essentials and a few crates of books and memorabilia. The TV set was still on the living room floor when a newscast caught her attention.

"Six weeks after the collapse of the Cypress Street Viaduct, an engineering report has finally been released," the newscaster said. "It confirms that design flaws in second-level columns led to a progressive collapse of the upper deck. Similar findings were issued for the Bay Bridge expansion joint failure.

"Even though no injuries resulted on either bridge, rumors still persist that it was sabotage, and the mystery woman remains unidentified. Many locals believe this woman to be Professor Julia Gathers, who has denied these rumors and recently resigned her position at the university."

✳✳✳

The afternoon drive up from Paso Robles gave Ethan time to think about the discussion with Julia.

"She suspects something," he said. "But I'm not sure exactly what."

"Suspects?" Sara asked.

"She asked me about you a couple of times," Ethan replied. "And I always deflected."

"When she meets me," Sara said. "She meets me."

"I'm not so sure it's that simple," Ethan said.

"It has to happen at some point."

"But when she meets you," Ethan questioned. "It could change her life, and you might never be born."

"I'm already here, in this timeline," Sara said. "With everything we do, we make changes. Our presence here is something entirely new to this timeline. There won't be a paradox because I won't meet myself, so I'm not going to snap out of existence."

Ethan shook his head.

"Look, let's say that I was never born because of this meeting today," Sara said. "But isn't what we've accomplished more important? Giving Julia a belief, an understanding, of what her life must become? Julia is more important than I am in the future, so maybe my part in all this has run its course. I've passed the baton that nature intended. Besides, I feel like there's nothing left inside me. I'm at a turning point between exhaustion and surrender. In a way, I almost hope I disappear in there."

Ethan said nothing. His retracted expression and pursed lips were response enough as he pulled up at Julia's house.

"It will be OK," Sara said with a detached smile.

"Are you sure you want to do this?" Ethan asked.

"Yes, I'm sure," Sara replied. "This is a loop that has to be closed."

Sara stepped out of the car and walked to the doorstep. She reached for the doorbell, but on cue, the door opened. Julia expected to see Ethan, but the face that looked up at her was Sara. Sara thought she was prepared, but she was not ready to see Julia, so young and beautiful. What seemed like hours of memory recall startled them into a motionless and speechless state.

Julia's thoughts swam. *This is the girl in the computer video with dead mammoths, the same girl pulled off the bridge by a helicopter. She's taller than me, even in flats, so I'm not the one being thrown through time.*

All the while, Sara was lost in her own thoughts as well. *This is my mother, but she can't be. This is the woman who raised me, the mother who took me to the beach, made me study, took me to horse races. I've traveled across time to get back here. But I'm older now, and she is so young, she can't possibly believe this is me. I'm not even born yet.*

Their eyes welled up; Julia covered her mouth.

"May I come in?" Sara asked.

Julia nodded.

Sara walked the main level taking everything in; a house she had only seen in pictures from a photo album but felt like she knew. Curious, Julia followed as Sara walked upstairs. There were bedrooms to the left and right and a bathroom straight on. Sara at once turned right.

"I remember this room from old photographs," Sara said.

This supernatural meeting could not be possible, or could it? Julia realized just who this stranger really was, with similar features, hands, and even her voice.

Fighting back the tears, Julia reluctantly asked, "When did you see these old photographs?"

"Many years from now." Sara sighed, crying, as she fell onto the bed.

Julia did not know this person but felt she did. She reached for a blanket, laid it over Sara, then ran her fingers through Sara's hair and rubbed her shoulders.

"I've toughened up since I was thrown back here." Sara wiped her eyes. "I thought this would be easier. I'm sorry. I guess I just wasn't prepared."

Julia couched her response.

"Ethan wouldn't tell me much about you," she said. "But after all that happened, I'm convinced you're both from a different time."

Sara sat up and pulled herself together.

"Yes, we are," Sara said.

"I understand now why Ethan reached out to me," Julia said. She stood and walked to the window. "At first, it was difficult to believe, but it's starting to make sense. He seemed to know everything about my life and my future.

"Hmm, I even accepted a new position at NOAA, as director, no less, just as he predicted. But as far as I know, without intervention from time travelers."

Julia turned back to Sara.

"So, why are you here?" she asked. "What do you have to tell me?"

"I suppose I could talk about how you convinced me to work for you at NOAA," Sara said. "Or all the missions you sent me on or other future disasters, but I don't want to talk shop.

"I'd rather talk about the times you took me hiking in the Rockies, helped me with my homework, and went horseback riding.

"When I was thirteen, we went on vacation, or maybe it was work for you, to California. We went whale watching at Bodega Bay and came across a dead gray whale that had washed ashore. It traumatized me but set me on a course."

Julia adjusted herself. Too much to take in.

"No," she said. "This isn't possible."

Sara thought about it.

"Imagine waking up in a desert," she said. "Alone, with nothing in sight but dust, brush, and blistering heat."

Julia's expression turned grim.

"That's what moving through time is like." Sara grimaced.

She stood and faced Julia.

"I know these past few months have been confusing and difficult for you," Sara said. "But there's one last piece you need to know."

"The things you speak of are not within the timeline template that I am privy to," Julia said. "I think I've had enough for one day."

Sara walked to the window, then turned back to young Julia. *How the world changes*, she thought.

"What is it?" Julia asked, sensing her thoughts.

"Things are the same," Sara said. "Yet different, in subtle ways."

Sara knew Julia's life was about to morph into something much more complicated than her life in academia. She would have to make adjustments.

"You need to surround yourself with men in power, outside NOAA," Sara said. "As the director, you will be dealing with future events that require cooperation between all branches of government and the military."

"There is a man in the military that you've already met, but like you, he is still relatively unknown. His name is Jackson, Matthew Jackson. I'm not sure of his current rank. Do you remember that name?"

"Vaguely."

"Something about a chemical agent hearing."

"Oh, yes," Julia remembered. "But that was a few years ago."

"You must reach out to him," Sara said. "Once you're settled into your new position."

"But what type of ecological disaster would possibly require military assistance?" Julia scoffed.

"In the coming decades," Sara said. "There will be a rotation of the Earth's core. We'll be amid man-made mass extinctions. Acidic waters killing off coral reefs. Ice sheets are melting, sea levels are rising, Florida beaches are giving way to levees, and cruise ships are crossing the north pole in January. Industry is moving into the Arctic, mining, oil exploration. Sinkholes in once-frozen tundra the size of small towns. Do you want me to keep going?

"A world crippled by human activity was in no condition to deal with the core flip."

Julia took it all in with a long gaze through the windowpanes.

"This is not a story with a happy ending," she sighed. "A battle we can't win."

"But we can fight it. At least we can say we did that much," Sara stated. "I know so much more about things to come that you can use as a tool to convince people."

"Like a core flip that throws the world into chaos?" Julia asked. "They will see that as Armageddon and wonder why even prepare?"

"The world can prepare," Sara said. "We can make a difference."

Julia sighed.

"When I was a little girl, you gave me jigsaw puzzles," Sara said. "And I would always get frustrated. But you would patiently sit down to help, always saying, 'You have to start somewhere, take baby steps.'"

Julia circled the room and searched for words.

"This Jackson," Julia asked. "Why him, why not anyone else in the Military?"

"I can't tell you that," Sara replied. "But with his help, many opportunities are made. The military can do things that NOAA can't."

Sara suddenly felt emotional and out of place. She quickly turned and left the room. Julia followed her downstairs to the front door.

"Where are you going?"

"I have to go," Sara said with regret.

She reached for the door, but Julia reached for Sara and held her close.

"I really don't understand any of this," Julia said. "But I can tell that everything you've said comes from the heart."

"I've missed you so much," Sara sobbed in her mother's arms.

"Sweetheart," Julia said. "Don't worry so much. It's going to be all right."

It took a few minutes and a few tissues, but Sara pulled herself together. They parted with smiles, good luck, and goodbyes.

Ethan sat on the hood when Sara finally walked up.

"You're still here," Ethan joked.

"Yes, still here," Sara said. "Alive and well."

And for the first time in this century, she beamed a genuine smile.

The new timeline

Boulder, CO
Two months later

It took some time for Julia to track down Captain Jackson at his new base, and he was surprised to hear from her. Shocked was more like it, especially when she asked that he fly out to meet her in Boulder. Julia was relieved when he was announced at the guard gate a week later.

When he entered Julia's office, Jackson noted its military-esque layout and décor. Definitely a government operation. Julia sat behind a metal desk, a window behind her, and two upholstered chairs across the desk from her. A man Jackson did not recognize was seated in one of them.

Julia crossed the room and extended a hand.

"I'm so glad you could get out here on short notice," she said. "Captain Jackson, I'd like you to meet Arthur Melton, an advisor."

"Captain," Melton said and extended a hand.

Jackson took a seat and studied both faces.

"You called for this meeting, Miss Gathers," Jackson stated. "And in a cloak and dagger kind of way. How can the US Army be of service to you?"

"As you know, NOAA monitors weather worldwide," Julia said. "We protect life and Earth's natural resources. In times of crisis, we could need outside assistance. Someone who can swing a bigger stick, so to speak."

Jackson's response was to the point. "Were you the one lifted off that bridge by helicopter in San Francisco?" Jackson asked.

"That was my helicopter," Melton said. He hung himself out on that since, up 'till now, no one had ever identified the mysterious black helicopter or the lady on the ladder.

"Do you work for NOAA, sir?" Jackson asked.

"No, I do not," Melton replied. "I work in the private sector."

"And you, Ms. Gathers, are the new Director of NOAA," Jackson said sternly. "A US government agency working covertly with the private sector?"

"At the time," Julia answered. "I was not with NOAA." Another first as Julia placed herself out there to protect Sara.

Jackson deliberated for a moment.

"OK then, how exactly do you envision the US Military and NOAA working together?" Jackson asked. "And on what kind of missions?"

"There will be many natural and man-made disasters," Julia said. "In the times to come."

"Lots of people in the military, Ms. Gathers," Jackson said. "Why me?"

"Because you're a man who gets things done," Julia replied. "What if I told you there was something more important than being a captain in the US Army, that you can use the service as a tool for things you never imagined? Something more far-reaching that could actually help an ailing planet."

Jackson stood and paced.

"People say you saw it was coming," he said. "The earthquake, that is. That you can see the future."

"I have some insight," Julia offered, stretching the truth. "But I think we take that one step at a time.

"There will be instances when a few cars blocking bridges is simply not enough. I need someone I can call on to mobilize men and machinery at a different level."

Jackson studied her face.

"One government agency working with another," Julia said.

Jackson measured his words.

"Ms. Gathers," he said. "I'll consider it."

He tipped his hat and left the room.

The Continental Divide

In the Rocky Mountains, about an hour west of Boulder, a makeshift podium was situated in front of two rows of folding chairs. The temperature was thirty degrees cooler than in Boulder. Julia patiently mingled with political, military, and other governmental dignitaries. Captain Jackson was part of the military contingent. Arthur Melton led a group of Big Oil representatives seeking alternative fuel sources as a show of endorsement. Opposite the podium, a crowd of reporters and onlookers waited for the introduction of the new Director of NOAA.

The rumor mill circulated that the first woman would be named Director. When the reception ended, and all dignitaries took their seats, young Julia Gathers stepped up to the podium. She addressed the need to mobilize aid and help for future natural disasters and extreme weather conditions due to global warming. But her message was only partially acknowledged. The press focused more on the US military presence and how the lady at the podium looked familiar. The question-and-answer session that followed was a bit heated and to the point.

"Any more questions?" Julia asked.

"Why did you bring us up here?" a voice cried out. "It's freezing."

A question Julia was hoping to hear. "The world is not prepared for things to come," she said. "Just like you did not prepare for a change in the weather.

"Look behind us. From this vantage point, you will see forests climbing up these mountains in less than fifty years. The delicate mountain tundra will give way to a new ecosystem. Trees at higher altitudes are a grim reminder of a warming planet."

"How do you know that?" another voice asked.

No answer.

"Why are military personnel here?" a reporter stood and asked. "NOAA is not a branch of the military."

"As the world warms and the weather gets more severe," Julia said, "there is a greater need for cooperation between all governmental agencies to mitigate hurricane damage, sea-level rise, and other natural disasters."

"Like earthquakes?" a man in the crowd shouted. "Look," he continued. "We all know you're trying to be a mild-mannered reporter, but we know who you really are."

"Who you think I might be is not important at this time," Julia said, dishing him off.

"How did you know about the bridge?" the man pushed along. "How do you know any of this?"

Julia took a moment to study the faces in the crowd. "Let's keep our eye on the ball, folks," she said. "We have a planet to save."

She stepped away from the podium and walked down an aisle between the military and private sector representatives, who at once stood in escort.

With hundreds of remaining questions, the crowd looked on in confusion and exchanged dumbfounded expressions.

***

Melton's flagship tanker pushed through choppy waters in a driving rain off the Oregon coast. At 6:00 AM, a team of eight men loaded supplies onto the helicopter platform down in the cargo bay. Curiously enough, there were no weapons or assault gear. These men were trained for any dangerous situation, but this was a first.

"Why do we need 1,000 gallons of water?" one man asked. "Are we going to a deserted island?"

"I'm not sure," another man replied. "But this big Chinook can carry the weight, so let's get it loaded."

In time, the supplies were loaded, and the crew strapped in. While they adjusted their helmets and checked their headsets, the pilot began start-up procedures.

Eventually, elevator doors opened and cast light out into the dark cargo bay. Sara and Mason stepped out and onto the helipad platform. They boarded the chopper and strapped themselves in. Momentarily, the giant hangar deck hatch rolled open, and the hydraulic lift pushed the Chinook upward. They finally cleared the main deck into a driving rain that rocked the big dual-prop chopper.

"Ma'am," a voice came over the headsets. "What kind of mission is this?" He pointed to the pile of water jugs in the holding bin.

Mason grinned and shook his head.

"There's a pod of Cetaceans, stranded near Coos Bay," Sara said.

"Excuse me?" a voice asked.

Sara's face became serious. "We're going to rescue some whales," she clarified.

"I thought this was a dangerous mission," the voice came back.

"It is," Sara replied.

The crew exchanged condescending smirks.

"Ha," Mason said. "You ain't seen nothing yet." He pulled out a Bowie knife and brushed the blade along his glove. "I should have brought this the last time," he said.

The crew's faces dropped.

Sara burst out laughing.

THE KUIPER ROGUE

A sci-fi novel from C.P. Schaefer.

Join the mailing list at cpschaefer.com

PROLOGUE

The World Space Council had great expectations for outward colonization in the late twenty-first century. Living biodomes on the moon and Mars set the standard for sustainable habitats that produced food and breathable air. These prototypes had proven a system ready for the challenges of the outer solar system.

Saturn's moon Titan proved equal to that challenge. At twice the size of Earth's moon, Titan had a substantial atmosphere, a rocky surface with mountain ranges of solid ice, and oceans of liquid methane at temperatures near absolute zero.

The Titan base was a statement project with advanced systems and high-tech add-ons that stretched the imagination. Even the designers were impressed when they realized what they'd created.

This crowning achievement among the gas giants was hailed as a milestone in space exploration. But no one anticipated an ominous threat lurking in the icy cold regions beyond the planets, or the ancient prophecy of its destructive effects on our solar system.

Chapter 1

GAIA 3 –
Titan Moon base

"All right, Sys," Will Vandolah said. "What exactly am I looking at here? A pinwheel in outer space?"

"Processing," Sys replied. "No similar configuration in file catalogues."

"Curved blue streaks but emanating from what?" he mumbled.

"Was that a question, sir?" Sys asked. "You seem frustrated."

"No, it wasn't," he replied. "*I* was just processing."

A long silence.

"It's four AM." Will rubbed his eyes and refocused on the artificial sky, but the throbbing stridulation of chirping insects was too distracting. "Fuck!"

No response from the System Operator.

"Okay, Sys, this makes no sense." He sighed. "My brain is fried, and I'm sorry I raised my voice. Save down and let's regroup tomorrow evening."

***

It was sunset in the Living Hemisphere with a faint orange glow on the horizon and a few stars twinkling into view. Will sat in a foldout chair on the desert plateau and ran his fingers through his sandy brown hair. He didn't care much for fashion, sporting a modest wardrobe and utility boots.

He considered the chance circumstances that got him here on Titan. His life and career were on a launch pad to the stars, as he had always dreamed. He was assigned to the new Gaia 3 station; with its high-tech planetarium and orbiting telescope, he could do research like no other astronomer in history. And it was his mother, of all people, who got him assigned.

Margaret had spent most of her adult life in space, leaving young Will behind with relatives. At first, Will watched each of her launches with pride and awe, but as he grew up without her, that pride turned into resentment and troubled him still.

But other, more complicated, events from his past lay waiting to play out on a stage he had not yet imagined.

Printed in Great Britain
by Amazon

47133096R00249